DISCLAIMER

This book is a work of fiction. The characters, incidents and dialogue are drawn from the author's imagination and should not be construed as real. Any resemblance to actual events or living persons is entirely coincidental.

Although events in this novel are fictitious, Thomas Moran, was an actual person, an artist and printmaker of the Hudson River School. Moran's work often featured the Rocky Mountains. He was held in high regard, and his paintings portraying Yellowstone Park influenced the decision to designate the Yellowstone area a national park in 1872.

DEATH ON CANVAS

Chapter 1

Rural Montana, 1918

John Running Bear swatted at a mosquito near his ear as he sat bolt upright on the rickety cot in the boys' cabin at St. Benedict's Mission School. Annoyance, rather than the bug, kept him from sleeping. Why had Sister Mary sent them all to bed so early? He was too old to go to bed like some baby. Maybe he could go check the schoolhouse for something to eat. Sister often had bread left over at the end of the day, and his stomach felt empty as a water bucket on a dry day. He swung his legs out of the whisper thin blankets and sat on the edge of his cot, slipping on his moccasins. Then he cocked his head, listening. He heard raised voices coming from the nearby cabin that served as the school. One was Sister Mary's. She sounded mad as a squawking hen with a fox after her chicks. So angry. So out of control. *What was going on?*

Curious, he left the cabin and crept stealthily the short distance to the school to eavesdrop below the window. The other voice was that of the visitor, the woman who told them Father Michael sent her to help out until he came back from his trip—a trip made to search for funding for St. Benedict's proposed new building. Now, the woman was fairly spitting words—words low and sharp as the edge of an ax. *Something about money. Whose money*, he wondered.

Sister Mary's angry retort ended mid-sentence with the sound of a heavy thump. John froze. He didn't like the scary sound of that solid "thwack". The silence that followed seemed

1

ominous. Holding his breath, he raised his head to peer into the window and by the low light of the kerosene lamp saw Sister Mary on the floor. Her head was bent at an unnatural angle and she wasn't moving. He gasped. *No, no, no.* Heavy footsteps came toward the window. Stifling a sob, John turned and, avoiding the direct path behind the schoolhouse with its lit windows, he ran to the nearest shelter, the outhouse. He flattened himself against the side of the building, its ripe stink filling his nostrils. Tears streamed down his face, but he didn't brush them away.

It wasn't yet full dark. The merest sliver of moon cast light over the treacherous Yellowstone River that ran swiftly past at the edge of the schoolyard, turning the flow to a metallic band of pewter. The silhouettes of trees stood against the deepening sky. If the woman had heard him and was searching, there was enough visibility for her to see John outlined against the outhouse wall. Cautiously, he slid to a prone position, ignoring the bites of mosquitos that homed in on his face and neck and the scratches from fireweed stems growing behind the outhouse. Horror and fear wrapped around him with the heaviness of a damp woolen blanket. He strained to listen.

Nothing. Wait. Just wait.

Lying on the ground as he did when stalking game with his father, John closed his eyes, letting them become better accustomed to the darkening night.

Later, when he began to tremble from the effort of remaining still, he heard the schoolhouse door open, and a sound came like that made by a deer carcass dragged across bumpy ground. John peered around the corner of the small building. Toward the band of silver river, he spied the heavy, squat woman pulling something large and pale, grunting with the effort. *Sister Mary.* Wincing, he realized she was in only her undergarments, and in sick dread, John watched the woman roll her into the water. Then she stood straight, rubbing her palms together as though at a job well done

As she began to turn, John's small heart froze, his mind racing as he again flattened his length against the earth. What to do? There were no options but to lie still as stone.

"Cover me with darkness, Great Spirit," John whispered inwardly. "Hide me with the fog that hangs over the Yellowstone on spring mornings."

Passing within yards of him, the woman trudged to Sister Mary's cabin instead of back to the schoolhouse. As soon as she closed the door, John ran to the river.

Too late. Too late. Too late.

There was nothing but the metallic gleam of the swift current. She was gone. The Yellowstone had taken her.

He stood and watched the door of the cabin until clouds rolled in, covering the moon. The killer hadn't once looked in John's direction. He was safe.

But what about tomorrow? Would this woman kill them all? The little ones in the girls' and boys' boarding cabins?

He had to think. John worked his way to the copse of cottonwood, letting the trees surround him. Yes, he could think better here than in the man-made building. *Think.* What should he do? If only he could speak to his father, but his parents lived a day's horse ride from the school. He cursed his slight stature. He couldn't fight the killer. An eleven-year old boy against the big woman? She was tall, and she was wide. An ax handle across, he thought. It was impossible.

Blending into the irregular shadows of the cottonwood trees, John Running Bear crouched motionless in the engulfing night. A slight whimper escaped from his throat, making him wince and clap a hand over his mouth. Closing his eyes, he stilled his ragged breathing, willing himself to be brave. His thin shoulders sagged, the weight of responsibility bearing down like a physical presence. As the oldest student at the school, he'd have to protect the others. Even if John could walk to his parent's home on the reservation, there were no horses for the smaller children. They couldn't go that far on foot. Without food. And without clean water. He pulled angrily at his thick hair. No, he'd have to protect them somehow. And not only the Indian children, but the little Irish girl with flaming hair. Her father had brought her to school only a week before. Kate. Her name was Kate. He snorted. Being the only white child at the school, she'd taken a lot of teasing the past week. She took it

3

without tears. Kate was tough, but tiny as a tick. No, it came down to him, John Running Bear.

Maybe the murdering woman would be gone in the morning. He hoped she'd disappear like smoke from a campfire. He yanked again at his hair, twisting it around his finger and pulling hard. If she was still there, he could no longer be a child. John grimaced. He was skinny. Young. Not big like the bear, and not yet skilled enough to fight like the smaller, quicker, wolverine. He'd once seen a determined wolverine run off a much larger bear. Vicious. Hmmm. He considered the animals he knew well. The answer came. He stood. The fox. The fox protected its den. But it was careful. Sly.

Small and young though he was, he was the son of a warrior. *No. It is not enough to be the son of a warrior. I must be a warrior. Cunning. Strong.*

While he hid and planned, the sky darkened to ink. The trees trembled in a light breeze and the stars twinkled, acknowledging his presence. John crossed his arms across his chest, wrist over wrist, fingers splayed wide like the claws of a great beast. Tears streamed from his eyes, but his heart swelled. A chill ran through his body as he whispered to the Great Spirit.

"Hear me, Great One," he whispered, tipping his head back.

With his eyes raised to the sky, he bared his teeth. He lifted his arms high over his head.

"I am John Running Bear. I am a warrior."

The next morning, John woke each child and told them to let him be the first to go to the schoolhouse, telling them, "Sister Mary left in the night. I'm not sure what happened. Don't worry. I'll go look, and I will wave to you from the school door if it is safe to come in."

His moccasin clad feet did not want to take him to the school cabin. They slowed and shuffled as if of their own accord. Finally, John reached the door and peered in. There the woman stood. She was dressed in the nun's stark black robe, leaning against the big oak desk, a steaming mug of coffee in her hands.

"Come in. Come in," she said, gesturing with her free hand. "I don't bite. Sister Mary had a family emergency. It was lucky I was here to teach you young'uns until Father Michael gets back." She smiled broadly. "Don't worry. You're safe with me."

Safe. John stood like a block of wood for nearly a minute. The word reminded him of the game of softball Sister Mary had been teaching them to play—the run and slide across the dusty square she'd called home base, her laugh when John let the little ones catch him and put him 'out'. Mixed with a sense of horror, was heartache. Sister Mary wasn't 'safe'. And she wouldn't be playing any more ball.

Bile rose in his throat and he swallowed hard. Then John gave himself a mental shake. Recalling the red fox he'd seen protecting its den near the reservation, he felt courage and cunning seep into him. He thought again of his plea to the Great Spirit. *So that's how it's going to be*. Straightening his spine, John Running Bear drew himself up to his full height. He smiled back at the woman, his grin not reaching his eyes. *I am a warrior*, he thought.

He stepped back through the doorway and waved the other children in.

Chapter 2

Sage Bluff, Montana, present day
Jessie O'Bourne pulled onto the shoulder of the country road, parked her battered pickup and gave the door a vicious shove to pop it open. The scent of alfalfa dredged up childhood memories. She yawned, then sat spellbound in the driver's seat, gazing out over the hayfield, the scene morphing to molten gold as daybreak spilled over the horizon. *Wow—great glow around Dad's haystack. If I can't make a dramatic painting with that backlighting I should have just hit the snooze button.*

She pulled out a block of sticky notes and a fine-point marker from the glove box. Peering through the windshield, she drew several thumbnail sketches of the scattering of new bales drying in the field, the massive stack of hay bales, and the windbreak of silver-leafed Russian olive trees silhouetted against the blushing sky. As she finished each tiny, two-minute sketch, she peeled it from the pad and stuck it on the dash, evaluating the new one against the previous drawing.

A low feline rumble filled the cab, emanating from the enormous orange tomcat stretched out on the Navajo patterned horse blanket covering the seat. Jessie reached over to rub his wide head and scratch behind his battle-scarred ears.

"Quit grumbling, Jack. I need several more landscapes for my display." She'd dropped paintings at several galleries during the trip from New Mexico to her dad's Montana ranch, so her inventory was low. As the judge for the upcoming painting competition, she was expected to exhibit at least a dozen of her own landscapes.

"I'll get a small one done this morning—then it's home for a decent breakfast." She yawned again as she rubbed little circles on her forehead with her fingertips. "Coffee first, though. Then I'll hit the easel."

She stepped out, reached behind the seat, and pulled out a thermos, travel mug, and a cake donut wrapped in a napkin. She broke off a nugget of the pastry and reached back inside the cab to wave it back and forth like a conductor's wand in front of Jack. His slanted yellow eyes followed the movement. His tail twitched in anticipation; a paw full of claws swiped at the morsel.

Jessie grinned and tossed it to the cantankerous cat, who snatched it in mid-air and leapt from the truck, prize held between sharp teeth. She chuckled.

While Jack munched with enthusiasm, she poured dark coffee into her travel mug and gulped a few scalding swallows, then set the mug on the hood of the beat-up red Ford with a thump. Humming to herself, she slipped on a red artist's apron, gathered her mass of auburn hair into a ponytail and pulled it through the adjustment loop of a denim ball cap gussied up with an embroidered tractor and logo 'Let's Ride – Get 'em at Yonky's Farm Supply'. From the truck bed, she grabbed a lightweight easel and set it up on the shoulder of the gravel road. The tailgate made a makeshift table for her fisherman's tackle box crammed full of painting supplies.

Jack gave the long grass by the edge of the field a predatory sniff while Jessie squeezed creamy globs of pigment onto her palette and mixed colors with a palette knife. She centered a canvas on the easel and the painting began in earnest, her brush dancing a ballet of bold strokes. A rich landscape depicting the ochre haystack and rectangles of hay littering the field rapidly materialized, the sky beginning with deep ultramarine blue at the top and feathering down to cool cerulean at the horizon line.

She glanced up. The clear sky threatened to make a liar out of Koot Lundgren, the weatherman. Old Koot, as he was affectionately called by his followers, said it was going to rain. Seems like he's right only half the time.

Jack returned to flop down under Jessie's easel, emitting guttural complaints. He narrowed his eyes with disapproval and drummed his tail in an impatient rhythm on the toe of Jessie's leather boot. She walked over, reached into the cab of the truck, and snagged another nugget of donut. But with her mind still on her canvas, she absent-mindedly put it into her apron pocket instead of dropping it to the tomcat.

"That'll hold you for a while. Not much longer 'til breakfast," she murmured to a grumbling Jack. She stepped back to the easel and worked her brush with furious speed. "Gotta catch the light."

She noticed a patch of turquoise near the side of the haystack.

Nice. A perfect little color note.

She mixed a daub of paint to match the turquoise splotch and flicked one brushstroke onto her canvas. On the bottom corner of the canvas she signed—J. O'Bourne, scribbled the location, time of day, and added the title, "*Morning Light, O'Bourne's Field*" in a small notebook.

She gazed up at the brightening sky, standing motionless for several minutes to admire a bald eagle soaring high above the fence line, hunting breakfast. Jack spied it as well and darted under the pickup. He turned to peer out, his reptilian yellow eyes glinting from the shadows. Jessie ducked at the waist and reached under the Ford to tickle his chin.

"Smart boy," she said, grinning. "No sense being eagle bait." She stowed her supplies in the truck and slipped the completed landscape into a storage box she used to carry wet paintings. Later, she'd work the bristles of her brushes with a special cleaner and use a little walnut oil to reshape the bristles.

She dumped the last drops of now tepid coffee on the ground before dropping the metal mug behind the seat. Her stomach growled a request for bacon and eggs, but she glanced with resignation over her shoulder toward her father's haystack.

The brilliant daub of turquoise. A neat touch for the painting, but damn it, litter was litter. Why are people such slobs?

She slammed the pickup door, strode to the barbed wire fence to shimmy under and trudge toward the trash to pick it up. Looking back, Jessie called the cat. Jack emerged from hiding, and scurried to catch up. He ambled next to her across the rutted field, stopping every few yards to tilt his nose upward and sniff the air.

As they drew closer to the stack, the tomcat moved closer to Jessie, slowed and stiffened. High above them, a wail erupted into the air, growing into a crescendo of agonized fear. Jack crouched low next to Jessie's foot, listening, claws extended. She sheltered her eyes from the sun with the side of her hand and searched the closest line of trees. The eagle had seized opportunity—and its morning meal. Her gaze followed the rhythmic sweep of muscular wings as the bird lifted and flew, a rabbit dangling from sharp talons. The keening dropped to a whisper and grew silent.

Poor bunny. But the eagle has to eat, too, I guess.

She stroked Jack's head as she glanced back down the field. Near the haystack, she set Jack down and zeroed in on the dab of turquoise. It was a running shoe edged with reflective tape. Too weird. One shoe? A narrow tire track curved around the edge of the stack. Motorcycle. Probably some teenagers had a party or a make-out session. Crap. I'll bet they left a bunch of trash.

Jessie followed the track around the corner of the haystack. Instead of the expected rubbish, an expensive looking, red and black motorcycle lay in the dirt. Eyes wide, she circled the bike, noticing a well-worn black touring bag and a daypack with a Harley-Davidson logo mounted over the fender. Past the cycle, several bales had been removed from the stack and scattered around. Jack crouched on a short pile of bales, staring intently down.

"Watcha got, big guy? Some poor mouse?"

Jack snaked a paw into the crevice between two 90 pound bales and yowled in the guttural tone he reserved for slithery prey.

"Ugh, that better not be a rattlesnake" She waved her hand at him. "Get down, Jack."

The cat held his ground, gave Jessie a contemptuous look and jumped into the crevice.

"Doggonit!" Jessie walked over and looked downward as Jack jumped out and avoided her grasp. An involuntary scream burst from her throat.

In the crack between two bales was a still form, clad in a brown leather jacket and torn jeans. The woman's body lay wedged on its side, arms tucked close to her torso. Long black hair matted with dried blood obscured her face. One foot was bare, the toenails painted crimson; the other wore the mate to the discarded turquoise tennis shoe.

Fearing the worst, Jessie squatted down, grit her teeth and thrust a bare arm between the body and hay bales, trying to feel her pulse. Stiff stems of dried alfalfa scored deep scratches into her skin, and as she withdrew her arm, it immediately began to ooze droplets of blood.

Can't tell. She stood up. Then she heard a low moan. *She's still alive...*

"Hey, can you hear me?" No answer. She patted her pockets looking for her cell phone. "Phone's back at the truck. I'm going to call for help. Hang on."

She raced back to her pickup and grabbed her cell phone and hit 911 with trembling fingers. While she listened to the ring on the other end, she yanked Jack's wool blanket from the seat, and pulled a utility knife from the glove box. Her stomach clenched the way it always did when she confronted sharp objects: knives, needles, broken glass. She grimaced, turning to start back. When the dispatcher answered, she explained the emergency, giving terse directions while she jogged back to the injured girl. Her breath came in gasps.

Another eagle—likely the first one's mate—circled above the haystack, something large clutched in its talons.

Oh, dear God, please don't let that be Jack. No, no, no.

10

She accelerated. Nearly to the stack, she spotted the orange tom squatting in the shade of a hay bale. Relieved, as she passed the bale, she stooped, grabbed the cat and hugged him close as she ran. Above, the eagle made a lazy U-turn to head the other direction.

Dumping Jack onto the ground, she sucked air between her teeth and opened the knife. As she cut the twine from the bales trapping the still figure, she pulled away clumps of hay and pitched them to the side until the limp body was released. The woman slumped onto her back, her leather jacket falling open.

Jessie stared. She looked young, teens maybe, and at least part Native American. Above the scooped t-shirt neckline peeped the edge of a thunderbird tattoo. As she covered the slim body with Jack's blanket, the girl's chest heaved.

"Don't worry, you'll be okay. Help is on the way."

Where's the damn ambulance?

As if her thought conjured the reality, she heard distant sirens and breathed a deep sigh.

When the sound drew louder, the girl's eyes opened. Her mouth moved as if she were trying to speak.

"It's okay," Jessie said soothingly. "Help is coming." She knelt by the girl's side, tucking the blanket more tightly around the slight form. "Where are you hurt? Who did this?"

At the raspy, indistinct response, Jessie shook her head, puzzled, certain she had misheard. When the sirens grew to an earsplitting crescendo, she stepped from behind the haystack and waved her arms. The ambulance pulled off the gravel road and ground to a stop near her truck, and the siren stopped.

Jessie turned back to the girl, whose eyes were wide and frightened.

"God, no," the girl said, "No, no, no. Not the police. Please. It was a cop. A cop! Don't—"

Her arms flailed weakly. Her eyes closed. She went silent.

Chapter 3

Rural Montana, present day

Sergeant Russell Bonham hit the gas, pushing his patrol car to eighty. He could hear other sirens wailing in the distance and then winding down.

They must be about to O'Bourne's ranch already, he thought. *I'm right on their tail.* As he rounded the next corner, he spotted the emergency vehicles parked on the shoulder of the lane behind an old red pickup. The field gate stood open.

His car swerved, fishtailing, and Russell eased off the pedal. Cranking the wheel, he pulled off the road and parked behind the ambulance. He shoved the door open, got out, and loped after two paramedics who were hurrying over the rough ground, hauling a stretcher. Another EMT carrying a Medical Field Kit ran ahead, already halfway to the haystack.

Russell picked up his pace.

"Don't touch anything around the stack, just pick up the victim," he yelled. "And you," he pointed at the tall figure holding a squirming cat. "Stay put, please. We'll need to talk to you."

He reached the others and looked down at the unresponsive girl the ambulance team was loading on the stretcher.

Nobody he knew, thank God. He pegged her about early twenties. *Indian. There'd probably be ID in the motorcycle bag, license and registration, at least.*

"Does it look like she's going to make it?" he asked the nearest EMT, a brown-haired beanpole who towered over Russell's six two by a couple inches.

The fellow shook his head, looking sad and bewildered.

Newbie. Volunteer, maybe, Russell thought. A female EMT looked up as she was tightening a strap on the stretcher, and he saw it was Cassy Adams. Her aunt worked at the station. His mind eased. Cassy was good at her job, and he'd seen her in action at some rough accident scenes. He gave her an inquiring look. "What do you think, Cassy?"

"Don't know," she said. "We gotta run with her, Russ. Anybody's guess, but we'll keep you posted." The EMTs hustled the stretcher down the field and slid it into the waiting ambulance.

Russell gestured with a beefy hand, waving the paramedics on, then he pulled his police radio from the holder on his belt and called the station. "Blanche, send Johnson and Kraft out to the O'Bourne's west hayfield."

He listened to the voice on the other end. "Yeah, where the injured girl was found. Tell 'em to bring a trailer. We have a motorcycle here we'll need to haul back to the station, and we'll need to dust it for prints."

He thought a minute. "Send Arvid with them, too. Sergeant Johnson can swing by and pick him up as they pass the Abrahmsens' place."

After listening to the voice on the other end he said, "Yeah, he's back. He called a few minutes ago and was just rolling into his driveway from his big fishing trip. Catch him on his cell phone. And tell him not to take time to clean up and get into uniform. When Johnson drops him off, I'll have him accompany the woman who found the girl back to the station, so he can take her statement."

Russell glanced around. Damn weather had been so dry he didn't expect to find any footprints. The woman who found the girl and the ambulance team had both stomped everywhere anyhow. They'd still have to check the area, take a few pictures. He squatted down, gazing across the field. He saw a slight trail of bent alfalfa stalks leading from the middle of the field directly to the haystack. Drag marks. Person must have tried carrying the girl. Got tired halfway, dragged her the rest of the way to the haystack and hid her, then drove the cycle over and hoped neither would be noticed for some time. It was a stroke of luck she'd been found so soon. Russell turned to speak to the woman who'd called 911 and did a double take.

She had her head tilted skyward, the long red ponytail of curls trailing down her back from under one of Russell's own caps, and a huge orange cat was held tightly in her arms. As he stood watching her, she swiveled toward him.

Oh damn . . . when did Jessie O'Bourne come home?

A twitch started at the corner of his left eye, and he forced himself to calm down, to let his face go blank. When he looked up, those amazing eyes were looking into his.

Yep, still mad.

"Hello, Russell," she said, winter frost in her tone.

"Hi, Jess. Didn't know you were back. Heck of a thing to come home to." He rubbed the back of his neck with a broad palm and then met her gaze. "She a friend of yours? Got any idea what happened? Did she talk to you before we arrived?"

God, now I'm babbling.

"No to all three questions. I've never seen her before." Jessie hugged a squirming Jack to her chest, her blue eyes like glacial ice. "I have no idea what happened. Poor thing did wake up for a second or two, but she didn't make much sense, Russell. The only thing I understood was that she was terrified the police would come with the ambulance. And now that I see who answered the 911 call, no wonder she was worried," she said in a tone Russell could only interpret as snotty.

He felt the heat rise up his neck but ignored her barb. "Hmmm. Could be the head wound. Could be drug related. Been a ton of drug problems around here the last couple years. The EMTs will likely need to send her by copter to Billings. We'll ID her and get her family notified. I'm going to ask you to go sit in the patrol car while we're waiting for the other officers to arrive, so you don't walk around the crime scene any more than you have, and you can corral that orange monster you got there."

14

"Oh, for . . ." Jessie gave him a steely look.

"And I need to go take a quick look at your vehicle." At her startled glance, he said, "Hey, just routine." He walked toward Jessie's Ford, then turned and looked back. "You look good, Jess. Been a while hasn't it? Still wearing one of my old hats, I see."

Chapter 4

Sage Bluff, Montana, present day

Arvid Abrahmsen rode shotgun in Jessie's pickup, his lumberjack physique wedged tightly into her small truck. He was holding Jack on his ample lap and regaling Jessie with stories from some of the Scandinavian settlers, especially tales of his Norwegian relatives. The Sage Bluff area had been settled in the 1800s by immigrants of German, Irish, Swedish and Norwegian ancestry.

"Yep, glad the great grandparents chose such pretty country. Nice people here, too. 'Course right now, we're all trying to outdo one another in the decoration of mail boxes."

"Mail boxes?" she asked in surprise.

"Better believe it. We've got a county-wide contest going for the most creative box, and it's a contest with some mighty attractive prizes." Arvid's blue eyes twinkled in a wide, sunburned face, and salt and pepper hair covered his head in a short, messy mop. He wore waterproof boots, khaki canvas slacks, and a blue plaid shirt topped by a vest that smelled ever so slightly of trout. Jessie liked the man immediately, mentally adding him to her list of "good people". It was a short list.

"Sounds like fun."

Miles of wheat fields, pasture grass and alfalfa flashed past the truck window, interspersed with an entertaining assortment of mailboxes. Miniscule tractors, metal dragons, milkmaids, horses, and pigs, some on fancy posts carved with the owner's name.

"This is mine, here." Arvid pointed to a narrow lane leading to a frame house, its Norwegian blue and red trim faded from the harsh Montana winters and even harsher Montana sun. The turn in was marked by a large mail box painted to mimic the ocean, complete with waves and topped with a kitschy homemade Viking ship.

"Oh," Jessie said, "Neat box. That ought to put you in the running."

"Hope I win."

"What kind of prizes does the contest have?"

"Second is a night at a local B&B. One of them fancy, schmancy places. But first place is a brand-new horse trailer from Carlson's Implement. "

"Oh, you have horses?"

"Nah. I'd trade it in on a small motorhome I been wanting. One perfect for fishing trips." As they turned onto Main Street in Sage Bluff, he changed the subject. "You were raised around here weren't you, Miss O'Bourne? You look familiar." Then Arvid slapped his knee, startling Jack. "Oh, you must be Dan O'Bourne's girl."

"That's right."

"Your dad and I were only a couple years apart in school. I played on the same football team, but back then, if you can believe it, I was sort of a runt. Haw haw."

"Hard to believe, all right." She smiled. "And please call me Jessie. Or Jess. Yeah. It's my old stomping ground, all right. But it's been a while since I've lived at home. Dad's place was mid-way between Sage Bluff and Baxter. I went to grade school in Sage Bluff but decided to switch to Baxter when I reached high school age. They offered an art class. I lost track of most of my old Sage Bluff crowd, but I still see a few friends from art class now and then when I come home." Out of the corner of her eye she saw Jack's mouth begin to open and saw the broad head tilt. "Don't let him bite you. He's not real good with strangers."

"Aw, he likes me. Biggest damn cat I ever seen. Pardon the Swedish." He snickered and rubbed Jack's ears. "Bit of Norsky humor there. I like to blame what I can on the Swedes."

17

Jessie grinned. She looked out the window at the once familiar streets as she drove and gazed longingly at the neon sign as she passed the Calico Family Café.

No breakfast today. I'm starving. And wouldn't you know it had to be Russell Bonham who picked up the 911 call? Blast . . . haven't seen him since the funerals.

"Looking at your sketches stuck there on the dash, I just realized you're the artist everybody's been talking about. Didn't think you'd be so young. You come back to judge that big art contest over in Baxter, right?"

"That'd be me. I hope we have a good turnout."

"I was surprised such a little town could sponsor a big, artsy hoo-ha like that. The newspaper says there'll be a couple hundred artists coming. So what's so special about this 'plain old painting' they have listed on the posters I've been seeing around town?"

She slowed to a stop at the intersection of Main and Third and waited for a young couple pushing a stroller to cross. The couple were smiling at each other and talking animatedly. A wistful feeling washed over her at the sight of the stroller before she continued on.

"It's called *'plein air'* painting, Arvid." She spelled it. "It's just a fancy way of saying 'painting in the open air'. Some painters think nothing compares to painting outdoors from life."

"How do you feel about it?"

"That's an interesting question. I guess I believe that a good painting is a good painting—whether it's plein air or done from photo references. It's still what the artist puts on the canvas that counts, and, even more often, what the artist leaves out. I do both studio and outdoor work. Sometimes I make a larger studio painting from a small outdoor study, but if I'm painting animals, I need photos."

"Huh. Interesting. My wife loves art. Bet she'd love to visit with you sometime. And Esther's a musician—writes her own music." He wriggled his eyebrows. "She's a beauty, too. You wouldn't think this overweight old Norsky could reel in such a catch as my Esther, but you'd be wrong. Just had to have the right bait." He looked down at the cat with a pensive

18

expression, then chuckled, scratching his head with one hand. "I can't remember what that bait was, but I must've done something right."

Jessie laughed.

"Say, I seen you looking at the café sign back there. You hungry?"

"Starving. I didn't eat breakfast before I went out to paint."

"*Ja.* Well, let me take down your statement, and I'll run back for breakfast sandwiches and some decent coffee. I'd give you some from the station pot, but it'd be weak as dishwater. The clerk there makes *terrible* coffee." He made a dramatic gagging sound, then grinned. "Don't say I said so. The gal doubles as a dispatcher, and she does a good job except for the coffee. Whoo-ee! She takes terrible offense when people criticize her lousy brew." Arvid shook his head sadly. "And I hate to say it, but that woman can be mean as a snake about the littlest things. Anyway, my opinion is that the only folks that can make decent coffee are Norwegians. Good and strong." He made a bicep. "Hold up the spoon."

Jessie smiled and tapped her own chest with her thumb. "You've got nothing on the O'Bournes there, my friend. We *dissolve* the spoon!"

A few minutes later they approached the building that served as Sage Bluff's Sheriff's Office. Like other towns around Montana, the historic buildings were still put to good use. High above the door, the old stone façade read *First National Bank and Trust.* At the side of the entrance door, a nondescript sign announced *Sage Bluff Courthouse and Sheriff's Dept.* All the parking places were filled, most by trucks with gun racks in the window. She circled around the block.

"All the hunters are in town," Arvid explained. "The hardware store remodeled, and the owner added on enough space to put in a sporting goods section. Today's the grand opening."

Next to the Sheriff's Department was a computer store whose rock pediment read *Post Office,* and whose parking lot held one empty slot. She hooted in triumph, whipped into the

19

opening and parked. She reached over to take the orange cat from Arvid before he exited the pickup. Jack hung limp as a dishrag except for one paw whose hooks were deeply entrenched in not only the Deputy Sergeant's fishing vest, but a bit of Norwegian flesh as well.

"Sorry." Jessie grimaced, then disentangled Jack's hooks.

"Aw, it's okay. See, he likes me, all right. 'Course, I got a comfortable lap."

She was positive a small grizzly bear would find the big man's lap comfortable but held her tongue and followed him into the station, Jack looped over one shoulder, his claws now digging into her back.

The Sheriff's Department was a relic with good architectural bones. Solid marble steps led to wide double exterior doors covered with a triangular pediment. On each side of the door were granite columns topped by scrollwork.

The heavy doors opened into a spacious lobby that had seen better days. The office door on the right was open, but there was nobody behind the desk.

"Blanche is out for a minute, I guess." Arvid said. "She said we'd need to use Russell's office. Hope it's open."

"You don't have an office?"

"Ja, I do. But while I was on my fishing trip, the guys surprised me and had the hardwood floors refinished. The varnish needs another day to dry. I planned to stay longer, but Sheriff Stendahl flew to California to visit family. He wound up having a heart attack while he was there, then a triple bypass. I was away fishing, so he made Russell acting sheriff. I knew Russell would be short staffed, so I came home to help out."

Arvid led the way down the hall, opened the door to Russell's office and seated her near the corner of a massive oak desk. A glass paperweight with a distorted version of Russell and a smiling youngster, both with fishing poles, sat on a stack of notepaper. Jessie looked closer.

Must be his son. Wish the photo wasn't so darn blurry. About five, maybe a little older.

Marker and crayon drawings of boats, trucks, dinosaurs and other animals covered the edge of the desk blotter. She looked closer. Darn good sketches for that age. More than darn good. How ironic that Russell, who she knew had so little appreciation for art, should have a child with such natural ability.

While Arvid muttered over the jumbled state of Russell's desk drawers, her gaze moved to the wall. She didn't see any photographs of Russell's wife, Trish. Everyone had expected she'd marry Jessie's brother, Kevin, but after Kevin's accident, Trish had married Russell within the month. Jessie pressed her lips tightly together. Not for the first time, she wondered if they'd been fooling around before Kevin's death. Russell was too darn good-looking. Tall and lean, with hair the color of home-made fudge, he looked so all-American he should've had Old Glory tattooed on his muscled biceps.

Yeah, he'd have attracted Trish all right.

She rose and walked over to examine the child's drawings again. One of a running horse—a horse spattered with green polka dots—stood out. It looked three-dimensional. Astounding for someone so young.

I hope he doesn't spoil it for the kid.

Russell had been against her going away to art school, calling it "a frivolous waste of time". She felt a flush creep up her face. Thank God she'd been able to go. It gave her some distance. She'd have died if he'd ever guessed that her feelings toward him were anything but sisterly.

Since Kevin's funeral, then her mother's only a week later, she hadn't bothered to get in touch with Russell whenever she came home to see her Dad. She had been too hurt. It still hurt. She bit her bottom lip. When she thought of him with Trish, it was hard to catch her breath. Worse, his odd attitude towards Kevin's death bothered her. *And that look on his face at the burial.*

Her emotions flitted through fear, then anger, then longing. *And here you are, Jess girl. Alone. With a biological clock that hammers like Big Ben ringing in the New Year. And there's Russell, with a kid that wants to draw. Life just isn't fair.*

21

Dousing the corrosive wave of self-pity as it flowed relentlessly through her, Jessie surreptitiously wiped her eyes with the tail of her apron while Arvid continued to dig in the desk drawers for a statement form.

"Damn British and their clocks."

"Huh?" Arvid asked.

"Oh, nothing." She forced a grin. "Just thinking stupid thoughts out loud. I like to keep the smart ones to myself. I'm selfish that way."

"Me, too! Why give 'em away when someone might pay good money for 'em? Look at that guy who invented the sticky notes you got all over your pickup dash. Millionaire," Arvid snapped his fingers and smiled. "Just like that." Then he reached back into Russell's drawer and withdrew a piece of paper and pen, holding them up in triumph. "Okey-dokey. We may as well get started. Unless you got more insights to share about England."

Twenty minutes later, the enormous cop leaned back in his desk chair and capped his pen. "That'll do." He grinned and patted his ample belly. "It'd be an honor to treat Sage Bluff's big-shot artist to two of Alice's special breakfast burritos from the Calico Café. Now, *they're* a real work of art."

"Sounds good, thanks."

Arvid heaved his bulk out of the chair and turned to leave.

"Sit tight. I'll go over and pick 'em up. Back in two shakes."

Chapter 5

Sage Bluff Sheriff's Department, present day
"Her name is Amber Reynolds. Ring a bell?" Russell looked over at Jessie, who sat on the metal folding chair opposite his desk. Her arms hugged her torso, long legs stretched out in front of her, crossed at delicate ankles. Under the chair, Jack sat contentedly and washed his fur. Jessie had removed the cap. Her long hair had escaped from the neat knot and a glossy, loose curl corkscrewed over one cheek. Russell noticed the other cheek sported a faint daub of yellow paint.

"Don't suppose you clobbered her yourself, Jess, then had second thoughts and called it in," he said. "It would make my job easier if you'd just confess now."

"No." Jessie glared at him. "I did not. And if you're making a joke, it's not funny. I've been kept waiting in your office for nearly two hours. I've been bored to tears sitting here. And I've already been over the whole thing with Detective Sergeant Abrahmsen."

While Russell and his team had been going over the scene with meticulous care, Arvid had supplied her with two succulent ham and egg sandwiches and a hot cup of caffeine— in the strongest brew possible that would still pour. After Jessie finished, with assistance from Jack on the ham, she'd whiled away the time filling Russell's desk blotter with intricate ball point sketches of the view from his office window. She'd carefully avoided the area of childish drawings that filled one side of the blotter.

"Jess, you've never been bored a day in your life." Russell glanced at the blotter, intrigued. The row of maples across the street, tiny pedestrians, dogs, cars, and belligerent crows paraded across his desk in delicate cross-hatching. All of the miniature drawings she done next to K. D.'s old drawings on the blotter were frame worthy. "You always find something to keep your hands busy. I remember when your brother and I—"

"Oh, stow the memory lane stuff," Jessie interrupted, "I don't appreciate being treated like a criminal just because I found some poor girl and called 911. What's the matter with you—small town cop syndrome?" She glared at him. "There's probably an acronym for that."

He grinned broadly, then tapped his face with a fingertip. "Got a big smudge there on your cheek, Jess. Look a lot like you used to when your brother and I would pick you up from Mrs. Johansson's art class . . . you know, when you *accidentally* missed the bus on such a regular basis. You might clean up some when we're done."

She sat up abruptly, scrambled in her apron pocket for a rag, and yanked one out. Part of a cake donut popped out of the pocket along with the cloth and dropped to the floor, where Jack attacked it with 'cat's got the cream' enthusiasm. She scrubbed at her cheek. A wide blue streak appeared across the smudged yellow.

Russell clenched his stomach to keep from roaring with laughter but tried to keep his face stony. "That's better." He rubbed a finger on the side of his nose so that his hand covered his mouth, where a smile threatened to erupt. "Listen, I can't picture you doing anything like this, but the injured girl was found on your dad's property and it's my job to cover all the bases. Whoever hit her smacked her with a heavy fencing tool. You know, one of those big suckers farmers use to stretch barbed wire? We found one lying in the grass with blood on it. Bet there's normally one in your dad's pickup. You missing one out there at O'Bourne's?"

"Heck, how am I supposed to know?" Jessie asked. "I don't put up fences, and I was driving my old pickup, not Dad's." She paused. "My Ford has been stored at the ranch for some time. I use it when I come home—Dad says a vehicle runs better if it's driven once in a while—and I don't want it to rust away in the garage."

She crossed her legs, swinging a foot nervously. "Dad always keeps a bull-nosed fencing plier in a waterproof pouch hanging on the main gate post—uses it to fix things when he drives out to check on his cows. A couple years ago he started dipping the handles of all of his screwdrivers and pliers in a liquid rubber. Did the tool have a red coating on the handle?"

"I really can't give that information out."

Jessie grimaced. "Probably Dad's if it does. Peel that rubberized layer back and if it's his, 'O'Bourne' will be engraved on the metal."

"Guess I'll talk to your dad then."

"Nope, you won't. Dad's been gone over a week. He and Marty are on their honeymoon and won't be back until next week."

"Long honeymoon. I thought he'd be back by now."

"Just for the record, there's no way he had anything to do with this." Jessie snorted, "I'll bet every farmer and rancher in the county has one of those tools. Gee, Russell," she said angrily, "maybe you should take a county-wide inventory."

"Huh. Think I'll pass." He watched the orange tomcat flip donut crumbs around the office, batting at miniscule bits before greed asserted itself and he gulped them down. "I know you went over your story with Arvid, but I like to cover the details, too. What made you go out to the haystack, Jess? I might need to add it to the report. For the record, just routine."

"For cripes sake. I was painting. I need to finish a bunch of paintings while I'm home—local scenes—for my upcoming exhibit in two weeks. The light is great in the morning." She sighed. "I saw a flash of blue over near the stack. Thought it was just trash—went to pick it up, saw it was a shoe. Jack wouldn't leave the stack, so I went to pick him up and there she was. The girl—Amber—she'll make it, won't she? I hope you'll be able to ask *her* what happened."

A knocked sounded and a woman pushed open the door. She was as tall as Russell and broad as Hoover Dam. Her Winston Churchill face was topped by tight grey curls. "I've got the Denver P.D. on the phone, Russell. They've spoken to the girl's family. Do you want me to transfer it to your desk?"

"No, Blanche." He stood. "I'll come out."

Blanche focused on Jessie. "Well, now. Dan O'Bourne's girl, isn't it? So nice to see you. My Gosh, you've grown up pretty. It doesn't surprise me, because I knew your mother. When you're done here, stop at the front desk and visit for a spell. I'm due for my break and I want to hear all about the art show coming up and your dad's new bride."

"Uh, okay," Jessie said in a surprised tone.

Blanche squinted her eyes at Jessie. "No offense, but you're welcome to use the ladies' room down the hall if you need to wash your face. You've got quite a splotch of war paint. About there." She tapped her own cheek, turned, and closed the door.

Jessie sputtered and stared daggers at Russell.

He chuckled at the mortified redhead on his way out the door, then leaned back in and said, "After your visit with Blanche you may as well go home, Jess." He gestured to the tomcat. "Don't forget to take the monster mouser with you. Leave your phone number at Blanche's desk after your gossip session."

Chapter 6

O'Bourne's ranch, present day

Russell raised his hand, hesitated a minute, then gave the front door a few decisive taps. He wanted to clear the air but was unsure how much to tell Jessie. *He'd have to lie, at least by omission. You loser, Bonham, you know you just wanted to see her—even for a day.* Maybe she wasn't home. He couldn't decide if that would be a bad thing, or a lucky break. Just as he turned to walk away, he heard footsteps. Then he heard Jessie yell.

"Who is it?"

"Pond scum," he yelled back.

The door popped open. Jack sauntered lazily out, and Jessie stood looking at Russell with a surprised expression on her face. Her glorious hair hung loose around her shoulders and she wore one of her goofy T-shirts. Today her pullover was an eye-popping green color, emblazoned with an image of Edvard Munch's painting, *The Scream.* Stone-washed jeans covered her long legs. In her left hand, she held a paring knife and a fat lemon.

Russell gave her his best cheesy grin, the one that had worked on Hannah O'Bourne when he and Kevin got into trouble as kids.

"Don't give ME that look, Bonham." But even as she glared at him, she handed him the knife, and motioned him inside.

27

He did a mental fist pump. Then he chastised himself. Getting too involved with Jessie would be as easy as sinking into quicksand.

Just mend fences and get out.

Stepping inside, he surveyed the room. Dan had repainted. What was once a robin's egg blue was now daffodil yellow. He scanned the room to make certain Jessie's lovely small paintings, the ones he'd been so fond of, were still hung. There were several new ones. As he sauntered over to the bowl of lemons on the kitchen counter, he scrutinized each piece.

Ten minutes later, he sat on a swivel stool at the black granite counter, his hand wrapped around an icy glass of homemade lemonade. Nearby was a depression era glass lemon squeezer. The tangy smell of citrus pulp and freshly grated rind permeated the air. He'd his share by cutting the yellow fruits, flicking the seeds out with a fork, and working the lemon halves over the ridges of the juicer.

The taste of lemonade always made him feel grateful to the O'Bournes. With the first refreshing sip, memories of summers he'd spent at Dan and Hannah's place waylaid him. If he shut his eyes, he could hear Hannah O'Bourne telling him to wipe his feet and come in for a BLT and "home squeezed". A lump rose in his throat. He missed her. Hannah, in this kitchen, had been the beating heart of the ranch for years. He'd helped out on the ranch from grade school to graduation for a few dollars plus meals.

Meals.

Man, he'd been so timid and scrawny when he first met Kevin. *Nine*, he thought. They'd become inseparable. Knowing his old man was useless as a broken toaster, Kevin's parents had simply taken young Russell into their fold. A niggle of sympathy for the lost little boy he'd once been passed over him. With it came a renewed determination that his child—his son—would never go hungry. Not for food. Not for comfort. Not for love.

Stay on task and stop feeling sorry for yourself. Talk to Jessie, you moron.

He set his jaw and glanced at her. Standing there by the counter, she was so close, yet as unreachable as Mars.

"Sorry to butt in on your morning, Jess. Uh . . . I figured I'd stop in and see if there was any heavy work you needed done while your dad was away."

"Nope," she answered curtly. "I'm good, thanks." She idly twisted one of her red curls around and around a finger.

"Nice of you to come home and house sit for Dan and Marty, so they could take a proper honeymoon. I'm real happy for them. Nobody can replace your mom, but Marty seems good for your Dad." He smiled. "Sure never pictured Dan flying off to Honolulu, though."

"Yeah," Jessie said, her expression softening, "me neither. Dad called and did a lot of complaining about the airline seats after the trip over, though. Swears they were made for city folk built like hoe handles."

Russell chuckled, thinking of the huge man stuffed into a tiny airline seat. Dan O'Bourne was not just a big man, but as canny as they came. He'd seen the naked longing in Russell's eyes whenever he looked at Jessie, starting when she'd just turned fifteen. He'd warned him, "She's too young. And I know my Jessie. When she grows up, she won't stick around Sage Bluff. And you—hell, you're a homebody. I can't picture you happy anywhere but here, can you?" It had given the smitten teenager something to chew on.

He frowned, remembering how he'd come to agree with Dan. So many years later, he still couldn't picture himself anywhere else. And he for darn sure couldn't picture Jessie coming home to live in Sage Bluff. She didn't seem to need people. Certainly not some broke son of a drunk.

Her obsession with art was the tool he used to put distance between him and the tantalizing redhead. All it took was a sharp criticism of her work now and then. A belittling comment pushed her away just as firmly as if he'd shoved her.

Heck, she was like his absentee mother, not content to stay where the good Lord had put her. But it didn't make him want her any less. He frowned and looked over at Jessie, ached to reach out, pull her into him, run his fingers through that mane

29

of hair and tell her everything. The whole sordid story. And now—now he needed her to finally come home for good.

"Say, Jess," he said, "uh . . . how long you going to be around?"

There was no answer. Jessie had walked over to stand at the dining table in front of the large rectangular window. He stared at her slim, shapely form. She stood awash in sunlight, her back to him, arms around her torso, hugging herself. He opened his mouth, then shook his head instead. As usual, he had waited too long to talk, and she was lost in thought, staring out at only God and Jessie knew what.

"Great lemonade," he ventured. "I love the way you mixed the pink broccoli in with the little plastic soldiers and the feathers from the albatross." He slurped loudly. "Deeelicious."

"Uh huh," she murmured, gazing raptly at the sky, "Thanks. You should see the clouds today, Russ. The sky is dazzling."

He sighed. "Blue. Looks about the same as any other day."

Same old Jess. Flesh and blood couldn't compete with color and light. Leastwise, not *my* flesh and blood. He stared out, trying to see what she saw. Well, the sky *was* pretty. His gaze swung back to Jessie and his heart nearly stopped.

Her auburn hair was a fiery halo. Then she turned and for just a second looked at him full on. Her eyes held an odd expression and he felt the intense blue of her eyes. Suddenly, he didn't just see the color. It slammed into him like an ocean wave. She immediately turned away, to look out the window, but it was too late. For the first time in his life he not only *saw* beauty but *felt* it—a soul-searing pain of realization.

She was silhouetted against the light, her back to him now, and behind her, the upper third of the window blossomed with richly-colored transparent glass in a grape and vine pattern. The sun tossed colors through the stained-glass window onto the tile floor with the challenge of a gauntlet, daring him to ignore the resultant play of prismatic blues, greens and reds. The effect was mesmerizing. The window Jessie had made was magnificent. Deep inside, in the locked piece of his heart he

30

hated to admit was reserved for Jessie—and Jessie only—the captive voice whispered, *"And Lord help me, so is she."*

Willing himself to relock that chamber, he shut his eyes. Shut her away. When he opened them, the window had become simply a means of looking outside, colorful though it was. With a pang of regret, he remembered Jessie painstakingly building the stained-glass window—a gift for her parents' twenty-fifth wedding anniversary. She'd cut and soldered the miniscule bits of glass during an unusual hiatus from her incessant drawing. He'd been so impressed when she'd started the project, knowing her fear of sharp objects made cutting the pieces a miserable undertaking.

What had he told her when she'd finished the project? Her eyes had glowed with excitement. She'd tried to explain how joyous the streaming colors of light made her feel, how the beauty of it made her heart swell to bursting. Finally, she'd told him, it was one, wondrous piece of glass where hundreds of shards had been. He'd said something about a waste of time.

Oh, yeah. He winced at the realization. He'd said, "God, Jess, grow up a little. It's just a picture of grapes. You're such a funny kid."

He wiped a hand across his forehead and pressed his lips together, his mouth suddenly tasting as sour as if the lemonade was missing sugar.

We only hurt the ones we love.

Pushing thoughts of the past away, he heaved a sigh and turned from the window to its creator.

"I know you're blasted mad at me. I'm sorry."

She stiffened but turned to face him. With a jolt he saw her eyes were moist. Moist, but angry.

"I am. After all my folks did for you, the years you spent as part of the family, you should've at least been at Mom's funeral. And . . . well, it just seemed like you got married so fast, that's all. And to Kevin's fiancée, of all people." She twisted her fingers together nervously. "So, yeah. I guess you could say I'm pretty damn mad. Disappointed, because I wondered—"

"I know." He frowned. "I'm sorry. But there wasn't anything going on between Trish and me while Kevin was alive." *Actually, not afterwards, either.* "Please believe that. I missed the funeral—"

Jessie put out her hands, palms up, the expression on her face anguished. "You don't owe me an explanation about Trish. But yes, you MISSED Mom's funeral. Dad and I needed you. And you went off and got married like you didn't have anyone to think of but yourself—you selfish...." Her voice caught. "You...you not only got married, but you never even invited us. Never even let us know. We had to hear it from Sage Bluff's gossip line. You absolute—"

"Don't say it, Jess. I didn't think. *I couldn't have gone through with the marriage if you and Dan had been there.* "I'll say it myself. I was a thoughtless bastard. I know. And I understand how it must have seemed to you. Irresponsible. Thoughtless."

Jessie snorted. "Don't hold back, but yeah, that about sums it up. Guess you know why I never sent a wedding gift."

"Can we shelve the marriage with Trish just for now?" He made a dismissive gesture with his hand. "I need to talk to you about Kevin and—"

Icy blue eyes chilled him to the core.

"Shelve it? Oh, s*ure*, let's just *shelve* it. After all, it's only been shelved for six years—"

"Jess—"

"You and Trish aren't any of my business. But Dad knows you had a huge fight with Kevin before his accident. So if it wasn't over Trish, what was it about? What was going on that day?" Jessie balled her fists at her hips. "The day Kevin died."

He stared back at her. Horror at what she was implying shot through him.

"THAT'S what you've been thinking this past six years?" He stepped toward her. "You think we fought? You think I hurt him? Or killed him? I . . . I just found him in the barn, Jess. He was already dead. There was nothing I could do."

32

He lowered his voice to a near whisper. "You can't think I had anything to do with Kevin's death, Jess."

She looked at him, blue eyes narrowed, her lips pressed tightly into a thin line.

He continued. "I thought you were mad at me because of the funeral. I missed the funeral because I had to—"

His cell phone buzzed. Russell and Jessie continue to stare at each other—each unable to break eye contact. Then he patted his pockets, reached in and pulled the phone out. He looked at the caller ID.

Hellish bad timing! Dammit! Without thinking, he reached for her and she drew back. He let his arms drop, the phone in his hand still insistent.

"I have to take this. And we both need to calm down. For Pete's sake, if I'd known you were thinking I might've hurt Kev, I'd never have let this go on so long. We ARE clearing this up before you leave Sage Bluff," he said emphatically. "And I hope you think about coming home more often. Actually, think about coming home for good."

He turned and strode out the front door, letting it bang shut behind him.

Jessie frowned. She hugged herself tightly and let her chin drop to her chest. Something was definitely wrong in Russell's world. She hadn't been sky-gazing when she'd ignored Russell's crazy comments. Not this time. She'd needed time to process what she'd unexpectedly seen in the window glass. The fleeting reflections of Russell's face had shown worry, sadness, and yearning. It was the yearning that had surprised her most. And yanked her heartstrings.

Forget the look. He's a married man with a son.

Her eyes filled and she blinked hard. She knew if she'd allowed herself to look back at him at that moment, it would have exposed her heart plain as the prairie grass. Come home for good? Who was he kidding?

Later, she'd paint the memory of Russ sitting at the table, holding the glass of lemonade, light bouncing from the blue shirt he was wearing to wash the underside of his strong chin in the same ultramarine. She had a sketchbook full of memory studies of him—page after page. Him and her Dad. Laughing with Kevin. Teasing her mother. And she knew she would draw one of him with that look in his eyes—the look she had seen in the reflection. Then, hopefully, she could lock those feelings away and simply concentrate on what to paint next.

Jessie took a deep breath and lifted her hand, making a few imaginary strokes in the air. Remembering his posture, his eyes. Cementing the picture in her mind. The tilt to his head. The color harmony of the yellow drink against the blue uniform shirt. His hair just a little untidy.

That *damn* Irish temper of hers. Would she ever learn to control those firecracker explosions? And worse. Now she realized that, after all these years, she wasn't as angry as she was afraid. Terrified of what he had to tell her. The week Kevin died and her mother collapsed, something had happened that changed Russell. She knew the man. And she knew the emotion on his face at Kevin's burial. She had recognized it with horror.

It had been guilt.

Russell stood on Jessie's back porch, phone pressed to his right ear. He pressed his left palm hard against the back of his head. A throbbing had started near his temple, the pain working its way to jackhammer intensity.

"Well, damn, Arvid. What did Doc Turner say about it? The last I heard, he thought the girl was stabilized. He told me she should make the trip just fine."

"Huh," Arvid grunted. "You know how he hates to lose a patient. He's upset, Russell. So is the EMT, Cassy Adams, who rode with her. But, like Doc says, nothing's ever guaranteed with head injuries."

"So now we have a murder. Did he have an idea on the time of the attack?"

"Nah, not really. He said probably late evening. The main reason she lived until morning is that hay bales hold a lot of heat, probably kept her from dying of shock. Probably whoever hid her body in the hay thought she was already dead."

"Maybe," Russell said, "or someone just didn't have the heart to finish the job and figured nature would do it for him."

"Maybe, but I wonder if there was more than one perp involved. After all, Amber was hauled about a hundred yards from the road. It had to be a fairly strong guy, even if he was dragging her.

"Could be there were two of them, I guess. Or of it was just one, he might've shoved her into his vehicle and drove right over the field to the haystack. I took another gander at the crime scene photos. It looks like someone probably drove over the field, then came back, got the cycle and hid it behind the stack. So . . . probably drove over it twice. Once with their own vehicle, once with the Harley. Look at the photos again and you'll see what I mean."

"Huh." Arvid mused, "Okey-doke."

"I think whoever did it knew right where Dan's fencing pliers were usually hung on the fence. That smacks of some— and I hate to say it—some local guy. Did you get much from the girl's parents?"

"Yeah, some. They said Amber had a boyfriend, Jake Ward. Seems this Ward got into some drug trouble at the college." Arvid snorted into the cell phone. "God, I *hate* drugs. Takes so many young people and wrecks their lives. Be kinder to run over 'em with a truck than get 'em hooked on that crap."

"I know. So, they have much info on this boyfriend?"

"Well, here's what they got. He got kicked out of college on his keister because he couldn't keep his grades up. Then, Amber dumped him because of the drugs. After that, he must have cleaned up some, because he was able to get a job up at the Bakken oil fields in North Dakota. Amber still considered him *"the ex"*, at least according to mama."

"We'd better verify that," Russell rolled his shoulders as he spoke, trying to loosen the tight muscles.

"Yep. Mamas don't always get the true scoop. Sometimes what their kids tell 'em as gospel is just so much snake oil."

"Well, follow up on that angle. Or give that chore to Baker if you're too stretched."

35

"Huh. You think that's why the little gal was so afraid of calling the station, Russell? Didn't want to rat out her boyfriend? Lots of abused women don't want to land their men in hot water."

"Could be. Could be something else entirely," Russell said glumly.

"I'll ask Denver P.D. to give the parents the bad news in person. They'd planned to fly to Billings to stay with her in the hospital. Now, the body will be flown back down to Denver. Sad."

"Depressing," Russell agreed. He paced back and forth on the wooden porch.

"Her folks gave the Denver police a list of Amber's close friends. Station down there says they'll fax the names to us, too, but they were going to talk to those in the Denver area to see if anyone has a clue what was going on with her lately."

"Good, good."

"You okay, Russ? You don't sound so hot."

"Yeah, I'm okay. Headache is all."

"Tell you what. Grab a couple aspirin from Blanche when you come in. She's got a regular pharmacy in that desk of hers. You want me to find out where this Jake Ward was when the girl was attacked?"

"Yeah, do that."

"Oh, and let me tell you the most interesting thing Amber's parents told the Denver cops who went to tell 'em their daughter was hurt."

Arvid began reading from his notes and Russell gave a sharp intake of breath.

Five minutes later, he said, "Man, that puts a weird twist on it, doesn't it? Give me Jack Reynolds' phone number, Arvid. I don't have it with me." He pulled a pen from his pocket and scribbled on a scrap of paper while the other detective spoke. Then he patted the palm of his hand repeatedly against his thigh, a concerned expression on his face. *Geez.*

"You get that, Russ?"

"Yeah, I got it. I got it, but I sure don't like it. I'll be back to the station soon, Arvid, and we can brainstorm on it." He

36

sighed. "But someone has to talk with Jessie about this. I'm already here, so I guess it better be me."
God, I'd rather take a beating.

Russell walked back into the bright kitchen and picked up his lemonade from the counter. He took a swallow, set the glass down on the black granite surface and looked at Jessie, his expression stony.

"Yeah, well, maybe you know why she was up here, Jess? Got something you want to share with me?"

"What? Of course, I don't, but I can tell you're in a twist about something, Russ. Is this Twenty Questions?"

Russell narrowed his eyes. "Don't be a smart ass. I'm serious. Guess what she was doing up here."

"Okay, I'll play along." Jessie struck an elaborate pose lowered her voice to mimic that of a prosecuting attorney. She held her fist in front of her mouth like a microphone. "I have no idea what this young woman was doing in my father's field. Can you please tell the court what Miss Reynolds was doing up here, Sergeant Bonham?" She grimaced at him and lowered her hand. "Heck, just ask her, for Pete's sake."

He gave her a disgusted look and said seriously, "I'm afraid we're not going to be able to ask Amber who attacked her. She died on the helicopter flight to St. Vincent's Hospital in Billings. When we find the guy who hurt her, he'll be charged with murder, not assault."

"Oh, no." Jessie covered her mouth with her hands. "I was hoping . . ."

"Yeah," Russell said wearily, "We were all hoping she'd make it. Doc Turner thought she was strong enough to make the flight to Billings, too."

"Poor little thing. She looked so young, too."

"Older than she looked. Twenty-three. Arvid found out she was going to college down at the University of Denver. Doing graduate work, writing a thesis."

"Wow. There's nothing in Sage Bluff that screams research opportunity. Hmmm, maybe if she was in agricultural studies, I suppose."

"That's the kicker. Arvid spent some time on the phone with the cop in Denver, the guy asked to notify the parents after we first found her. Amber had phoned her folks as recently as two days ago, and they knew why she came to Sage Bluff."

"Oh, really. Why?"

"Jess, she was on her way to see *you*."

Chapter 7

O'Bourne's ranch, present day

"Geez. I've told you everything I could possibly tell you, Russell." Jessie said, scraping her chair back from the kitchen table and standing. "We've been at it for half an hour. There isn't one blessed thing I could possibly add. Do you want me to write it in blood?"

"Oh, don't be a drama queen."

"I'm serious. I'm done. I don't care if you do have a badge."

A noncommittal grunt escaped him.

"Speak up," she grumbled. "Were her folks *positive* she was coming here? Here, to this house?"

He sighed and leaned back, tilting the chair onto two legs until Jessie gave him a dark look. He straightened, letting the chair thump back down, then stretched his long legs out and crossed booted ankles. "'Fraid so."

"But . . . to see me?"

"Uh, not to see *you* specifically. Mrs. Reynolds said Amber wanted to talk with the O'Bournes in Sage Bluff. It concerned her Master's thesis. She was making a big loop, interviewing anyone she thought could contribute information for her paper."

"So our family wasn't the only place she planned to stop. I wonder what she thought we could contribute. And I'd sure like to know what her thesis was about."

"No clue. And Amber's parents didn't know where else she'd been in the past few days. But there she was—in *your* family's field." He frowned, looking at her expectantly.

Jessie saw his knee jerking rhythmically up and down and winced. It had always been the sign that Russell was stressed or worried. "There's something you aren't saying, Russ."

"Yeah. After Amber died, we spoke to Jack and Shelly Reynolds again. They have a request. They asked if you would please call them tomorrow."

"What on earth for?"

"I'd like to know that answer, too. Families of victims often have odd requests. I guess it's okay if you give them a call. Here's the number." He leaned over, pulled a piece of paper from his pocket and copied the information onto a grocery list on the table. He handed it to her and sat back, the knee jerking immediately starting up like a car revving its engine.

"You've been lying to me, Jess. It's time to come clean."

"Lying? Clean? You're nuts. What makes you think I've been anything but totally honest with you?"

"Because when they heard who found their daughter, according to the Denver cops one of Amber's parents said, "Oh, we *know* her.""

She wracked her brain. "I—"

"I'll be speaking to them again today. But I'd like to hear the truth from you first."

"I told you the truth. Oh!"

"Oh, what?"

"I'll bet they're art collectors, Russ. They might mean they know *of* me from galleries or articles, that type of thing. Not know *me* personally. Most people who read the art magazines or follow major shows have probably heard of me."

Russell gave her a doubtful look. "Hell, Jessie . . . don't be so full of yourself."

"I . . . I'm not." Hurt stabbed through her. "You asked me and . . . I just—"

"Never mind," he interrupted, waving his hand dismissively. "We can follow up on that, Oh, Queen of the Art

40

World. I'd appreciate it if you'd phone them and then let me know how the conversation goes. And we'll be checking with them, too, of course," he said coldly.

She nodded, his chilly tone cutting her to the quick.

"Now. In your statement to Arvid, you said the victim spoke to you before the ambulance came, but was somewhat incoherent. Did you understand any of what she said?"

"I put it in my statement, Russell. Didn't you even read it? She was worried about the police coming. Terrified, actually. She kept saying 'No police'."

"So, nothing else? Are you sure that's all you heard?"

"She wasn't making sense. I asked her if she knew who'd hurt her. Her voice was so raspy—so weak—but it sounded like she said, *Thomas Moran*'."

"Are you nuts?" He stood, fairly spitting the words at her. "She told you who attacked her, and you didn't share it with the police? What in God's name were you thinking?"

"Oh, get a grip." Jessie stared at his dumbfounded expression. "Thomas Moran was an artist who died way back in 1926. Several of my old relatives knew him. He was the one who taught my aunt Kate to paint—the aunt who was murdered. Remember? Someone set the school on fire trying to cover it up. Moran was famous. He gave St. Benedict's Indian school a couple paintings worth a bundle, but the priest who ran the school died before he could sell them. The artwork got lost somehow."

"Yeah. That rings a bell." He rubbed his chin.

"It was only a day after Kate located the paintings that she was killed. It happened while she was teaching school here in Sage Bluff."

"Oh, yeah, Dan told me about that. Still, we have to keep the name in mind. Maybe the killer actually *is* named Thomas Moran, or something that sounded like it to you." Russell stood, picked up his glass and set it in the sink.

He looked out the window. An enormous barn with steps leading to the upper area of the building filled the side yard. Man-high hollyhocks grew in profusion along the front of

41

the building, the crimson blossoms camouflaged against the red barn. He wished they'd paint it white. An overwhelming sadness threatened to crush him. He looked at Jessie. She'd followed his gaze out the window. The wounded expression in her eyes stabbed him through the heart.

He cleared his throat. "Jess, we really need to talk."

"No." She flung her hand up in a blocking gesture, tilting her head to the side away from him. "I don't want to talk about anything right now." She wouldn't look at him. "All I can think about is that poor girl."

"Well, we'll do it on your timetable. You've been gone for several years. Whenever you've come back to visit your dad, nobody let me know. But sooner or later you, your dad and I have to talk. I miss—"

Her face took on a stony, stubborn look that he knew well.

Let it drop.

He sighed. Giving himself a mental shake, he reminded himself she thought of him only as a family friend—and a married man.

So be it. I'm also a patient man. A very patient man. And Jess girl, I have something you are going to want.

Through the window, he glimpsed Jack coming from the barn, heading toward the house with something dangling from his jaws. The big tom had a purposeful stride, his belly wobbling a little side to side in time to his swishing tail.

"Okay then. Getting back to the business at hand, I want you to be careful out here by yourself. Lock your doors and windows. Keep a phone handy." He placed one of his business cards on the counter. "Here's my number."

"You don't think it could have anything to do with the missing Thomas Moran paintings, do you? Maybe that's what Amber was trying to tell me."

"Hmph. Get real. We already have a lead we're following. And nobody's going to kill someone over a couple of paintings."

"No? You'd better rethink that, Mr. Smarty Cop. Today they'd be worth, oh . . . upwards of ten or fifteen million. Each.

I read that one of Thomas Moran's paintings of the Green River area of Wyoming sold for nearly eighteen million dollars in 2008. You may not appreciate art, but plenty of people do."

"You're yanking my chain. Eighteen million?" He laughed. "You were always lousy at math. You probably misread the amount and added a few zeros."

She glowered at him.

"Besides, I *do* like art. I appreciate it as much as the next guy." He bit his bottom lip. "Hey, I'm sorry I used to give you such a hard time about drawing every minute of the day when you were in school."

She ignored the comment. "Yeah sure, you're a connoisseur, all right. There's nothing quite as artistically pleasing as the tapestry of dogs playing poker you used to love. And I'll bet you still have it."

He felt the telltale flush creep up his neck.

"Thought so." Jessie smirked.

"K.D. likes it."

"Yeah. Little kids would," she said sarcastically. "Better wrap your mind around that art disappearance as a motive. You know, I've always been surprised nobody was still looking for those two missing paintings."

"Oh, Jess. Nobody around Sage Bluff today would have a clue about the value of a painting like that. Not a clue. My bet is on a hopped up ex-boyfriend." He walked to the door and glanced over his shoulder. "Don't forget. Call her folks."

"Tomorrow."

He started to push open the door, telling himself the first thing he'd do when he got home was pitch that tapestry. He turned back to Jessie.

"By the way, that window ...," he cleared his throat, the words coming almost of their own volition. He flipped his hand toward the stained glass. "The window you made, Jess. It's—it's goddamn gorgeous." He stepped through the open door.

Jessie stood there, open-mouthed as Jack strolled proudly in, dropping the still live mouse on the welcome mat. The big tomcat squinted at her with a pleased expression. A small grey blur bolted for the narrow space under the kitchen range.

Chapter 8

O'Bourne's ranch, present day

Stars were scattered across the sky like confetti when Jessie finally gave up on sleep. She tossed the covers aside, got out of bed and padded barefoot down the stairs in her green silk pajamas. She looked at the kitchen clock, mentally computing the time difference between Sage Bluff and Honolulu. Grabbing her phone, took the slip of paper from under the magnet on the refrigerator, and punched in her father's number.

What a way to interrupt a honeymoon.

"Hey, Dad. Um, getting a good tan?"

"Having a ball, little girl. So, what's wrong? You sound funny. Tell me fast, we're heading to a luau. It's a fancy word for barbecue." He yelled something unintelligible to his wife, Marty, in the background, then came back on the line. "What?"

She tried to give him a shorthand version, but he interrupted every sentence to say, "Oh God, on MY property? That's just awful." Then to Marty he said, "Go get yourself one of those coconut drinks. This is going to take a while."

"Yes. And they hid her in your haystack. It was hideous."

"In my haystack—oh dear Lord."

"Yeah, sorry. This gets worse. Russell called after dinner to say your big bull-nose pliers, the one you use for fence repairs, was definitely the weapon." She heard muffled swearing. "Did you ever hear of Amber Reynolds?"

45

"Don't think so."

"She was coming here. I don't mean to Sage Bluff. I mean here, to the house!"

"What the—?"

She bit her lip and closed her eyes.

"Yeah. I know, Daddy. It's all awful. There was a message on the answering machine from her saying she wanted to stop by, but the beeper was turned off and I didn't hear it until tonight."

"Lord have mercy. What an awful thing."

Again, she heard him yell to Marty.

"I'm telling you, honeypot, go down to the bar and get yourself a piñata colada or something, I'll be down in a few minutes."

Muffled tones came through the earpiece, then, "I don't *care* what they're called. I need to talk to Jessie, so I might be a few minutes late. Go enjoy yourself with the tour group. For god's sake, don't let them leave without my fat behind sitting in the bus. Try to get one of those bench seats in the back."

"So?" Jessie prompted.

"No, honey. I didn't know her, but you'd better go check the mail on my desk. There's a letter there you'll want to share with Russell. It's from an FBI agent."

"What? You're kidding, right?"

"No, it's the doggondest story. It seems the FBI has an art theft Office. The Thomas Moran paintings that disappeared years ago . . . well, there's an agent following a new lead."

"I know the old story, Dad. What about the FBI fellow?"

"Someone called Christie's auction house and described the little painting Moran had given Kate Morgan, asking if they could list it on consignment. It's been on a list of stolen Moran work ever since it disappeared, and the employee at Christie's was well aware of that. Sounds like all of the auction houses have a list of "hot" art—full descriptions, the whole shebang."

"Did they find the person trying to sell it?" She paced back and forth holding the phone to her ear, wishing she'd put on her slippers. The tile floor felt like ice on her bare feet.

"No. The guy was calling from a disposable phone. They couldn't track the number. And something spooked him and he hung up."

"Wow. How did you find all this out?"

"I talked to the FBI agent." He paused. "If the girl did say Thomas Moran, then Russell is on the wrong trail. You'd better call that FBI fellow and tell him about this girl. And tell Russell again to check the Moran angle."

Jessie groaned. "Like I can get him to listen about anything."

"I know you and Russell don't get along, but you used to be as close as brother and sister. He's a good guy." He cleared his throat. "I know you're mad that he married Kevin's girl. And there's something—"

"Don't get me talking about him, Dad," she interrupted. "You'll never get to your luau."

"Yeah, yeah. Methinks you doth protest too much."

She ignored him. "But what if the girl was afraid of the police for a good reason? What if it *was* a cop who hit her? If the FBI wrote to you, they may have touched base with the Sheriff's Department in town, too."

"But that would have nothing to do with the girl. Where would *she* fit in?"

"No idea. When I talked with Russell this afternoon he said they have a lead. Something about a druggy boyfriend. I don't know if the girl had any drugs in her system, or in her bags, but he wouldn't tell me if there was. He'd probably say 'police business' if I asked."

"But—"

"I'll tell him about the letter from the FBI, but he already thinks I have a screw loose. And if it really was a cop who murdered that girl, what if he shares my info with the wrong guy?"

"Hmmm. I don't know. I just can't imagine any of the police . . . ." His voice trailed off.

"Dad," she said hesitantly. "I've always wondered. Several friends from school told me Kevin and Russ had a huge fight the day he died. Did you know that? Do you think Russ was involved somehow in Kevin's—um— accident? Dad, what if Russ *is* the cop the girl was afraid of?

A belly laugh erupted into the phone. "Honey, if you think Russell is the guy, you do have a screw loose. No way. There is no way in hell he would hurt anyone. And no damn way he'd use one of *my* tools to do it. Hahahah. And not on our property." He sighed. "I don't care if Russell's old man was a louse, the kid is *not* his old man. He loves our family."

"But—"

"Aw cripes, I'm not going to argue with you about it on the phone."

"Sorry, Dad. I'm just worried. There aren't that many cops in Sage Bluff and—"

"Just be careful. If someone hurt this college student— on our property, damn it—because they thought she knew something about the missing Moran paintings, they must know she was coming to see you. Sweetie, you might not be safe there at the ranch all by your lonesome."

"Don't worry. I'll be fine," she said reassuringly.

"Hope so, honey. You know, it always seemed like one of those wild treasure hunt stories. Buried gold. Missing jewels. But those paintings would be worth a lot of money. Enough for some jackass to kill for." He cleared his throat. "I think I'd better grab a plane ticket and come home."

"Oh no you don't! I wouldn't be safe from Marty if I ruined your honeymoon. No. Absolutely not."

"Hmph. I'm getting homesick, anyhow. The trees are weird here and there's too damn much water." She heard a crash and then, "No, I did NOT say I was sick of the honeymoon! No, I'm not putting off the luau trip. I'm *coming*."

"I'm sorry I upset you," Jessie said, trying not to chuckle. "I'll call Russell tomorrow. Go to your luau. Eat some roast pork. Watch some hula dancers. Go—"

"You do that. I gotta go."

Click.

She sat on the kitchen stool with the dead phone in her hand, twirling a long strand of red hair around and around her finger. Something was bothering her. Just out of reach. Then she had it, and her stomach clenched. *She really hadn't noticed there was a message. The answering machine only turned off the beeper if someone had already played the message.*

It was nearly 10:45, too late to call Russell. She went to the window and looked out. She considered going out to the studio over the barn to get some painting done, but she was just too keyed up, too worried. Her eyes found the Big Dipper in the inky blackness, the constellation surrounded by stars as numerous as salt poured from a shaker. She latched the window, then moved on, locking and checking each of the others in turn.

After flipping on the porch light, she went down to the basement to secure the windows and visit her father's Browning gun vault. It was a black steel monster as tall as she was, adorned with a picture of an eagle and American flag. Her fingers spun the combination lock, and she opened the heavy door and lifted out a Remington pump-action shotgun and a handful of shells.

When she was in high school, she used to shoot it at the local range. She didn't much like the noise, but her dad pushed hearing protection headphones at her and told her it was something important to learn. She smiled. She could almost hear his gruff voice saying, "Since we're going to have them in the house, everyone in the family should be competent with every single model. Don't give me that 'But Daddy, I'm a girl' crap."

Up in the guest room, she propped the shotgun in the corner nearest the bed, put the shells in the nightstand and locked the bedroom door. She crawled back under the covers and made a mental list: do some target shooting to get back up to speed, phone the FBI fellow, call the folks down in Denver.

And call Russell to tell him someone must have been in the house and had listened to the answering machine message.

Chapter 9

Rural Montana, April 1918

Thomas Moran, a bent reed of a man, stood on the hill, thumbs and gnarled index fingers touching to form a rectangle. He peered through this makeshift picture frame at the picturesque scene below. A smile creased his grey beard. Then he mounted and nudged his horse downhill toward St. Benedict's Mission schoolyard. Behind his patient chestnut gelding plodded two pack animals with panniers holding well-organized art supplies, finished paintings, a ragbag of foodstuffs and several water canteens, most a half sip from empty.

In Thomas's mind, a painting was already in progress, with color brushing onto the mental canvas in bold strokes to shape the dilapidated school, the two rustic cabins, and the tangle of Blackfoot Indian children playing tag nearby. A scattering of colorful chickens were quick swipes of a loaded brush. Beyond the drab buildings, the Yellowstone River flowed, blue and rough, its banks lined with blood-red willow and the contrasting mustard green of budding cottonwood trees. Waving his hand in the air, he filled in swatches of color only he could see.

"I think I'll title it *Spring on the Yellowstone*. Not real imaginative, but accurate."

Thomas, sitting on a plump pillow strapped to the saddle to cushion his thin bones, continued on, lost in thought. He was unperturbed by excited yells and giggles erupting from the irrepressible small brown bodies who now swarmed like bees toward his pack train as he entered the schoolyard.

The artist's imaginary painting was interrupted when a scowling, black-robed figure emerged from the doorway of the schoolhouse. A sour-faced nun stood watching him. She shooed the children away and gestured to the left toward the water pump and hitching post near the building. It was hospitable to let a stranger drink at the well before pleasantries or business—anyone riding in would be coming from a distance. Thomas gave her a quick wave and tipped his hat. He guided his horses to the pump area and climbed, saddle-sore and weary, from his high perch.

Yep, the old bones are getting arthritic.

A redheaded girl of nine or ten, her hair in disheveled braids, sat cross-legged on the ground, not looking up as he pumped a dipperful of water for himself, drank, filled a canteen, and drew a bucket for each horse. He looped their reins over the hitching post and walked over to the girl. She was drawing in the dust at her feet with a twig, the tip of her small pink tongue smothering her upper lip as she concentrated.

"What are you working at, sprout?" he asked, peering over her shoulder at the drawing scratched into the hard soil. Several other sticks and twigs of various thicknesses were scattered on the ground around her feet. *Remarkable—a makeshift sketching set—working with dirt instead of paper, and still getting a better drawing than most adults.*

She jumped up, startled, and stood to face him, smoothing her threadbare calico dress with grimy hands. The pale fabric hung baggy and wrinkled on her small frame, the name 'O'Bourne' embroidered over her heart.

"Good gravy, mister, you liked to scare the bejeezus right outta me!" she yelped. She smiled wide. "I don't hear nothin' when I'm drawin'. I'm making a picture of them hills over yonder." The girl pointed toward buttes in the distance. She surveyed her handiwork with a solemn expression. "Wish I had colors." She tugged thoughtfully on one braid, then looked apprehensively around and saw the nun steaming toward them. Her little foot darted out and obliterated the detailed landscape.

The youngster focused on the approaching woman with a shimmer of fear in her blue eyes. Involuntarily, her small hand flew to her cheek and touched the shadow of a bruise on the delicate skin. Her face paled, the freckles peppered across her cheeks lending the only hint of color. Then Thomas saw her straighten her back, lift her chin, and all emotion vanished from her expression.

"Kate! What have I told you about such language? You rinse your filthy hands at the pump and get right in there and work on your reading. Maybe extra work will teach you to use better manners. The good Lord knows you need to find something more practical to do with your hands. Always drawing lines in the dirt—it's disgusting. Now git!"

Kate stiffened and turned to the pump, grabbed the pump handle and hung her weight on it to pull it down, drawing several gushes of water. On the ground under the spigot, a metal tub was placed to catch the flow. Kate squatted and swished her hands in the cold water, then yanked her hands out, wiped her fingers on her dress and sprinted toward the school.

The nun glared after the running child, then swiveled an acne-blanketed face toward Thomas. Her eyes were the pale green of spring moss—almost startling, he noticed with interest. *They'd be beautiful,* Thomas thought, *if she didn't have the expression of a rabid badger.* His mind went immediately to what colors he'd need to mix to get that shade of luminous green. Thomas gave himself a mental shake when he realized the nun was speaking to him.

"Sorry, mister—that one has her head in the clouds. She's more work than the rest of the students put together. I'm the teacher here. . . Sister Mary Campbell. What can I do for you?"

"Name's Thomas Moran, Sister Campbell." Thomas removed his hat. "I'm traveling through Montana to do some painting." He turned his head and watched the small figure run to the schoolhouse and disappear, braids bouncing, through the door. The artist stroked his chin thoughtfully and scratched his head. "I had some business with the priest, partly concerning that little gal. Leastwise, I imagine that was Katherine O'Bourne—heard you call her Kate, and that flaming red hair runs in the family. I'm afraid I got here several days before Father Michael expected me. Is he here?"

"No. Sorry. Father Michael is away hunting for funds to pay for the new building the church hopes to build near Sage Bluff." She bowed her head slightly. "I pray for his success every day, Mr. Moran. However, I'm filling in. I'm stuck here until he returns, and I expected him to be more reliable. He's way overdue."

"Well, that's unfortunate, Sister. I saw Kate's dad a while back, and he asked me to check on his daughter when I rode through. He'll come for Kate as soon as he can. Might be another month. He's managing the crew at the Anaconda copper mine, can't get away. His wife got that terrible influenza, and now her doctor's worried she could lose the baby they're expecting. They're keeping her in bed under a nurse's care." Thomas reached into a saddlebag, withdrew a canvas sack of coins and offered it to the nun. "Jim said they owed the school for her keep, so he sent along what's due."

The nun took the heavy bag, tossing a surprised look at Thomas. She hefted the payment, and Thomas felt an odd jolt as an unexpected look of avarice flitted across her face. She jiggled the packet up and down again, smiling slightly.

"I'm grateful, Mr. Moran, for your trouble –and it's high time they sent us something for taking on that little gal—she's a passel of extra work." She looked down at the bag of coins. "Well, you'd best come in and see the school, and have a bite to eat while I put this in a safe place. There's a pot of stew left on the stove … might still be warm. You rode in during our noon break."

Thomas followed the billowing habit of Sister Campbell through the door of the small schoolhouse building, immediately inhaling the familiar gamey scent of cooked venison. His stomach growled. Thomas glanced around at bare walls, the tattered books on battered desks. A narrow scrap of faded green curtain fluttered above the open window. Flour sack fabric, he reckoned. *Sure a bleak schoolroom,* Thomas thought. A tall white kitchen cupboard loomed in the corner, its flour bin ajar, and a dusting of white flour had drifted over the worn pine floor. At a nearby stool, pretending to read her primer, sat the nun's nemesis. Kate snuck a peek at Thomas out of the corner of her eye. Thomas winked at her, and her elfin face erupted into a smile warm enough to kindle a fire in the schoolroom's pot-bellied stove. Then, seeing the nun whip through the schoolroom door, she abandoned herself to her fate, lowered her head to the book and began to read, her finger leading the stumbling words across the page.

The nun frowned, narrowing her eyes at Kate, then turned to Thomas. "Help yourself, Mr. Moran, while I get you some bread from my cabin. I thought there was a slice left, but I guess someone took it," she said, looking pointedly at the small child. Kate kept her eyes directed downward at her primer. Sister Campbell turned and left.

A sooty, cast-iron Dutch oven sat on an imposing cook stove in the back of the room and the nearby table held blue granite-ware bowls and spoons. Thomas ambled over and peered hopefully into the pot. An unappealing brown mass sat in the bottom of the pot. "Looks like cookin' isn't Sister's strong suit," he said aloud. He was rewarded by a titter. He sniffed. *Smells okay, though.* Thomas chose a bowl and ladled a generous portion of venison stew into the tin bowl. Seeing nowhere for an adult to sit, he perched his bony bottom on a sturdy desk as the nun came toward him carrying a wrapped loaf of homemade bread. The first spoonful of stew was heaven—lukewarm, but tasty. On his painting trips, Thomas pampered his horses, but seldom took time to make himself hot dinners. He made short work of the lukewarm meal. Thomas swallowed the last spoonful, mopped the bowl with a piece of the chewy bread until it was wiped clean, and put his bowl into a nearby dishpan.

"Sister, what a delicious change from my own poor cooking. Much obliged." Thomas thought a minute, watched Kate struggle over her primer, then fibbed, "I hate to leave without seeing Father Michael. We go way back. And he promised the O'Bournes I would stay a week or more—wanted me to teach the wee gal some art. She's a prodigy, they say. I assume that arrangement is still acceptable." He continued in a mild tone, "Shall I camp over by the river?

"Well ..." began the nun.

"Must be hard feeding all these kids," Thomas jumped in. "I'm old, but I'm not decrepit, and I'm good with a fishing pole. How about I catch you some trout or catfish, 'bout every other day. When I'm ready to move on, I can leave you any leftover canned goods from my packs, since I can replenish most everything in Great Falls." Thomas looked at Sister Campbell with his best poker face, judging her reaction to the offer, then upped the ante, "Think there's still some tins of ham."

She smiled. "You're welcome to camp here, of course, Mr. Moran."

Sister Mary gazed out the window. Her eyes sidled to the horses, and Thomas had the feeling she was assessing the bulging saddlebags.

"Fish would be appreciated. But if you plan to break bread with us while you're camping, we'd still appreciate a donation to pay for your meals. The bacon, beans and flour needed to cook for so many children are expensive. Venison and rabbit brought in by trappers and hunters is our mainstay, with eggs from my small chicken flock." She went on, "And of course, Kate can't have her schooling interrupted. You can teach her in her free time if you think she'll listen to you. But why Father Michael asked you to teach her art, of all things, is beyond me."

"Think he felt the sprout needed a lot to occupy her mind, what with her mother sick and all. And I'll sure respect your class schedule, Sister Campbell. I reckon I'll feed myself at the camp, but I'll bring some fish most days when I pick up Kate, depending on my luck. Might take you up on buying some eggs, though, if you have a few to sell . . . hungry for those."

She nodded. "I'll keep some out for you tomorrow."

Thomas shifted from one tired foot to the other. "I'd appreciate it. Thank you. Also, I have some items in my saddlebags that O'Bourne and some friends sent along for the school. Want to take a look?"

"Yes, I sure do, Mr. Moran. We're always begging for even the basics—pencils, paper, books, more desks. And more Bibles, of course." Her forehead wrinkled in thought. "Students who sleep in the shed out behind the school need new blankets. St. Benedict's feeds, clothes, and teaches the little heathens, but the Indians can't give us much."

Hearing a ruckus outside, the nun fluttered toward the window and peered out, checking on the children playing outdoors. Her eyes widened. "Heathen hooligans!" she yelled out the open window. "Quit chasin' my rooster!" She yanked her head back in. "Excuse me a minute." The nun darted through the door, vulture wings of black whipping around her. As she pulled her foot through, a toe caught on the doorjamb and she stumbled on, muttering with annoyance.

Thomas chuckled. "I wouldn't want to be one of those young folk right this minute. That nun looks like a bit of bad weather." He sauntered over to Kate.

"Got somethin' for you, little miss. First, got a note here from your daddy," He handed her a scribbled letter from Jim O'Bourne. Then he reached into his pocket and pulled out several drawing pencils, a fat eraser, and a small brown booklet half-filled with his own sketches and script. The other pages were empty – ready for Kate's fingers to fill them with tiny masterpieces. He put them on her desk. Joyful eyes looked up at Thomas.

"Drawin' stuff! Real art pencils," she whispered in awe. "How'd ya' know? Thanks, mister!"

"Well, I didn't. But your daddy said you had an artist in you scrabbling her way out, Kate. Didn't really believe him until I saw you drawing on the hardpan. Artists need supplies—and lessons. I'll hang around for a while and teach you what I can. Read that notebook. It'll help you learn to draw. The words might be too big for a little sprout, but you'll grow into 'em if you keep practicing with your schoolbooks. When you read, think of each letter as a tiny drawing—it'll help you get by." Reaching into his pocket he pulled out a small penknife. "For sharpening those pencils." Thomas said. "Know how to use one?"

Kate nodded at Thomas with a look that said, "Christmas came early".

He lowered his voice. "Might be best not to let Sister Mary Campbell know you have any of it, though. The Sister, she seems all business. Might think you were wastin' time." As Sister Campbell's steps approached the open door he whispered, "Don't lose 'em, now." A tiny hand slipped treasures into a calico pocket.

Sister Campbell walked in, wheezing, the gleam in her eyes heralding victory over the chicken chasers.

"Well," Thomas said to the winded nun, "As I was saying, come on outside and we'll see what I've got for the school from Jim O'Bourne and his pals."

Reaching the horses, Thomas dug into his panniers, pulled out a dictionary, several rulers and a world atlas, four parcels of lined paper and several packs of pencils. He presented them to Sister Mary. From another pannier he withdrew a large bag of horehound hard candy and added it to the pile. As the candy sack appeared, the nun's expression changed from boredom to delight. "Thank you! Oh, my goodness, these writing supplies are like a gift from God! And I don't think most of these children have ever tasted candy. Horehound's my favorite." A fleeting squint of greed marred her features.

Well, Thomas thought, *guess if you've never tasted it, you don't miss it. Adding that candy to the pot did the trick, though.*

Thomas gestured to the distant grove. "How about I take my horses over by that stand of cottonwoods near the river and set up camp?" With a feeling of satisfaction he said, "You can send little Kate over in the morning for her first painting lesson."

The nun nodded and went back into the school.

As Thomas untied the last horse from the hitching post, he noticed a slight Indian boy of about eleven watching him curiously from several yards away. When Thomas tossed him a wave, the boy nodded his head, then looked Thomas up and down as if he was a wagon boss inspecting a new horse wrangler. The child opened his mouth as if to speak, then abruptly snapped his mouth shut, turned and walked stiffly away.

Strange.

Thomas gave a mental shrug and swung up into the saddle.

Several miles downstream, a slim Blackfoot woman put her minnow bucket down on the gravel next to her husband's fishing pole. She flicked her hand toward their favorite fishing spot, a deep backwater of the Yellowstone River where the trunks of massive dead trees rested on the sandbar and long branches dipped like graceful arms into the water. The woman put both hands on her chest and raised stricken brown eyes to look inquiringly at her spouse. In her native tongue, she said, "Trouble. Always it finds us."

They stood together and gazed down at the bloated body of the white woman, embraced by the waterlogged tangle of driftwood.

"I think it is the woman of God."

Chapter 10

Sage Bluff, Montana, present day
"Mrs. Reynolds? This is Jessie O'Bourne from Sage Bluff, Montana. I am so sorry about your daughter." Jessie sighed.

"Oh, yes. I'm so glad you called."

"One of the men here at the Sheriff's Department said you believed your daughter was on her way to our home, and that you asked me to call. Ma'am, I didn't know your daughter. But I thought I should call as you requested."

"Miss O'Bourne . . . my daughter Amber. . ." She stopped. There was an audible gulp then she continued, "I'm going to have my husband talk to you."

"This is Jack Reynolds, Miss O'Bourne," a voice boomed. "We realize you didn't know our girl. But I'm sure you can understand we need to know what happened to her."

"I don't think I can help with that, Mr. Reynolds. I know absolutely nothing helpful."

"What we want to know . . . we wonder if there was something in her research—who she talked to—whatever—that got her killed. On Friday, we are burying our baby girl."

"I am so very sorry," Jessie said again.

Jack Reynolds coughed. "Since she was killed on her way to visit with your family, we wanted to speak to you in person."

"But I don't know *why* she was coming to see us, Mr. Reynolds," Jessie protested.

"The O'Bourne name is mentioned many times in the last few pages of her work. She told us you and your family would be some of the key interviews for her thesis."

"That's just astonishing. We know nothing—"

"Miss O'Bourne, her mother and I think her research got her into trouble with someone. We want *you* to look at her laptop, but we don't want to ship it for fear it might be lost or damaged. As you can imagine, it's now pretty precious to us. It has copies of the research she's doing—did—for her thesis."

"I'm just an artist, Mr. Reynolds. I'm not sure what I can do. Why me? The police—"

"The police?" He snorted in derision. "They don't seem to take the idea seriously. The police are only searching for a drug link. Well—that ex-boyfriend of hers wasn't a winner—not by a long shot—but our girl was *clean*. Clean." He hesitated. "And we want every possible motive explored."

"But I don't even know what Amber was studying. I have no idea why she wanted to interview our family." Jessie scrunched up her face.

Geez, could it have something to with the old stories?

"Surely one of her professors would be a better choice. I'm just a painter. I also have to be here to judge a large art competition in two weeks, and it's a long way to—"

"Miss O'Bourne, please indulge us. I am familiar with your work. And I looked you up online. You're more than just a painter. You're a master artist. We know you have the right education to search through her research and see where it was headed. In the course of doing so, you might notice if something appears—I don't know—odd."

"Well . . . ."

"How about I get online right now and book you a round trip to Denver?"

"Mr. Reynolds, I can't just drop everything and come to Denver."

"I know I'm being pushy. But I already checked the schedule. If you'll drive to Billings this evening, we'll reimburse you for a hotel. A ticket can be waiting for you at the check-in counter and you can catch a plane at 7:20 in the morning—"

"But—"

"— and you'd be here by mid-morning. Our visit should only take a couple hours."

"Mr. Reynolds, I don't think I can possibly do that."

There was silence on the other end, then he said, "I see I've come on way too strong." His voice became soft. "My apologies." Silence. "But please. Please help us."

"Sir, what was your daughter's thesis about?"

"I have a draft of it here. Let me read the title."

Jessie could hear papers rattling.

"Amber kept changing it. She has . . . had . . . enough information for a book, actually, not just a thesis. Hmm, yes. It's titled *Thomas Moran's Expeditions in Art—Capturing the West on Canvas*," he said in a flat tone. "But while she was working on her thesis, she became interested in two Moran paintings that disappeared in Sage Bluff in 1939."

"Omigod." Jessie swallowed. "When my aunt Kate was killed."

"She was obsessed with them. Not just because the paintings worked into her paper, but because she wanted to find them. Amber wanted to be the one to give them back to the St. Benedict's school."

"Moran's paintings . . . they're so valuable. If someone thought she had a lead . . . ." Jessie didn't want to finish her thought.

"Exactly, Miss O'Bourne. Exactly. Will you come?"

"Yes. I will. I'll be there as soon as possible."

"Oh, thank you." Jack Reynolds' breath came out in a whoosh of relief. "We're so grateful."

Jessie felt Jack rubbing against her ankle. Like a toddler, he wanted attention most when she was on the phone. She reached a hand down and petted his soft back.

"Don't book me a flight, though. I'm driving. I'll leave in half an hour. She looked at her watch. Let's see—that puts me there by late evening."

Jack flopped down by her foot and proceeded to lick his tail.

"Um . . . do you like cats?"

Chapter 11

Rural Montana, April 1918

"Seems like I been workin' on mixing paint all this week." Kate said. "And I still can't get the color right for paintin' that old rooster. Mean old thing anyhow."

"Keep at it, sprout," Thomas encouraged. One of his old shirts covered Kate's clothes, and she stood with a rectangle of linen canvas tacked on the board he'd placed on his easel. She was using one of his palettes for mixing paint. He sighed. He was readying to move on and it was going to be difficult to leave. Interrupting his packing, he handed her a palette knife and a tube of sienna paint.

"You want to do it right, don't you? You have to pay your dues—means you got to work at it like a demon. Every great painter had to start from scratch. That's the same way you're learning, sprout."

For almost three weeks, Thomas had taught Kate, filling her notebook with illustrated suggestions and watching her absorb the painting process that seemed as natural to her as drawing breath. He watched her sparingly squeeze out paint and begin to press the palette knife down into the color.

"Don't hurry it," he said.

A few minutes later, she tilted her head and tugged on her left braid, squinting at the mixed glob of paint. She grinned.

"Think I got it already." She held up the palette knife triumphantly and showed Thomas. "Looks just like the color of that ratty old chicken tail, don't it?"

He nodded, and sighed again.

I'm going to miss her. She's a prodigy, all right. No wonder Jim insisted I stop by. Heck, he could've had any number of people drop that payment off. He knew I couldn't resist the little toad. But where on earth is Father Michael?

"They're not hers, you know." Kate dropped into the silence.

"What aren't hers?"

"Them chickens," she shot back. "Daddy brought 'em for Father Michael. If they were her chickens, I wouldn't even paint that stuck-up rooster."

"Mad at her, are you?" He looked at her, noticing for the first time a bruise darkening on her thin arm. His jaw clenched. "What happened—you still dawdling over your reading?"

She jerked a shoulder up. "Naw. Sister Campbell was mad I got some paint on my skirt. At least I *wash*. She don't even wash that robe, neither. It's dirty, and it's too short. That's 'cause it ain't hers neither."

Curious now, he asked, "What do you mean, sprout?"

"Ain't her robe," Kate said with conviction. "The other nun left it here. John Running Bear said the first teacher took off after a big argument with Sister Campbell and the new one just started wearing her black clothes."

Her brush flicked.

"Anyway, she said I wasn't clean, and I said, 'Least if I had on someone else's clothes I'd take care of 'em'." Kate wiped her brush on a rag. "That's when she got mad. Mean old bat."

"Why didn't you mention this before?"

"Never thought of it 'til I started paintin' ornery, old Big Bud. He's as wicked as she is. Guess it reminded me."

"Hmmm," Thomas mumbled thoughtfully.

I'd like to pitch that woman in the Yellowstone. Feed the catfish. But I'm betting if I interfere, it'll be harder on Kate after I leave.

He took a deep, slow breath. "Well, don't worry your head over it. Stay out of her way. Let Father Michael sort it out when he comes back. Sounds right up his alley."

He picked up a brush and made several strokes on her canvas.

"Fix this part here. Your brush strokes should be made in the direction the feathers grow."

While his small charge concentrated on bringing life to the meanest chicken in the schoolyard, he resumed his packing, methodically stashing brushes and the paint Kate was through using in special compartments of his panniers. But his mind was on the little girl.

Heck, I never even liked kids much. Sure like this little bugger. . . hate to leave. Might send a telegram from Great Falls, tell Jim to come and get her as soon as he can. Something is wrong here, and why in heck does that older boy, John Running Bear, keep giving me the fish eye?

"We've got to have a talk, little miss." The light was beginning to fade. "You clean up now; then we'll discuss a few things."

Kate hummed to herself, while cleaning her brushes in a bit of turpentine and blotting the bristles on a soft cloth. Then, in the way Moran had instructed, she dipped the brushes in a container of walnut oil and reshaped the bristles so they would dry with a good point.

He went to the tent and withdrew his packet of sketches and dry paintings done on sturdy linen canvas. He could roll the dry paintings, but instead he always packed them flat. He placed them between two sheets of thin wood and wrapped the final package in a blanket. Then he stored them in a specially constructed pannier so no weight rested on them.

"Hate to head out tomorrow, Kate, but I have to. People are counting on me to deliver some work." He frowned. "I'm not good at sugary goodbyes, but I have something for you."

Thomas opened the packet of artwork. He shuffled through the sketches and took out a small drawing of several mule deer.

"This is for you. It'll fit in your suitcase. Keep it there until your dad picks you up." He withdrew a pencil from behind his ear and at the bottom right of the drawing he scrawled, *"To Kate, my student and friend, Affectionately, T.Y. Moran"*. He

65

captured her gaze. "I'll pack it for you." He put a finger to his lips. "Remember, 'til your daddy comes, this gift is a secret—like the notebook. Keep it mum, sprout."

Thomas sat down heavily on a fallen log and searched through the rest of his work, Kate peering over his shoulder like a horse expecting oats. His sketches of Kate and the Blackfoot children filled a leather folder. He withdrew the drawings and had his protégé identify each child by name. He wrote the name lightly in pencil before signing each sketch and adding it to the pile of drawings.

Another packet of work contained oil paintings that had completely dried. He chose three and set them aside. Then he rose, tucked the sketches back into their leather folder, wrapped the remainder of the small oil studies and with utmost care packed everything into his saddlebags.

He looked at the three pieces he'd left out. One was a miniscule sketch of Kate looking over her shoulder at the far off hills across the Yellowstone. Jim Morgan would like this one. He inscribed it, *"Kate, St. Benedict's, May 1918, T. Y. Moran"*. He slipped it, along with the mule deer study, between two pieces of thin alder wood, wrapped a piece of twine around it as if readying the package for travel and handed her the packet.

"Give the sketch of you to your poppa."

He couldn't meet her eyes.

"Do some drawing every day. And remember, when your daddy moves, send me a letter—maybe send a drawing now and then, too, okay? When I get the address, I'll mail you a painting kit. Now, sprout, I need you to promise you'll do something for me. You big enough to keep a promise?"

She nodded solemnly, her eyes wide.

"When Father Michael comes back, tell him straight away that I left two paintings with Sister Mary Campbell, as a gift for him to sell if and when he needs money for the new school. I'll write him a letter telling him how to go about the sale. Wouldn't want that ornery Sister to forget to give 'em to him or anything, right?"

He cleared his throat. It seemed very tight for some reason.

66

"They're too big to leave with you, or I would. I'll give 'em to the nun before I go. Now, you'd better hightail it back to your bunkhouse." He glanced over at the schoolyard. "Good time to go, because I see Sister Campbell is busy with some company. It seems that sorrel mare's been tied at the hitching post quite nearly every day lately."

Kate nodded again and gulped. A tear leaked from the corner of her eye and drizzled a trail down her freckled face. She ran to him and hugged him hard. Then she picked up the two sketches and her notebook, pulled them tight against her chest, turned without a word and trudged toward the bunkhouse. Halfway there she began to run. She ran in a jerky motion, her red head glowing like a lit match bobbing along the path.

The next morning, Thomas walked his loaded horses to the school. From one of the packs he withdrew a thin parcel tied with twine. The package contained one sunlit canvas depicting the Missouri River Breaks and a larger painting of the banks of the Yellowstone River near Billings, a scene blushing with pink wild roses blooming against a backdrop of sandstone cliff.

Someone will need to put them back on stretcher bars and frame them. But, I reckon they'll bring around twenty, maybe thirty thousand—enough to do some good. Don't think I'll mention that sum to the nun.

He carried the package to the school and beckoned Sister Campbell to the open doorway. "I'd like to leave you a couple paintings for the priest, Sister. When Father Michael returns, tell him they're a little gift from his old friend, Thomas. Got them all wrapped up here. I'm afraid they aren't worth much except in sentimental value," he lied.

"Well, bless you, Mr. Moran, how kind. Yes, how kind," she repeated, accepting the package. "Of course I'll tell him. I'm sure he'll be pleased to have them." Her tone was dry, her green-eyed expression skeptical.

Thomas grimaced. Hope Father Michael comes back soon. He turned to peer over his shoulder, throwing a wave to a small figure in a faded calico dress.

"See you, sprout." He urged his horse forward.

Be safe, little one.

As the sound of Moran's walking horses faded, Sister Mary Campbell stopped at the trash barrel and tossed the two paintings by the master artist inside. Kate watched in horror.

Behind the nun stood her friend, John Running Bear. He looked at Kate, inclined his head toward the barrel and closed one eye in a slow wink.

Two minutes later, the schoolyard filled with the grunts and yells of two scuffling young boys, mingled with raucous squawks as chickens scattered across the grounds. A varicolored rooster flew out of the melee. Landing, he strutted away without haste. Kate got a glimpse of John Running Bear ducking swiftly behind the school.

"I saw you, you little heathen!" Sister Mary Campbell yelled after the retreating form, then barreled past Kate on her way to gleefully administer a bit of prairie discipline,

As the nun rounded the corner of the cabin, Kate rushed to the barrel, snatched the packet and ran toward the dormitories.

"Hiding spot, hiding spot, hiding spot," she repeated, her breath coming in distressed gasps. In a panic, she burst into the first sparse room and looked around.

Chapter 12

O'Bourne's ranch, present day

The barn door slid open with a swish. Jessie backed her Greyhawk motorhome out through the double doors, and drove over to park near the front door of the log house. She went back to closed the barn and grab Jack from where he sat mesmerized near a mouse hole in the hollyhock patch. He hung limp and heavy as a sack of wet laundry, rumbling and complaining, until she got into the motorhome and put the big tom on the floor of the diminutive bedroom. He leaped to the middle of the bed and settled in, sniffing a catnip filled cloth mouse he'd left in a bedraggled state on the bedspread the week before.

"You like to travel and you know it, you old grump." Jessie told him.

She pulled the door closed. The Greyhawk was usually packed, loaded with enough art supplies, clothes and non-perishables to take off on a whim, even for a week-long jaunt. However, the last trip she'd taken had been a long looping drive from Santa Fe to California to deliver paintings to galleries, then to Sage Bluff to house sit. Peering into the refrigerator, she took inventory. *Need a few things from the house and a gas stop on the way out of town.*

She hurried to the house and raided the fridge, grabbing milk, lunch meat and a dozen eggs. Then she transferred them to the motorhome's tiny refrigerator. Remembering the shotgun upstairs, she ran up to the bedroom, grabbed the shotgun and shells, and locked both in the Browning gun vault. It was a family rule–never leave a gun out if you were going on a trip.

Looking into the open safe, she thought about the long stretches of empty road through Wyoming. She reached in and took the 9mm ammo and an extra magazine for the pistol she kept in the Hawk. Painting on location sometimes meant 'middle of nowhere'. The pistol was a constant companion when she traveled.

The phone rang, but by the time she reached the top step, she'd decided to let the answering machine pick up the call.

A husky voice came from the machine.

"Mr. O'Bourne, this is Grant Kennedy from the FBI art theft division again. I'll be in town Monday and would like to visit with you. Please call me back at this number to set up an appointment."

Jessie jotted down the number, then picked up the phone, but instead of taking time to call Kennedy back, she dialed the Sheriff's Department. A syrupy female voice answered.

"Sage Bluff Sheriff's Office. Blanche speaking."

"Hi, Blanche. This is Jessie O'Bourne. Is Russell in?"

"You just missed him."

"Darn. Please tell him I'm going to Denver. I'm anxious to get on the road and don't want to wait around until I can get hold of him. I hope to be home Sunday evening at the latest."

"Are you flying?"

Jessie laughed. "No, I'm driving, but you still might call it a flying trip, all right."

As the gas poured into the cavernous motorhome tank, Jessie unfolded her map. She always planned her trip routes to give her the best opportunities for interesting painting. It made sense to drive to Denver using the quickest possible route, but on the leg home, she wanted a few hours to paint on location. Her finger traced the interstate on the map. Billings, then south through Casper and Cheyenne—an almost straight shot to Denver—looked like a given for the trip down. Coming back, she'd angle over through Yellowstone Park. Just the thought of the photo and painting opportunities made her smile. She replaced the gas cap and grimaced at the total she read on the pump. Her next credit card bill was going to read like the national debt.

Back inside the big Greyhawk, she stowed the map and looked in the cabinet to make sure she'd packed her digital camera. She checked the Nikon battery and then the spare. Good to go and ready for the open road, except for picking up some extra snacks. She pulled away from the pump, drove the motorhome to the side of the convenience store and parked.

In the "Get and Go Gas", she bought a cup of coffee and a couple croissants. As she backed out of the door, pushing it open with her hip, she bumped into Arvid Abrahmsen going in.

"Just the Norwegian I wanted to see, Arvid. How would you like to get treated to lunch in a couple of days?"

"Hmm. Sounds like a bribe to me." He propped open the door open for her. He lowered his voice conspiratorially. "And if you watch TV, you must know small town cops are easily bribed. That lunch include pie?"

With a smile, she nodded. "In fact, do you have a few minutes now?"

"Sure, I was just going to grab a coffee."

"Go get your caffeine fix and come on over." She pointed to the Greyhawk. "That's my motorhome there. I'm about ready to hit the road, but I want to tell you about it before I go."

"Whooo-ee." Arvid's eyes gleamed when he saw the Jayco Greyhawk. "Mama, I want one of those."

She laughed. "I'd be glad to give you the ten-second tour."

When Arvid pushed open the Greyhawk door a few minutes later, Jack was in his carrier. He reminded them of that fact every few minutes with a plaintive yargle ending in a squinty-eyed high soprano. Jessie knew from experience that once she let him out and they got under way he'd be a fine traveler, but she didn't want to chance his getting loose in traffic while she showed off her home away from home.

Arvid set three chocolate covered donuts and a mega go cup of Colombian coffee on her small kitchen counter and grinned. He looked around at the rich cherry cupboards, the comfortable driver and passenger seats. A small overstuffed sofa and swivel chair covered in a subtle, autumn leaf pattern and a tiny table was the extent of the living room furniture, but it had a flat screen television, microwave, stove and all the storage cubby holes to make life easy for someone who wanted to get away from town, yet drag a little civilization along.

"Wow. This is just what I need for my fishing trips. Then that elegant wife of mine wouldn't have any excuse to stay home. Her idea of camping is a night at the Super 8."

He opened the bathroom door and peered in.

"I'm a little concerned she might have to use a pry bar to get me out of that tiny shower, but maybe I could just take a dip in the lake. Besides, Esther's always telling me to go jump in. Har, har," he chortled again.

"She'd love it. I take it all over the country. I've been in about eleven states the past two years, going to art shows and giving workshops. If Esther doesn't like roughing it, this is just the ticket."

"She doesn't. About the only thing my wife thinks is good about camping is the grilled fish. They're great done over an open fire. I brush 'em with butter, wrap 'em in tin foil and . . . hey, does this thing have a barbecue grill?"

"Come outside and see." She stepped out of the motorhome with him close behind. Jessie showed him the push-button extendable awning, the pull-out grill, and the outdoor shower.

"Oh, baby! I'll have to be extra good this year . . . have Santa stuff one of these in my Christmas stocking."

Jessie giggled, then said, "Let's go back in and have our coffee before it gets cold. It's story time. And it starts way back in the 1900s."

"So you see," Jessie said, as she finished telling him the story of the vanishing Morans, "for whatever reason, Amber *was* afraid of the police. I guess it might not be the police from

72

Sage Bluff, though. Maybe before she got here, she came across a policeman whose ethics deserted him when the possibility of finding a couple multi-million dollar paintings walked in the door."

Arvid nodded thoughtfully. "Lot of temptation."

"I'm going to trust you, because you're the only cop in Sage Bluff who wasn't even in town when Amber was killed." She smiled wide. "When I was visiting with Blanche the day Amber was found, she said you'd been back such a short time you still smelled like fish. She commiserated with me for having you in my truck still in your fishing clothes."

"Huh. Better scent than the perfume Blanche wears, if you ask me. I don't have much sense of smell, but she drenches herself in that stuff." Arvid frowned, his tanned moon face wrinkling in thought. "You know. I heard that story about the paintings way back. When I was just a kid. I always wondered what happened to the woman—the painter, Kate. A lot of people here said their elderly relatives told them that when the school burned down, the fire had actually been set to cover up a murder. Murders didn't happen much around Sage Bluff, but several people died in strange circumstances that year, according to my grandma."

"Yeah, my aunt Gemma said the same thing."

"Unusual enough for people to remember, I guess. You know how people get excited when something scandalous happens? Just human nature, so take it with a grain of salt. But, Grandma said there was a rumor Kate Morgan found the paintings Moran had promised the school just a day or two before she died. Maybe when the school burned down they burned too, but people didn't think so. There was a girl in the art class who said she'd mailed a large flat package for Kate Morgan, a package big enough to be paintings. Of course, they could have been your aunt's artwork. Let's see—she'd be what we call your 'double great'—your great grandmother's sister, right?"

Jessie nodded. "To keep it simple, let's just call her my aunt Kate. Or maybe just Kate?"

"Kate it is."

"According to my family stories, the package contained her own work she was shipping to a framer in Boston. But, I suppose if other people heard about the package, they might've imagined it held two Moran masterpieces worth more than most people make in a lifetime."

He nodded.

"Where I need your help," Jessie said, "is in locating folks who would remember the old stories. You seem to know a lot about the area history and the people. I'd love to find those old paintings. What say we join forces and see what we can find out? I have a second motive for asking."

"And what would that be?"

"I'm a little nervous." She shrugged. "Okay, maybe even scared. I think this girl from Denver might've been onto something. What if she let the wrong person know she had a lead? She was on her way to our place, and with what she said about not wanting to call the police here, the sooner her killer is found, the better I'll sleep."

"You really think Amber's death had something to do with the Moran paintings?"

"I do."

"Well, if you're right, finding the artwork would help," He said, scratching his chin. "If there's no treasure left to find, the killer wouldn't be looking around your Dad's place for it—or maybe thinking you know something he wants to find out."

"Yeah. But I *don't* have any clues. I'm hoping the research I plan to pick up in Denver will have some tidbit. I'll ask elderly relatives what they recall, too. Will you join forces with me? And keep it under your hat—secret partners?"

"Normally, I'd say hell no, police just do not—do not—work with free-lancers. But Amber's fear of the police worries me, too. As long as we can look at this angle with you playing it real safe—letting me know if someone or something seems off, and without doing anything illegal—or that might make me lose my job—I'm in. How's that?"

Jessie gave him a wide smile. "I'll be careful. I won't ask you to do anything I wouldn't do."

"Okay." He rubbed his chin. "Now—remember you're helping me find the paintings, not trying to solve Amber's attack. Let's get that clear as crystal. We're just trying to figure out what Amber knew, what it was she thought would help find the paintings."

"Scout's honor." Jessie held her hand up, palm out.

"When you get back, let's take a trip out to Minna Heron Woman's place on the reservation. She's the oldest person I know—heck, that I ever knew—but sharp as a young girl. A fascinating woman. And she knows the history of any subject or family from town." Arvid grinned and nodded his head up and down. "Probably the whole county. And I guarantee you'll like her."

"It's a date." Jessie gave him an answering smile. "When I get back, I hope to have a few trails to follow from Amber's schedule, too. Her father seems to think her laptop might hold some clues as to who killed her."

"It could, but don't get your hopes up. And what did I say? You aren't looking for her killer. That's my job."

"Yeah, I hear you. If I'm lucky, it'll have a list of who she has already visited or interviewed by phone. Why do you think the police haven't tried to decipher her notes about the past few weeks?"

"It's anybody's guess." The big Norwegian grimaced. "Mostly because they still think it's a random assault, and they could be right. Right now the force here is blaming everything on drugs, and it's usually an accurate guess. Illegal substances are seeping into the county somehow. If her boyfriend was connected, there could be all sorts of reasons for someone to hurt her—to steal money, to get revenge on her boyfriend who owed someone for drugs. That kind of scenario. She could've carried the drugs, and so on and so forth. But, sometimes a pig is just a pig."

"And is that a bit of Norwegian philosophy, Arvid? What's it mean?"

"It means sometimes what you see is all there is. If the police in Denver aren't sharing that laptop with us, and don't think it's important, maybe they're looking too hard for a drug connection. That connection might not exist, and there they go—missing what's right in front of their noses. This poor college kid wanted to write a thesis, graduate and get a good job. Instead, maybe she stumbled across something and someone who saw it as a way to get tremendously rich. So rich he'd never have to work another day."

Jessie nodded in agreement. "Or she. It could be a woman."

"Yeah, but I bet it was some guy."

"Well, Mr. and Mrs. Reynolds are expecting me tonight. I'd better get a move on."

"I'm not even sure you should go, Jessie. But it might be safer for you in Denver than it is here in town. Be careful." He handed her a card. "Here's my cell number and my desk phone at the station. My home number's on the back."

"Thanks."

"Listen, don't leave a message on *any* of the Office numbers. I trust the men here at the station, but I've never seen them tested with temptation like this. If I don't answer the phone right off, call my home number. My wife Esther can let me know you need to get in touch."

"Okay." Jessie pocketed the card.

Arvid tipped his hat back and scratched his head. "Eighteen million or more. Gee, I'm not sure you should trust ME with that at stake." He stared off into space with a dreamy expression. "I could retire and fish away my golden years. Get that fancy fly rod I been wanting." He looked at her, his eyes wistful, then he looked serious. "Remember, I do not want you blabbing on the phone what you found out from the Reynolds's. I could be in the middle of something at work, an arrest, a meeting. Maybe surrounded by people, but unable to answer the phone. If I don't pick up, like I said, I'll return your call soon as I can."

"That'll work."

"Call me when you're on your way home, so I can get hold of Minna Heron Woman and set up a visit."

"Will do," Jessie opened the motorhome door and held it aside, letting Arvid descend the small step before she grabbed her purse and followed him down. "You have all my info at the station, but let me give you my number anyway . . . so it's handy." Jessie reached into the zipper pocket and pulled out a pen and sticky note. She scribbled out her number and handed the scrap of paper to Arvid. "This is the cell I use when I'm traveling. And I'll be real careful, don't worry."

Standing by the patrol car, Arvid stared at Jessie, his eyes distant. "My grandma always said the past never goes away. Her expression was, 'It haunts our present like smoke curling from a blown out candle'. We *could* be on the wrong road here." He tapped his fingers on the hood of the car. "Especially in thinking a cop is involved. I sure hope we are wrong there. "But I think we're on the right track."

From inside the motorhome, Jack's howls mimicked screeches of the damned, since he'd heard Jessie leave the Greyhawk without him.

"Dammit, that's a *huge* tomcat you got there, but I wish you had a Bull Mastiff or a Rottweiler."

"Heck," Jessie gave a crooked grin, and tossed him a wave. "I like dogs, but they're a lot harder to take traveling than Mr. Fancy Pants in the Hawk. Besides, I've got my little 9mm pistol." She patted her pocketbook. "I need to practice a bit. Maybe hit the shooting range when I get back, but I do know how to shoot."

"Monday or Tuesday, after we get caught up on the particulars of your trip, I'll take you out to my gun club," Arvid promised.

"Great. That'd be fun."

"And you'd better have a concealed carry permit to go with that pistol you've got hidden away, young lady," He said in his best policeman's growl, pointing at her purse.

She gave her best sassy look. "Sure do."

Chapter 13

Trip to Denver, present day

After promising herself it would be a straight shot to Denver, Jessie broke that promise several time for photo opportunities. First, she spotted a number of sandhill cranes in a field near Sheridan, Wyoming. She'd mistaken their large bodies for deer at first, then drew closer in the motorhome and found herself with the photo opportunity of a lifetime. Parking by the side of the road, she yanked out the binoculars and focused on the flock of cranes for several minutes. Their long necks were topped with red feathers. They swayed and dipped as they gleaned stray grains of wheat from the harvested field. She soaked in the scene. Then she grabbed her Nikon, stepped out of the motorhome, and slowly worked her way near enough to get clear photos.

"Hey, those are huge birds," she told Jack when she got back into the motorhome. "If you could catch one of those, think what I'd save on cat food."

At a pull-out near Casper, she filled the camera card with image after image of running antelope. Their bodies were the amber color of the dry grass and with their nimble hooves maneuvering over the rough ground they seemed to skim rather than run like ghosts of the prairie. The big heads and white rumps flashed by in a herd of forty or fifty. Jessie watched intently, burning the image into her mind, savoring the feel of it, the energy, wanting her next painting to bring the fleeting moment to life.

She stopped for a break and a snack of instant coffee, cut lunch meat, and whole wheat crackers in mid-afternoon in the small town of Douglas, Wyoming. The town's claim to fame was a large jackalope sculpture—a rabbit with antelope horns. *Kitschy*, Jessie thought, *but fun*. She set the timer on her Nikon, grabbed Jack from his perch on the motorhome sofa, and stood clutching the cranky fur ball in front of the sculpture, smiling and waiting for the camera to click.

Across the street, a block-long tour bus was parked and nearby picnic tables were full of laughing Japanese tourists, many pointing at her. Before Jessie could hop back into the Greyhawk, she was mobbed. Eighteen Japanese pulled cameras from pockets and totes and each nodded, gesturing toward her, and then pointing at their digital cameras. She smiled at them. They were so gracious. How could she not oblige?

It was a snap fest. Jessie, wearing her *Starry Night* tee, and holding a squirming Jack, was sandwiched between so many posing strangers she began to feel like the B in PB&J. Afterward, she ducked back into her vehicle, dumped Jack unceremoniously on the passenger seat, and grabbed a small box from a cubbyhole before stepping back out.

When they climbed back on their bus, each tourist had one of Jessie's glossy business cards tucked into a pocket or purse. Some were already accessing her website with their smart phones, waving from their bus windows, pointing to their phones and giving her American looking "thumbs up" gestures.

Jessie got back into the driver's seat and laughed heartily while she started the engine. She told the tom, "Free marketing, grumpy puss. And you just never know."

Jack sat in the passenger seat, twitching his tail and washing the taste of strangers from his fur. He gave her a haughty look.

"Yeah, you were magnificent, Jack. A huge hit." She scratched him behind his ears and crooned. "And you didn't bite anyone."

He looked up in her direction and closed his eyes to slits.

Chapter 14

Denver, present day

Sitting in the South Platte River Valley just east of the Rocky Mountains, the twinkling lights of Denver filled the sky long before Jessie reached the exit. The ten-hour drive had stretched to twelve grueling hours. She stopped at a gas station, yawned, and then dialed the Reynolds' number. Jack Reynolds picked up on the first ring.

"Hello, Jack Reynolds speaking."

"Hi. It's Jessie O'Bourne. I wanted to let you know I did make it to Denver. But it's so late, I can hold off and come over in the morning."

"Nonsense. Shelly and I are both night owls. And you're welcome to stay here at the house."

"Actually, I'm driving a motor home."

"Perfect. You can park it in our driveway. Don't worry. There's enough room for a city bus. Let me give you directions."

"That's okay. I already have the address keyed into the GPS."

She navigated the streets easily, the route finally winding into an upscale residential area of huge homes with fancy lighting and long, sinuous driveways. At Highland Drive, a gated community, she gave Jack Reynolds's name, and her own, to the tired looking gatekeeper.

At 10 o'clock, Jessie parked the Hawk in the Reynolds' driveway. Gratefully opening the door and stepping out, she lifted her arms over her head and stretched her muscles. A mansion loomed above her. The arched door flew open, yellow light throwing Jack and Shelly Reynolds into silhouette.

Jessie sat in a living room with twenty foot high vaulted ceilings, and walls hung with richly framed western and Native American art. An enormous multicolored Navajo rug depicting the Blessing Way Yei ceremony, with the traditional spirit figures woven into the pattern, hung on one wall. Other Navajo rugs in pictorial patterns were used on the dark hardwood floor or scattered on the backs of leather furniture. Niches built into the wall held baskets or pottery from different tribes, and Jessie noticed several black Santa Clara pueblo pots that were magnificent. She wished she weren't here on such a sad mission. It would be wonderful to feel free to just look around. A painting near a walnut sideboard caught her eye.

A Frederick Remington. And I'd bet it's an original, not a reproduction.

The room contained such a collection of art and artifacts Jessie almost expected a museum curator to walk in at any moment.

"Amber was our only child," Shelly Reynolds said in a soft voice as she set a cup of herbal lemon tea on the side table by Jessie. A pale, slim, youthful looking woman, Shelly had a mane of glossy black hair that draped her shoulders. Her flowing blue robe was decorated with faint images of stylized running horses, and she wore leather sandals. She went to join her husband on the sofa.

"She was adopted, you see, and never felt she fit in. At school she felt uncomfortable as the only student with Indian heritage. Being half white, she thought she'd never fit into the Indian community, either. At college, her nationality seemed less important, but most of her friends were working part time jobs trying to pay tuition and then she was out of place because she felt over-privileged. Too much money." She cleared her throat and took a sip of tea. Tears filled her eyes. "I know. It's a problem many people wish they had."

"Teen years are difficult for most people," Jessie said quietly. "We all have something that eats at us at that age, and anything that sets us apart from the crowd makes us feel uncomfortable."

"So true." Shelly looked at her husband, sitting next to her and took his hand. "Well, no matter *where* she was, Amber felt out of place. In time, she would have outgrown it. I understood it. I'm part Assiniboine; the Assiniboine are a Siouxan people, but I also have some French in my ancestry."

Jessie nodded, and made an encouraging gesture for Shelly to continue.

"I was born to a woman of the Missouri River Dog Band, the Minisose Swnkeebi. Children raised off the reservation lose much of their culture, and I was raised in a white family and a white community."

"I thought most tribes refused to let children be adopted by parents living off the reservation," Jessie said.

"You're right. Many tribes do not allow it. I never knew how my adoptive parents managed to complete the red tape." She gave a short harsh laugh. "Maybe they stole me, who knows? Or maybe it was done with money. They certainly had enough." She went on. "They always made sure we had acquaintances that were Indian, but there is quite a difference between having an acquaintance, and having a friend. I never seemed to mesh with either culture until I moved into middle-age. That's partly what led us to adopt Amber."

Jack Reynolds broke in, "Amber was an abandoned baby. Her parents were never found, and that made it easier for us to keep her. That, and the fact that because of her lighter skin tone, tribal members were sure she was not full blooded Native American and were more willing to let her be adopted away from the reservation."

"We believe Amber was part Flathead, or perhaps Salish," Jack said. "There's no way to know. We didn't care. We gave her everything we could, but we couldn't erase the slate. We couldn't give her a culture that embraced her."

"All we could do was love her," Shelly said. "We loved her so much."

Jack sighed and continued, "When she began work on her Master's degree in Art History, her thesis was going to cover

82

the effect of major artists on the National Park system, especially the Hudson River School of Artists—Albert Bierstadt, Thomas Cole, Thomas Moran, and the rest. She narrowed her thesis to cover only Moran. Then she researched his involvement, his influence actually, concerning Yellowstone Park."

"I should know about this connection," Jessie said with interest. "Refresh my memory."

"It was partly through seeing Thomas Moran's paintings of the Yellowstone area that the Office of the Interior designated it the first national park in the world. In 1872. Somewhere, either in Amber's reading or interviews, she found out about two missing Thomas Moran paintings. The painter supposedly gave them to a priest in Montana to sell. The money earned at auction would have funded a new and better school at Sage Bluff, Montana—St. Benedict's Indian School. At least, that's what Amber told us."

"Interesting. That's where my aunt, Kate Morgan, went to school for a short time when she was a little girl," Jessie said. "Our family has a photo of her in front of that log school. It's a true story, Jack. If Amber was coming to see us to verify that, we would have done so."

"How can you be sure?"

"Moran not only visited the school, he gave my aunt art lessons, a notebook of painting tips and sketches, and a small painting. He even paid to send her to the San Francisco Art Institute when she grew up. At that time, my great grandfather wasn't as well off as he was later in life." Jessie thought it would be too depressing to mention that the painting Moran gave Kate disappeared and that Kate, herself, had been murdered.

"Your family was mentioned on several pages of Amber's research." Shelly fiddled with her teaspoon, twisting it between her fingers. "Finding the paintings became her obsession. She knew their worth was immense, but she wasn't looking for them because of their value, Amber thought if she could recover them, she'd gain esteem in her field."

"That isn't all she hoped for," Jack said. "If she found them, and if they were finally sold to build a fabulous new school and set up a perpetual fund for Indian education in Montana, she would feel she'd contributed to her Indian culture. I think our daughter hoped it would give her some acceptance."

"We know that it was never likely for Amber to find Thomas Moran's stolen work, Jessie. It was only a dream she had. But her research is still valuable, isn't it?"

"Of course it is," Jessie said reassuringly. "Is all her research on the laptop you wanted me to take home?"

"No. We have a large box of folders, too. Some, but not all, of the information in the box may have been scanned and added to the laptop, but we don't know which pieces. We'd better send the box home with you, too."

Jessie thought of her stop at Douglas, Wyoming. About half those tourists hadn't used an actual camera. Some had snapped Jessie's picture using their smart phones, some the built in camera on an iPad. And many of the tourists were speaking into their iPad or digital camera while they took Jessie's picture, probably narrating where the photo was taken and immediately forwarding the photos to friends and family back home.

"How about video or audio? Anything like that?"

"I never thought about recordings," Jack said. "I guess I'm so old fashioned I've been thinking more of written notes."

"Not in this electronic age, Jack. She may have done interviews and recorded those who spoke to her with a digital camera that recorded sound. Did she have one?"

"Yes," Jack said, his brow furrowing, "She had a new phone, and a camera—a good digital SLR. Amber was never without it. On holidays, she'd take family photos and make us say things like "Merry Christmas" while she took them. She certainly might have used her phone or iPad for recording interviews." He nodded at Jessie.

"I can't imagine a young person these days travelling without their electronics. Do you know if she had them both with her? I think her phone is a given. Kids don't go anywhere without one.

Jack turned to Shelly. "Her digital camera and iPad weren't on the list of personal items the police said they'd be returning to us, were they, Shelly?"

His wife shook her head. "I don't think so. There wasn't much on the list. What there was, we hope to pick up after the funeral, when we travel to Sage Bluff to pick up her motorcycle.

Jack turned back to Jessie; his eyes wide. "And she had to be staying in or near Sage Bluff. Her iPad and camera could be at a hotel there somewhere. There was a motorcycle saddlebag listed on the inventory, but I'm pretty sure Amber had an extra backpack, too. I. . . I don't know. Shelly and I didn't like the motorcycle. We kept trying to get her to agree to buy a car. There isn't—wasn't—a good way to haul a suitcase, so she made do."

Shelly put her head against her husband's shoulder and slumped into him. Her eyes filled. "Honey, we're probably missing so many of Amber's private things."

"I'm sure the Sage Bluff Deputies will check all the local lodgings. There aren't many," Jessie said encouragingly. "I can call Detective Sergeant Abrahmsen. He's the one who has promised to help me with the Moran angle of your daughter's death."

"Thanks, Jessie." Shelly rubbed her eyes, and said in a tired voice, "I hope you begin work soon with the papers we have here. I'm sorry. There's a lot, but without the missing iPad it might be a lot like starting from scratch. Please let us know."

"Shelly, it's late." Jack stood up, took Shelly's hand and drew her up from the sofa. "Why not get some rest? I'll take this young lady to Amber's room to get the computer, and we'll gather whatever paperwork we can find."

"The guest room is made up, Jessie. Let me get you some fresh towels." Shelly stood shakily.

"I offered her our guest room for the night while you were getting our tea, but she insists on staying in her motorhome. She can leave it in the driveway."

"Yes, that's perfect," Jessie said.

Shelly Reynolds stared at her. "But our guest room is always ready for visitors. Are you positive you want to stay out in the little trailer?"

"Oh, yes." Inwardly, Jessie smiled to hear the huge Greyhawk described as a little trailer. "Believe me, Mrs.

Reynolds, you don't want my cat around your lovely rugs, and I don't want him left alone in my motorhome, either." Jessie chuckled.

That won a faint smile from the lady of the house. "I understand."

"I hope you don't mind my asking for a short tour of the western art you have collected, though. Maybe tomorrow morning before I leave?"

"Of course. And we'll have a nice breakfast in the morning. I'll see you at 7:30 or so, then, Jessie. I believe you mentioned you wanted to get an early start home. Thank you again for coming." She looked at her husband, her eyes brimming with tears, and gave him an apologetic look.

He looked back with understanding, his grey eyes darkening. "Goodnight, dear," Jack Reynolds said, as his wife walked haltingly to the elegant curving staircase.

"Goodnight, Mrs. Reynolds," Jessie said.

Once his wife turned the curve of the landing, Jack Reynolds turned to Jessie. "We'll retrieve the items we'd like you to take charge of, and there's something else in Amber's room my wife and I want you to see."

Jack Reynolds opened the door to a bedroom gleaming with mellow cherry wood furniture. The room was accented with the intense indigo, burgundy and ochre of traditional Native American rugs and pillows. Amber had used them with a lavish hand. A featherweight down comforter the color of clotted cream with a border of stylized running buffalo covered the queen-sized bed.

A walnut roll-top desk was placed against the north wall. It looked antique, but was actually a reproduction designed to hold a computer. Jessie was stunned to see that hung above the desk was a vivid oil painting of a horse herd and wranglers running through a snowy meadow. The mix of roans, palominos, paints and duns was joined together in the composition by billows of churning snow and the bright colors of the cowboys' shirts. Leading the herd was a magnificent reddish-brown bay with a white blaze and white stockings. It was one of the largest and most dynamic oil paintings Jessie had ever sold, in fact, one she regretted putting on the market. The gallery sold it the first week it was displayed.

"Amber discovered your work while she was working on her thesis. We bought this piece for her birthday. She wanted a painting done by your great Aunt Kate as well, but we couldn't locate one that was for sale. Her love of your artwork was another reason we wanted you to work on her research, Jessie."

"Oh, I'm delighted she liked my work. I wish that she'd found one of Kate's. Our family has a number of them, but we couldn't bear to part with any."

"Of course not."

"Most of Kate's are quite small, but we do have two large ones in my father's bedroom. My favorite is an autumn painting of the Missouri River breaks near Great Falls, Montana. It was painted after the cottonwood trees had turned yellow and gold and the scrub oaks a deep red."

"And the other?"

"The other painting is a pioneer ox cart pulling onto the bank after fording a river. The oxen are lunging forward against the yoke, rolling their eyes with the effort of hauling the wagon out of the water." She sighed. "They're magnificent. I wish your daughter could have seen them."

"My wife would still love to see them, Jessie. So would I. Perhaps someday it will be possible for us to come and visit to discuss the research. Or, when we can come to Sage Bluff to retrieve Amber's belongings. I didn't argue with Shelly about it, but I plan to have the motorcycle and belongings simply shipped to Denver when they're done with them."

"Yes," Jessie said with understanding. "That might be more practical."

"We'll see how stubborn she is about it. I'm afraid she'll feel it's necessary to see where Amber was found." Jack Reynolds bowed his head for a second, seemed to give himself a mental shake, and looked at his guest. "Shall we get busy?"

Amber's computer booted up slowly, and began an automatic slide show of photographs—mostly college kids enjoying life in their free time. Jack Reynolds sat in a leather chair on Jessie's right, his face solemn. Jessie was seated on the chair that matched the roll-top desk, leaning over and peering at the monitor intently.

"Her computer is not password protected. That makes it easier. It seems like an invasion of privacy, but I would like to look through her email and see who she'd been in contact with during the course of writing her thesis." Jessie looked at Jack.

"Go ahead, Jessie. You have free reign."

At his okay, she tapped a few keys. "I'll need a copy of the list of friends you gave the police, too. Kids today usually go by nicknames—I'll need to be able to match them with full names. For instance, how about this entry that just says 'the Web'?"

"That's Amber's best friend, Monette. Monette Weber. There will be photos of her in Amber's picture gallery on the computer—a tiny woman, older than Amber, with a mass of white blonde hair."

All of a sudden Jack Reynolds leaped from the chair and looked at Jessie in horror. "My God. We haven't heard from her. I would have expected her to call. She went along on some of Amber's trips, but I don't know about this trip." Jack looked down at his watch. "It's way too late to phone. I'll call her first thing in the morning."

"Was Amber good about telling you who was along for the ride when she traveled?" Jessie said.

"Yes. Usually, she called us as soon as she settled into a hotel on one of her research trips. If anyone else was along, she'd give us their phone number, too. Just in case of traffic accidents, and such. We never heard who was going along this time, but it was nearly always Monette."

He pulled a cell phone out of his pocket and stared at the screen. "There aren't any missed calls. I can't believe I didn't think about Monette before." He looked at Jessie with a haunted expression. "Now I'm very concerned. It isn't like her not to call or come by if she knows what has happened to our daughter. What if she was hurt, too, and nobody even knows?"

"Mr. Reynolds . . . Jack, do you have her number? I think we should try it tonight, or you simply aren't going to be able to sleep."

He looked stricken. "No, I don't think I do. And it was a cell phone. There's no way to look it up."

"We'll figure out something in the morning," Jessie assured him. "Maybe by calling mutual acquaintances. Your wife will know a few other girls we can phone and ask."

Jack looked slightly relieved. "Yes, you're right. I think she will."

"It *is* getting really late." Jessie reached over to shut down the computer. "Why don't I take this back to the Greyhawk, along with the notebooks and thumb-drives you gave me? I want to get a small start on them tonight. That way, I'll know if I have other questions you'll be able to answer before I leave tomorrow."

"Yes, that's a good idea."

Jessie stood up and stretched, putting her hand at the small of her back. "And I imagine I have a cat who wonders if I have abandoned him."

"Ah. We used to have a very demanding Siamese and still miss him. He was an elegant, smart beast, Amber's baby. She called him Zebedee."

"Siamese are beautiful animals."

"What kind of cat is yours? And what do you call him?"

"I'm almost embarrassed to tell you," Jessie said, smiling broadly. "He's an enormous, perverse, orange tomcat named Jack. He's named after a boxer my granddad used to like, Jack Dempsey, who was in the ring in the 1920s. Dempsey had a killer left hook, and held the World Heavyweight Championship from 1919 to 1926."

"Yes, I know the boxer you mean," Jack said with interest.

"Well, this cat is a heavyweight, has a little notch missing from one ear, and has lots of hooks. He likes to fight, too, so I keep him close to me when I can."

Jack Reynolds beamed. "A fighting cat named Jack, huh? We have to remember to tell Shelly that in the morning. It might brighten her day a little. She might even have to come out to your Greyhawk and get acquainted. I assume he's a handsome devil."

Jessie thought of Jack's ragtag ear, his loopy grin when the cat's front tooth sometime became snagged over his lower lip, and when his pink tongue decided to protrude just a bit for no particular reason, and said with a smile, "Oh yeah. He's a looker."

Back in the motorhome, Jessie grabbed her cell phone and called Arvid, apologizing for the lateness.

"They don't know where she was planning to stay. Her folks already told the Denver police that. I don't know why that info wasn't passed along to the cops in Sage Bluff. Jack said she definitely would have had reservations at a small hotel. She hated the big chain hotels. Or maybe a B&B. Amber had plenty of money for travel, and Shelly and Jack told me she hated camping." She flicked a cat treat to Jack, and then yawned loudly. "Sorry, it's been a long day."

Arvid yawned back. "Uffda, don't get me started. It's been a bugger of a day here, too."

"Anyway, she could have been staying anywhere. Surely everyone in Sage Bluff would have heard about her death by now. Do you suppose someone thinks they can keep her stuff if they don't fess up about her staying at their place?"

"Yeah. People love free things if they think they can get away with keeping them."

"Hers had to be nice things, too. The missing digital camera was very expensive, if the Reynolds' place is any indication. It's a *mansion*."

"I hear you. Good quality. Tempting for innkeepers. Yes, people must have heard about her death. The newsman on Channel 8 made an announcement for us. They also announced that if anyone has any knowledge about Amber they should call the station. No takers."

"Too bad."

"Yep. But she had to be staying somewhere local, and she must have offloaded some of her personal items at that

90

lodging. There wasn't enough in the motorcycle bag to get her through even a two day trip. Especially not the way most girls travel with extra clothes, makeup, junk like that—heck, Jessie, there wasn't even a hairbrush in there. In fact, it looks to me like it's mostly dirty clothes she was planning to take to a laundry, and a pair of sandals."

"Well, I know she had a duffel besides the black leather saddlebags that fit on her motorcycle. But no regular luggage," Jessie said with authority. "Her folks say that besides the camera, which probably could take a short movie, if she was interviewing people she may have an iPad with her to record interviews. College kids these days don't take notes on paper. They do everything with electronics, and nearly everything portable has a microphone—iPads, smart phones. Amber would be using something easy to travel with. Her parents think it was probably her iPad. And of course, the phone is a given."

"Yeah, kids practically have phones stitched to their ears," Arvid said. "Huh, I'm surprised they haven't made the smart phones into earrings. Say, Russell said you called him and told him there was a message from her on your dad's answering machine?"

"Yes. After Russell told me her folks said she was coming to see us, I listened to the messages. All Amber said was that she wanted to stop by when she was in town. Her voice seemed professional and calm. She didn't give any specific time she might stop by, either, but it seems odd that she'd plan to show up unannounced—especially so late in the evening, doesn't it? It makes me think that maybe after she left the first message, she found something that she couldn't wait to share."

"Nah, bet it's just that most college kids are night owls, so they expect everyone else to be up. I have a nephew who calls my sister at 11:30 nearly once a week. He can't seem to understand she's been in bed for at least an hour or two by then. Inconsiderate little bugger. My sister keeps threatening to call him at 5:30 in the morning when she hauls herself out of bed. Ha ha." He went on, "I'll want to listen to that message when you get home. What else did you find out?"

91

"Arvid, there's this girl . . . " Jessie told him about the little blond who may have been with Amber.

"Damn. Since this Weber girl hasn't checked in with anyone and never called the Sheriff's Department, maybe she didn't go along. She may not have heard about Amber's death." Arvid paused. "Or, blast it, we could have a missing girl."

"Yeah," Jessie said. "Woman, actually. She was older than the usual student. And the Reynolds know Monette was raised by a maternal grandmother, but that's about it. They don't know the woman's last name or phone number. The college may have her contact information since Monette was registered for classes this year, though. Her information would be on Amber's phone. If it ever shows up." Jessie thought a minute, feeling like she was missing something obvious. "Heck, I must be having an idiot day," she said, thumping the palm of her hand against her forehead. "Her email address ought to be on Amber's computer Jack Reynolds just gave me—and an email would go right to a smart phone. She'd get the message in two seconds." Jessie heard a slamming sound.

"Jessie, I'm on my way out the door, heading to the station. Boot the computer back up before you take off, and send me that email address when you find it."

"Will do."

"When I get back to the office, I'll try to get hold of her. And Baker, our new hire, has been real interested in how the investigation's been going. I might get her to do some follow up."

"Okay."

"Tell Amber's parents that Russell and I *will* find where she was lodging and track down her things." He wrinkled his forehead with worry that Jessie couldn't see over the phone, but heard in his voice. "You be real careful, Jessie. Russell could still be on the right track, thinking there might be a drug angle, but if I asked one of them magic eight balls kids I had when I was young, I think when I flipped it over it'd say the 'outlook is poor'."

The next morning Jessie bit into the last sliver of her warm caramel roll and nearly swooned with pleasure.

"You're right; your wife is the best baker I've ever met. Thanks for talking me into staying for breakfast. But, I've got to get on the road soon."

"I never lie, Jessie. At least not about something as good as Shelly's cooking."

They sat at the breakfast bar in the Reynolds' custom kitchen on high stools whose cushions were covered in vivid, southwestern Zapotec patterns. A shoe box of correspondence from Amber's bedroom sat at the end of the counter ready to be packed in the Greyhawk. Jack had handed her the box with an apologetic look as soon as she entered their home that morning. It had been overlooked when they searched for computer disks the night before. A quick glance through the box piqued her interest. Jessie planned to go through every word as soon as she returned home. The box of letters had also reminded her she had forgotten to look for the letter from the FBI agent her father asked her to give Russ. Well, she'd do it tomorrow.

She slid down from her stool and reached into her pocket for a pad of sticky notes. She got a pen from Jack Reynolds, jotted down Arvid's name and personal cell phone number and handed it to him.

"This is the contact information for the cop there in Sage Bluff who I know will help as much as he can. He'll call you when he finds out if Monette Weber was actually traveling with your daughter. Arvid's a sweetheart." She handed a business card to Shelly. "This has my cell phone number and email address. Contact me any time."

Shelly looked at the card, then placed it on the counter. "Monette." Shelly made a small moue of distaste. "She's been good to Amber. And I like her okay, Jessie, but she's what you'd call a 'man-eater'. Monette is older than Amber, closer to thirty. She isn't the bit of fluff that she looks, either. Monette is what people call a computer geek, and like Amber's address book says, my daughter simply called her "the Web". But of course, we gave her full name to the police."

"Man-eater, huh?" Jessie said.

93

"And a woman that beautiful is even more dangerous when she truly enjoys the same type of things men like— camping, fishing—that kind of thing. Don't you think?"

"Oh, Shelly," Jack Reynolds said in a tone full of exasperation, "Monette's full of life, one of the most intelligent people I have ever met, and she and Amber were very close." In an aside to Jessie he said, "Shelly imagined Monette was flirting with me when she came to dinner here, Jessie. Imagine—thinking some young thing would flirt with this old duffer. She was just trying to be kind."

Shelly gave Jessie a knowing look, ignoring her husband's comment. "Plus, she has this little girl, southern drawl that makes men fall over their own feet trying to take care of her. She's smart, but she knows how to get what she wants."

Jack Reynold's rolled his eyes. ."Still, she was good to our daughter."

"We don't expect you to search through Amber's research or put it into book form for free, either, you know. We'll pay you."

Shelly looked down at the caramel rolls on the kitchen table as if seeing them for the first time. She had picked at breakfast, putting tiny bites into her mouth only when her husband encouraged her to eat.

"I'm going to send the rest of the rolls home with you." She removed the plate of rolls, busied herself at the counter and handed a foil-wrapped package to Jessie. "Make sure Detective Abrahmsen gets some, please?"

"Yum. Thanks. I'll try," Jessie grinned. "I'm not driving all the way home in one day, so I won't promise all of these are going to make it back to Sage Bluff. I have a reservation at the Fishing Bridge Campground in Yellowstone tonight." She gave Jack and Shelly each a quick hug before going out to the Greyhawk and climbing in.

Jack Reynold's namesake sat placidly on the passenger seat, ready to travel. As usual, the cat had one tooth hooked over his bottom lip in an insolent catty grin. Jessie buckled her seat belt. Then she started the engine and turned to look at Jack with twinkling eyes.

"Let's roll, you handsome devil."

Chapter 15

St. Benedict's Mission School, 1918

A blocky cowboy tied his sorrel mare to the hitching post, removed his hat and called out, "Hello! Virginia, you there?"

The figure the students knew as Sister Mary Campbell darted through the doorway.

"Cal, shhh," she whispered, "You keep forgetting—call me Sister Mary, you idiot! If these kids find out I'm not a nun, they'll blab to their parents. Then the whole valley could find out where I am. You trying to get me killed?"

"Sorry. Just checking up on you and bringing you the latest—and it's good news. They caught him, the bank robber from down in Dillon. His name was Gordon Harris. The Sheriff shot him in self-defense."

"Aw, that's great," Virginia said, enthusiastically.

"Too bad you were there when he robbed the bank in Helena. You must've been so worried knowing he thought you could identify him, sweetheart. I'm proud of the way you held yourself together."

"Is he dead, Cal?" Virginia asked.

"They never found the money, though. Darn shame, for all those people who lost their savings."

"Sure is," Virginia muttered. "A cryin' shame. But is he *dead*, Cal?"

He looked at the black robed figure. "I think so."

"Good." Her green eyes sparkled.

"So, *Sister Mary*, I talked to my cousin yesterday." He laughed. "He'll sell me a horse and I'll bring it for you next week. Then we'll head over to Billings."

"I can't wait," she said.

"It's a good thing you decided to help out here, or the kids would have been all by themselves when their teacher ran off."

"Yeah, those kids were lucky I was here to fill in all right."

"They ever find her?"

"Not yet." Her hand clenched.

The nun had given her a place to stay after Virginia spun a sob story about her non-existent abusive husband. Unfortunately, that same evening she'd caught Virginia counting the money from her saddlebags. The brown wrapper on each bulky package she hadn't opened was labeled Helena State Bank.

I didn't have any choice, Virginia thought. *Stupid nun. I wonder if you go directly to Hell for killing a nun.*

She'd lured the real Sister Mary into the schoolhouse, telling her the rest of it was hidden in the cupboard by the stove. She still felt the heft of the cast iron skillet. The dull thud of it hitting the woman's skull. That nun wasn't any lightweight, either. She'd been heavy, and it had been slow work undressing her, then dragging the body to the river.

"Sure a fine fix, her running off like that, leaving you to do all the work."

"Yeah, some people are sure inconsiderate She probably got tired of all the work here. Them kids are a lot of work."

Surely the strong current carried the body so far downstream it must be long gone, thank God.

Her mouth twitched, thinking how funny it was for her to thank God, and mean it. She chuckled aloud. She turned her chuckle into a flirtatious giggle as she turned her attention back to Cal and saw him looking at her in a curious way. She linked her arm with his.

"Aw, I been treatin' these kids just as good as that sissy-faced nun ever would, I'll bet." She smiled at him, her green eyes sparkling in her pock-marked face. "So, they killed Gordon Harris, huh? Well, then I must be safe now."

"Don't worry, honey. I'm sure you're fine, now." Cal looked at her with an adoring smile. She was so tall, they stood eye to eye. "They'll have to have a replacement for you here."

"Yah, sure. I'll make sure they do."

Right now I'll just tell him about the baby. Later, when I tell him about the money . . . well. If he acted strange about it, the money—and Cal's nice ranch—could both be hers alone. She thought again of that satisfying "thwack!" *She always wanted to raise some horses.*

At that, Virginia smiled broadly and gazed into Cal's eyes. She reached out and laid her hand on his arm.

"I got some news for you, sweety," she said coyly.

"Oh, you don't say, now," The cowboy slipped his large hand over hers.

"In fact, I got some real good news." With her free hand she rubbed her growing belly, smoothing the black habit.

Several days later Jim O'Bourne walked out of St. Benedict's schoolhouse with his little girl. The black robed figure of Sister Mary Campbell stood in the doorway watching the tall redheaded man and the girl who looked up at her father with unconcealed happiness. After taking photographs of Kate in front of the log schoolhouse with his newfangled Brownie camera, Jim swung his daughter up in his arms and whirled her around while she squealed with delight.

"Kate, we're going home. Go pack your things," he said. He set her down and gave her a wide smile. "I've got a huge surprise for you when we get there. Bet it'll be an even bigger surprise than having my friend Thomas teach you to paint." He chucked her under the chin. "You owe your old dad a hug for that one," he said.

Kate's eyes clouded at mention of Thomas. She pulled her dad's head down and whispered in his ear.

"You did fine," Jim said. He gave her a reassuring hug, but his expression was somber. "I'll go talk to John Running Bear on the quiet while you pack," he whispered back. "I know his family. I trust him to explain to Father Michael when he gets back. He'll tell him where the paintings are, and why you hid them." He patting Kate gently on the back.

"Now, go pack. Scoot."

Chapter 16

Rural Montana, May 1918

Father Michael urged his horse down the incline, the sweat running in rivulets down the priest's back and trickling down his forehead, stinging his eyes. He was heartsick at the recent discovery of Sister Mary Campbell's murder.

Who could have done such a sinful thing? May God forgive him.

It was unchristian, he knew, to hope God would punish him *before* He forgave him. Punishment with God's own fierce, mighty, and powerful sword.

Yes, that's what the murderer deserved. He grinned at the thought, then made the sign of the cross.

Lord, forgive me, for I have sinned.

He mulled over the puzzling story of the mystery woman who had acted as the nun's replacement. A person would need an awfully good reason to want to stay at a poor school like his. The woman had left before he returned, but he believed the children when they told him that until a day or two before he arrived back at St. Benedict's School, there had, indeed, been an unauthorized teacher there. *I'm glad I sent John's description of the woman on to the Bishop. Not sure what good it will do. What a shame.*

How disappointing that the Sheriff wouldn't at least listen to John Running Bear's story of the woman hitting Sister Mary Campbell, killing her. John was a reliable, smart child.

Once the Sheriff belittled the older child, saying he was just trying to draw attention to himself and making up tales, none of the younger children were willing to speak.

Sad. People are so blind to their own faults but their eyes see color all too vividly on someone else's skin.

He removed his hat and fanned his ruddy face. Then he said a quick prayer for the Sheriff.

Bless the cranky, bigoted old bastard.

The bay he was riding shook her head and nickered. The priest patted her neck, whispering sweet nothings into the horse's ear to comfort the big animal. They were nearing the small creek and the horse probably smelled the water. Father Michael sniffed. He could smell the sweetness of the blooming chokecherry bushes that grew near the bank, and see the clouds of white blossoms.

A good crop this year.

He'd come back later with several of the children once the tangy fruits ripened to rich black. Pick the berries. Make syrup and jelly. His stomach rumbled in anticipation. How he hated to leave the school, but they had to have supplies. Many of the supplies had been pilfered in his absence, likely disappearing with the woman imposter. It was dangerous to go into town, with the spreading of this horrendous influenza. Life was so uncertain.

So many dead. Probably the majority unbaptized. An awful toll in lost souls.

He made the sign of the cross over his chest. What if he, himself, fell ill? It worried him that he'd forgotten to tell anyone he'd moved the two beautiful paintings to a more secure hiding place. He would let John know where the paintings were as soon as he returned. And before the end of the month, he'd send them to an auction house. Thank heaven for Thomas Moran's generosity.

Rider and horse had reached the edge of the stream and the bay lowered his head to drink. Father Michael dismounted, knelt down, and with cupped hands sluiced some of the cold, refreshing water over his face. He wetted his hair and neck.

A shot rang out and a piece of stone ricocheted off an outcropping, striking the priest on the cheek. The priest put a hand to his face and turned in alarm as his horse lunged sideways and began to trot downstream. Then he heard another blast, felt a hot pressure on his side and grabbed the wound, saw red trickle between his fingers.

My God, dear heavenly Father . . .

Chapter 17

Sage Bluff, Montana, present day

Grant Kennedy unfolded his tall frame from the rented pewter Toyota Camry. He removed his sunglasses, tucked them into the pocket of his twill shirt, and walked down the block toward the Sheriff's Department. Twice he'd circled the block before he parked, not trusting his GPS and not realizing that the old bank building was now the Sheriff's Office. He looked around at the sturdy old buildings.

Picturesque. Probably a great place to raise kids, if someone was into that. And here comes Mayberry R.F.D. He grinned to himself.

Walking the other direction down the sidewalk was a sturdily built dark-haired man in a Deputy's uniform, holding the hand of a small boy in a green T-shirt and blue shorts. The young boy had a tousled head of red hair, more freckles than Grant thought God could fit on such a small face, and a large bandage on one knee. The Deputy and youngster turned and went up the steps leading into the station. Grant walked over to the building, climbed the stairs and followed.

He walked into the first open office he saw. A large woman in a floral patterned blouse sat behind the desk, intent on a fashion magazine she held open in front of her.

"I would like to speak to the person in charge of the Amber Reynolds murder. And I'm sorry, I don't have an appointment."

The woman looked up, and when she saw Grant, she smiled.

"Sheriff Stendahl is out for a six-week rest—doctor's orders. Sergeant Russell Bonham is who you want. Go down the hall, then to your right," the woman explained. "If Russell isn't in, take a left and visit with Detective Sergeant Abrahmsen."

"Thank you."

The big woman stared at the blond man, taking his measure as though he was on the auction block at the annual "Bid on a Bachelor" night the Baptist church sponsored annually the week after Thanksgiving.

"I'm Blanche." She splayed her hand across her ample chest, fingertips glossy with dark red polish. "Let me know if I can help you with anything else," she purred. "Or if you'd like some coffee while you talk to the fellows."

Kennedy thanked her again, and saw the Deputy with the child disappear around the corner. As he turned to walk away, he heard the clerk mutter inscrutably to herself, or perhaps into the phone, "I'd go three hundred, not a penny less."

He continued down the hall to the right hand corridor and knocked on the door marked "Sergeant Bonham". Hearing a deep voice say 'come in', he pushed the heavy oak door open and took out his badge. Grant Kennedy approached the desk with his badge flipped open.

"Hello, Sergeant Bonham. I'm Agent Grant Kennedy, with the FBI."

"FBI?"

"Yes. I would like to speak to you regarding a case I believe you're working on—Amber Reynolds."

Russell picked up a tablet from his desk and handed it to the young boy, along with a small box of colored pencils. Then he reached for the proffered badge and gave it a serious look. He narrowed his eyes, comparing the badge's photo of a blond man with hazel eyes and a slightly crooked nose to the features of the tall man standing in front of his desk. Satisfied, he handed the badge back, stood, walked around the desk and shook Grant's hand. Grant was about four inches taller, and Russell looked up to meet his eyes.

"The FBI is getting involved? This is a brand new case. How the heck did you even hear about it, and what's the FBI's interest in it?"

"It's a long story. In fact, a real long story." Grant Kennedy looked at the little boy, who sat on the floor cross-legged, happily opening the tablet and starting a drawing. "First, I'd like to hear your story about the Amber Reynolds attack. You tell me yours. Then I'll tell you mine. The woman working the front desk promised me some coffee. I've been driving all morning. I'd sure love a cup if you've got it."

"Well, we got something that almost passes for coffee, but I don't want to piss off the FBI." Russell said. "Think you'd be a whole sight happier if we got some from the restaurant down the block." He reached into his pocket and withdrew a twenty dollar bill, handing it to his son. "K. D., go down to Arvid's office—ask him to walk you to the Calico Café. Get yourself a milkshake. Pick us up three coffees—three—and some donuts. Tell Arvid we need him to bring it back here to the office and join us. Think you can handle that?"

K.D. nodded. Russell looked at Grant. "Cream and sugar?"

"Black, thanks."

Russell turned back to the boy. "K. D.," he said in a conspiratorial whisper, "Tell Arvid to come in the back way. Remember—the back way. Don't let Blanche see you with that coffee, or we're toast. I swear that woman has a mean streak." K.D. bolted into the hallway.

"My babysitter was sick today," Russell said. "Sorry, but I didn't want K. D. to hear the gruesome details. We can cover that before they get back, and Arvid won't miss anything new."

Russell retrieved a file from a drawer, pulled photos and the medical examiner's report from the manila envelope and laid them out on his desk, waving a hand at an empty office chair to indicate that Grant should take a seat. Grant Kennedy thumbed through the file while Russell spoke.

105

"We suspect Miss Reynolds was attacked by someone she knew or recently met. Bashed in the head and hidden between two hay bales out on a local ranch. We think he meant to kill her outright, but misjudged how hard he'd struck her. We've been having a lot of trouble with drugs here in Sage Bluff. At this time we are checking out the possibility her attack was related to that issue."

"Do you have any leads that indicate it was drug related?" Kennedy said.

"Yeah, there's an ex-boyfriend who is definitely a person of interest. Jake Ward was a heavy user and pretty upset not only that Miss Reynolds broke off their relationship, but that she was so successful in college while he was booted out. Supposedly, he's working in Williston, North Dakota, driving a truck for one of the companies doing the fracking at the Bakken oil fields. I spoke to the police in Williston yesterday and they're going to locate the kid and get back to us. Find out if he was actually in Williston when the attack happened." He hesitated. "In fact, I'm surprised we haven't heard back from them yet."

"Well, your hunch *could* be right. The death could be drug related, but if I were you, I wouldn't be running down to Vegas anytime soon." Grant continued nonchalantly reading the thin file, flipping to the last page, then looking sadly at the pictures of Amber Reynolds. "It's more likely a connection with what I am working on. I don't want to mislead you. I am an FBI agent, but I'm in the art theft division of the bureau. I think she was killed because she was looking for something worth twenty million or more—two Thomas Moran oil paintings."

Russell guffawed. "You've been talking to Jessie O'Bourne already, I'll bet. I think the world of her and her dad, but the whole family has always had an inflated view of how much art is worth. Especially Jessie."

Grant Kennedy put his head down and began to chuckle as well. Russell looked at him in amazement. "Well," Grant said, shaking his head and looking up at Russell. "Miss O'Bourne and the rest of the world, then. In 2008, one of Moran's large paintings sold for $17,737,000."

Russell stared at him. "Nearly eighteen million dollars for a painting? I thought sure Jessie'd added a few zeroes."

"No. Eighteen million, I assure you. Miss O'Bourne is not exaggerating when she says they're valuable. I'd call that amount high enough for anyone with a vicious streak to kill for. But I'll wait until your partner gets back with the coffee and we'll have a talk. No sense trying to explain it twice."

Russell leaned back in his chair, laced his fingers behind his head and gave Grant a hard look. "Art theft, huh? I didn't even know such an FBI division existed. Bet you have a lot of interesting stories to tell."

"Actually, you'd be right, but when it comes to paintings lost or stolen in the past, history itself is what makes the stories so fascinating. The two missing Morans are a special project of mine, because I'm a western art history buff. They were paintings of the West, donated to benefit a poor Indian school in Montana."

"Yeah. I've heard that old story."

"So often we are trying to recover old masters of typical European scenes. It's all beautiful work of course, but not of American subject matter by an American painter, and rarely work donated to a good cause here in the States. Of course, Moran was a bit of a character. He once bought a gondola in Italy and had it shipped back to California so he could paint scenes from Venice."

"You're kidding, right?"

"Not at all. Pure truth." Grant grinned, and gave a brief laugh. "Artists," he said. "You have to love them. They see—actually see—the whole world in a different way, I think. It comes alive for them in some manner the rest of us miss. Or maybe it's only that they take time to look."

"Yeah, I imagine you're right," Russell returned Grant's smile. He looked down at his desk blotter, covered with drawings by K.D. and Jessie, then back to Kennedy. "Guess I'm kind of a 'velvet Elvis' guy when it comes to taste in art, so I'll have to take your word for it."

A few minutes later, while Grant was regaling Russell with a story of art recovered from an Illinois attic, Arvid and K.

107

D. snuck in with coffee and a bulging sack of glazed donuts. They slipped through the door and shut it quickly. Arvid held the sack of donuts up like a trophy, looked at the two men and raised his eyebrows.

"Gentlemen," he said. "Our clandestine mission has been successful." He put the coffee and donuts on the desk and, as Russell made the introductions, held out his hand to Grant Kennedy.

Arvid looked at Agent Kennedy and whistled softly through his teeth. Over the past hour, they'd skimmed most of what the FBI had in their files about the missing Morans and the death of Kate Morgan, while finishing the coffee and donuts.

"So, what you're telling us, Agent Kennedy, is that you believe people have been dying since 1920? Maybe earlier, over these two Thomas Moran paintings? Including our recent grad student." He scratched his bristled chin.

"I assure you we do."

"Then do you think Jessie O'Bourne, the gal who found Amber in the hayfield, is safe? She went to Denver to talk to the girl's parents."

Grant and Russell erupted at the same time, staring at Arvid.

"Jessie went to Denver?" Russell asked.

"Miss O'Bourne talked to the girls' parents?" Kennedy asked.

Arvid looked back at them, his expression closed. "I ran into her on her way out of town. She was filling her fancy motorhome with gas. Mr. Reynolds phoned and asked her to come and pick up their daughter's research. They didn't want to ship it. They wanted Jessie to look it over, see if she can continue organizing it into a paper or book form."

"Motorhome? Jessie?" Russell said in a stunned tone. "What about her old pickup?"

"She don't use that old beater except when she comes to visit. Takes less gas." Arvid looked straight at Russell. "When you went over to O'Bourne's the other day, I don't think she was

108

planning to go to Denver. Guess she had her motorhome, a nice big Jayco Greyhawk, parked in the barn." Arvid got a far-away look in his eyes. "Man, it's a lollapalooza. I'd love to—"

"Where would she get the kind of money to spend on something like that?" Russell interrupted. "She's just a painter. Jessie probably makes about enough to buy groceries and gum. Hell, she wears jeans hanging together by a thread, and she's still wearing one of the hats I left at her dad's when I was in high school, for Pete's sake."

Grant threw his head back and his rich laughter started up again, filling the room.

"I know a bit about Jessie O'Bourne. I have two of her paintings. One of her paintings hangs on my office wall in D.C., and I certainly paid a gold plated price for it," he said. "Perhaps I paid for her motorhome. At least for half of it." He continued to chuckle.

Russell glared at him.

Arvid smiled, and said, "You don't know much about our little Jessie, Russell. She's one of the best artists in the country."

"I knew she was good." Russell shook his head. "But Dan never said she was that good."

"Well, I'm thinking you maybe never asked. Why did you think Amber Reynold's folks already recognized her name before this terrible mess with their daughter? Now, shall we get back to business?" Arvid's mouth tightened like he tasted something nasty. "Someone didn't want Amber Reynolds to reach O'Bourne's, and it's possible they'll be going after Jessie next. Like I said, I don't think she's safe."

"I agree," Grant said. "If she's the only one out at the O'Bourne ranch, Jessie is in the thick of it. We know that back in 1939 Kate found the two missing Moran paintings a couple days before she was killed. And there isn't any doubt that her death was a murder."

"That's for sure, huh?" Russell asked.

"Yes. The police at the time looked at all possible suspects, but never solved it. The paintings never showed up. It was only when someone called an auction house several months ago trying to sell a little Moran painting with a deer in it—a painting that sounded suspiciously like the one originally given to Kate Morgan—that we got any sort of lead."

"Someone called? But how on earth do you know it was that specific painting they were trying to sell if it was just discussed over the phone?" Russell asked.

Kennedy repeated the story he'd told Dan O'Bourne in a letter. "When that small Moran painting was stolen, word went out all over the United States—a detailed explanation of what it looked like—the color harmony, its size, the inscription. The same thoroughness of description was given for the painting of Kate Morgan's that was stolen at the same time, but that's another part of the story. Perhaps a case of mistaken theft—stealing a painting they thought to be more valuable than it was."

"So finish the story about this phone call," Arvid said.

"The caller not only described the Moran perfectly, he even read the inscription over the phone. He asked if the auction house would cover shipping from Montana. Then something made him edgy and he hung up before the auction house could get any contact information."

"So this was the first time someone tried to unload it?" Russell asked.

"As far as we know, yes. There was a painting we checked out ten years ago. We had high hopes it would be a lead—Moran rarely ever painted animals and this one was a deer painting just a little larger than the one reported stolen. But, it was missing the inscription, and the oil painting itself was evaluated and judged to be a forgery."

"Really? A fake, huh," Arvid said.

"And a damn good forgery, too. We wasted a lot of time on it, but got a handful of nada." Kennedy waved his hand in the air.

"Interesting," Arvid said. "Where did the forgery show up?"

"This one had been consigned to a gallery in New York by a man from Manchester, England as part of an estate sale. The heir, a grandson, didn't have a clue where his grandfather had purchased it. Since Moran so rarely painted animals the FBI believed the forger could have been working from the original but didn't realize he was making something so different from Moran's usual subject matter. He, or she, probably made it larger because a bigger painting would bring in more money, and because they were afraid to market Moran's stolen piece."

"I see." Russell rubbed the back of his neck. "Still, that's got to be pretty unusual, isn't it? Art forgery?"

"No, it isn't, actually. We've discovered numerous forged Moran oils and watercolors. They're easily sold to collectors and devilishly hard to spot. Someone in the 1950s was busy turning out good quality fakes. Funny, isn't it? A good painting should be a good painting, but the monetary worth is so often set simply by the signature."

"So let us in on the bit you aren't saying, Agent Kennedy." Arvid folded his arms across his chest and narrowed his eyes. "Why exactly did you come to Sage Bluff?"

"I wondered when one of you'd get around to asking me that." He looked at the massive Norwegian. "Amber Reynolds called me on the way to a B&B here in town, the White Bison Inn."

Arvid and Russell exchanged glances.

"And why did Amber Reynolds call the FBI?" Arvid asked.

"It wasn't the first time. She'd been in touch with me earlier as well. First, she wanted some background information to add to her thesis. I sent her copies of a few items unimportant to us, but pertinent to her thesis. Last week, she called again. And this is where it gets interesting."

"Go on," Arvid said.

"Amber was excited. She was convinced she'd uncovered new clues to finding the two Moran paintings left at St. Benedict's school in the early 1900s."

"Did she say what she'd found?"

"All she said was that she had found some unexpected results through her research, in fact, a possible tie-in with a bank robbery, and that she had discovered some photographs she felt were of paramount importance. I asked her to send what she'd

111

found. Amber said she could send me copies—have the pictures scanned somewhere here in Sage Bluff. I was intrigued, but frankly, I didn't want her to scan them in a public place. We made arrangements to meet here, instead of having her send on copies. Actually, the original appointment would have been for the day after she died."

"So were you in town when she was attacked, Agent Kennedy?"

"Just call me Grant, please . . . enough of the Agent Kennedy. No, I was not in Sage Bluff. I had to postpone the trip because of another job. Unfortunately, once I arrived, the day after Amber was attacked, I heard about her death when I watched the news at my hotel."

"Huh," Arvid grunted. "Mind if we ask your office to confirm that schedule?"

Russell looked at Arvid in surprise.

"Hey, I'm just sayin'. No offense. Nobody's immune when it comes to something worth that kind of money."

Grant Kennedy nodded his head approvingly at Arvid. "No offense taken, Detective Sergeant. Yes, my office will confirm my flight arrival late last night in Billings. Sergeant Bonham here tells me you were on a fishing trip when Amber was attacked."

"Trout fishing," Arvid said.

"After reading Jessie's statement that says— emphatically—Amber was afraid of the police, can I confirm you landed a bunch of those trout the day of the murder? And I'd like to get the name of any fishing buddies you had on that trip."

Arvid grunted, but nodded.

Kennedy then turned his smile on Russell, but it didn't reach his eyes. "I'd also like to verify Detective Bonham's whereabouts at the time of Amber's assault, and the whereabouts of any other officers as well—with your permission, of course. I have no authority over your murder investigation, just trying to tie up loose ends in my own. Perhaps we can work together?"

"We only have two officers on night shift, Grant. Lenny Svensen and the newbie, Baker Donovan. There was a bad head-on collision on the state highway that kept them busy until the wee hours of the morning. After the initial accident a couple other cars piled into the wreckage."

"Sounds hairy."

"Our local paramedics were there in minutes, but they were pretty overextended. Too many cars involved. Baker left the scene for a few minutes to set up warning flashers and cones."

"Was he gone long enough to have been the girl's attacker?"

"I don't think so. And Baker's a gal—our newest officer."

"I see. Can you account for your own whereabouts, Sergeant Bonham?"

"Just Russell is fine. I'm afraid I was home in bed the night Amber was attacked. Nobody can confirm it, because I live with my little boy, no other adults." Russell said coolly, "You can speak to any of the staff here at the station. Can we have a contact number for you and for your office?"

"Of course," agreed Kennedy, handing Russell a business card. "So gentlemen, how far back do your records go? I will be studying the records in Sage Bluff that relate to the murder of Kate Morgan, but I would appreciate being able to view any files relating to other crimes in your area during that year, and extending to a five year span before and after.

"Why would you want those?" Russell asked.

"Just in case some major thefts were solved since the disappearance of the artwork, thefts that could have been perpetrated by the same thief, but were never tied together. Surprisingly, we do recover some paintings by following such links. It isn't likely I'll find anything that other agents have missed over the years, but can you humor me? I plan to start from scratch as though it were the first time the disappearance of the paintings was reported. So . . . do you have records that go back that far?"

"Yeah," Russell said slowly, "And I don't see why you shouldn't have access to the records. But it may take Blanche some time to locate them. We can call your cell phone when we have them pulled if you want. Geez, they're probably so old they'll crackle."

Arvid said, "While you wait for us to find those, you might check with the Sage Bluff Courier newspaper office. Maybe they have records going back that far on microfilm or even archived in a digital format. Their articles might have more than just the local area crimes. Not much happens here, so they'd have reported any newsworthy crime that happened anywhere in Montana."

"Thanks," Kennedy said, "I'll check that out. When is Miss O'Bourne due back?"

"Sunday night, I believe. But she was going to stop here and there in Yellowstone to paint on location, so it's anybody's guess how early she'll get home."

"I can guarantee it will be late. When Jessie starts painting, she loses track of time," Russell said. At Grant's puzzled look, he explained. "I was a close friend of her brother's, so Jessie and I kind of grew up together. The woman is obsessed. Totally obsessed. Been that way since she was in grade school. Zones out when she works. She's even worse when she sings. It's like she becomes a different person, and that person changes, too, depending on the music."

"When she sings?" Arvid asked. Then he chuckled and said, "Ah hah!"

"What's gotten into you, Arvid?" Russell asked.

"I thought Jessie looked so familiar because I had seen her around with Dan O'Bourne once in a while, but she used to sing every year at the fairground competition, didn't she? Won them, too. No wonder I remembered her." Arvid smiled broadly, eyes twinkling. "Why, I remember one year she did this amazing Tina Turner version of Proud Mary. It was . . . hmmm, uh, she wore. . ."

A red flush crawled up Arvid's shirt collar.

"Yeah, yeah, I know," Russell said, glowering at him. "I remember. I imagine half the men in the county remember. The

114

chef over at the Wild Bull restaurant has been trying to get her to come and sing for one of his charity benefit nights ever since. But it wasn't what she wore, Arvid."

Grant looked questioningly at Russell.

Russell said, "What she wore was just an old shirt of her brother's and a pair of cut-off jeans. Nothing sexy. It was the moves." He gestured toward K.D. on the floor and made a zipping motion across his lips.

Grant looked down at the little boy humming loudly while merrily sketching his way through sheet after sheet of paper. "You're going to have an artist of your own, I see. Maybe a singer, too."

Russell nodded.

"Well, maybe one of you can give me directions to the O'Bourne ranch so I can call on Miss O'Bourne this coming Monday," Grant said with a grin. "My GPS system doesn't seem to think the O'Bourne address exists. And if I bounce across any more pot-holed gravel roads to nowhere, listening to its creative misdirection, I'm going to be hitting those high notes, myself."

Chapter 18

Yellowstone National Park, present day

The morning dawned crisp and clear. Jessie had spent the night at the campground in the park, and now stood by the Fishing Bridge overlooking the Yellowstone River as it leaves Yellowstone Lake. A ring of a dozen white pelicans simultaneously dipped and bobbed, hitting the water with their wings in a fascinating display of cooperative group fishing. Periodically, one would lift his gigantic orange bill to gulp down a silvery flash of fish.

Jessie raised her Nikon camera and snapped photo after photo of the circle, and then shot close-ups of several birds. The photos would be fantastic painting references. Humming to herself, she browsed through the pictures to make certain they were crisp, then sauntered back to the motorhome. As she approached she saw Jack sitting on the back of the sofa, watching for her out the window. When he saw her coming, he turned his head away with pretended disinterest. She thrummed her fingers on the glass as she went past and he turned toward the window and twitched his tail in impatience.

She unlocked the Greyhawk, hurried up the steps and ruffled the fur on Jack's head. She put the lens cap on the camera and put the Nikon into its case. Then she slipped into the driver's seat. Jack jumped down into his accustomed seat and settled in to ride shotgun.

"Off we go, Butter Tub," Jessie said. "Next stop, Inspiration Point." She chuckled. Then, in her best faux French accent, she said, "Prepare to be inspired, mon ami."

Twenty miles later, Jessie pulled into the parking area at Inspiration Point. She could already see a breathtaking view of the Grand Canyon of the Yellowstone. She slung her camera and small backpack over her shoulder, hurried from the motorhome and locked the door.

Jack would have to guard the Greyhawk while she made a whirlwind sightseeing trip. She didn't dare take time to hike the three miles of the North Rim Trail, instead opting for the shorter walk to the Inspiration Point overlook. Following an enthusiast group of German tourists, Jessie reached the overlook and peered out, shading her eyes with the side of her hand.

With vibrant colors rioting upstream and down, the sculpted canyon lived up to its name. She stood in awe. The sheer immensity of the landscape made her feel small—insignificant. She added a note to her mental wish list. In future, she'd allow an entire week to amble through the park, time to stop and put brush to canvas. No wonder Thomas Moran spent so much time painting the area.

Jessie took several photos, then stored the camera and pulled the backpack from her shoulder. So much for a whirlwind sightseeing trip, she thought, pulling out a 5x7 watercolor tablet and a travel sized watercolor palette. She could do some small studies, then make a larger oil later from memory and the mini paintings.

She unscrewed the cap of a water jug, took a healthy swig and then poured water into a mug-sized plastic tub useful for wetting and cleaning her brush. Jessie stood on the viewing platform, looking out and down. Way down. Below her, clusters of plastered mud nests clung to the vertical wall and cliff swallows darted about in frenzied flight, feeding unfortunate insects to their young on the fly, with fast food efficiency.

The lofty canyon walls were painted with orange, yellow and rosy hues. Grey rock, and the contrast of evergreen trees clinging to the sides added more dimension of color and in the gorge far below glistened a silvery sliver of whitewater. Jessie could hear the roar of the falls.

Goosebumps rose on Jessie's arms when she realized she stood on the edge of the Inspiration Point promontory where, in 1975, an earthquake severed a massive section of the point, including 100 feet of the original viewing platform, and dumped it into the Yellowstone River far below. She shivered. Then she picked up her small paintbrush and made several color sketches of the scene in front of her, finishing the last miniature landscape surrounded by awed tourists marveling at Jessie's skilled rendering of Inspiration Point.

She was too engrossed in her work to notice them at first. When she did, Jessie nodded and smiled at the people who had been watching her paint. She reached into her backpack, pulled out a small stack of business cards and fanned them out with an inquiring gesture. Most of the entranced tourists took a business card. Then she said a firm goodbye to her audience, stored her supplies into her pack, took a last long look at the impressive gorge, and began the hike back to the Greyhawk.

Curious bystanders are one thing Thomas Moran would not have had to cope with when he painted the east wall of the canyon.

Reaching the Hawk, Jessie slid in behind the wheel. Jack sauntered to the front of the motorhome, leaped to the passenger seat, kneaded the cushion into submission and flopped down, looking at Jessie with his usual "get this show on the road" expression.

"Homeward ho, Jack," she told the cat. "Why can't you be a burly chauffeur named Tom, instead of a lard-bottomed, old Butter Tub? And don't look at me like that," she said to his feline smirk.

She backed out of the parking space, put it in drive and stepped on the gas. As she moved forward, the motorhome pulled drastically to the right, bouncing erratically over the pavement.

"Blast it," Jessie slammed her hand on the dash. "That's a flat tire, for sure. Shoot. We're not going anywhere soon," Jessie said to him. "

She drove with care to the side of the parking area, killed the motor, and got out to check the tires. The back dual tires on both sides were fine, but the front right tire was flat as a popped balloon. She sighed, squatting down and looking disgustedly at the tire, hand on her hip. Whenever her pickup had a flat, she'd changed it herself. There was a spare in the storage of the motorhome, but this was more than she wanted to handle.

She was just straightening when a huge Gulfstream trailer pulled into the parking area and slid into the spot next to Jessie's Hawk. As soon as the engine died, teenagers poured out of the motorcoach, followed by a wide-shouldered, middle-aged man with a shaved head. He nodded his head up and down, counting the teens as they headed off down the trail to Inspiration Point. Then he muttered something to himself and turned around to stick his head into the doorway of the Gulfstream and yell. In a couple of seconds, a teenager as broad as himself scrambled down the steps onto the parking lot, a sleepy look on his face.

The man clapped the boy on the back and gestured down the trail, but the boy had noticed her standing dejectedly by her punctured tire and pointed toward her. The two walked over to the Greyhawk, the man lumbering like a bear, the teen with the swaggering walk of a sixteen-year-old. The big man nodded at Jessie, then squatted down as limber as a child and peered at the tire.

"Say, Miss," he said, standing back up to tower over Jessie. "They don't get much flatter'n that."

The father and son stood side-by-side, arms folded over their chests, big feet spread apart, like mirror image oaks. Both looked questioningly at Jessie, the older man doing a mechanical head-bob that matched a nervous, tapping foot.

"Yeah, it's a good one," Jessie said. When it became clear she was reluctant to ask for help, the father spoke.

"You got a spare?"

Jessie nodded, looking hesitant. She pulled her phone from her pocket and checked it. "But, I see we have coverage here. I can call emergency road service."

119

"Nah. They'll charge you an arm and a leg. I'm used to this. Back home I run an auto shop. We'll whip that tire off and slap it on while Lukey's cousins are off admiring the view. Where're my manners? I'm Ed, and this here's my son, Lukey."

Jessie gave them a twinkling smile and Jessie held out her small hand to shake Ed's wide mitt. "Jessie O'Bourne."

While the two rolled out the spare, Jessie punched in Arvid's number to let him know she'd be later than expected getting back to Sage Bluff. Before the call connected, Ed pointed to her flat tire.

"You know, Miss. This looks like somebody ruined this tire valve on purpose. Shoved something sharp into it—knife or something. Ask your repair guy what he thinks when you get home."

Jessie gawked at him. "Vandalism?"

"Could be."

"Hello?"

As Jessie heard Arvid's voice, she felt a spasm of guilt. She was going to be giving away his caramel rolls.

Chapter 19

Yellowstone Park, present day

As father and son loosened the lug bolts and put her spare tire in place, the thought of Moran painting the park distracted Jessie from their efforts. She'd spent most of the previous evening dipping into the shoebox of Amber's correspondence. There were copies of letters addressed to a lawyer's office in Sage Bluff, Montana and to the Bureau of Catholic Indian Missions. It was correspondence Amber had begged from Moran's descendants and so many other sources that Jessie marveled at the girl's ingenuity.

The grad student had included copies of old newspaper articles from 1918 and 1940, and one manila envelope contained original letters from Moran to Father Michael, the priest who was head of the old Indian school. The outer envelope was marked 'return to Lucille Sullivan'. Jessie had no idea who that was, but suspected her to be a relative of Father Michael's. Luckily, an address accompanied the request. It was a Helena, Montana, address, she recalled.

"There you go." Ed interrupted her thoughts. "All done."

Jessie thanked him profusely and handed him the foil wrapped package. As he walked away she heard him say, "Hey, Lukey," he said, "Look at this. Caramel rolls. We hit the jackpot."

Climbing back into the Greyhawk, Jessie hugged her cranky cat. Jack gave her a slant-eyed look and a tail twitch. She grabbed a bag from the glove compartment and shook out a couple treats for the tom. Then went to her small refrigerator and grabbed a cold soda.

Sipping from the can, she thought back to one wordy letter from Moran to Father Michael that gave her a sense of the man behind the paintbrush. In it, Moran described the visit to St. Benedict's school while the priest was absent, and he gave specific instructions about where to sell the donated paintings to get the best price. The letter was full of colorful description and humor as well. There was an odd comment about the nun who was teaching the children at the school. He described the nun's appearance as though the priest had never seen her before, and asked. "Does this sound like the regular teacher? If so, she's a mean one." Amber had attached a sticky note by the comment with a cryptic 'compare photo from Jim O'Bourne' written in ink. *From Jim O'Bourne! What photo?* Jessie thought. *And compare the missing photo to what?*

She looked out through the motorhome windshield. It was obvious from the letter to the priest that Moran really wanted his missing paintings to help fund St. Benedict's. Reading that letter had jolted her memory. As a teenager, she read a journal Thomas Moran gave to her Aunt Kate. It was a family keepsake, and was probably still in the den bookshelf. The style of writing was exactly the same, even though the journal was written in a tiny hand to save space and was meant to be instructional. It was full of advice on choosing colors and materials and developing brushwork, with comments about scenery or wildlife encountered in Wyoming and Montana. Lively anecdotes about Moran's experiences were sprinkled in. The last quarter of the journal was written by Kate Morgan. Jessie made a mental note to locate the hundred-year-old journal when she got home and read it again—this time, for clues instead of painting tips.

Stashing the soda in her drink holder, then rummaged through a kitchen cupboard until she found a granola bar. She opened it and munched it thoughtfully. She crumpled the empty wrapper and added it to a trash bag behind the seat. Feeling refreshed, she reached over and rubbed Jack's head until he purred in a deep rumble, then Jessie sat back and started the engine. She looked both ways for traffic before she pulled out onto the Wyoming highway, but as she drove, her thoughts were still on the past.

What happened when her great, great aunt Kate was a little girl at St. Benedict's school?

Chapter 20

Sage Bluff Sheriff's Office, present day
"I can't believe Jessie would just take off to Denver and not give me a heads up. She should stay in town, since she's on the suspect list for Amber's attack."

"Did you tell her not to leave town, Russell?"

"Well, no, but—"

"I got the feeling you and her don't get along, so maybe she didn't see any point in jawing with you." Arvid narrowed his eyes. "She just happened to run into me when she was getting gassed up for the drive."

"We get along just fine," Russell said indignantly.

"Naaah. You shoot sparks off each other."

Russell glared. "First of all, we do get along fine, she's like a kid sister. Second, I don't like her taking off to Denver by herself just because of some dumb idea. I—"

"Huh," Arvid said. "A sister, eh? And you think that girl don't drive all over the country with that Greyhawk going to her art shows and galleries? Probably handles it fine, too." At the dark look on Russell's face Arvid cleared his throat to hide a smirk. "She'd probably call you a chauvinist. You're not a chauvinist are you, Russell? Because that comment's sort of—you know—oink, oink."

"Never mind, Arvid."

"Well, what she told me was that the Reynolds couple wanted help searching through the research their daughter left in Denver. Mostly because the officers in Colorado didn't believe her thesis had anything to do with the attack. There was too much stuff to gather and ship."

"Arvid, the cops there aren't stupid," Russell said. "They probably felt the idea was just too iffy, an art history type of thesis getting someone killed. It is an odd angle, you have to admit."

Arvid ignored him and went on, "Course, even if they did wonder if the girl's findings could be important, would the Denver cops know what they were looking at? Doubt it, when it comes to the art research. You or I wouldn't neither."

"Hmph," Russell grunted. "So what's Jess going to do? She can't be butting into a murder investigation."

"Nup, she can't. But Jessie does think she can pull Amber's documents into some sort of paper, or even a book, that would wind up with Amber Reynolds' name on it. Might be a clue in there somewhere that helps her find the Morans. But Jessie says even if there isn't, it's a worthwhile project anyway. And the parents would feel a tad better. It's gotta be hard to lose a kid."

"I can imagine. No, actually, I can't." He looked down at K.D., who was stretched out on his stomach on the floor, coloring furiously on a brown paper bag Russell had saved from grocery day. "I don't want to even think about it."

Arvid watched the little boy for a minute as well. Thinking hard, he pushed his lips in and out, in and out. Finally he said, "You know, I think you're hunting for a drug angle that isn't there. No drugs in her belongings. None in her bloodstream. No record of her ever being involved in drugs in any way. Now—"

"Yeah, yeah Arvid, I'm beginning to think you're probably right." Russell waved his hands in resignation, and flopped into his desk chair, swiveling back and forth in the seat. "We got word this morning from North Dakota. Amber's ex-boyfriend, Jake Ward, has been in the Williams County jail since last Monday—before she was assaulted."

"What'd they tag him on?"

125

"Running a drug business on his truck route delivering supplies to the oil field. Someone in Williston got wise and turned him in."

"I'll be danged. Enterprising little booger. How was he working it?"

"The jerk would drive a big loop—pick up oil rig drilling parts and other legitimate supplies for one of the companies pulling oil out of the Elm Coulee Oil Field. But every time he stopped for fuel, he'd also pick up and deliver his own special goodies, including prescription drugs. Especially pain killers. . . Hydrocodone and Oxycodone."

"What a scheme." Arvid shook his head. "It's a shame, too, isn't it? Kid smart enough to plan all that could have done okay in college if he'd just applied those smarts. Mighta made something of himself. No guarantee he only made sales where he got his gas, though. And I bet he's responsible for a lot of the dope coming through Sage Bluff. Anybody verify that?"

"Yeah. Well, we don't have it locked in, but Sage Bluff was on his route, all right. Detectives up in Williston are working through his gas receipts, thinking he wouldn't have stopped long at each place—might have made his deliveries right at each fuel stop. Or at the café where he picked up lunch. Most of the towns are in a tri state area and are just spots on the road—places like Spearfish, North Dakota, Douglas, Wyoming, Dillon or Custer, Montana. Places where it's harder to get drugs."

"It could be anyplace he stopped two seconds for a stop sign, Russell."

"I know, but Jake Ward won't say. He keeps swearing he wasn't the brains."

"Will he give the ringleader up?"

"Don't know. The Williston police keep pressuring him. They think it's a good bet. Jake keeps saying he's gotta check on something before he makes a deal."

"Huh. How does he think he can check on diddly from prison?"

"An extensive 'con network', I guess. Beats me. Anyway, the fuel bills are a start. I already sent Lenny down to the Get and Go Gas—that's where the receipt was from here in town. It might take some time to find proof he had a cohort here in Sage Bluff. And, the drug problem here could be a separate matter—might not have anything to do with Jake Ward."

"Bet it does, though."

"Yeah. And I suspect his accomplice here is one pimply-faced teenager whose teeth chatter every time a patrol car pulls up to the pump."

"Hey, I know which kid you mean," Arvid said. "Always looks guilty, like he has the whole cash register hidden in his shirt pocket, when I walk in. He's a blond shrimp with an Adam's apple that always has a Band-Aid plastered to it. Like he can't learn to shave. He's not real short, but he's kind of slight built." Arvid snapped his fingers. "Duane, that's his name."

"You nailed it," Russell grinned. "They're pressuring Jake to open up about his partners, but so far he's so close-mouthed you'd think his lips were super glued. No luck. All he'll say is that it's such a wide network, we'll never close it down."

"Kind of strange for him to make that comment when he's behind bars himself." Arvid stroked his five o'clock shadow. "Makes me wonder if he isn't even close to being the top rung on the ladder."

"I'll bet you're dead on there, too." Russell paused. "You could be right that Amber had nothing to do with the drug route, too. The cops up there told him about Amber Reynolds. They say Jake's a big, strapping guy, but he broke down and blubbered like a baby."

"What about his buddies? They have any reason to hurt her?"

"Jake insists his friends didn't know Amber. He'd never introduced her to them. Said she dumped him as soon as she figured out he was doing drugs. Poor schmuck hadn't wanted her to know he was dealing, not just using. He didn't think she'd found out. Jake said he always hoped he could make a bundle, get himself straight and maybe make amends."

"Poop," Arvid said. "Not likely. Druggies lie to themselves all the time. Once you get hooked, the habit just reeeels you in—you can't wriggle off the line."

127

Blanche knocked lightly and stuck her head in the door. "Oopsey. I forgot to tell you that Jessie went to Denver, Russell. She said to tell you she'd be home Sunday."

Russell glared at her, then cocked his thumb at Arvid. "I know, Blanche. Mr. Know-It-All here already told me. Thanks, though."

"You're welcome," Blanche murmured sweetly, retreating.

"So, Arvid," Russell said, getting up from the chair. "I'd like to get a step ahead of the FBI agent. And I still think Jessie misheard the Reynolds' girl. I can't believe anybody on our team would be involved in something like that. And like I told Kennedy, no cops on the night crew could even have been in the vicinity." Russell nudged K.D.'s Spiderman tennis shoe with his own large boot.

"Daaaad," K.D. grumbled. "You almost made me mess up."

"Sorry, kiddo. But time to pick up. Let's get ready to go, buddy. I'm dropping you at playschool or at your friend, Joshua's, for a couple hours."

Arvid looked thoughtfully at Russell, remembering how certain Jessie had been about Amber Reynolds' fear of the police, but he said nothing.

Russell didn't notice Arvid's speculative look. He was bending down with a look of awe at his son's drawing of a horse and rider. He whistled. K. D. looked up at him with a gap-toothed grin. His father gave him a thumbs up, tousled the boy's hair and then straightened. "Well, let's get at it. C'mon, K.D."

Then to Arvid, "I'll see if I can drop my budding artist here at a playmate's house. After that, you and I can run over and make growly noises at the White Bison Bed and Breakfast. Maybe we can turn up Amber's belongings."

"Sure. Hey, after that how about we hit the Calico for lunch?"

"Sounds like a plan. While we eat, you can educate me about these so called works of art you and Jessie think are worth making such a fuss over."

After lunch, Arvid and Russell stood side by side under the wagon wheel chandelier in the rustic lobby of the White Bison Inn. They had their arms folded across their chests and feet spread wide, looking at the B&B owner, Clarence Vilhauer. Both men treated Vilhauer to their best 'annoyed cop' expression.

"But it *wasn't* a dark haired Indian girl like the fellow on the news said you were looking for, so why would I call you?" Vilhauer whined. "I'm telling you, the only lone female who stayed here that night was white. She was white. A tiny blonde woman, older than college age, with a mop of curly hair. Sexy gal. The name she gave was Monette Weber. She didn't have a reservation. She said she saw our sign out on the highway. I always ask how they heard about the B&B, because I like to know where my ad money does the most good."

"Was she alone?" Russell asked eagerly.

"Yes, but she did say a friend would be sharing the suite, so I should plan on two for breakfast." The pot-bellied man gave an exasperated shake of his head, causing both chins to quiver like poorly set gelatin. "Heck, I figured some guy was going to show up and join her, but not even the girl turned up for breakfast."

"Did she tell you she might miss breakfast?"

Vilhauer shook his head in the negative and grimaced. "And I'd made my signature French toast, potato pancakes and enough Canadian bacon to feed all of Edmonton—even fresh squeezed orange juice. My potato pancakes alone are worth getting up for. You see, I take the potatoes and grate—"

"Did Monette Weber give you the name of the friend who'd be joining her?" Russell interrupted.

"No. And I didn't ask. I didn't need it, and I try to be circumspect. People like their privacy." He looked down at his feet, shuffling one foot. "But like I said, the way girls are nowadays, they're so slutty, I figured it would be some guy."

"That happen a lot here, Mr. Vilhauer?" Russell asked with slanted eyes.

Vilhauer held both hands out palm forward. "We don't encourage that kind of behavior here. I run a clean place. But man, that blond was hot." The man gave a lecherous leer and fanned his face with a pudgy hand. "Woman like that wouldn't be alone for long, if you know what I mean."

"Hmph. Did you notice if she had anyone come and visit during her stay, even for a few minutes?" Arvid asked.

"Nobody I noticed. Course, they could have come in by the back stairs. Most guests use the entry by the parking lot."

"How about your check-in process, Mr. Vilhauer? Do you have contact information and a vehicle listed?"

"Yep. I have an address in Denver listed as her place of residence. I can pull the info up for you, and the vehicle was . . . let's see. Hmmm." He thumbed through an old fashioned rolodex. "Yeah, she had a motorcycle. Little tiny gal like that, and she had a big Harley. Well, big for a little slip of a thing like her, anyhow. It looked like the one they call an Iron 883." He shuffled his foot. "Used to ride myself," he said.

"We'd like the license number she gave you for the cycle, and can we look at the room she used, sir?" Russell asked.

"Uh, sorry. I can make a copy of this for you, but she paid for the room with cash, and we didn't write down anything except 'motorcycle.' Oh, but I recall they were Colorado plates. You can look at the room. But you'll be disappointed. Nothing was left behind, and we cleaned it the next morning. Several guests have used that room since then."

Russell and Arvid looked at Vilhauer expectantly. The man sighed, opened a drawer and withdrew a key.

"But, I'll be happy to let you in. It's empty right now, anyway."

Arvid and Russell followed Vilhauer down a wide hallway covered in cedar and decorated with framed photographs of nostalgic Montana ranch scenes, mostly cattle drives and cowboys. Stopping at room six, he inserted the key and pushed the door open, gesturing for them to enter. The room was a double. A multicolored log cabin quilt covered each queen bed, and a snowy white sheepskin rug was tossed with elegant casualness over the end of each.

"We couldn't get a white buffalo, of course, so we made do with sheepskins," Vilhauer commented. "Heck, most tourists think they're the real deal. I'd like to know where they think all the albino buffalo come from. I mean, duh."

Fifteen minutes were enough for Russell and Arvid to completely search the room. Nothing. No sense trying for prints, either. The room had been used by other visitors, and the maid informed them she had wiped every slick surface, including door knobs and faucets, with cleanser after each guest's departure. It was a total bust.

"Well, at least we know she wasn't traveling alone," Russell said. "Let's call Blanche and have her contact the Denver P.D. with Monette's address. See if they've located Monette Weber's grandma—and find out if she knows where she is. If they have, we can ask the granny to email us a couple recent photos of Monette. Also contact info. Pics of her closest friends. We can print the photos out and come back with them—make sure Vilhauer identifies the one of Monette as the right person. Have him look at the other photos, too, just in case he's seen one of them hanging around."

"I'll do that." Arvid pulled his cell phone from his pocket, dialed the station number and waited for Blanche to pick up. His stomach rumbled, and he grimaced at Russell. "Need some lunch. Remember, today's the day Alice makes her famous huckleberry pie. Cuts it into six pieces, too, not eight."

"What's this?" A cranky sounding female voice said. "Now you're calling me to give me *menu* information? By god, now I got a hankering for a piece of Alice's huckleberry pie. You'd better bring a piece back for me."

"Oh, sorry about that, Blanche," Arvid said. "Didn't hear you pick up." He relayed Russell's requests. "If we can't get the photos from the granny," he said, "call Jack Reynolds and see if Amber's parents can locate some and email them to us."

Then he ended the call as Blanche said, "Don't forget, Arvid. Huckleberry pie."

Arvid muttered under his breath. Then gave a disgusted shake of his head.

"So Russell, how about that lunch? And don't let me leave Alice's without an extra piece of pie. Blanche don't like

131

me much, so I'm trying to earn a few brownie points. Course, maybe she just don't care for big, good looking Norwegians."

Grant Kennedy looked through the box again, disappointed, thinking he must have missed something. Blanche had helped him locate the archived files from 1915 to 1930—old musty boxes he hauled up one at a time from the basement storage area and set on a folding card table in Blanche's office. The boxes smelled of mildew and were stuffed with disorganized, hand-scrawled notes on yellowed paper. A few folders included crackled black and white photos. But none of the archives held anything whatsoever from 1918 to 1924.

He looked over at Blanche, who sat reading a romance novel, the genre evident by the amorous couple pictured on the book jacket. The big woman's face wore a rapt expression.

"Blanche," Grant began, "Was there a fire in which Sage Bluff records may have been destroyed? Or somewhere else old file folders may have been stored?"

"Not that I know of, Agent Kennedy," Blanche said in her little girl voice.

"Well, unfortunately, the years I need don't seem to be in these files."

"Would you like to go back downstairs and look again? I'll come with you."

"Maybe," Kennedy said. "Yes, I think we'd better check one more time. See if the files from those years wound up in the wrong box."

"Sure," Blanche said, looking up at him over her reading glasses and fluttering her lashes. "I'm real good at searching the records. If they're there, I will absolutely find them for you. Absolutely. But, I think that someone back then probably just didn't think they were worth keeping."

"You might be right, but I'll feel better if we do a more thorough search, Blanche, if you don't mind." Grant pushed his chair back and stood, raising his arms in a stretch that tightened his blue dress shirt over a muscled chest.

"Oh, no, honey," Blanche said in a simper. "I really don't mind a bit."

Grant reached the door to the basement ahead of Blanche, opened it and reached into the gloomy space. He yanked the pull chain, which turned on one bare light bulb to illuminate the steep steps.

As they trudged down the dingy stairway, he heard Blanche mutter enigmatically, "Maybe I'd even go five hundred."

Chapter 21

Calico Café, Sage Bluff, present day
Arvid put down his cell phone. Russell looked questioningly at him, raising one eyebrow. "She's fine. She was calling from Inspiration Point. She had a flat on the Greyhawk."

"Well, heck, I suppose she needs someone to go get her? That's the trouble with her running around all over the country by herself. Women!"

"Anybody can have a flat, Russell. A good Samaritan changed it for her, some burly guy who runs his own mechanic shop in Tennessee."

"Hmph," Russell said.

"He thought the tire might've been ruined on purpose. I think we should have Lou down at the repair shop take a look, just out of curiosity."

"We could, but stuff like that happens all the time. It doesn't mean someone was out to cause Jessie trouble. Especially not way in Yellowstone." Then he squinted at Arvid. "You realize you have a big glob of huckleberry or something on your uniform? What'd you do, bring Blanche's piece of pie back on your shirt?"

"Oh, poop," Arvid said looking gloomily down at the uniform shirt stretched over his girth. "Good thing I have a spare uniform in my office closet. I'll have to drop this by the cleaners on my way home."

"Say, Arvid." Russell said with a puzzled expression on his face, "Why was Jessie calling *you*, anyhow?"

"She said she was just checking in. Wanted to let us know she was on her way back."

"But she must have had your number with her."

Arvid scratched his head. "Nah, probably got it from Blanche or looked it up on one of those smart phones. Hey," he said, changing the subject, "Next thing you know, they'll have a smarty phone app that can air up your tire if you get a flat."

Chapter 22

Abrahmsen's home, present day

Esther Abrahmsen stepped over a cockapoo the color of a dirty mop stretched out by Arvid's foot. "Shoo, Minnow." She fluttered her hand at the little dog. "Shoo!" The dog squinted its eyes, flopped one paw over its face, and rolled to its side on the hardwood floor. She scowled at the dog, then at her husband, setting the plate of meatloaf and mashed potatoes down in front of Arvid with a thump, accentuating her displeasure.

"I know you're worried about Jessie O'Bourne, but why on earth are you suspicious of Russell? You can't seriously think that nice man had anything to do with that poor grad student's attack. For Pete's sake, he's a fine cop. And Russell is your friend."

Esther walked back to the stove to dish her own plate. Arvid's eyes followed her with appreciation. Today, Esther had on designer jeans that fit snug against her willowy form, and a black knit top decorated with music notes, treble and bass clef symbols. Her white hair was cropped short, spiked with gel into a punk rock look. Several bangle bracelets hung from one wrist. She looked back over her shoulder at him, waiting for his response.

"Are you listening to me, Mister?"

"*Ja,* I know, I know," Arvid said in a placating tone. "Amber could've been attacked by someone we don't have on our radar. But the girl told Jessie O'Bourne she was afraid of the police. Deathly afraid, Jessie says. The two rookies we have on

136

night duty are cleared. They both have ironclad alibis for the night of the attack."

"What kind of alibis?"

"A three car pile-up out on the highway and they were stuck until the tow trucks hauled the totaled cars away."

"So you're thinking the only one left is Russell?" She gave him a look of disgust. "Heck, you aren't even thinking about Baxter. It could be a cop from Baxter. "Russell might have an alibi—"

He looked at Esther with the expression of a child whose brother just ate his chocolate Easter rabbit. "Russell is the only one who *don't* have an alibi. Just says he was home with his son. I hate feeling suspicious of Russell. He's a likable guy, and he gets his job done. That little boy of his is great. Russell takes good care of him, too. But, Esther, I'm just saying, what if?"

"What if? 'What if' seems to be your catch phrase lately, Arvid. You think Russell hit that girl on the head and left her for dead? I know you. Even after six years, you're still thinking of Jessie's brother again, thinking Russell had something to do with his accident, aren't you? Am I right, Arvid?"

"Huh," Arvid grunted, frowning down at the laden plate. "Yup." Arvid gave his plate an even dirtier look, the schooled his features into a bland expression and looked up at her. *No sense making her mad as hell.*

Esther nudged mop dog with her foot. Minnow rolled again onto his back and curled his front paws over his chest. "Aren't you ready to let go of that idea? In the past six years, you've never found anything to indicate it was anything other than a tragic accident. Not one thing, Arvid. And you've been feeding this moocher at the table, haven't you?"

"Hmmm," Arvid muttered noncommittally. He looked around the cheerful kitchen, thinking about his friendship with Russell. He wondered how he could care so much about another person, but when it came to trusting him, it read like a whole different book. Kevin's death had somehow slammed a door between himself and Russell. And driven an even bigger wedge between himself and Sheriff Stendahl, who had insisted Arvid close the case.

"Maybe I'm just getting paranoid as I get older, Esther, but yeah. I admit it's bothered me since the day Kevin was shot. Something about his death smelled bad as field fertilizer."

"Those two were like brothers, Arvid. You said so yourself."

"That don't matter. Look how you and that sister of yours bicker." He pointed his fork at her, a fork laden with meatloaf and dripping catsup. "You practically yank each other's hair."

"We do not," Esther said emphatically. "We just like to fuss at one another. It isn't fighting."

Arvid rolled his eyes. "Well, sometimes even brothers have major disagreements. I know they'd been at each other's throats that week because I saw Russell get right up in Kevin's face in the station parking lot. You know how Coach Anderson loses his temper and reams the referee after a bad call? Well, I only saw it through the window, but the body language was the same."

"You never mentioned that to me," Esther said in a surprised tone.

"Well, at the time I thought I was crazy to think Russell would do anything to hurt the O'Bourne family. But I asked Russell about it anyway, after Kevin died. He looked me right in the eye, Esther, and lied through his teeth, denied there'd been any argument. Lied through his teeth. To me, his friend."

"What did he say exactly, honey?"

"Said they were just talking sports." He put the forkful of food into his mouth and chewed thoughtfully. "Russell's not only the one who found the body, but it was odd the way Russell and Kevin's fiancée Trish got married so soon after he died."

"I'll give you that point, Arvid. But maybe they were just a comfort to each other. Sometimes it happens when two people have lost someone they both cared about."

Arvid grunted and mixed melting butter into his mashed potatoes, the fork making a furrow like golden wheat in a field of snow. "Yeah, but do you think she cared about Russell? She couldn't have cared much. By God, she took off right after their son was born." He snorted. "Left Russell to raise K. D. by his lonesome. Don't think the gal's ever been back."

Arvid took a bite of the stirred, mashed potatoes. *I wonder . . . .* Then he put down the empty fork.

"Esther, I'm no T.V. detective, but the angle of the bullet didn't look like it could have been an accident. Nobody knew why Kevin had the gun in the barn to begin with. The ground around the body was disturbed, kinda like there'd been a struggle. And where the gun was laying after the so-called accident just seemed wrong." He shook his head. "Aw, I can't explain it. I guess it was more of a feeling that something was off."

"I still think it was an accident, or he committed suicide," Esther said. "People do things on impulse when they're depressed. It was too bad there was no note, but unfortunate as it is, people don't always leave an explanation for those left behind."

"Suicide. Yeah, it's sad." Arvid reached for the meatloaf dish and slid another slice onto his plate. When Esther glanced to her plate, he surreptitiously flicked a tiny piece onto the floor near Minnow.

"Suicide is a heartbreaking thing," Esther said. "Worse than an accident. Worse than murder. And I saw that Arvid Abrahmsen. You're going to make that dog fat, and guess whose turn it is to mop this weekend."

Arvid gave her sorrowful look.

"Don't give me those puppy dog eyes. It's your turn."

"Aw, okay." He grinned at her. "Anyhow, it wasn't suicide. The gun couldn't have landed where it did if Kevin shot himself, honey. Besides, Kevin had life figured out. He had a girl. He had a good job. He had good friends."

"Maybe he was depressed anyway. People get chemically depressed."

"Everyone I spoke to said they'd never seen Kevin in a gloomy mood—not ever. Oh, well, everyone except Blanche."

"Blanche from work?"

"Yeah, Blanche claims she saw Kevin down at the bank, and he was in a foul mood the day before the accident. 'He looked awful', she said. But something about it just didn't ring true."

"Why do you say that, honey?"

"Seemed to me that Blanche was just being overdramatic. Wanted to chip in her two cents just to be in the limelight for a sec." The Sheriff was satisfied, Arvid remembered. He wanted the case closed. 'Cut and dried', he'd said. "But there was something about the way Russell acted every time we discussed Kevin's accident that month that just didn't ring true, like he was acting a part."

"Oh, honey," Esther said, running her hand through her short hair, ruining her do, making it stand up in feather spikes like an angry hen's. "We discussed this before. I still hope you were imagining that. I *like* Russell. Besides, not only did his best friend die, but you remember Hannah O'Bourne went into such a state, that's when she had the heart attack."

"Yeah."

"Hannah was about the only mother Russell had ever known. When she died, he must have been as devastated as Jessie. Of course he acted odd."

Arvid glanced around the room, noticing the hand-penciled music scattered across the bench of the Steinway baby grand, Esther's pride and joy. She spent most of her time sitting at the piano. He loved the way her fingers danced over the keys when she played. She was probably in the middle of a new composition, and here he was, dumping his worries on her.

But something about Kevin's death still niggles at me worse than mosquitos down at the lake. I wonder if the two men had gotten into a fight over something important—the girl, Trish, maybe. He rubbed his hand across his wiry five o'clock shadow. *And now, here's these damn Moran pieces clouding the issue.* Why did his gut tell him Kevin lying dead in the barn six years ago was somehow involved with those bits of canvas? *It don't make sense.*

"I like him, too, Esther," he said finally. "In fact, Russell 'bout seems like part of our family, too. But, that don't mean I'd let him get away with murder. Being so close to the O'Bourne family, he's had plenty of opportunity to hear about the Thomas

Moran paintings. Does it seem logical he wouldn't know how valuable they were? He acted like he didn't have a clue." Arvid scowled, wrinkling his forehead into a deep furrow.

"Well, if he's not interested in art, maybe he never paid any attention," Esther said.

"Maybe he was tellin' me the straight scoop, maybe not. Something's going on with Russell right now, too, just since that little Colorado gal died."

Esther rolled her eyes, but said nothing.

"And if he's a good enough actor to have pulled the wool over my eyes when Kevin died, he could be capable of anything." He gestured with his fork. "If that's the case, I'm going to get him."

"Oh, Arvid," Esther said, her usually cheerful face dropping into a frown, "Eat your meatloaf. And your carrots. I cooked them in apple juice with a spoon of brown sugar, just the way you like them. Now, let's change the subject. It isn't good to talk about unpleasant subjects at dinner." Esther watched Arvid reach for the catsup bottle and squirt another glob of red on both his potatoes and his meatloaf. Then she looked at her husband with crystalline blue eyes that gleamed with steely resolve.

"By the way, we need to beef up our mail box. Have you seen Gunderson's?"

Back at her dad's ranch, after Jessie unloaded the motorhome, she took a steaming hot shower and pulled on fleecy pajamas and her comfy red flannel bathrobe. She sat on the sofa in her father's den, Jack purring contentedly by her side and the box of research from Jack Reynolds on the square coffee table in front of her. The box of folders wasn't as interesting as the shoe box of correspondence, but Amber had not scanned the papers into the computer. Jessie would have to go through both boxes one piece of paper at a time.

The folders in the big box were loaded with notes on Thomas Moran's paintings of the Yellowstone region. Most of his larger works had been painted partially from memory, and partially from small watercolor studies he made while traveling

141

with the 1871 Hayden Geological Survey. Jessie skimmed over long and boring phrases Amber had copied from textbooks— phrases like 'Entranced by the colors and natural wonders, Thomas Moran painted numerous large canvasses depicting the grandeur and scale of the scenery'.

"Huh," she said to Jack, "Same composition as I planned when I did the small studies at Inspiration Point. You know," she said, "while you sat on your pudgy tumpa and let some creep wreck our tire. Lou says it was vandalism sure as anything. Heck, I wish you could talk. You could probably tell me who did it."

Jack stretched a paw out and placed it on Jessie's leg, opening his mouth in a silent meow. Jessie tickled his chin and returned to the paperwork.

"Well, I love you anyway," she told Jack. "Get this. According to this paper, I can blame Thomas Moran for the tourists that bug me when I paint in the park."

Amber's notations verified that Moran's work helped influence President Grant and Congress to set aside the land as the first National Park. His name was so closely linked with Yellowstone that the artist incorporated a 'Y' for Yellowstone into his signature. Amber had included a close-up photo of Thomas Moran's signature. Jessie recognized it. She had seen Moran's actual signature on a few pages of Kate's journal and on the drawing of Aunt Kate her dad had inherited from Jessie's grandpa, Nate. It hung in Dan's office.

As she read through folder after folder of Amber's documents, Jessie grew excited. The grad student had been meticulous in citing references, and everything in the folders was in chronological order. Amber's work should be published, just as Jack and Shelly Reynolds said. It would make a noteworthy book—not just a dissertation—a book.

Once she had all Amber's research joined into an organized whole, she would either search for a publisher, or publish it with the Reynolds' financial help. *It would mean time away from the easel, a lot of time*, she thought. Jessie absent mindedly scratched Jack's head. *I'll need some help.*

Jessie pulled the next folder off the stack left in the box. It was intriguingly labeled 'Forgeries' and contained only a blue notebook. She opened the notebook and read through the long list of works that were at one time attributed to Thomas Moran, but later shown to be fakes. How odd, Jessie thought, for someone to have the technical ability to paint in the style of a master, but not want to make his or her own art. It was probably too lucrative to sell a copy of someone else's already famous work instead. She flipped a page. The photo showed a study of a mule deer, supposedly painted by a forger. Amber had made a notation: *Original was inscribed to Kate Morgan.*

Jessie gasped. Jack jumped down, whirled around and hissed. "Good gosh," she said to the alarmed cat, "Someone had my Aunt Kate's painting long enough to make a copy." She looked to see what Amber had written about the forgery. In small neat writing the girl had written: *'maybe one of the art students Kate taught in 1939? Any of them had the opportunity to steal the painting and Kate Morgan had taught them to paint in her own style, a style which was a lot like Moran's.'*

Yes, Jessie thought. *Amber might have something there.* It was the first mention Jessie had seen that referred to the two small paintings that disappeared when Kate was killed, not the larger Moran works. If Amber had been actively looking for them, as the Reynolds said, where was the rest of the information she'd gathered on the hunt?

A copy of an old black and white photo was inserted into the notebook. It was Kate Morgan's class, the art students casually gathered for the portrait. The back of the photo had each student's name listed. Kate stood to the left, a tall woman with wide-set eyes, even features and a heavy braid of hair draped over her shoulder. She wore an artist's apron. Her expression was serious. Jessie stared at the photo in shock. It was like looking in a mirror.

Jessie quickly skimmed the rest of the blue notebook and saw nothing as startling as the note about the forged deer painting or the photograph of the class. Then she became curious about Kate's journal. She remembered it used to be on one of the highest shelves in her Dad's bookshelves. She brought a stepstool from the kitchen and searched the top shelf. *Yes, there it is!* She pulled it down. As soon as she opened it she realized it was priceless. The first page held a small Moran sketch, a tiny three inch by two inch pencil drawing of a waterfall. *Good lord, this notebook could be worth a million dollars and Dad leaves it here in plain sight? It belongs in a museum.*

Jessie reached down and scooped Jack onto her lap as she sat down again to read. He purred and she studied the pages until her eyes felt like sandpaper. The last half of the journal was written and illustrated by Kate Morgan.

There was a definite similarity to Moran's drawings in Kate's self-confident sketches, a simplicity of line and strong composition. Jessie's eyelids drooped.

Bedtime, she thought. *How many more pages are there?* She flipped ahead to the last page and read Kate's last sentence out of curiosity. Surprised, she said a word Arvid would blame on the Swedes, then got up and carried the precious journal down to her father's gun safe. She unlocked the safe, added the book to the shelf with the extra ammo, pulled the shotgun from its slot, picked up half a box of shells for it, and relocked the safe.

She was now wide awake as she climbed back up the stairs to the main floor. She checked the doors and windows and went up to her bedroom, locked the door from the inside, and slipped the shotgun and shells under her bed. Jessie crawled between the covers, snuggled into their warmth and sighed.

On the last page in the journal Kate had written simply, 'next notebook'.

Chapter 23

Rural Montana, present day

The noon sun beat down, brutal in its assault, causing steam to rise eerily from the black asphalt. Had the road been filled with writhing souls instead of the occasional flattened road-kill, Dante could have mistaken it for the River Styx. Jessie fanned her face with her John Deere cap, doing little except to stir the dust in Arvid's old beater pickup.

"There's the sign for 'Bison Creek Buffalo Jerky'," Arvid said, pointing to a rusty metal sign peppered with bullet holes. "If you come out by yourself, remember you want to take the next right turn." He put on the blinker. He drove off the highway onto a poorly maintained secondary road, rumbling over the parallel metal bars of a cattle guard, a grid over a ditch designed to keep cattle from straying off the reservation into traffic.

"Keep your eyes peeled for livestock on the road, Jessie. You probably remember it's free range here on the reservation, but there's a lot more livestock than when you were a kid. It's always an obstacle course of new potholes, too," he said with a grimace as they bounced along, landing hard on the worn springs of the truck seat with Arvid offering a repeated chorus of "Sorry.". . . "Uffda!" . . . "Blast it!"

Jessie looked out the window, up at a ridge textured with blue grey sage and the acid yellow-green of blooming rabbit brush. A game trail meandered downhill, worn into the hillside by countless animals walking the same route to available water, winding through sparse cedar trees to end at Bison Creek.

"Maybe better keep an eye out for antelope or deer. I see some antelope up on the bluff to the right."

Arvid looked from the road long enough to follow her gaze and spot five or six pronghorns bounding up the hillside, the lead animal gaining the top of the rocky ridge. He turned and, silhouetted against the bright sky, looked back at his harem as though to hurry them along.

"Ayup. Sharp eyes," He said. "You paint much wildlife?"

Jessie nodded. "It's my favorite subject. Most of the work I do in the studio is of animals in their native habitat, using my own photos. I get a better painting if I work on it as soon as possible after I take the pictures. Then I still have a sense of the animal's movement and I remember the lighting. It's all about the light, Arvid."

He grunted. "Got any antelope or buffalo paintings in that 'art thing' you got coming up?"

"I guess you mean the art competition over in Baxter at the end of the next week. No, my wildlife paintings had to be put on hold while I painted some on-location landscape pieces. Since I'm the awards judge for the contest portion, the gallery hosting the plein air competition—Reuben White Fine Art— wanted me to display work." She fanned her face again with the cap. "But if you'd like to see it, I do have a large bison painting nearly finished right now. The reference photos of the big bull were taken at Christmas time, early morning, when the brush and trees were still covered in frost. I'd gone down to ski at Grand Targhee near Jackson, Wyoming and drove out near the Tetons. I was sure glad I had the camera along."

She pointed out the window at another small herd of pronghorns before continuing. Arvid nodded his head.

"I see 'em. You got it here at the ranch?"

"Yeah. I brought the painting with me hoping there'd be time in the evening to work on it. This mess with the Reynolds girl is more important, though. Instead of painting, I'm reading an old journal of my Aunt Kate's and going through Amber's computer and research papers."

"I suppose you don't have anywhere to paint at your dad's anyway, huh?"

"Oh, believe me, there's a great place. I paint in a space over the barn that was originally built as an art studio."

"Your aunt Kate's?"

"It was. I use it when I come home, so I keep it completely outfitted. Paint, canvas . . . extra easel. But, a lot of Kate's things weren't ever removed. Even her old pochade box is still up there. Hoo boy, is it heavy."

"Bet it has a lot of sentimental value, though. You using it?"

"Oh, heck no. Art materials and supplies have come a long way since she was painting. My portable easel is handier— new light-weight materials, better design."

"Huh," Arvid grunted. "Same with fishing tackle and creels." He continued, "So, you found Kate Morgan's journal, huh?"

"Yeah. You'd think Dad would know how valuable that little book must be. It has sketches all through it by Thomas Moran and Kate." Jessie put her hand dramatically over her heart. "I'm almost afraid to turn the pages, for fear I ruin something. If a painting by Moran is worth well over a million dollars, think what the journal, with all the tiny sketches and notes must be worth. It should be appraised and stored some place with temperature and humidity control. Heck, Arvid, it really belongs in a museum."

"I have to agree with you there. Any clues in it, Jessie? Something you think might help locate the Moran paintings?"

"No, darnit. In fact, after you get past Moran's art tips, much of the journal is written in a childish scrawl. She told about being left at the school the year 'everyone got sick'. That was when Montana was hit hard by that global Spanish Flu epidemic."

"Yeah, everyone lost a relative to that nasty influenza."

"Kate's mom recovered, but she lost the baby. Kate's aunt and uncle both died, so Jim and Margaret O'Bourne adopted their son Nate."

"Terrible times for a lot of folks. Good thing the little boy had family to take him in."

"Kate wrote about learning to mix paint, and a few odd notes about a nun who sounded too mean to be very religious, but there I'm sort of reading between the lines. It sounded almost as though she'd written it while being very careful, for fear the nun might find it and read it."

"Interesting. Nothing about the two missing paintings?"

"Nope. Only about one Moran gave her to give Jim O'Bourne. A gift. The journal was abandoned for a few years after her father came to retrieve her—no more personal notes. When she began writing again, it was mostly notes on painting technique. Now that was fun. Aunt Kate must have been as obsessed with painting as I am. I have to try some of her tips. Oh, and the last page made it clear there was another journal."

"Huh," Arvid said, glancing over at Jessie. "Well? You have that one, too?"

"Nope. Guess there must be another notebook somewhere at the ranch, Arvid. If I can't find it, I'll ask Dad about it this evening. Slow down, Arvid. Cows!"

Arvid looked back at the road, took his foot from the gas pedal and stepped on the brakes, seasoning the air with a few choice phrases he again blamed on the unfortunate Swedes. A pregnant Hereford cow, sides bulging with unborn calf, stood in the center of the road, looking at the oncoming GMC truck with bovine disdain. She chewed, standing her ground. Arvid slowed to a stop. Another cow scrambled up from the roadside ditch, a white-faced calf bawling behind her. Jessie grinned.

"Poop, it was a mistake to stop," Arvid said. "Sure as shootin', now they'll think I'm dropping off a bale of hay." The accuracy of his statement was apparent as cows stopped grazing on the slim pickings along the road and headed with purposeful strides toward Arvid's truck, gaining momentum as they came.

Jessie lunged for her camera bag on the floor of the pickup, hurriedly unzipped it, and grabbed her Nikon. As she hung out the window snapping photos of bellowing cows and calves, Arvid revved the engine, his foot still on the brake, then leaned on the horn, which emitted a deep 'woogah, woogah!'

148

At the sound, a bull in the distance raised his head, interpreting the noise as either a dinner bell or competition. He charged down the hill toward the pickup, massive bulk swaying side to side, hooves churning the dry hillside into billowing dust.

"Whoops! Better get a move on."

Arvid put his foot gently on the gas, inching the truck forward until the cattle crowding the center line decided to inch away. With tosses of disgruntled heads, rolling eyes showing whites, accompanied by loud bellows, the cows grudgingly gave ground. Arvid pulled forward and slowly picked up speed. In the side mirror, Jessie saw the bull reach the road and stand looking after the truck, his head jerking up and down and his tail swinging in agitation.

The heavy truck bounced over the lane to Minna Heron Woman's home, a house the faded blue of last year's robin's egg with a weathered wooden door. The surrounding yard was scoured of grass. A twiggy geranium blossomed in red profusion on the porch, the only living foliage in Minna's front yard.

The side-yard was littered with enough worn out appliances, used vehicles and broken down machinery to start a parts store. A yapping dog darted from behind a rusted station wagon to welcome their arrival. He scuttled on his short legs in excited circles near the interloper's vehicle like a beetle on hot tin.

"Don't mind Muggs," Arvid said. "He doesn't bite."

"What the heck kind of dog *is* that?" Jessie asked. "He's got the biggest head I've ever seen, especially for such a stubby-legged little guy."

"Best guess is his mama was a yellow Lab, and his pop some kind of nighttime opportunist." Arvid chuckled. "Minna doesn't know the breed."

"Well, my guess would be a Lab and a dachshund," Jessie grinned. "Not sure how they managed. I swear, Esther's right when she says everyone in Montana must own at least one dog."

149

Jessie and Arvid opened the truck doors and stepped out. Arvid reached into the pickup bed and grabbed two large grocery bags. The front door opened and a withered Native American woman in a floral print housedress stood framed in the doorway. She hunched over a diamond-willow walking stick, her skin as dark and furrowed as tree bark. The two hands covering the knobby head of the cane reminded Jessie of inverted bird's nests, the gnarled brown fingers intertwined, the backs of her hands full of raised veins twisted like twigs. A rope of silvery-grey hair hung over her right shoulder to touch her thigh, and it swayed as she tilted her head to one side as though listening. The mutt continued to bellow.

"Muggs! Pipe down." Arvid commanded. The dog grew less animated, studied Arvid as though to judge the seriousness of the request, and settled on snuffling first Jessie's shoe, then the loaded grocery sacks. Arvid raised his voice. "Ma'am, it's Arvid."

"Ah, Arvid." The woman lifted a wrinkled hand from the supporting cane and held her arm out to Arvid, who stepped in closer to clasp her hand in both of his, before introducing her to Jessie. "Ma'am, I brought company. I have a friend, Jessie O'Bourne, with me. I told her you were the best historian in the county."

Jessie held out her hand and felt it firmly gripped in a leathery palm.

"Come in, come in. If you're going to flatter me, Arvid, let's go inside where I can sit down while I listen. You, too, young lady." The old woman turned to shamble through the doorway of her home, and waved her hand at her visitors in a beckoning gesture. "I see you didn't forget about my shopping list."

"No, ma'am, and I added a couple packages of trout I outsmarted on my last fishing trip. They're frozen. Should I put them in the freezer for you?"

"That'll be a treat. Better leave a package on the counter to thaw, I think. It will be your job, too, to pour cold drinks. Thank you, Arvid. And don't ma'am me."

She looked at Jessie with rheumy eyes as Arvid went to put away groceries. "Stay here and keep me company while Arvid does those chores, dear. He knows where to put things. I don't see as well as I used to, and Arvid is always kind to this old woman."

She sank heavily into an arm chair, leaning her walking stick against the chair. Her eyes seemed cloudy and unfocused. Jessie realized she had cataracts, a common curse of elderly Native Americans.

Jessie looked around the small room. The walls were covered with photographs in cheap plastic frames, mostly of children at various ages. A smell of old dog, old person and fried fish permeated the air. Jessie looked around for somewhere to sit.

"Move my garden catalogues out of your way, Jessie, and sit yourself down. I can't read well anymore, and I'm too old to have a garden, but I still enjoy the big flower pictures."

"I get the garden catalogues, too. I'd love to have a small garden," Jessie said, "but I'm gone too much to keep one watered and I hate imposing on neighbors who'd be willing to take care of the garden when I'm away. Still, Mom always had one. Sometimes I get homesick just for the smell of tomatoes fresh from the yard."

Jessie shoved the stack of catalogues to the side and sat carefully on the ripped vinyl sofa, patched in places with silver duct tape. No matter how she squirmed, a sharp edge of peeling plastic poked maddeningly into her bottom.

Muggs, exhausted from the effort of sounding the alarm, collapsed onto the shabby carpet as though his weight had overcome his runty legs. He plopped his large head across Jessie's feet, still snuffling her ankles, until Minna reached for her cane and tapped the rubber tip on the floor with a sharp command.

"Come!" The dog raised reluctantly and went to Minna, settling in next to her chair and flopping heavily onto his side.

A wasp bounced against the window pane behind the old woman's chair, and the elderly woman turned her head listening, trying to identify the noise.

151

"There's a hornet on your window, Mrs. Heron Woman. Shall I get a swatter?"

"No, just open that side window, Jessie. There's no screen." She waved her hand vaguely in the direction of the insect. "It'll go out eventually. Never kill anything if you don't need to, child."

Jessie rose and tugged the window up a foot. Then she realized it wouldn't stay raised, and she looked around for something to prop it with.

"There's a stick on the shelf—just there by your hand," the old woman said. Jessie was wedging the window open as Arvid came back in and sat.

Thirty minutes later, while drinking cold root beer, they'd made the polite conversation one must make before 'getting down to business'. The conversation had covered the health of Arvid's relatives, Dan O'Bourne's recent wedding, problems with local teenagers, the weather and the inaccuracy of Koot, the weatherman and—Minna's obsession—how little the young Blackfoot learned of their heritage and language. Finally, Minna Heron Woman turned to Jessie.

"Arvid told me you have questions about the old days, Jessie. About St. Benedict's Mission School when I was a girl. Stories that might have been told me by the elders when I was a child."

"Yes, I'd love to hear some of the old stories, Minna. Especially about people who might have known my aunt Kate Morgan before she died in 1939."

"Ah, more questions about the painter? There isn't much I can tell you." She looked at Arvid. "I told the young woman from Denver the same thing. Poor thing, I heard she was attacked near your father's farm, too. How upsetting for you."

Jessie and Arvid looked at each other. "Amber Reynolds was here, ma'am?" Arvid said.

"Yes. She'd stopped at the library to do some research and asked for the names of area historians. My name was the only one that came to mind, I'm afraid. It's unusual when young people are interested in history, don't you think?"

"Yes it is," Jessie said. "But—"

"And Arvid, you know you're supposed to call me Minna. You too, Jessie. All the 'ma'am this' and 'ma'am that' makes me feel old, and I'm only 103."

"Minna," Arvid said, smiling. "Did she have anyone with her?"

"Yes, she did. A friend she called Webby."

Jessie and Arvid exchanged looks.

"Such an odd name. Especially for a girl. Even with my poor eyesight, I could see her friend was tiny, just a slip of a thing. Skittish as a deer. I was sorry to hear about Amber." She frowned. "A lovely name, isn't it?"

"Yes, it is," Jessie said.

Minna's face wrinkled into a frown. "It didn't suit her, even though I could see she was a pretty girl. Amber. The gemstone is supposed to balance the emotions and release negative energy."

"You feel she had negative energy, Minna," Arvid asked.

"Yes. She was troubled—conflicted—over her heritage, her worth. She asked questions about the Blackfoot. I told her she needed a talisman—perhaps a pendant of amber—as soon as possible. I offered to help her make one."

"And did you," Arvid asked.

"No. She said she could wear an amber pendant she already owned. I don't think she understood how important it was." Minna broke off and sat very still. "I used the past tense when I spoke of her. She died, didn't she, Arvid? I heard about the attack, but I never heard if she lived."

"Yes, I'm afraid she did, Ma'am. And she wasn't wearing any amber jewelry when we found her. I'm sorry."

"Young people seldom believe, Arvid. And she was such an independent young woman, riding that big motorcycle."

"What questions did she ask, Minna? Were they by chance about some old paintings?" Jessie asked.

"She had a lot of questions." Minna rubbed the side of her nose. "Hmm. Yes, she did ask about a painter from the old days. Thomas Moran. He painted many of the Blackfoot children from St. Benedict's school. The first school, not the modern building they have in Sage Bluff now. It was made of log and some of the outbuildings were old railroad ties. Ugh, they had to be sweltering during the summer. And the flies . . . when I was a child, oh, the flies were awful. But I'm getting off track. Let's see."

"What else can you remember?" Arvid asked. "We're trying to piece together some of her research."

"Oh, she asked if I ever heard a story about the body of a white woman being found on the reservation round about 1918."

"And had you?" Jessie asked.

"Oh, sure," Minna said. "I heard about it. But I was away at the time it happened, so I had little to tell. Then, she wanted to know about John Running Bear's family, wondered if I knew where they lived."

"John Running Bear? He was a student at the school when my aunt Kate was there. My aunt mentioned him in her journal." Jessie said. "Why did she ask about him, Minna?"

"Amber had some old newspaper clippings about the discovery of the body. The dead woman was later identified as the nun, Sister Mary Campbell. Her skull had been crushed."

Jessie said. "But Minna, why did Amber want to find John Running Bear's family?"

"It was an odd story. While she was researching the time Thomas Moran spent at St. Benedict's Mission School, Amber came across a note to a Catholic Bishop in which John Running Bear claimed a strange woman impersonated the dead nun for several weeks. She didn't act much like a nun, according to John. Amber had some photographs that she thought might prove who the imposter was. Isn't that remarkable? After all this time."

"Remarkable," Arvid agreed, "But where did she get the photos?"

"She found several in a letter from Jim Morgan—your great grandfather on your mother's side, Jessie—written to Father Michael Connor, the priest who was head of St. Benedict's Mission School. The letter was part of the correspondence Amber was given by a relative of Father

Michael's when she was working on her research. She compared one of the pictures with a photo from the school records of 1918. Amber said the photos proved John was right, someone masqueraded as the nun." Minna shrugged. "That imposter could have been the true Sister Mary's killer. Or perhaps knew who murdered the nun.

"Wow," Jessie said. "What did you tell her?"

"I said, 'of course'. That's the story John's family said the child told local police at the time, but nobody would listen to him."

"Why not?" Arvid asked.

"John was only ten. People thought he was making the story up to get attention."

"Too bad," Arvid said. "But why would anyone pretend to be a nun? And why didn't the priest say anything?"

"According to John, the woman took off before the priest returned. Left the kids there with no adult. The tribal members knew this had happened, but kept silent. All of them were afraid they'd get blamed for something, somehow."

"Bigotry?"

"Yes, Arvid. Whenever anything went wrong close to the reservation, the Blackfoot tribe got the blame. It was a problem then," Minna said, with a tone in her voice that made it plain she thought the issue had improved little.

"That's sad," Jessie said, then asked. "Did you tell her how to find John's family?"

"No. I told them to ask John. If he wanted to give that information, it was his to give," Minna said.

"Minna," Arvid said in a surprised tone, "you mean John Running Bear is still alive?"

"Oh, yes, he's over a hundred years old. The rascal. He loves telling stories about the old days. Of course, when he was a child he had many people tease him and accuse him of making things up about the murder. Now he's so old, they think he doesn't remember correctly, or dreams things." She gave a rueful smile.

"Where does he live, Minna? Can you give us his address?"

155

"He's easy to find, dear. John is at the High Butte Senior Living Center in Sage Bluff, in the nursing home half. The center is divided between elders who can do most things for themselves, and those who are unable to do much at all."

"We'll go see him," Arvid said, glancing at Jessie. "I'd love to know his version of what happened."

Minna waggled her index finger at Arvid.

"Now, don't you believe any of the stories he tells if he mentions me," she said with a rasping chuckle. "He's a scoundrel, that one."

Arvid and Jessie both smiled broadly. Arvid noticed how the smile transformed Jessie's features from striking prettiness to unexpected, startling beauty. *Good thing she don't smile like that around Russell. It was plain that Russell was tense as a spring around Jessie already. Smitten. Trying to say she was like a sister. Huh.*

A smile like that might be the end of his willy-wallying around. And that, Arvid thought, might not be a good thing for Jessie. Not if Russell knew something about Kevin's death or— God forbid—Amber Reynolds' attack. *Or drugs. And a crooked cop somewhere in Sage Bluff.*

Something was eating at Russell. It worried Arvid, Russell's attitude smacking as it did of a guilty conscience. Arvid swore to himself he would find out what was going on if he had to cancel every fishing weekend until winter. *Dammit, and I broke down and ordered that new custom Pryor fly rod, too.*

Hmm. Jessie's smile. It reminded him of someone. *Who was it?* Then it struck him, and his eyes widened. *Well, I'll be damned*, he thought, filing the information away in his mind to be revisited later. He stood up abruptly, gave himself a mental shake, and thanked Minna for the visit.

Minna Heron Woman's cloudy eyes stared at Jessie as the two visitors walked toward Arvid's truck. She stood as she had when they first arrived, framed in the open doorway, one gnarled hand resting over the other on the head of her cane, leaning heavily on its support. Arvid was opening the door to the truck for Jessie when he heard Minna yell after him.

156

"Arvid! Arvid! I need to talk to you again for a minute!"

"Be right back," he said, and trotted back to see what the old woman wanted. Probably some grocery item he'd forgotten.

"What is it, Minna?" Her face was set in intense concentration and she reached toward him, clutching at his arm.

"Arvid, I'm a silly old woman. I wanted to tell you . . . ," She looked sheepish, gesturing toward Arvid's truck. "I'm worried for your friend. Worried. Take extra care of Dan O'Bourne's daughter."

"Of course I will," he assured her, giving her a gentle hug.

"Arvid, it's important," she said.

"Nobody better than a big, old Norsky for jobs like that, huh, ma'am?" He looked at her with a more serious expression. "Are you okay here, ma'am?"

"Yes, Arvid. I'm fine. And I told you, quit ma'aming me," she said. "Now, don't keep that girl waiting in that stifling rust bucket you pretend is a truck."

"Is she okay, Arvid?" Jessie asked as Arvid slid onto the driver's seat. "What did she need?"

"Oh, she just wants me to take care of a little something."

As the outer door closed behind Arvid, the bedroom door opened behind Minna. A round-faced girl of about twelve, still carrying ten pounds of baby fat on her road to womanhood, walked into the room. Her straight black hair hung to her shoulders and thick glasses perched on her pug nose. "Did you see something, Grandmother?"

"Yes, but don't worry, child. Always have faith. Nah-doo-si, the creator, will protect her. And Arvid will, too, of course. But, I think I will make her a small medicine bundle. We will have to gather some things for it. You must be my good eyes and my hands. I will tell you what we need."

"Why did you lie to them, Grandmother, when you teach me to tell only the truth? I heard you. You told them you are only 103."

"White people," Minna scoffed. "Do you think they would believe me if I told them the truth?" She raised her hand, thumb and index finger almost touching, as though to measure half an inch. "It was a little fib—this small. But," her leathery face split into a grin showing several missing teeth, "many times I feel Arvid is no fool."

"You like him, Grandmother? He's big."

"Yes, child. He is big outside. And he is big inside." Then she said somberly, "The woman, Amber, is dead. Do you remember where you put the note with her tiny friend's number on it? Find it, and put that on the refrigerator, child. Under a magnet."

"Okay. But why didn't you tell them you had her number, Grandma?"

"Did they ask me, dear? Tomorrow you will help me call. I know she's been camping over in a gully near Peter's house. They have seen her several times, plugging in what Peter calls a 'smart phone', into the outside outlet after they go to bed at night. How smart can it be if it must steal its electricity?" She laughed, the effort ending in a rasp.

"And fish for dinner, Grandmother?"

"Yes, dear. Fish. Now, let's continue your lesson." She patted the little girl on the shoulder. "You must learn to speak Aamsskáápipikani, our Blackfoot language. And then, you will learn to cook trout."

"I guess you didn't see a photo in Amber's research labeled 'clue', Arvid said, looking both directions and then pulling out of Minna's lane onto the gravel road.

"I don't think so. There is a photo of Kate in front of the old school. I can't see why it would be evidence of anything except Kate being there at the time, though," Jessie said in a perplexed tone. "I haven't read through all the correspondence. There were quite a few pictures in the letters I've already read. I'll go back and be more thorough."

"Seems like she was real thorough with her research. She couldn't have used all of it in her thesis, I bet."

"Gee, she'd use a lot, Arvid. It's going to be a job putting it into book form, and it will be a pretty thick book when I'm done. And the newest interviews and papers wouldn't be with the items I brought from Denver. She surely used the iPad Jack Reynolds said she hauled on all her trips. But her phone hasn't even shown up, has it? Or her iPad."

"Nup," Arvid said. "I gotta say, somebody else has the rest of her research. Probably the attacker, or her friend Monette."

"We need the phone and iPad, Arvid."

Arvid nodded. "You know, it's weird, but I got a hunch Minna wasn't telling us everything she knows either, Jessie," he said. "She's a canny old woman. There's something she was holding back."

"Minna? I don't know see what it could be, Arvid. But I'll take your word for it. You know her well, and I just met her."

"Yeah, I've known Minna Heron Woman for a lot of years."

"How often do you always take her groceries?"

"Once every two weeks. I take turns with her niece. She's too healthy and too stubborn to go to a nursing home, and it's important for her to feel independent."

"Must be hard for elderly people like that, especially with her bad eyesight. Do you realize how beautiful she must have been once?"

"Minna?"

"Yes, she has wonderful bone structure, and so much character in her face. I'd love to paint her portrait. I wonder if she would let me take photos, or paint her while she sits in that big armchair of hers."

"Ask her sometime. I bet she'd at least let you take a few pictures."

"Speaking of painting, I'm still trying to get some done so I have inventory for next week, and I have to plan the workshop portion of the competition. I'm running behind." Jessie looked at her watch. She needed to call the gallery before they closed.

"Hey, 'behind' is my middle name."

"I'm so curious, though. Do we have time to go talk to John Running Bear before I get back to work?"

"Let's take time," Arvid said.

The architect who designed High Butte Senior Apartments, the assisted living facility in Sage Bluff, was originally from the deep South. The white building sprawled across half a city block and looked like a transplanted Georgia plantation house, complete with tall round columns. Elderly men and women sat contentedly in rocking chairs on the wrap-around porch, staring at Jessie and Arvid as they navigated the steps, crossed the wood porch and walked through wide, double doors with leaded glass windows.

A receptionist sat behind an antique mahogany desk with curved Queen Anne legs; a desk whose provenance no longer mattered because of the large hole drilled through the top to accommodate a snarl of computer cords. The bored looking, middle-aged woman looked up as the two visitors came in. Her face broke into a wide smile.

"Arvid!" she crooned. "How the heck are ya?"

"Good, Sally." He introduced Jessie and asked, "Is this a good time to visit one of your residents, John Running Bear?" Arvid asked.

Sally pushed a button on the desk intercom and buzzed another station, then looked at Arvid and Jessie with an apologetic expression as a male voice said, "I'm sorry, but I just helped Mr. Running Bear to bed and he's resting. He had a morning visitor for a change. It tired him. If it's really important, I can wake him, but if not. . . "

Arvid shook his head. "No, it isn't that important. Never mind. We'll come another time."

The receptionist smiled. "Regular visiting hours are from 2:00 until 4:00, and 6:00 until 8:00," she recited. "And Arvid, thank your wife again for the free piano concert last week. It's kind of Esther to come and play the old songs for the folks here. They look forward to her sessions, and every rocker on the porch fills when they know she's coming. They sit outside and watch for her," she shook her finger at the big

160

Norwegian, "and you'd better watch it, Arvid. At least half the men propose to her. They just love her."

"So do I," Arvid laughed. "So maybe I'd better pick up a box of chocolates on my way home tonight, huh? Gotta keep myself in the running." Arvid turned away from the desk and then swiveled back. "Say, Sally," Arvid said, "you didn't happen to see who came to visit John Running Bear, did you?"

"Don't know who she was but, yeah, I saw her. A young woman. Lot of curly blond hair. Big hair, the kind you see on women in honky-tonks. Cute little bit of a thing not more'n five feet tall."

Jessie stepped up on the running board of Arvid's pickup and heaved herself in. "So, at least we know she's in the area and alive. But she never checked in with the police. I wonder if she's called her grandmother or Jack and Shelly Reynolds yet."

"I'll call Amber's parents and ask, and I plan to ask again about Amber's other friends, too. See if anything has come up." Arvid looked at his watch. "I wanted to tell Sally that it was police business and maybe she could forego the rules, but old people like their routine and need their naps." Arvid yawned. "Heck, sometimes I need a nap, young and robust as I am."

"Don't get me started," Jessie said, covering her mouth with her hand.

"Shall we get together later this evening and try our visit again? I'll go back to the station and get some work done after I drop you off. Why don't you meet me at our house about six o'clock? I'll introduce you to my better half."

"Good plan. In the meantime, I'll get a quick 8x10 painted and then look for the other journal. In fact, I'll pull the art studio inside out like an old sweater."

"Go for it," Arvid said. "Doesn't seem likely it'll be around after all these years, though."

"Well, if that doesn't turn it up, much as I hate to bother him on his honeymoon, I guess I'll call Dad. He might have an idea where to look for it. There could be something in it that helps us find the paintings now that we can add Amber's research to the notes in the journal."

161

Arvid paused. "Heck, my priority is to catch who killed Amber. But—I'd love to find the paintings. Do you mind if I read both of them journals myself? That is, when and if you find journal number two?"

"Not at all, Arvid. You're more than welcome to take a look."

"It would be nice to find out what happened to the Morans before anyone else gets killed over those damn canvases."

"It isn't like the Moran paintings were responsible for people being murdered, Arvid. Art doesn't kill people."

"No," Arvid replied with a serious expression. "But greed can. And greed does."

"It sounds like Amber had information on one of the oldest unsolved murders in the county, doesn't it, Arvid? That poor nun's murder. But, it's probably nothing to do with the Morans."

"Huh. Let me tell you, a case doesn't get much colder'n that. I hope the photos Amber told Minna Heron Woman about turn up."

"Yeah. And if they do, I hope to heck we can figure out why they're important."

"Me, too," Arvid said. "Why on earth would someone kill a nun?"

Chapter 24

Sage Bluff Sheriff's Office, present day
Blanche knocked on Arvid's office door and pushed it open
without waiting for a 'come in'. An overweight, middle-aged
woman only half Blanche's height strolled in with her. Her hair
was over-permed, resembling nothing so much as a child's
stuffed animal, and still reeking of the beauty parlor smell.
Arvid recognized her and groaned inwardly. It was Violet
Adams, Blanche's sister.

"You know, Mrs. Adams, like I told you on the phone
yesterday, Cassy is a grown woman." He gave Mrs. Adams a
look of sympathy. "Maybe she just took off on a trip she wanted
to keep quiet? Boyfriend, perhaps? Girls don't always want their
parents to know."

Blanche and Violet both glared at him. Then they settled
in like wet bags of concrete into Arvid's extra chairs, their
ample thighs flowing over the chair seats and draping like plush
pillows over the edges. Arvid sighed in resignation.

"I'm telling you, my daughter is responsible about her
job. But she hasn't showed up for work for two days. Two days.
Eric Jensen, her boss, called me. 'If she doesn't have a good
reason for missing work', he says 'tell that girl she's fired'. Fired.
Instead of wondering if she's in trouble. That's the kind of boss
she has. Fired. What a jerk." Violet tightened her mouth into a
line as thin as a pencil mark.

"Huh." Arvid said.

"That girl of mine helps me out with grocery money and rent," Violet Adams said. "How am I supposed to make ends meet if Cassy doesn't come back? Why, I'd have to go to work! At *my* age! You do something about this, Arvid Abrahmsen. You find her."

"Oh, all right." Arvid said grudgingly. "She probably just wants a bit of time away, but I'll help you fill in a missing person form. I'll have to find one. It sure isn't something we need in town much," Arvid said, digging in his desk drawer. "I'll start checking into it and I'll fill Russell in when he gets back."

"Isn't he taking an awful long lunch?" Blanche asked, her bulldog face set in a disapproving scowl.

"No. He isn't. The poor guy didn't even get any lunch, Blanche."

"Why not?"

"Aw, some kid was driving with beer in his truck. Middle of the afternoon. No license and no common sense. Shame you can get one without the other." Arvid located the missing persons' form, patted his empty pocket hunting for something to write with, then rummaged in his desk drawer for a pen. "He's taking the teenager home so he can read the parents the riot act."

"Well, that shouldn't take him long, and when he gets back, maybe he can help you look for my niece," Blanche said.

Arvid pulled out the gnawed stub of a pencil. "Let's get started. Go ahead. Give me her cell phone number, list of her good friends, whatever you can think of. Guess I'd better have a photo, too, although nearly everyone knows Cassy. Still, I think you're worrying for nothing."

Blanche smiled sweetly at Arvid, her wide face wrinkling into folds. She got up and waltzed out, saying, "You start, Violet. I'm going to go get us all some coffee before I go back to my desk. Just made a fresh pot."

Violet and Arvid looked at each other in dismay. Arvid groaned and said quietly, "I'm glad to help you, Mrs. Adams, but I've got to tell you, swallowing your sister's coffee goes beyond the call of duty."

Eric Jensen pushed a copy of the form across the desk toward Arvid. "This is the application we have our EMT applicants fill out. Nothing on Cassy's that most everyone in town don't already know about her. She never even left a message saying she wasn't coming in. Just didn't show up, damn her," he said.

"Never let you know, huh?" Arvid said. "Was that like her?"

"Nah, not really. She was usually reliable as clockwork. And it made me *two* employees short, not one. Travis Simpson is out of town for a family emergency. Left a message on my cell that his dad had a heart attack. He seemed pretty upset."

Arvid felt a flicker of alarm. He skimmed Cassy's file, flipping pages, then asked. "Travis Simpson—that's the beanpole that was on the scene when we found Amber Reynolds, right? Tall, skinny guy, dark brown hair?"

"Right, Travis Simpson."

"Was he the one that rode in the helicopter when they flew Amber Reynolds to the Billings hospital?"

"No. Cassy Adams rode with her. She's real good at her job. Leastwise, she was until she stopped showing up for work. It was a shame that college girl died on the copter ride. Cassy was pretty broke up about it. Only thing I hate about having a gal for an EMT. They've got to cry at everything that goes wrong. A guy just goes out for a beer."

"Was Travis the kind who went out regularly for that beer?"

"Oh. I got off track there. No, he wasn't a drinker. At least not to my knowledge."

"Did Travis Simpson and Cassy happen to leave on the same day, Mr. Jensen?"

"Yeah. It was the same day, now that I think about it."

"Was Cassy involved with Simpson? Maybe took off with him?"

"Don't think so. They didn't seem involved that way. In fact, I can't remember seeing Cassy with any special fellow. She was a pretty enough girl, but I don't think any of the guys here thought of her like date bait. She was kinda just one of the guys."

"She gay?" Arvid asked. "Maybe I should be looking for a girlfriend."

"Naw, I don't think so," Jensen replied, flushing. He paused, rubbing his chin. "But her mother is right. The girl's been real responsible until now. She was always on time, never missed a day. Neither had Travis. Course, he's pretty new . . . been here just a month or two."

"Huh," Arvid said. "Did you verify that his dad was ill?"

"Heck, I just took the kid's word for it. Well, he's not a kid. I guess neither Cassy nor Travis is that young, but the older I get the more the new hires look like babies. Anyhow, I never pulled his employee info except to grab his cell phone number. Tried it, but all I get is voice mail."

"Oh, yeah? That's kinda odd. Kids these days live with their cell phone on."

"Well, nobody ever picks up," Jensen said.

"You mind if I look at his job file? Just in case Cassy did wind up tagging along with him?" Arvid flipped through Cassy's file. "I see next of kin is listed on your forms. I can try Travis's next of kin and see what they got to say."

Jensen opened a file cabinet and rifled through the contents. He yanked out a thin folder and held it out to Arvid.

"Knock yourself out," he said as Arvid reached out and took it.

"Say, did either of them have access to prescription drugs that might have value on the drug market?" Arvid said, as he opened the blue cover.

"Hey, we all do, but I run a real tight office," he said in a sharp tone, giving Arvid an angry look. "We really screen our new employees, too. Travis seemed like a perfect fit for the team. After we hired him, we realized . . . well, we decided he was a little paranoid, or something, always looking over his shoulder like someone was watching him. A tad weird. But he was efficient. And a decent enough guy."

"Not saying he isn't a great guy. Not implying any of your crew is involved, either. I'm just sayin', we have a lot of

166

drugs coming into town." He looked at Jensen. "And maybe going out of town, too." Arvid looked at the application.

"Not from our Fire Station," Jensen said emphatically. "I'd know."

"Travis Edward Simpson, huh?" Arvid said, ignoring Jensen's comment. "Well, guess his folks had to call him something other than 'bean pole'." Arvid skimmed the resume. "Army medic in Iraq. Fire crew medical team during the summer for BLM. Hospital experience in Helena . . . ."

"Yeah," Jensen said. "And we verify that stuff when we hire. He checked out. Checked out all across the board."

"Huh. Pretty impressive experience. No wonder you hired him," Arvid said. "The past two or three years he doesn't seem to have had very steady employment, though. Wait a minute, this application just lists a sister as the next of kin. Says no living parents. Thought you said his dad had a heart attack."

Jensen looked startled, grabbed the file from Arvid and took a look.

"Well, for heck's sake," he said in annoyance. "Kid maybe pulled a fast one on me."

"Mebbe," Arvid replied. "Who do you have working today that knows Travis the best?"

Jensen walked over and stuck his head in the break room and motioned with his hand. A stocky young man with brown hair tied back in a ponytail and a day's growth of beard stepped out.

"This here's Rick Hansen. He worked with him on Sundays. Sundays are our slow shifts. More time to chew the fat, so Rick probably knows Travis even better than I do."

Arvid nodded, introduced himself, and shook hands with the EMT. "We're hunting for Cassy Adams, Rick. Is it possible she went home with Travis last week when he said his father had the heart attack? "

"Nah, I saw her Friday evening at the hospital," Rick said. "We both do a few hours a week at the ER there." He thought a minute. "So did Travis. When I heard you got a message about his dad having a heart attack, I was surprised. Travis told me he didn't have any family. I mentioned a fishing

167

trip I wanted to take my dad on and Travis said he envied me. Said he didn't have folks. Maybe he just meant they weren't close."

"Oh, yeah?" Jensen said, grabbing the file back from Arvid and looking down the entries. "Bet he lied about his dad's illness. Damn kid must have an out of town girlfriend."

Rick shrugged his shoulders. "Don't think so. He never mentioned one, anyhow, when I told him about my girl. Travis seems like a stand-up guy to me, too. That all?" His eyes went back to the television in the break room where a ballgame was playing.

"Hold on a minute, Rick," Arvid said. "Do you have any idea where Cassy Adams may have gone?"

"No." He pulled his gaze back from the TV and met Arvid's eyes with a worried expression. "She was stewing over something though, lately. Real out of sorts. Guess I should have asked her if she was okay. You don't think something happened to her, do you?"

"Don't know. Hope not," Arvid replied. "Thanks. If you think of something, give me a call." He handed Rick a card with his cell phone number on it. Rick nodded and returned to the break room, flopping heavily down on the loveseat and gluing his eyes to the big screen.

"If you never pulled his application file, I guess you didn't call the sister. Think I'll try her number right now." Arvid reached over and retrieved the folder, took his cell phone from his belt and keyed in the sister's number, noticing the Montana area code. He leaned both elbows on the desk.

"Hello," said a female voice in a clipped tone. "Who are you trying to reach?"

"Ma'am, this is Detective Sergeant Arvid Abrahmsen with the Sage Bluff, Montana Sheriff's Office. I am trying to reach Travis Simpson to request some information. Is he there, or do you know how I can reach him?"

"Regarding?"

"Just an issue here in Sage Bluff, Ma'am. We have a matter we'd like to discuss with him. Travis isn't answering his cell phone."

"We have not heard from Travis," the voice quickly cut in. "I would prefer to first phone the Sage Bluff Sheriff's Office and verify your employment, after which someone may get in touch with you. Your number is now on my caller ID." The phone gave an audible click as she severed the connection.

Arvid took the phone from his ear and looked at it. "Well, I guess that's why the kid is a bit paranoid. The whole famdamily is paranoid," he said.

"So what about Cassy?" Jensen asked.

"I'm beginning to think we'd better put a whole bunch of effort into locating that young woman. And the Simpson kid, too.

"I'll help any way I can, Arvid. Not sure how to help though. I can take care of injured people, but I haven't got a clue how to go about finding one that's gone missing."

"Ayup. Not something I get a lot of practice at, either. Have to fly by the seat of our pants, I guess," Arvid said.

Jensen looked glum.

"Two employees dropping their job at once is quite a coincidence. Maybe if we find one, we find the other. Blanche Michaels and Violet Adams are both on my case," Arvid said. "They're worried because of what happened to the grad student from Denver," *I hope this Simpson isn't a psychopath.*

"God, I never even thought about a connection with that girl who was attacked," Jensen blurted. His eyes had a worried expression. "I sure hope nothing like that has happened to Cassy."

Arvid nodded his head. "Me too." He looked at the form. "The application asks height and weight; guess that's so you know if someone can lift a patient if they need to?"

"Yeah, and Travis seemed strong as hell for someone so skinny. Some of them wiry guys are like that."

"How about hair? Guess I know that one already, dark brown," Arvid scribbled. "Eye color?"

"God, who'd notice? Blue or grey, I guess."

"You wouldn't have a picture, would you?"

"Nah," Jensen said. "Well, yeah, there's a tiny one in the back of his folder. Take a look." Arvid flipped to the back page and looked at a miniscule picture so blurry it was almost unrecognizable as human.

"Oooo-kaay," Arvid said in a disappointed tone, "Well, I'll go talk to Travis's landlord. See if he can add anything. I've already talked to most of Cassy's friends. Nobody's heard from her."

"And Cassy's mother is her landlord," Jensen said, "Or maybe she's her mom's landlord. Don't know."

Arvid snapped the papers under the clamp on his clipboard. *This is starting to look like a can of worms*, he thought.

"And, oh boy, Cassy's mom is a piece of work," Jensen said warming to his subject. "She came by here ranting and raving about me maybe firing her 'little girl'. I think she was more concerned about the money she gets from her than the fact her daughter is missing. She acted like I might've had Cassy locked in the back room or something."

"Hey, that reminds me. All the EMTs have lockers, don't they? Can I take a look at the missing EMTs' assigned storage space?"

Jensen scratched his head. "Well, I guess so. Come on back."

"You have the key?"

"Heck, nobody locks their lockers."

He led Arvid into the room where Rick sat, one leg thrown over the side of the loveseat, a thick sandwich in his hand, eyes still on the ballgame.

The room held a battered trestle table and benches, refrigerator, microwave and a row of metal lockers similar to high school gym units. Jensen walked to a locker with a white label that read 'Adams', the name written in thick black marker. Underneath the label was a drawn happy face. The locker's only other decoration was a shiny, silver padlock.

"Well, I'll be damned," Jensen said in surprise. He looked at Arvid.

"Well, I guess some do lock their lockers. I take it you don't have a key?"

"No," Jensen said.

"If it takes too long to locate Cassy, we may have to saw through that padlock."

Jensen nodded assent. "Fine with me. Hey, she might just be a little shy about being the only woman firefighter or EMT here." He gave an embarrassed laugh. "Might have some female stuff she wants to keep private." He looked back at the locker. "Padlock's new, though."

"Good to know. So, how about Travis, what else do you know about him? Anything important that's not on his application form here?"

"Nah," Jensen said. "Oh, wait. Yeah. The guy wore an ankle holster. Pistol."

"You're kidding. Did you ask him why?"

"Heck yeah, I asked him about it. I noticed it when we were working at the nursing home the other day and he was squatting down by this old fellow who'd had a heart attack. He said he couldn't help it, he was paranoid, and to please keep it under my hat. He did say he had a concealed carry permit. That's another reason we all thought he was a little paranoid. The ankle holster . . . it made him seem like a bit of an oddball."

"Huh," Arvid said. "I'd guess so."

"Good paramedic, though. I like him okay, I guess. Don't get me wrong, I hunt, and I own guns myself. But he was one of those quiet people. Lot of people like that would make you a little uncomfortable when you see a gun strapped on his ankle like that. Kind of give you the creepy crawlies, you know?"

"Shoot," Arvid said. "I know a lot of folks with concealed weapon permits, but I never saw anybody with an ankle holster, either. So, did Travis give you that creepy feeling?"

"Well, no. I have to admit that until today when you came in here asking questions, he never did. Now, with Cassy disappearing the same day he left, and now finding out he probably doesn't even have a father, let alone one with a heart problem . . . well, now I don't know what to think." Jensen scratched his head thoughtfully.

Arvid nodded and told Jensen he might have other questions later.

"Can we take a quick look in his locker?"

"Guess so," Jensen said. He walked over to the locker labeled 'Simpson' and yanked it open. A single EMT shirt hung on the hook inside. "Nothin' but the spare shirt we all got."

Arvid peered inside. Then he pulled his cell phone from his belt clip and called Blanche, giving her a terse request to call the hospital with Travis Simpson's particulars.

"No, we're not calling him a missing person yet, Blanche," He said into the phone. "Probably just a coincidence they seem to have flown the coop the same day. He may have gone home for a family emergency, but if so, his sister says she hasn't heard from him." Arvid didn't mention the sister had hung up on him.

He heard Blanche muttering to herself, "Dear, dear, merciful heavens. I can't imagine what my sister is going to do. We just don't get these cases here. And now another one missing. It's like an epidemic, and Arvid won't have any idea what to do." She gulped in air and sniffed loudly into the phone.

"Gee thanks for your vote of confidence, Blanche," Arvid said. "We'll start by checking out all the angles. Ask your sister if Cassy and Travis Simpson ever got together after work. I wondered if it was possible she went along with Simpson and they ran into trouble along the way." He listened, then said sharply, "No, I'm not trying to give you palpitations." More muttering. "Well, I'm not a total boob, Blanche. And yeah, yeah, of course I know the hospital should have called Violet if someone brought Cassy in. Call anyhow. Now listen." He looked at Travis's description in the folder he held and read the particulars aloud to Blanche.

Poop, she could probably just ask the desk if anyone hauled in an injured bean pole. Bigger and bigger can of worms. Wish I was out somewhere fishing with 'em instead of getting them dumped in my lap.

As soon as Arvid hung up, his phone buzzed. Before he could say hello, the same woman he'd spoken to earlier said, "Detective Sergeant Abrahmsen?"

172

"Speaking."

"This is Leona Hanfield. I believe someone will be down this afternoon to speak with you and the Chief of Police about Travis Simpson. If someone does not arrive today, make sure that the earliest possible appointment is available for tomorrow morning. Thank you." Again the click of a severed connection.

"Huh," Arvid grunted into the dead phone staring at the small blank screen. "Someone missed third grade the day they covered telephone manners."

Chapter 25

Rural Montana, present day

Russell steamed as he walked from Miller's house to the patrol car. He hated dealing with anything that involved teenagers. As he slid behind the wheel, he vented his frustration with Tommy's folks by slamming the patrol car door. *Damn nitwit parents,* he thought. *People ought to need a license to have kids, not just to get married or to drive a car.* He turned the ignition key just as his cell phone hummed. He answered and heard Arvid's deep growl demanding to know his location.

"Just heading back from Tommy Miller's now." Russell said peevishly. "What's up?"

"Didn't want to use the radio. Too many busybodies monitor the channel. Blanche's niece, Cassy Adams, seems to be missing, and that new EMT, the one who was out at O'Bourne's when we found the grad student, seems to have dropped out of sight as well. Cassy might have been gone just a couple days, but it doesn't make me feel too good that this fellow—his name's Travis Simpson—disappeared the same day. He left a message on his boss's cell phone saying his dad had a heart attack and he had to go out of town—"

"What's the big deal then?" Russell interrupted.

"The deal is, that story's as fishy as five aces in a hand of poker. One of the other EMTs says Travis never mentioned any family. I asked Jensen if I could look at his employment application. It lists only a sister for next of kin. Looked like a Billings number."

"You call it?"

"Yeah, I called it and got some woman who acted like she didn't wanted to talk to me. The phone call gave me a bad vibe."

"Weird."

"But get this, Russell, she made an appointment for someone, '*someone*', she says, no name, no info—to meet with us tomorrow morning and she requested the Sheriff to be at the meeting." Arvid laughed. "Tag! You're it."

"Oh, joy," Russell said sarcastically. "I wish Sheriff Stendahl would get his tail back to work. I assume you're checking on Simpson because he had access to the drugs Jake Ward delivered on his route? Seems pretty suspicious that Simpson disappeared right after Jake was arrested."

"You got it in a nutshell. But it also seems odd Cassy hasn't come in to work. I can't imagine her being involved in anything shady, Russell, I really can't. But it's too much of a coincidence they disappeared the same time. Could be Simpson's disappearance has something to do with her. Dang it, Blanche's sister, Violet, is going to have a cow when she hears the station is missing a male EMT as well. A big old Hereford cow."

"You bet," Russell said. "Glad I'm not going to be in before *you* tell her." He laughed. "What else you find out about Simpson?"

"Well, he had a small basement apartment. He paid month to month, no lease. The landlord, Michael Ralston, teaches music here in town. He didn't want to let me into Travis's apartment."

"You get in?"

"Yeah, he changed his mind when I explained we were also hunting for Cassy Adams and she'd worked with Simpson. It helped that Travis's rent was due last Friday and Ralston was ticked he hadn't received it."

"Yeah, money changes people's ideas faster than anything. I think the drugs were coming into Sage Bluff way before this new EMT came to town though, Arvid. What else you got?"

"Well, nothing weird in the apartment. It was neat as a pin. I noticed the last three issues of the Sage Bluff Courier were piled unopened by Simpson's apartment door. I'll fill you in when you get back if I find out anything else. In the meantime, keep an eye out for his car, a blue Ford Taurus with a dented back fender."

"Sure."

"And say, call me nuts, but since you're already out that way, can you take a run by the field where the Reynolds girl was dropped? It would ease my mind. I'm worried about Cassy. Some people have no imagination, you know. I just want to rule out a repeat performance, or a copycat."

Russell swore and did a quick U-turn, tires spitting gravel.

"Yeah," he said into the phone, "will do." Russell looked at his gas gauge, hovering at the quarter tank mark. "Arvid, maybe you'd better send Lenny back out to the gas stations. Have him ask every clerk if they saw anybody filling up a blue Taurus in the last few days. When I hit town, I'll swing through the drive-in on my way. My stomach thinks I forgot how to eat, it's been such a long day. You want me to bring you a couple burgers?"

A few minutes later, Russell eased his vehicle onto the shoulder of the road near O'Bournes' hayfield. He sat in the car and looked past the field, staring at the sprawling log house he'd spent so much time in as a pimple-faced teen. He smiled, thinking about all the hours he and Kevin spent shooting baskets behind the barn or fixing fences with Dan. And the welcome sound of Kevin's mother, Hannah, calling them to dinner. Hannah fed him just like she did the O'Bourne youngsters, fussed at him about homework. Hugged him goodbye every night.

And I missed her funeral. No wonder Jessie is still so mad.

Russell looked away from the log house. He rubbed his temples with tired fingers. He had been ready to come clean about Kevin's death when Hannah suffered the fatal heart attack, but at the time, he couldn't load more sorrow on top of that. Now, when he finally might act like a man and tell Dan and Jessie what happened, they weren't likely to understand.

Might not even believe me. God, what a mess. I'm just no good at dealing with people. Why did I leave it so long? His stomach roiled. *Lord, I'm not a praying man, but I need some help here.*

Russell shook his head to clear his thoughts. He got out, slipped through the barbed wire fence instead of taking time to open the gate, and power walked to the haystack, examining the entire perimeter of the stack of bales before jogging back to the car. As he was walking around the car to get in, he glanced back again toward O'Bourne's.

He saw a dust cloud kick up as Jessie sped out of the yard in the red pickup, heading his way. Russell leaned against the car and waited, wishing Arvid had come out himself to check the field. It wasn't in his best interest to see too much of Jessie. He chided himself for wanting to see her so badly his heart lurched even before the battered red Ford pulled up and stopped.

She must have been out painting earlier. She was wearing another of the old hats he'd left at the ranch, an old brown Rocky Mountain Elk Foundation cap. Like usual, she'd twisted her hair into a ponytail and pulled it through the fitting on the back of the ball cap. He had purposely left two of the hats at the O'Bourne house years ago, liking the idea of her wearing something of his.

His breath caught thinking of that tumble of red hair, the way she threw her head back when she was happy and the way laughter bubbled from her like clear water from a spring.

Man, if he'd thought it would complicate things to approach Jessie then, now it would be like K. D. trying to do calculus with a crayon.

Jessie leaned out of the open window, her face serious. "What's going on, Russell?"

"Hey, Jess. Just checking for dead bodies."

"That's not funny after what happened out here."

"Sorry. Actually, I'm looking for a guy that was part of the EMT team when you found Amber Reynolds out here. The tall skinny guy."

"You think he just stuck around or something, Russ? Thought he'd hang out for a week or so?" Jessie asked.

"Now who's being funny?" Her expression became grave. "You aren't kidding, are you? The EMT is missing? And you expected to find him here?"

"Two. Two missing EMTs. Cassy Adams and Travis Simpson. They were both on the scene when Amber was found. It was Arvid's idea I check out here at the same place we found Amber. It was a hare-brained long shot, and thankfully, there's nothing here." Russell started to reach for his car door handle. "Sorry to have alarmed you."

"Oh, no you don't, Russell Bonham. I needed to talk to you anyhow. Follow me back to the house. I've had a break in at the barn."

Jessie pointed to the broken window of the Greyhawk door and a series of impressions in the dust of the barn.

"They aren't my footprints. My feet aren't nearly that big. I'd been out painting this afternoon and I needed to grab some more supplies from the studio upstairs," she said. She had pulled the cap off and now gestured with it toward the shattered glass.

"Someone broke the window so they could open the door, and whoever it was has been through everything, all the cupboards, even the art supplies. I checked the studio upstairs and the door was hanging off its hinges. Same thing there. Things were pulled out of shelves, dumped on the floor and stuff."

"Take anything?"

"That's what's weird. I don't think they took a darn thing. At least, I don't see anything obvious missing. I never noticed the damage to the Hawk until a half hour ago."

"The Hawk? Oh, the camper?"

"Yeah," Jessie said.

"Well, it could just be kids, thinking your dad left the place empty. But then I think we'd be seeing vandalism, spray paint, probably a case of empty beer cans."

"I think so, too."

"Was the barn door padlocked?"

She shook her head. "No, there's no lock. Dad never thought we needed one."

"Geez," Russell said. "Guess I knew that. I don't think most people around here even lock their houses."

"I'm going to the hardware store tomorrow morning though, grab a nice big one," Jessie said angrily, slapping her cap against her leg.

He looked at the footprints. She was right. The footprints were as large as his own. Squatting down, he took a photo of the prints with his cell phone. As he stood, his eyes traveled from her tennis shoes, up the long slim legs, the almost boyish curves hidden under a denim apron with stenciled writing that proclaimed "Paint the Town", and to her worried blue eyes surrounded by waves of now loose coppery curls. His eyes came back down to the "Paint the Town" area.

No, not boyish, not boyish at all. His breath quickened. *Concentrate, Bonham. This is serious.*

"Take a good inventory Jessie, of everything you can. And how about the house? Anything been disturbed in the house?"

Jessie shook her head. "No, and I had locked the house. I've been spending time in a lot of big cities. It's gotten to be a habit for me to lock up whenever I go out."

"I'm going to assume neither you nor Arvid is way out of line about how valuable those two Moran pieces were. Maybe someone knows you picked up Amber's research in Denver. Maybe thinks you have something that might be a clue to their whereabouts."

"How could they, Russell? Unless someone at the police station . . ." Her voice trailed off.

He looked at her with worried eyes. "Keep the barn and house locked when you aren't here. In fact, lock it when you're here. Keep your cell phone with you . . . and hell, if someone

179

breaks into the barn, and you're up in the studio, does the studio door lock? Jess girl, maybe you shouldn't be out here at the ranch by yourself."

"Yes, but Russell, I don't want…"

"Jessie, everything isn't about you. Your dad would die if something happened to you. He'd just die. So don't be careless. Someone obviously thinks your family has something valuable. Maybe valuable enough to kill for. Have some common sense."

"I've got plenty of common sense, thank you very much," Jessie said with irritation.

"I'll be out tomorrow to install a hasp and padlock on the barn door. And maybe get someone to come out and stay with you." He bit his lower lip. "Maybe you could have Blanche come out or something."

Jessie's chin shot up and her eyes shot fire. "I can put my own damn lock on, thanks, and I'm perfectly capable of looking after myself. You can't dictate to me, Russell. You aren't my father. OR my brother."

"Oh, I know," Russell said, his eyes glinting. "Believe me, I know." He looked again at the large motorhome parked in the center of the barn.

The Hawk, huh? Arvid wasn't exaggerating. It's huge. And likely luxurious inside. Jessie's making good money to afford something like that. A poor cop wouldn't have much to offer her, he thought with a sinking heart.

He turned and strode to the open barn door, then started to turn around. *But I do have something she's going to want,* he thought. *And she'll want it bad. I just have to decide whether to louse up her fancy life in order to give it to her. Am I that selfish?*

"Jessie . . ." he began. Then he noticed a pewter Toyota Camry pull into the driveway and park near the house. The car door opened and Grant Kennedy stepped out. Russell looked at Jessie, who had stepped up beside him at the sound of the car engine. She was looking with interest at the man getting out of the car.

180

"Never mind," he said sourly, "It looks like you've got company. FBI."

Chapter 26

O'Bourne's ranch, present day

As Jessie and Russell walked toward the house, the tall man strode toward them. He wore casual dress clothes, a soft blue polo shirt and grey slacks with an expensive look to them. And he wore them well. He also wore an air of self-confidence as though it were a tailored suit. A good looking man, Jessie realized. Blond hair. Athletic.

When he reached them, he nodded to Russell, then he showed Jessie his badge and slipped it back into his pocket. "Grant Kennedy. Miss O'Bourne?" he said, introducing himself and holding out a large hand.

"Yes, I'm Jessie O'Bourne," she said. She gestured to Russell. "This is Sergeant . . ."

"We've met," Russell interrupted.

Kennedy flashed a bright smile at Jessie, causing deep crow's feet to appear by his brown eyes, giving the appearance that a smile was his usual expression.

"It's my lucky day, Miss O'Bourne, to meet with you instead of your father. I understand he's soaking up the sun in Hawaii while you're house sitting."

"Yes, he is. He and his new wife are honeymooning through the Hawaiian Islands. Their next stop is Kauai."

"I hope he warned you I might be stopping by. Or you heard my phone message. "

"He did," Jessie said. "And I did hear the message. Sorry I didn't get back to you. I've been out of town." She cocked her

182

head at him. "You've made Dad and me very curious, Agent Kennedy."

"Grant, please. I not only have questions I hope you can answer, but I'm delighted to meet the artist who painted two of my favorite paintings. I collect your artwork."

"How nice." Jessie gave him a wide smile, then glanced at Russell. He nodded back at her, one corner of his mouth turned up sardonically, then he snapped a half salute at Kennedy, got into the patrol car and roared off.

"You seem to have annoyed Detective Bonham," Kennedy said.

"Maybe a little," Jessie admitted sheepishly. "We're old friends. He seems to think that gives him carte blanche to tell me what to do." She shrugged. "And I don't. Won't you come in, Grant?"

She poured iced tea, glancing surreptitiously at Kennedy, who had leaned down and was scratching Jack under the chin. The cat jutted his chin out and tipped his head back, accepting the attention as his due.

"What's his name?"

"That's Jack. Don't take his purring as a compliment," Jessie said. "It's three o'clock. He thinks the world stops spinning at three if he isn't fed. And be careful. When he figures out you aren't planning to feed him, he might bite." She added ice cubes to the glasses. "Do you take lemon or sugar in your iced tea?"

"Neither, thanks." Kennedy straightened, smiled and stepped back from the cat, who immediately swiped at his foot, claws extended.

Jessie picked Jack up and dumped him unceremoniously out the door with a small dish of food. She gave Kennedy an apologetic look. She picked up the two glasses from the counter and handed Kennedy his tea. They sat at the big oak table.

"I'm sorry you went to all the trouble to drive out, Agent Kennedy. I can't imagine what you think I can tell you. In fact, I hate to broadcast my ignorance, but until Dad said you'd written, I didn't know the FBI even had an art theft division."

183

"Most people don't. When I introduce myself while I'm hunting for a painting, people think I'm yanking their chain. But stolen art is a multi-billion dollar business. The FBI has always worked on major cases. We run a database of national and international art thefts. You probably know that I'm here because of the old missing Morans."

"Yes. We knew it had to have something to do with either them or Aunt Kate's missing piece."

"I'd like to find that one, too. But the two Moran paintings that went missing are high priority on my list because we had a recent lead."

"Really? That's wonderful," Jessie said in an excited tone.

He recounted the story he'd already told Dan O'Bourne about the call to the auction house in an attempt to sell Kate Morgan's small deer sketch.

"So we know someone in Montana has at least that one drawing. If we can find out who it is, we may find the paintings. I think Amber may have suspected who tried to sell the small Moran, but if so, she never got a chance to tell me. Unfortunately, it seems when valuable pieces like these surface, they sometimes wreak havoc. The Moran paintings caused Kate Morgan's death, and now that there's the slightest hint they may surface again, Amber Reynolds has died. We think she told the wrong person that she had a clue to their whereabouts."

"It could be. Isn't it sad that greed is such an inherent part of human nature?" Jessie said.

"Our office suspects that Father Michael Connor, from the old St. Benedict's Mission school, was probably killed because of the Moran oil paintings, too. However, what was left of his body wasn't found for months, long after the coyotes and other scavengers had been at it, and it was impossible by that time to tell if his death was accidental or murder. In those days, forensics were almost nonexistent."

"How awful," Jessie said.

"Some people thought he was killed because he had the paintings with him. Until it was rumored your Aunt Kate discovered the paintings in Sage Bluff years later, our division

184

figured that they'd been stolen in 1918 and were gone for good. Many paintings of that caliber wind up in European collections."

Jessie nodded, then said. "But it isn't the paintings most people want, it's the money they think they'd bring."

"Yes. Thomas Moran donated the two large paintings for such a worthy cause, but for everyone who came in close contact with them, they've been death on canvas."

"Death on canvas. Aptly put," Jessie repeated. "Tell me, how does a thief market such an expensive painting once he steals it?"

"They have less trouble turning them into cash than you might think. There's a black market for stolen art, so often they simply sell them at reduced rates. Another way is to use them as collateral on a loan."

"On a loan?"

"Yes. Some unscrupulous banks simply verify the value of a master work, issue a loan for much less, and the thief disappears. The loan is never repaid. But the bank has something worth much more, if they know what to do with it. And now, drug lords have discovered the marketability of old masters. They're easily transported to international markets as well."

"How so?"

"Think about it," Kennedy said. "A large amount of cash takes more space than a flat piece of canvas. A crook can get on any airplane with a painting in their suitcase, or rolled in a mailing tube."

Kennedy looked around the inviting kitchen, admiring the stained glass windows Jessie had made when in her teens and two small paintings that hung on the side wall. The snow scene was painted by her grandmother, Gemma, and the floral of brilliant poppies was one Jessie had painted as a 'welcome to the family' gift for her new stepmother. Kennedy stood and walked to the poppy painting to take a closer look. He turned around to see Jessie's slim form framed against the window, much as Russell had several days earlier—sunlight blasting her curls with flaming color as brilliant as that of the red poppies in the oil miniature.

"A treasure," Grant said ambiguously. "Quite remarkable."

"Thank you," Jessie said.

"Jessie, I've spoken to Jack Reynolds. I have his permission to look through the research he sent to Sage Bluff with you. I gave them my word, however, not to remove any of it from your property. This afternoon I'm pulling newspaper archives to study, but I would like to start on Amber's research tomorrow. May I take over your kitchen table in the morning?"

"Of course,"

"If there's as much of it as Jack Reynolds mentioned, it may take me several days. A huge imposition, I know." He grinned broadly and said in a mock serious tone. "But it is, after all, FBI business. And," he said, "the FBI has been known to spring for donuts."

"Oh," Jessie laughed. "I thought it was cops who did that." Jessie said, "Make mine chocolate covered, and you're welcome to use the table. But, you'll have to share, if that's something I can say to the FBI."

"The table? With you?"

"Yes, I plan on going through the boxes of research more thoroughly, but so does Detective Sergeant Abrahmsen, one of the local policemen." She looked at him inquiringly.

Grant chuckled. "Ah yes, the big, ruddy-faced fisherman I met at the station. Ask him to meet us here and join forces, if you like. Three heads are better than one. Do you have a computer scanner I could use?"

Jessie nodded. "Sure."

"And may I burn files from Amber's laptop to a thumb drive?"

"No problem. I was surprised at how little information Amber had on her laptop, though. I imagine you know her iPad, phone and camera haven't turned up."

"Yes," Kennedy said, "That's something Russell Bonham and Jack Reynolds mentioned, too. They still hope Monette Weber will get in touch with them and that she has

186

Amber's iPad. They're worried about Monette." His voice dropped to a low murmur as he noticed the doorknob twisting. "Someone is trying to open your door."

"Yeah, someone fat and pumpkin colored," Jessie said. She walked over and opened the front door. Jack sauntered in with his tail and chin up, one sharp tooth protruding over his lower lip in a feline sneer. He made a beeline for his water bowl.

"Ah," Grant said, "Clever cat."

Jessie smiled. "Personally," she said, "I think Amber would have been carrying at least the phone on her way to our house. I think the attacker took it."

Grant nodded. "I think you're right. No girl that age goes anywhere without a phone."

Jessie and Grant Kennedy talked for an hour. The conversation covered the long search for the paintings, the discovered forgeries of Moran's work and those of other great painters' work, and the art market in general. Kennedy asked intelligent questions about Jessie's art.

When the conversation drifted to trips Jessie and Grant had each taken to Europe, their individual experiences with airlines, food and books, Jessie realized it had been a long time since she'd visited with a good looking, well-read single man. She enjoyed his company. As if on cue, Grant Kennedy said. "How about taking pity on a lonesome stranger in town and joining me for dinner?" He inclined his head toward her. "We can resume our fascinating conversation."

"I'd love to," Jessie said. "But it would have to be a late dinner. I have an appointment in Sage Bluff at six."

"Late is fine." Then Kennedy looked uncomfortable. "As small as Sage Bluff is, is there anywhere decent to eat?"

Jessie laughed. "Pick me up here at 7:30, I'll point out the hot dinner spots and you can pick one," she teased. "Mickey D's, Burger Barn." Then she relented and admitted, "Okay, I'll be honest. There's only one restaurant worth visiting, the steak house. Dress casual. I hope you aren't a vegetarian. You'll be run out of town."

Kennedy's hazel eyes twinkled. "Not a chance."

Chapter 27

Sage Bluff, Montana, present day

Russell pulled up to the Burger Barn drive-through speaker and barked his order. He followed the line of cars forward to the next window, handed money to the teen working the checkout, and accepted his bag of cheese-burgers and fries. He pulled around to the front of the building and steered the patrol car into an empty parking space.

Russell reached into the bag for a French fry and popped it into his mouth. He sat, savoring its salty flavor and thinking. Then he picked up his cell phone and dialed Blanche. "Blanche, you get off work right after the swing shift arrives. Did you mention to any of the fellows that Jessie O'Bourne was driving to Denver?"

"No. You know I never talk about police business. My job wouldn't last long if I did."

"Anybody there by the desk when she called?"

"Maybe, Russell." There was a pause. "I seem to remember Baker had just come in. I'm so sorry. Is it important?"

"No, Blanche." Russell thanked her and clicked the phone shut.

Chapter 28

As soon as Grant Kennedy's car headed down the driveway, Jessie jogged over to the barn and ran up the studio steps. Between the consternation of realizing someone had broken into the Greyhawk, and the distraction of talking with the FBI agent, she'd forgotten about looking for the other journal. Her dad probably knew where to find it, but she dreaded interrupting his honeymoon with another phone call. Her new stepmother was going to think she was intentionally trying to interrupt their honeymoon. She grimaced at the thought. She'd make a quick search before she drove to Abrahmsen's home to meet Arvid. It was unlikely she would find the notebook in the studio, though. In the early years growing up she had used the studio above the barn. She would surely have discovered it then. Although, she had been cautioned as a youngster to leave Kate's things pretty much alone. Why, she wondered? Had her parents thought Grandma Gemma, who was Kate's niece, may decide to take them after all?

Jessie took inventory. A shelf of art books Jessie had already read, a few boxed art materials and a pochade box, a box that expanded into an easel with wooden legs, were the only things left of her aunt's belongings.

Her eyes fell on the wooden pochade box and she went over to open the lid of its main compartment. Tubes of petrified

189

paint, a few good sable brushes, and several with bristles stiff as toothpicks, were the only contents.

Several tubes of oil paint were still pliable and Jessie was delighted when she read the labels. The cobalt and cadmium colors she'd found were no longer made with those toxic elements, since artist safety requirements had become stricter. The original colors were richer, more vibrant than the synthetics that had taken their place. She was as safety conscious as the next person, but she would use them.

Setting the good tubes aside, she tossed the ruined supplies into the trash. She inspected the pochade box, pulling the shallow drawer all the way out. It contained several sheets of fine quality drawing paper, and underneath those were a few written notes about art supply companies and several old receipts. Ancient, Jessie thought. Jessie sifted through the small stack. Most of the receipts were from the same framer, Kenneth Worth, in Boston.

Worth. Surely that isn't the famous Worth Gallery. Have they been in business for a hundred years?

She glanced at one of the receipts, marveling over how cheaply artwork could be framed in her aunt Kate's era. The invoice was for two "double-framed" pieces, and Jessie recognized the titles as those of the fairly large paintings hanging in her Dad's bedroom.

She grinned to herself when she realized why the receipts had not been tossed in the trash long ago. On the back of each invoice was a tiny little sketch signed by Jessie's grandma Gemma in a childish hand. Gemma had stopped drawing when Kate died, Jessie knew. Too bad, Jessie thought. The little sketches were adorable and showed remarkable ability. *I should have these framed for Dad.* There was no drawing on the back of the receipt listing "double framing", and Jessie frowned thoughtfully. This invoice was dated after Kate died. It had to be for framing paintings Kate shipped shortly before she was killed. She set the items carefully aside and turned the drawer upside down, examining the bottom. *Nothing.*

The large studio closet was designed to store both clothes and art. One wall was fitted with a rod for hanging items, but the other was floor to ceiling shelves with built in vertical slots to hold spare frames or paintings. Many of the slots contained Jessie's still wet paintings for the upcoming show, but most were empty.

Jessie searched the shelves that contained blank canvases and paintings Gemma had started and then abandoned. One shelf held several partially finished sketches. Another contained unfinished paintings stored after Kate Morgan's death. The canvases could be lightly sanded, primed and reused, but she hated to paint over them. Maybe someday. She gave up the search and picked up the phone to call Dan O'Bourne.

Her stepmother answered on the first ring. "Your father is fit to be tied," Marty shrilled into the phone. "He's worried about you, Jessie. Since you phoned, unless I keep him busy every minute, all he does is talk about coming home. He's spoiling our trip, the big lug."

"I'm so sorry, Marty. Don't let him do that," Jessie said emphatically. "I can always call Arvid Abrahmsen, one of the policemen here, if I need to, and I'm perfectly fine. In fact," she said with satisfaction, "I have a date. I met the FBI agent from the Art Crime Team today, and he's taking me out to dinner."

"Yowza . . . a date!"

"Yep. It would be a shame for you to come home early. Tell Dad that surely an FBI hunk is a good enough body guard. Only don't use the word hunk."

"Oh," Marty's snickered and her tone brightened. "Don't worry. He checked with the airline. When they told us they would charge us two hundred dollars—each—to change our tickets, I thought your dad would have a cardiac arrest right on the spot. You know how your dad is so... er ..."

"Frugal?" Jessie supplied.

"Yes, how frugal your dad can be," she said. "He's downstairs checking our schedule for tomorrow's tour." Marty continued in a conspiratorial tone. "What's the FBI agent like? Young? Good dresser?"

"Both," Jessie replied with a chuckle. "Listen, will you have Dad call me? I need to. . . "

"Oh, he just walked in, Jessie. Here he is."

191

A few seconds later, her father's voice boomed. "How's my girl, Jessie? Guess what we're doing tomorrow. We're taking a bike tour of Kilauea Volcano! Real lava."

"Great, Dad," Jessie said. "Have a hot time. Listen, I only have a minute because I have an appointment." She filled him in on the high spots of Amber's research, then said, "Did Aunt Kate have a second journal? If she did, I assume grandma kept it, didn't she?"

"Yes, she did." Dan O'Bourne said. "Check the old trunk in the basement. It's been years since I saw that journal. My mother said that when Kate died, the police read every word. It didn't get them any closer to finding out who killed her. However, your great grandfather, Nate, seemed sure it was someone at the school."

"Oh, really? Did he have any specific person in mind?"

"I think Grandpa Nate changed suspects every week, Jess. He was very bitter about her death. He felt the paintings had somehow caused Kate's murder."

"Well, I'd like to read the second journal, even if it isn't any help. Kate Morgan was an interesting woman, and I like the art tips and tricks she mentions in her writing, too," Jessie said. Then she told Dan O'Bourne about the visit with Minna Heron Woman.

She avoided telling him someone had broken into the motorhome after she got back from Denver, and ended the call on a cheerful note. Jessie checked the clock. If she grabbed a quick shower, she could still meet Arvid at six. The trunk would have to wait.

Jessie turned into Abrahmsen's lane, a huge smile on her face after passing the mailbox. The big box, painted with ocean waves, was topped by a well-carved Viking longship with a red and white striped sail, a longship that was now being threatened by a green sea serpent. The front half of the scaly serpent was attached to the left side of the mail box, its dragon-like head lunging up toward the ship. The forked tail of the sea monster had replaced the mailbox flag, and was in the 'up' position. Leif Ericson would be so proud.

192

Steering the red pickup into the driveway, Jessie admired the neat two-story farmhouse, painted a bold blue with white Scandinavian style shutters. She stepped out of the truck and walked to the house on a cedar walkway flanked by blooming red rose bushes as high as her waist. *Someone puts so much loving care into this place.* Jessie bent to smell a rose just as the door opened and Esther Abrahmsen smiled down at her.

Esther wore a long denim skirt with a soft pink tank top and sandals. Her short white hair was glossy and spiked almost punk, but it suited her delicate features. Her eyes were spaced wide, and were the blue of the summer sky. *A dazzling woman,* Jessie thought, remembering how Arvid had described his wife as a 'good catch' the first time they met.

"You must be Jessie. Come in. I'm supposed to give you the ten minute tour. Arvid is running a few minutes late."

"I'd love it," Jessie said, "And I have to know who carved the mailbox."

Esther laughed. "Aren't we silly? Arvid made the Viking ship, but my sister carved the sea monster. Arvid is determined to win the mailbox contest, or at least place. Oh," she laughed again, "I guess I'm just as bad. Norwegians are terribly competitive. The funny thing is, if a Norwegian wins something, it's part of their nature to belittle themselves and claim they don't deserve the honor."

Jessie smiled. "Self-deprecating, huh?"

"Yes, but cut-throat. Especially the women."

They walked through the house, Esther pointing out various pieces of furniture Arvid had made, all solid oak pieces of clean design. Then Jessie looked out the large picture window to the back and noticed a chicken coop, about fifteen feet long. Half of it was sided with cedar and had a small window, and the other part was an enclosed run of chicken wire with a half dozen chickens scratching in the dirt. Esther saw where Jessie was looking.

"Arvid made that, too," she said proudly. "It's even heated for winter, and it isn't just a chicken yard. The back third of it is doghouse."

"Neat," Jessie said.

She grinned when Jessie looked at her expectantly. "I put the dogs away when I saw you turn into the lane. I hate it when they bark at company. Don't let Arvid tell you they're mine. He likes to tell people he bought the cockapoo for me, but that little dog is his sweetheart."

"That big house is for a cockapoo?"

"No. For the other one . . . well, watch," she said. Esther opened the back door, put her fingers between her teeth and gave a shrill whistle. A massive brindle head draped in wrinkles appeared in the window of the doghouse. "That," Esther said, "is Bass. He's a Neapolitan mastiff. I could feed three teenagers on what it costs to keep that big boy in kibble. Have Arvid show you his tricks some time."

"My god, he's enormous," Jessie said. "But he's gorgeous, isn't he? And by the way, you're my hero, Esther."

Esther looked quizzically at the smaller woman.

"I always wanted to be able to whistle like that." Jessie and Esther both laughed.

A second later, a small white puffball appeared to be standing on the big dog's back. "The cockapoo," Esther explained. "That's Minnow," she said, shaking her head. "I'm afraid the only trick he knows is how to hoodwink my husband out of dog treats. But, he's a master at that." Esther turned to walk back through the living room. "I think I heard Arvid's car door slam, so he's home. I'm glad he was late. It gave us some time to visit."

"Me too," Jessie said. "Come to the studio one day, and we'll get better acquainted. I'd also like to come back to hear you play."

"While we're talking about music, did you have a music teacher in high school named Karen Montgomery?"

Jessie looked startled. "Well yes, I did. She was one of my favorite teachers. Do you know her?"

"She's my sister. I met Arvid when I came down to visit her. And I just remembered why your name was so familiar when Arvid mentioned it. Karen said she had a student named Jessie who sang the birds right out of the trees. She had been talking about a talent night when you sang songs from several jazz and rock singers. Karen is a great judge of music, so now, I would like to hear your music, too, Jessie, as well as see some of your artwork."

Jessie's cheeks turned pink. "Oh go on, it's just something that comes natural, like breathing. I know it sounds silly, but I have a weakness for the Karaoke nights some places hold. It's more fun to sing when there's some accompaniment. Everyone in our family sings and plays a musical instrument. Everyone except me. That is, my art took so much time that I never had time to learn an instrument." Jessie's thoughts turned inward. She said, "My brother Kevin could hear something once on the radio and play it by ear on his guitar. We used to have a good time. He'd play his old Gibson guitar, and we'd sing duets. Sometimes, mom or dad would join in, but usually it wasn't their kind of music."

At that moment, Arvid opened the door, greeted Jessie quickly, gave Esther a peck on her cheek, and hustled Jessie out the door and into his patrol car.

"Sorry to rush you out," Arvid said. "After we're done visiting with John Running Bear, I want to go back to the office and talk to the night shift."

"That's fine," Jessie said. "I'd like to be home by 7:15 anyhow."

Arvid continued, "I also want to see if Jack Reynolds has heard from the Weber woman. We've called so often with no response, that we turned the job of phoning her number over to Blanche. 'Course, caller ID would show Sage Bluff Police Office, and she may not want to pick up."

"You think she's left town?"

"Probably. When Amber never showed up at the White Bison Inn, the normal thing for Monette to do would have been to call Amber's parents, then come and report it at the station."

"Wait a minute, Arvid." Jessie said. "You don't know she never showed. You only know the B&B owner never saw her. Amber might have gone to the inn, dropped luggage and then left again on her motorcycle. When she never returned, Monette might have heard about her death on the evening news.

195

Knowing her friend wasn't coming back, she could have taken Amber's things when she left."

"Yeah, you're right. In fact, since she was stuck in a hotel room, Monette probably watched some T.V." Arvid lifted a hand from the wheel and ran a hand through his thinning hair. He said. "There are a couple of possibilities. One, Monette heard Amber had been killed and hightailed it out of town, worried someone might be coming after her next. Two, she killed Amber herself. Maybe after traveling with Amber and helping with her research, she thought she could find the paintings. Turn them into cash."

"Those aren't the only choices, Arvid. Maybe she just didn't come to the station because she's as frightened of the police as Amber was." She paused. "Or . . . maybe she's dead."

Arvid looked grim. "Yeah, I didn't want to mention that last one."

The patrol car jounced over the poorly maintained steel bridge that spanned the swollen waters of the Yellowstone River. Below the structure, whirlpools spun enormous chunks of driftwood like riders on demonic carousels. Arvid looked down at the swirling flow as he drove across. "Water's too high and full of snags to be good fishing. There's always some idiot losing his line trying to fish off the bridge, though."

"I hear you. And those lines tangle up any other wildlife unfortunate to run across them."

Her comment was answered by a grunt and a bit of "Swedish" as the vehicle hit a pothole.

"You know, Monette might be camping somewhere, Arvid. Even if she didn't have camping gear with her when she first came to Sage Bluff, she could have picked some up."

"Yeah, I can check the stores that sell sporting goods . . . see if anyone remembers her."

"Might check the thrift shop, too. You think there could be any connection with Amber's death and Blanche's missing niece?"

"Nothing we're smart enough to put together yet, if there is." Arvid thought a minute. "Course, we're not batting a thousand so far."

196

The two rode in companionable silence until they pulled into the parking lot of the High Butte Senior Living Center in Sage Bluff. Jessie pulled a small notebook from her purse. "Thought I'd take a leaf out of my Aunt Kate's book and start a journal," she said. "Might write down anything interesting John Running Bear says."

Arvid stopped at the desk and asked the receptionist for John Running Bear's apartment number, then hurried down the hall, Jessie matching his long stride. As soon as they passed the reception desk, the flavor of the facility changed. "Ugh, Arvid. You'd think they would spruce it up for the elderly residents." Bare walls of white were unbroken by anything resembling décor, the effect making the senior living center seem industrial instead of homey. They passed several large alcoves where a homey chair could be placed by a window, but they stood empty and unwelcoming. "It's like a prison. I wonder if they'd welcome a suggestion of a mural competition." Jessie made a face as the rounded a corner and turned into another hall of white walls. "My Gosh, they could at least paint the doors bright colors. I'll bet plenty of artists would help spruce it up."

"Needs something," Arvid agreed grumpily. Then he muttered, "I always hope I don't end up in a place like this."

"Each hallway could have a themed mural. It would be free decorating for the senior living facility if enough businesses would donate paint and prizes. In fact, High Butte Senior Living could charge each artist a small entry fee and use the money for a special dinner or something for the residents."

Arvid looked at her. "Talk to Esther," he said. "She'll fuss at the manager for you. The residents need some cheering up, Jessie. Every time I come here I wonder how such an attractive exterior can have such gut-wrenchingly, gawd awful depressing halls. I used to hope the apartments were nicer inside. But I've been in a couple and let me tell you, they aren't."

"That's too bad."

"Let me tell you another thing, if I ever get put in the nursing home half of this place, and those people put that scratchy terrycloth over the arm of my chair I'm gonna take my dentures out and use 'em to bite somebody."

Jessie laughed, the melodic sound echoing down the cavernous hallway.

"This one's John Running Bear's." He knocked loudly at apartment number twenty-seven.

A tobacco-etched voice yelled, "Who is it?"

"Arvid Abrahmsen. I'm a Sage Bluff Deputy, and I would like to visit with you," Arvid yelled back.

"Go away!" the voice cackled. "I ain't robbed any stores! I'm sick of visiting with old men! And I hate cops. And what kind of name is Arvid? You sound like some kind of foreigner to me."

Arvid looked at Jessie. He thought a minute, then yelled. "I have a good looking young woman with me, Mr. Running Bear."

"Well, don't stand out there, then. Get your butt in here. And shut the door after yerself. Don't let that cow pie faced widow from next door waddle in with you, neither."

Arvid opened the door and gave a gallant hand gesture. "Ladies first, Jessie."

Inside, the walls of the apartment were an assault of empty white, but a multi-colored bedspread softened the room. A wizened man sat in a blazing blue recliner, his feet up, and several striped wool blankets over his legs. He wore a sweat shirt emblazoned with a buffalo skull, the horns filling the sunken span of John Running Bear's chest. The effect was macabre, the skull on the shirt topped by the skull-like, shrunken head of the old man.

"By god, if you'd told me it was a redhead, I'd have let you in the first time. Got a real likin' for red-heads."

Jessie smiled at him and stepped in to take the withered hand resting on top of the mound of blankets. John Running Bear peered at Jessie and his body jerked. He drew back from her and shut his eyes.

"Am I dead?" he whispered.

"Of course not, Mr. Running Bear," Jessie said, startled. "You're sitting here in your own apartment visiting with me."

He opened his eyes and looked closely at her. "Kate?" he asked.

"Oh, no. So that's what startled you, Mr. Running Bear. I've been told that I look like my great aunt, Kate Morgan. I'm Jessie. Jessie O'Bourne. Arvid and I wanted to ask you some questions about the old days—St. Benedict's school, my Aunt Kate—any stories you can share."

"Ah," he rasped, "and the paintings. Everyone wants Thomas Moran's paintings." His eyes shuttered. "Don't bother asking. I don't know where they went. They were supposed to help pay for a new school."

"Those too, Mr. Running Bear," Arvid said. "Minna Heron Woman told us to come to you. She said you know all the old stories. And she said you told the truth."

He curled and uncurled his bony fingers, clutching at the wool blanket while he looked again at Jessie. "Minna? Minna sent you?" He seemed to consider that. "Yes. I did. Nobody would believe me when it was important, but I told the truth. I was at St. Benedict's Mission School when I was eleven or twelve. Forget which. I should start at the beginning of the story." He coughed. "Besides, I like to draw my visits out. I don't get many."

"Take your time, Mr. Running Bear, "Arvid encouraged.

The old man sucked in a deep breath. "That year, school had been going on for about a month when a big woman came to St. Benedict's. She told the nun who was teaching there that Father Michael sent her to help out. Said in return the nun was s'posed to give her a place to stay. She'd been there for three or four days, and then one night there was a terrific argument. The next day—poof— our teacher was gone. The big woman told us someone rode in during the night to tell Sister Mary Campbell she had a family emergency and she'd been asked to take the nun's place. Said we should call her Sister Mary Campbell, just like the teacher who left. A day or so later, the woman began wearing the nun's robes."

Jessie and Arvid looked at one another.

"Go on," Jessie said.

"About a week or so before that, Jim O'Bourne had brought Kate to the school. Kate's mother had Spanish flu and

199

couldn't take care of her. That's the flu that killed millions of people in 1918." He shook his head. "It was a terrible killer that bug, even worse on young, strong adults than it was children and old people. It started to die back, but when the war ended, people held parties to celebrate, and it broke out again. Killed ten times more people than World War I," he said. Running Bear was thoughtful for a moment.

"Yes, I heard about that from my grandpa," Arvid said somberly. "Now, about Kate?"

"Sorry, I get sidetracked," the old man said. "Anyway, the new teacher hated Kate. Maybe because Kate was a pretty little thing and she stood up for herself. That little girl was like a spirited horse, something wild about her. Ever chance she got, the woman hassled that little girl. Damn woman pinched her. Things like that. Kate took it, set her jaw, and refused to cry."

"What about when Moran came, sir?" Arvid asked.

"When Thomas Moran came, I think he knew things weren't right for the little girl, but didn't know how bad it was. He stayed for weeks, camped out nearby. Gave Kate art lessons, and he handed two paintings—big ones—to the so-called nun when he left. We knew the woman had been leaving Kate alone while Moran was there, and as soon as he was gone, Kate would catch hell for somethin'. So a couple of us bigger boys got together and decided to cause a ruckus—chased a couple of the chickens around. That was guaranteed to get a rise out of her. Haw, haw. It was great. You should've seen that woman flappin' after us kids. I'll never forget it."

Arvid's deep laugh and Jessie's chortle joined Running Bear's hoarse laugh.

"She came running after us. Tossed those paintings in the barrel where we burnt our trash on her way past. In the trash! Kate took 'em out while we kept her busy. She couldn't find any place in the school to hide 'em so she ran right into the woman's own cabin and slipped 'em between the woman's bed mattress and box spring. She was a brave one!" he cackled. "Then, a day or so after Jim O'Bourne picked up his daughter, the woman skedaddled. Took off the same way she came."

"Are you sure she left, Mr. Running Bear, or did she disappear like the other nun?" Jessie asked.

"Nah." John Running bear avoided Jessie's eyes. "She left. Rode out. Took everything not nailed down with her. Didn't leave us kids much food, so I took that mean old rooster and we put him in a pot. Tasty, too. You know, things taste better when your belly's got such a hankerin' to eat." He grimaced and looked at the cold meal sitting on his bedside table. "Yeah, well. I don't have much appetite anymore."

Jessie took the man's hand again. "Did Father Michael take the paintings somewhere else after that, Mr. Running Bear? Town, maybe?" she asked.

"I told the priest where the paintings were—under that old bat's bed— and he moved 'em. I don't know where. But I know the priest didn't want to go to town to put 'em in the bank or try to sell 'em."

"Why not," Arvid asked.

"Too dangerous, that's why. The influenza was terrible in town by then. People were sick, dying. Father Michael was afraid he'd bring the germs back to the school. When we were down to almost nothing but venison my dad brought, and needed supplies—flour, salt, that kind of thing—he rode out, saying he had to take a chance on going to town. Said he'd pick up his mail and get groceries. He never came back." He coughed, the effort racking his withered body. "School ended early that year."

"What do you think happened to the paintings, Mr. Running Bear?" Jessie asked.

"I thought about it some. Thomas Moran sent a fellow out to ask about them when they heard Father Michael was dead. The only place the priest could have put them was in the old white cupboard in the classroom, but nobody asked us kids, and the cupboard had been taken somewhere." He plucked at the blanket again. "You sure look like Kate," he said. "I used to see her in town when she was all grown up and teaching at the new school. Poor Kate."

"What about the body they found on the reservation, sir?" Arvid asked. "Minna Heron Woman said it was the real nun, Sister Mary Campbell."

John Running Bear didn't meet Arvid's eyes. He plucked at the blankets nervously. "It was. Some Blackfoot couple on the reservation found the body several miles downstream of the school. She'd have been mortified if she knew she'd been found dead in nothin' but her undershorts and crucifix. The couple who found her were so afraid of the Sheriff, they covered the body with rocks and never told anyone until after the other nun left us kids high and dry. Guess they felt guilty for not coming forward earlier. Only way people were sure it was Sister Mary Campbell was the cross necklace. We kids thought the second nun might've killed her."

"What an odd story. Did they ever figure out why she came to St. Benedict's?" Jessie asked.

"No, but I know who she was, the fake nun. I saw her and her little boy when I went to a pow-wow in Browning years later. She came to the rodeo at the gathering wanting to buy an appaloosa horse my friend listed for sale. I didn't realize who she was at first, and she didn't recognize me. She was too busy trying to get a cheaper price on the horse. I was a grown man by then. But I never forgot those mean piggy eyes. They were just as green as grass. When I saw him talking to her and saw them eyes, I took my friend aside and told him to tell her the horse was already sold. Too late. He'd already made the deal."

"You said you know who she was, though? Her name and all?" Arvid asked.

"Yup. When she left, I asked my friend what name and address was on her check. Her name was Virginia Grayson. I looked up her address. She had a fine spread way out of town. I always wondered where she'd got the money. Somethin' like that, you don't pay for with old snuff cans and bubble gum wrappers."

"You ever tell anyone, Mr. Running Bear?" Arvid asked, as the elderly man's focus seemed to fade.

The elder man's eyes again slid away from Arvid's gaze. "What'd be the point? Nobody believed me when I was a boy, they sure weren't going to believe I recognized her so many years later." He shook his head. "And there wasn't any way to prove she killed Sister Mary, even if she mighta." Running Bear's eyes were drooping.

"You're probably right, sir," Arvid said. "You've been very helpful. I think we'll let you get some rest now."

"You want to ask me anything else, come again." Then John Running Bear roused and cackled. "And if you see that Minna, you tell her I still think she's a pistol."

Chapter 29

Sage Bluff, present day

Lenny bypassed the gasoline pumps and pulled under the metal carport where loud rock music filled the Get and Go parking lot. He got out of the patrol car and went resignedly into the convenience store. Last time he'd tried to talk to Duane it had been as easy as herding ducks, and he didn't expect it to be any different today.

He walked in and plunked the photos of Travis Simpson and Cassy Adams down in front of the skinny kid behind the counter and turned them toward him. The kid looked worse than usual, Lenny thought. His face was an acne farm, his shirt had seen cleaner days, and a lump was purpling to impressive blue-black on his cheekbone. He looked like a kid who'd get sand kicked in his face at the beach, if Sage Bluff had sandy beaches instead of amber waves of grain.

"Duane, seen these two lately? Either gassing up or stopping for snacks? And did you ever see them together?"

The clerk swallowed visibly, his Adam's apple bobbing on his scrawny neck. It reminded Lenny of the chicken necks he'd plucked on the farm where he grew up and, unfortunately, of the thin, lanky, insecure kid he himself had once been. And sometimes still was, deep down. The thought made Lenny scowl fiercely at the clerk.

"Nuh uh," Duane stammered. "I haven't seen Cassy all week. Don't know the guy. He gets gas here at the pumps but he pays outside . . . never comes in except for a Mocha Grande once in a while. I don't think he's been in for a couple weeks. Leastwise, not while I've been working." He pushed the photos back toward Lenny. "What's up?"

"Missing, both of them, and we're trying to figure out if there's anything to worry about is all. Cassy normally lets her boss know if she's not coming to work, but not this time. You ever see her with a boyfriend, Duane?"

The clerk looked uncomfortable, eyes flicking left to right before he answered Lenny.

"Nah, can't say I ever saw Cassy with a guy except another EMT. Then, only because she was working." He looked away from Lenny. "I'm sorry she's missing, though," he said.

"When you did see this man, Travis Simpson, did he ever have someone else along?"

"Don't think so."

"Travis Simpson drives a blue ford Taurus with a dented fender. You remember seeing someone else gassing one up the past four days, maybe?"

"Not that I remember." Duane looked at the door as a middle aged man walked through it and made a beeline to the back restroom. "I'm gonna need to get back to work."

"Yeah, I can see you're real busy," Lenny said sarcastically. He handed Duane one of his cards. "Listen, remember when I came in and asked you if you knew Jake Ward, the truck driver who drove an oil field supply loop? He's in custody up in North Dakota for selling and receiving drugs across state lines. You feel like changing your story on that?"

"Don't know him. Dude, I told you. Why are you hassling me about him again?"

"Duane, my name is not 'Dude'. It is 'Deputy'. Now, we were on his truck route. He had to get gas here in town somewhere every trip." Lenny reached into the manila envelope and pulled out a photo of Jake Ward, they'd received from the Williston P.D. that morning. He placed it carefully on the counter next to the images of Cassy and Travis, all the while watching Duane's face.

205

The clerk gave Lenny a blank stare. Lenny said. "And don't tell me he might've gone to Anderson's Station here in town. They don't have diesel."

"But he could've gotten gas in Baxter . . . wouldn't have had to stop here in Sage Bluff," Duane said.

"More convenient here, though. Closer to the interstate," Lenny said.

Duane made no reply, but his right eye twitched and he pressed the palms of his hands so tight on the counter the knuckles whitened.

"Well," Lenny said with a sigh. "Give me a call if something jogs your memory. If you're into something, anything, that concerned Jake Ward, you need some help. Better wise up and get it from the police station."

"Don't need help."

"What happened to your face, Duane?"

"Fell off my bike yesterday on the way in to work," Duane answered. "I might work at a gas station, but I can't afford to fill my tank. I pedal in."

"Huh," Lenny grunted, and slid the three photos back into their manila envelope. He grabbed two Twix bars from the candy display, slapped the exact change for them on the counter along with his personal business card. "Call when you're ready to level with me, Duane." He strode out, slid into the patrol car and shook his head. Then he tore open a chocolate bar and began to munch. *Poor damn kid is scared to death*, he thought. And something happened to his face. That bike spill was a load of bull. Something is going on, even if it has nothing to do with Travis and Cassy. He pulled out onto the road back toward Main Street. He wondered if Baker had any ideas. He'd have to pick her brain.

As soon as the middle aged man slammed the rest room door and went through the outer door, Duane grabbed his cell phone. He punched in numbers, waited for the call to be picked up and said quietly into the phone, "You told me to tell you if someone came around asking about Cassy or Travis. That weird looking cop was just here again—the one that has the curly hair,

206

looks like a cheerleader on steroids or something. He was asking a bunch of questions. He asked about Jake Ward, too. Asked, did he get gas here, did I remember him—"

"If you know what's good for you, you'll act deaf, dumb and blind, because if you aren't, don't forget I could make it really happen," said the voice on the other end.

"I know, I know," Duane said quickly. "I didn't tell him anything. All the same, I didn't sign on for this, none of it. It's gotten really ugly, and I want out. I want out as of today."

"Oh, for cripes sake, grow a spine. The only way you'll be out, Duane, is if you want to join Cassy and her 'oh, so friendly' fellow. I'm sure they're enjoying one another's company. Is that what you want?"

"No, no, no," Duane hurried the words. His voice sounded like that of a whimpering kid, even to himself. Tears welled in his eyes.

"Then are we clear? Hang in there. Or just hang, Duane. We can arrange it, you know. So don't call me here again," the voice said, severing the connection.

Duane dropped his cell phone back into his pocket. A bead of sweat glistened on his forehead, and his brow furrowed. There had to be something he could do to get away, something that wouldn't get him killed. Maybe he could find someone who'd get word to Jake Ward in Williston . . . let Jake know why Amber was killed. Maybe. Ward had connections. Duane's head nodded up and down as if in time to invisible music. Yeah. Let Jake get even. Thoughts twisted in his head like snakes in a pit, but every option seemed as deadly.

Chapter 30

Sage Bluff Sheriff's Office, present day
Russell stomped into the station, thinking of the smile Jessie had given Grant Kennedy. He glowered at Blanche when she started to speak to him, and headed down the hall to his office. Then he stopped short. A blocky, grey-haired stranger in a business suit and tie sat in a spare chair near his office door.

Blanche bustled down the hall, her attitude apologetic. "I tried to tell you, Russell. Your visitor has been waiting for nearly an hour." She turned and headed back down the hall.

"Sorry," Russell said, opening the door and ushering the man in. "What can I do for you?"

The man reached into his jacket and pulled out a badge, opening it for Russell.

"FBI?" Russell exclaimed. "You have got to be kidding me. Another FBI agent?"

"No, Detective Bonham, not FBI," the stranger said, offering his hand. "DEA, Agent Samuelson. We may have a drug enforcement agent missing from your town."

Russell stood for a second, letting Samuelson's statement register. Then he picked up the phone and dialed Blanche's extension. "Blanche, find Arvid. Get him in here."

"I already know where he is. He's out talking to Cassy's friends, trying to locate her, Russell."

"I don't care if he's talking to the Governor. Go call him, Blanche. Now."

* * *

208

Samuelson took a sip of coffee and winced. "Travis Simpson was sent to Sage Bluff over two months ago. The Drug Enforcement Agency had him investigating a lead on the drugs flowing through Montana. He called to notify us his father was ill, but Travis knew he was still required to check in. He did not call in yesterday as scheduled, and we could not reach him."

"Are you sure it was Travis who called?" Arvid asked. Russell looked at him in surprise.

"Yes. Our admin, Leona Hanfield, took the call. She recognized his voice. It was indeed Travis Simpson. And, as one might expect when there's a family emergency, he sounded quite upset. She told him to keep us updated. When he didn't call again, Leona called his emergency contact number to check on him and that was when we discovered a major screw up. We got his sister and she informed us her dad had passed away three years ago. Ergo, no father."

"Uh oh."

"That about sums it up. Deputy Bonham. I was already on the way to Sage Bluff when Detective Abrahmsen called the office to ask about Simpson."

Russell and Arvid exchanged glances. "An office number, huh? I am assuming it was not his sister I spoke to on the phone," Arvid said.

"No. That was Hanfield," Samuelson said.

"So what kind of lead was your agent following?" Russell asked.

"He was following fraudulent orders of prescription drugs. Large orders for certain pain killers have been sent to Sage Bluff. More than we feel are warranted for a small town hospital. We had the hospital do a surreptitious audit. The orders didn't come from the hospital, but were made to appear they were ordered and received by Sage Bluff General."

"The hospital, huh? We have a missing girl that worked part time at SBG," Arvid tapped an index finger on the desk.

Samuelson acknowledged the comment with a thoughtful nod.

"And she also worked full time at the Sage Bluff Fire Station with Travis," Arvid said.

Samuelson's attention went on high alert. "I want to hear all about her. Let's come back to that in a minute." He continued, "We understand you know about Jake Ward, the dealer they picked up in Williston, North Dakota. We've been trying to get names of his associates, but so far no luck, and nailing down all the stops on his route hasn't been easy. Where hasn't he been would be simpler to figure out."

"I imagine he was supplying Sage Bluff, but you don't think he picked up here, too, do you?" Russell asked

"Don't be so sure your fine town isn't supplying as well as receiving. We suspect one of the drugs that he picked up in Sage Bluff is Fentanyl. It's a pain killer that gives the user an immediate high."

"I've never even heard of it," Russell said.

"Yeah, most folks haven't. And you don't get Fentanyl just anywhere. Someone in the medical field has to be procuring it. Since Travis has some medical training, we had him apply for a part time job as an EMT with your emergency services in town. We also placed him undercover two evenings a week at the local hospital. He's young, somewhat inexperienced, but enthusiastic."

"We saw him on duty when we first picked up Amber Reynolds after her attack."

"Yes. When Amber Reynolds was found beaten, he was worried he'd missed something. He was one of the agents that helped arrest Jake Ward, and he recognized Amber Reynolds from a photo Ward had in his wallet when he was jailed. He was taken aback to see her here in Sage Bluff. Anyway, Travis called us right after the ambulance dropped Amber at the hospital. We were all over Jake Ward, trying to discover if she'd been in on the drug deliveries, but he swears not. Could be coincidence, could be he's lying through his teeth."

Russell said, "We asked Jack and Shelly Reynolds to allow an autopsy on the girl's body. She was clean."

"Yes," Samuelson agreed. "And we had the autopsy findings double-checked, simply because of the tie in with Ward. It was correct. There were no drugs in her system except those given by your doctor here to stabilize her for the flight."

"Has it been verified that the head wound actually was the cause of death?" Arvid asked, earning another of Russell's sidelong glances. "Hey, I'm just asking."

"You Montana cops are a little paranoid, aren't you?" Then Agent Samuelson smiled, and he nodded to Arvid. "Yeah, good question. You're not the only ones with a streak of paranoia. We had the M.E. look for everything. He thinks it was the head injury."

"He wasn't positive?" Arvid asked.

"There are ways to stress an injured person, even when one is unconscious. The level of carbon dioxide in the blood was inconclusive. Her eyes were somewhat bloodshot. That also happens with suffocation. However, the victim was allergic to alfalfa, according to her parents. She had been forced into a position that caused her to breathe dust from alfalfa for her entire ordeal. What can you tell me about the EMT who rode in the copter?"

"Well, we can tell you she's gone. It was the missing girl who worked part time at the hospital—Cassy Adams," Russell said. "We put her on our missing persons list today."

"Oh, crap," Samuelson said. "Never rains but . . . well, you know the saying. However, we have no reason to suspect that the EMT was involved with the drug route. We need to explore that possibility, though. The money involved is enough to tempt anyone."

"How about Travis Simpson?" Arvid asked. Russell and Samuelson both smiled. "Hey, call me paranoid, but I'm just asking."

Samuelson looked quietly around Russell's tidy office. He noticed the photo of the little boy standing by Russell, the drawings tacked on a piece of corkboard. He swiveled and looked seriously at both Russell and Arvid. Samuelson let his breath out in what any horse wrangler would call a snort.

"No, Travis wouldn't be tempted. He's as trustworthy as the Pope. We think someone else forced him to call our office. Whoever made him phone knew he wasn't calling his sister, or Travis would have played it that way to give us a heads up. They wanted him to plead a family emergency and Travis was a quick enough thinker to come up with the concocted story. He probably relied on me to catch on immediately that the message about his dad's heart attack was bogus." He studied his hands as though they belonged to someone else, then looked up. "I let him down. I think if it was possible for him to get in touch, it would have happened by now. We are beginning to wonder if he's dead."

"I hope not," Russell said. "How much money do you think we're talking about here, Agent Samuelson, with the drug route? A few hundred thousand? A million?"

"I can't give you a number, Detective Bonham. Multiple millions, I'd say."

Russell asked. "Did Travis know much about Amber Reynolds?"

Samuelson looked surprised. "No, I don't think he knew anything of Amber Reynolds except her old connection to our drug dealer. Why?"

"Well," Russell said, looking at Arvid resignedly, "According to our local expert and the FBI, Amber Reynolds was looking for twenty million dollars' worth of paintings. The head of a drug ring might be tempted to branch out for that much money. I wonder if the cases overlap. To finish your saying, Agent Samuelson, yeah, sometimes it just pours."

"Well, I'll have to dump a little more on you, Detective Bonham. Before Travis disappeared he said he was beginning to wonder if someone from the Fire Station or Sheriff's Office—actually here or in Baxter—could be connected with the drug distribution. Frankly, I brushed it off as unlikely."

"God, things just keep getting better and better," Russell said sarcastically. "What made him suspect that?"

"Don't know," Samuelson said. "He just said he was looking into it, and that he'd bet his pension the connection was here in Sage Bluff. It was a joke between us. He knew I was getting ready to retire, and his retirement fund was non-existent."

"Agent Samuelson, Amber Reynolds was afraid of the police," Arvid said. "Scared to death."

212

Samuelson's eyes opened wide. Russell nodded confirmation.

Arvid continued, "I wonder if Jake Ward let slip to one of his cronies that his girlfriend was hunting for those Thomas Moran paintings? Maybe bragged a bit about how much they were worth. Can you get someone to press him a little? See if he remembers mentioning it to anyone?"

"Yes, of course. I'll call Williston after we're done here. Now, regarding Travis Simpson, I'm afraid at the present time, with hopes that Travis's cover was *not* blown, that we have to pass the responsibility of looking into his disappearance to you two gentlemen. We don't want to give the drug runners a heads up that Travis was DEA, or that a DEA agent is in town. I wanted to meet and speak with you in person, not over the phone. Perhaps I wanted to get a look at the two cops that I was going to ask to find Travis."

Russell and Arvid stood, ready to show the man out. Samuelson looked at them with a serious expression.

"You realize no other officers can be told he was one of our agents, just in case he was right about the police connection. Please keep our meeting under your hat."

"Yeah," Russell said, "You have our word. Still hope he shows up, but we'll beat the bushes and see what we can find out."

Samuelson looked down at his half-full Styrofoam cup and pitched it into the wastebasket. "Thank the woman who brought me this . . . uh, coffee...tell her to button up her lip, too."

Russell nodded at Samuelson. "Hit the café down the street if you need a cup to cover up the taste of that one. Good place for dinner, too."

Samuelson stood, shook hands with Arvid and Russell and handed both men a business card. "I'll be checking in with you," he said. "And tonight I'm staying at the B&B a block over, the White Bison Inn." He turned at the door, grasping the handle. "I feel responsible for Travis. Please find him." He turned and left, pulling the door shut as he went.

Arvid and Russell looked at one another. "Not the normal case for Sage Bluff is it, Arvid?" Russell asked quietly.

"Nah. Probably not normal for any town our size. Say Russell," Arvid asked stroking his chin. "Got a hacksaw?" Russell looked at him questioningly. "There's a locker down at the Fire Station I think I want to take a look at."

Chapter 31

Wild Bull Restaurant, Sage Bluff, present day

Grant Kennedy walked around to the passenger side to open the car door for Jessie. Jessie caught her bottom lip between her teeth as she stepped out. Grant could see she was trying not to laugh, probably at the expression he imagined was plastered on his face.

"You're sure this is Sage Bluff's best restaurant, huh?" Grant said, looking up at the black fiberglass bull revolving on the pillar above the restaurant. Its eyes glowed eerily with red electric lights, and below the bull whirled a brilliantly lit sign that proclaimed 'The Wild Bull Steakhouse - Fine Dining'. Picnic tables full of rowdy diners as noisy as a flock of magpies cluttered the patio in front of the entrance. One of the black and white birds strutted hopefully between the benches of diners looking for handouts. The exterior of the building was sided with rough cedar shingles; here and there one hung precariously as though a stiff breeze would blow it into the next county. The aroma of spilled beer and smoky barbecued meat filled the air.

His stomach rumbled. He'd been looking for something a little nicer than a burger, though.

"You won't be sorry, I promise." Jessie looked amused. "The patio area has a different menu than the indoor restaurant. The outdoor area is meant for family barbecue get-togethers, teenagers and such: burgers, beer and barbecue pork. We'll eat inside. You might want to leave your jacket in the car, though.

I told you casual dress. I can't help it if you FBI types won't take advice from a woman.""

Jessie's hair was curling around her shoulders and she wore black slacks, a peacock blue silk blouse and soft black high heeled leather boots and silver hoop earrings. Over her arm she carried a sweater. She looked great.

Grant glanced around at the people sitting at the outdoor tables, most dressed in shorts and t-shirts, and he slipped off his jacket, removed his tie and tossed them into the back seat.

"Oh, man up, Agent Kennedy," Jessie said in a teasing tone. She cocked her head at him and tucked her arm through his. "Shall we?" She gave him a brilliant smile.

He looked down at her radiant face. The peal of a warning bell echoed through his head, and he made a dismal attempt to heed it. The woman was altogether too appealing. When he answered, his voice was husky. "You talked me into it," he said.

Grant and Jessie strolled to the entrance and were greeted at the door by a twiggy teenaged girl dressed in jeans, cowboy boots, and a heavily embroidered western shirt. The teen swung the door wide and stepped in, holding the door to allow the couple to enter the dim interior. Then she stepped in front of Jessie and Grant and yelled 'Seating in the back!' giving Jessie a broad wink before she turned and went back outside. A waiter hustled over, ushered them to the back of the restaurant, and seated them at a booth covered with a canvas top made to look like an old covered wagon. Old sepia-toned photographs of the Wild West hung on the wall. The table was covered in a pristine white tablecloth and set with silverware wrapped in red paisley cloth napkins tied with rough twine. A pitcher of ice water and two glasses had been placed in the center of its surface.

"Our special tonight is rosemary-garlic rubbed elk medallions with your choice of potato—garlic mashed, baked or funeral." the server said, placing dinner and drink menus on the table.

"Funeral potatoes?" Grant asked.

"Yeah," the waiter said, "It's a version of scalloped potatoes from an old Mormon cookbook. Chef Perry isn't Mormon, but a friend of his gave him the recipe. He jazzed it up a little, but kept the name. Yowza, they're cholesterol city, but real good." He patted his stomach, and smiled.

"How about this note?" Grant pointed to the bottom of the menu where it stated *Vegetables will be supplied on request at no extra charge*.

"Yeah, we can add any veggie but the kitchen staff doesn't add them to the plate unless someone asks. Guess our dishwasher said they were always getting scraped off the plate, so now the veggies are on request. I'll leave you two to look at the menu. Nice to see you again, Jess."

Jessie nodded at him with a "You, too." After the waiter left, she told Grant, "Todd was a couple years behind me in school. Seems like a lifetime ago."

"I know what you mean. I just missed a fifteen year class reunion. Man, this menu is amazing." Grant skimmed the choices. "I've never had the opportunity to taste some of these meats. Actually, I've never even seen them offered in a restaurant."

"Try something new, then. If you're hungry enough for an appetizer, try the bison carpaccio with mushrooms on toast points. Ooh, they're yummy. I like the hickory roasted pheasant soup, too. And, I should warn you that the portions are "Montana sized". You know how they say everything is bigger in Texas? Well, those folks haven't been to the Wild Bull."

Grant looked at Jessie in amazement. "How can they offer meals like this for so little?"

She gave a delicate shrug. "Well, it's all local. It's illegal to serve wild game in restaurants, so the bison, elk and pheasant come from local game farms. I've heard that they give Chef Perry a break on price, too, since his restaurant gives them so much business. It's similar to the restaurants on the coast that offer inexpensive lobster or other fabulous seafood. Food that doesn't have to be shipped long distances is fresher and cheaper."

Grant looked at the wine list. "All the wines on this list claim to be Montana vineyard specialties," he said. "Wine? In Montana?"

"You'd better believe it, City Boy. The Ten Spoon Winery in Missoula has a roster of award winning wine. Several of their bottles won the silver at the 2012 Indy International Wine Competition." She looked again at the list. "You might try the *Farm Dog Red*. It would go well with the elk medallions."

Grant continued reading the wine list, then skimmed the short paragraph about the Missoula winery, pressing his knuckles to his lips to prevent a chuckle from escaping when he noticed the address for Ten Spoon Wineries was "4175 Rattlesnake Drive". He smiled at Jessie and signaled the waiter.

They placed their orders, both having decided on the special, with the addition of asparagus spears. Then Grant ordered a bottle of *Farm Dog Red*.

Chef Perry, a burly man with a blue kerchief tied biker-style over his thinning hair in lieu of a chef's hat, was adding the garlic mashed potatoes to a T-bone steak plate. He was decoratively piping the hot spuds through a pastry tube, when a pudgy waiter carrying a tray of dirty plates pushed through the swinging doors.

"Randy, guess who I saw with some city boy, ordering the elk medallions in booth number eleven."

"What, it isn't enough I'm short-handed in the kitchen tonight? I gotta play guessing games with my waiters, Todd? I don't care if it's the Pope. Hey, Craig," he yelled to a man working at the next counter, "Get them pheasant breasts ready."

"I'll give you a hint," the waiter said, "Think redhead."

"For cripes sake, gimme a break! I got four—"

"Another hint. Think songbird. Then think redhead . . . ."

The chef's head swiveled around.

"Reeeally?"

"Yeah. Jess O'Bourne's home. I know you've been trying to think of a good ploy to pack this place for the fundraiser this weekend. After she blew away the crowd at the open mike night a few years back you couldn't stop talking about it. She'd be just the ticket. Man, we'd rake in the bucks. People donate more when they're having a good time."

"Yeah, they do. We need her. I'll give them time to enjoy dinner and then 'bam!'," he said, giving his best Emeril Lagasse impression, "I'll ask her when she's full of our best elk medallions. She won't know what hit her."

"That ought to do it," Todd agreed.

"Besides, who can resist donating to this benefit? Everyone knows how much the High Butte Senior Apartments need repainting. Especially the nursing home section. Shoot, it'd sure be nice if we could make enough to add some comfy furniture or a little library." Chef Perry added a garnish to a plate of venison steak, then handed the plate to Todd and waved him out.

"Of course, maybe Jessie hasn't ever been there. Her dad is still healthy as a teenager," Craig reminded his boss.

Perry thought for a minute, absent mindedly piping whipped cream in a decorative swirl onto a dessert plate. The swirl rose higher and higher. "You know, I think I'll just give her a certificate for dinner for two, and beg Jessie to come and sing that night."

Later, the chef untied his dirty apron and reached into a drawer for a fresh one, slipping it on and securing it behind his back. Then he slid two pieces of cobbler onto dessert plates, put a dollop of fresh raspberries and whipped cream on each, and pushed through the swinging doors. He headed for booth number eleven to make a personal delivery, compliments of the chef.

Grant looked at Jessie and asked, "So you're house-sitting for your dad. Where's home?"

"New Mexico. I'm gone a lot, delivering artwork, traveling to shows and teaching at workshops. But I own a small house and studio in Santa Fe. It's a cute little place, stucco and terracotta roof tiles, with a small courtyard. I love it there."

Jessie paused. "Of course, the area is a tourist haven, so it's also a great market for my work."

"I've been there. It's a great town. It was hot as blazes when I visited, though. I ski, so most of the tourist areas I visit are in snow country."

"Too bad. Actually Santa Fe gets enough snow for skiing. But I can paint outdoors nearly all year long. As much as I appreciate a good snow scene, I don't get excited about painting in zero degree weather for a third of the year, freezing my fingers like I used to do here in Montana."

"I imagine you're absolutely inundated with out-of-town company, friends escaping Montana's below zero winters?"

She chuckled, a rich throaty sound. "I wish. I'm not home enough to be overwhelmed by house guests. Art friends come to visit when they bring work to the galleries, and Dad and Marty plan to come to golf or gallery hop later this year." Jessie made a zipping gesture across her lips, then she smiled, her eyes twinkling. "Now, you've been letting me do all the talking, so it's your turn. I want to hear about some of your interesting art theft cases."

Just as Jessie spoke, their waiter returned with two steaming plates and Jessie and Grant looked appreciatively at the well-presented meals. While they enjoyed the chef's special, Grant regaled her with story after story of fascinating art recoveries—and a few tales where the thieves had never been caught.

As they finished their dinner, Chef Perry came bearing down on them with a dessert tray and an affable expression. Grant's eyes widened. He'd seldom ever seen anyone who would look more at home on a big Harley instead of in an apron. The white T-shirt Perry wore was stretched tight over thickly-muscled biceps. The kerchief and thick neck, along with one dangling earring shaped like a cross, made him resemble a Hell's Angel rather than an accomplished chef.

The big man presented the desserts with a flourish and then smiled wolfishly at Jessie. "So, Jessie, I have a proposition for you . . . ."

A few minutes later, a coupon for a free dinner was tucked in Jessie's purse. While they savored their chuck wagon raspberry cobbler and sipped Chef Perry's special gourmet cowboy coffee, an aromatic dark-roast, Grant was mentally thumbing through his schedule, hoping he was free the evening Jessie agreed to sing.

The conversation turned again to the missing Morans and Jessie mentioned the journals Kate Morgan had written.

"I'm sure they aren't mentioned in our data," Grant said with interest. "May I read them when we go through Amber's research tomorrow?"

"Sure. At least the one. I haven't found the second journal yet, but I plan to look for it this evening."

"Speaking of tomorrow, I'd better get back to the hotel and do some work," Grant said reluctantly. "I hate to end our evening, but if you're done with your coffee, I'll take you home."

"I'm ready. In fact, I take a walk almost every night about this time just to enjoy the sky," Jessie said. "The sun doesn't set until 9 o'clock or after this time of year, and sunset is quite a show—the most eye-popping mixtures of red, orange and violet. If I painted a landscape that vivid, people would think I was hallucinating. That would mean a 'no-sale'." Jessie stood, and Grant held her sweater as she slipped her arms into the sleeves.

"I'm not sure I agree with that," Grant said as they walked to the cashier's desk. "Claude Monet painted sunsets that were vivid and very popular."

"Oh, yes. I like the piece from Venice called *San Giorgio Maggiore at Dusk*," Jessie replied, "It's beautiful, but Monet was an impressionist whose style lent itself to such pieces. I'm not an impressionist."

"How about Turner's work?" Grant asked in a challenging tone. "Surely you aren't going to fault his sunsets? Or Van Gogh's *Starry Night*, or Edvard Munch's *The Scream* with its tumultuous orange sky? People love them." He handed the clerk his credit card and added a generous tip to the total. They left the restaurant and walked to Grant's vehicle, where he opened and held Jessie's door for her before they resumed their conversation.

"Listen, *Starry Night* is remarkable in its brilliance, and Munch's is full of intense emotion and color. In fact, *Starry Night* has such appeal it's been made into—get this—a T-shirt," Jessie laughed. "I have one. Every time I wear it I find myself singing Don McLean's song all day—the one called *Vincent,* about Van Gogh and his painting. But, I'm talking about realistic skies. Try again, mister."

They bantered back and forth about famous sunset paintings until Grant deposited Jessie at the front door of O'Bourne's rambling log home.

"I enjoyed myself, Jessie," Grant said as he opened her car door, helped her out, and kissed her lightly on the cheek. "Tomorrow I'll pick up the donuts on my way to the ranch, and during our breaks from reading Amber's research, I expect you to be prepared to argue sunrise scenes."

"Sunrise, huh? I'll be ready," Jessie promised with a laugh and a wicked gleam in her vivid blue eyes. "And don't think I'll go easy on you just because you're FBI, either."

Jessie walked to the front door. Instead of rummaging through her purse for the key, she retrieved one her father kept under the small planter near the front porch. Jessie turned the key in the lock, humming *Vincent.*

Dang, Here I am, already so busy and I let myself get sucked into singing in that benefit. As if that isn't bad enough, that song's going to stick in my head all night. Maybe a walk will shake it out.

An irritated blur of orange darted out as Jessie opened the door. Jack scampered to the patch of hollyhocks near the barn, his favorite hunting ground, to check out the possibility of long-tailed grey snacks. Jessie put the key back and shut the door. As she walked past the kitchen window, she saw the tom disappear into the thicket of tall plants.

Time to get some exercise, too, before I blimp up like Goodyear. The Wild Bull sure doesn't let you go home hungry.

222

She went quickly upstairs to her bedroom and changed into jeans, a light pullover, and tennis shoes. She pulled a house key from the kitchen drawer, grabbed her iPod and headphones, then hurried down the stairs and out the door for her evening walk.

Jessie locked up, circled around the house and followed the rutted gravel lane leading west past the alfalfa field, instead of heading toward the main road. She lengthened her stride, walking toward a line of tall steel grain bins—'Montana skyscrapers'—in the far distance. Small animals scurried into the brush beside the road as she passed. Several gophers, a mouse.

Jessie saw them but, because of the headphones, her world was soundless except for the audio book she listened to. On the iPod clipped to her pullover, Randy Wayne White described the mangrove coast of Florida, while Jessie watched the Montana sky begin to lower and Canada geese fly overhead, searching for a wheat field or river backwater to settle into for the night.

After thirty minutes of fast hiking, she stood to watch the edges of the silhouetted grain bins turn the color of glowing apricot, kindled by the setting sun. The sky roiled with purple grey clouds and ever changing swathes of crimson, orange and yellow. Across the dying light, the last flock of geese winged in a V formation. Jessie removed her headphones, turned off the book, and listened to their calls until she could no longer hear them. Then she turned around, settled her headphones over her thick hair, clicked *The Mangrove Coast* back on, and headed home.

Returning to the house, Jessie paused the audio book, looped her headphones around her neck and shook her hair out. She walked through the garage, unlocked the back door to the house and stepped into the moonlit kitchen. As she reached toward the light switch, she wrinkled her nose, sensing an unexpected odor. Cigarette smoke? Standing motionless, she listened, and heard a light footstep. *There was something wrong.* The door to the cavernous pantry stood open. Jessie

223

quietly stepped back, slipped into the space and pulled the door almost shut.

Through the crack she could see the microwave oven on the counter, and the moonlight on its glassy surface reflected the kitchen and the arched entrance to the dining room. The view showed no movement, no hint of an intruder. She allowed her breath to escape in a soft, cautious sigh, but continued standing, tense and still, heart thumping—straining to hear anything beyond the usual creaks of the log house. *There it was—a butterfly breath of sound.*

As her eyes became accustomed to the gloom in the pantry, she scanned the pantry. The shelves were full of canned goods and the pegboard wall held kitchen and small tools for household repairs. Then she saw something useful. Stretching to reach the highest row of hooks she took down a small ax, one her granddad, and now her dad, used to chop wood into fireplace kindling. She held it close to her chest, listening intently.

Five minutes later, she still stood behind the pantry door gripping the kitchen hatchet so tightly by the thick oak handle she wondered what would be first to snap, the old wood or the bones in her fingers. She stiffened her resolve and waited. She could sense rather than hear someone moving toward the hall.

Looking at the small ax in her fist, she shivered, recalling her childhood fear of the razor thin edge. The thought of using it against flesh and bone made her stomach clench.

"God, You know I hate sharp objects," she mouthed heavenward. "Couldn't you have given me something dull, but deadly? Something that made me less queasy?"

Jessie remembered watching the rhythmic rise and fall of the wicked blue-black blade in Grandpa O'Bourne's gnarled hand. In her mind she heard again the thumping sound of kindling dropping to the side of the wide cottonwood stump he used as a chopping block. It was her job to gather the split wood and carry it to the house. Giving a mental sigh, she focused on the reflection in the microwave door.

If there's someone in the house looking for trouble, I guess the Almighty wants him cut down a peg. All the same, if I could rub a lamp, I'd wish for my pistol.

The small hatchet grew heavy in her grasp, and Jessie was beginning to lower it, thinking she was just being paranoid, when she heard the front door being carefully opened. It was closed with equal care, and she heard an odd scraping sound, then the loud crunch of running feet churning the gravel in the drive. She ran to the darkened living room and peered through the blinds in time to see a figure run behind the barn. Seconds later, a motor revved and a figure hunched tight on a motorcycle sped from the yard, the cycle and rider a blended silhouette against the moonlit sky.

Her chest heaved, breath escaping in a loud, relieved sigh. Jessie returned to the pantry and hung the small hatchet on its customary peg before her legs began to tremble. She walked shakily back through the kitchen, grabbed the phone from the hall desk and froze.

Who should she call? She thought again of Amber's panicked voice begging her "no police". She thought of the smell of smoky clothing. To her knowledge, Russell had never smoked, and Russell lived closer than Arvid. It was crazy to suspect Russell. Wasn't it? She tapped her finger on the kitchen counter, thinking. Then she grabbed the business card Russell gave her a few days before and punched in his number. She gave him a brief rundown of what had happened, and hung up. She tapped her heel on the floor nervously. *Oh heck,* she thought. She picked up the phone again and called Arvid, too, and told him about the intruder

"I don't need you to come, Arvid. I guess I'm just covering all my bases. I don't really suspect Russell of being a killer, but it's hard for me to get past the fact he's the only one we could see had no alibi for Amber's attack." She gave a weak laugh. "It's ludicrous for me to be bothering you."

"No, it isn't. It was the right thing to do. I'm a night owl, anyhow. Call me again after Russell leaves."

"No, Russell. We've been over this twice already. Just like the break-in at the barn, I don't think anything is missing. I didn't recognize him. I couldn't judge how tall he was. He was bent over the motorcycle handlebars."

"And you can't tell me what color the motorcycle was—not even a guess?"

"I told you." Jessie's eyes flashed with indignation. "It was just too dark."

"Hmph." Russell folded his arm across his chest and glared back at her, feet spread wide in a cop stance. "You should have gone back out and called me from the yard."

"My phone was up on the bedroom dresser. I was afraid to walk through the kitchen to get Dad's portable."

"So you hid in the pantry. Geez, Jess, if they'd come looking for you, you'd have been trapped in there."

"Well, I grabbed the little ax we use for chopping kindling for the fireplace, that little hatchet Granddad used to call his baby. I waited and whoever it was simply went out the front and took off running. The motorcycle must have been parked behind the barn, hidden from view. When I was sure he was gone, I called you." She met his intense gaze with a calculating one of her own. "You got here faster than I expected."

"Well, I thought you sounded terrified." Russell said. "I blistered the road getting here," he admitted. "But a hatchet, Jessie? You picked up a hatchet with your phobia about sharp things?"

"I got over that a long time ago," she fibbed. "And it might have been someone violent."

"Yikes, someone violent, huh?" Russell grinned with relief. He still stood with his feet slightly apart, and his arms crossed over his chest. His cop pose. "I worried all the way over here, and probably should have been worried for the intruder instead," he teased.

Jack wound himself in and out between Russell's spread feet. Finally Russell relaxed, glanced down and bent over to rub the cat's head, scratching behind his ears, but when he stood up, he was still grinning.

226

"The poor burglar was probably some flighty teenager hunting for beer or DVDs, and here's you with an ax? An ax!" Russell shook his head. "Ha, ha, ha! Probably scared the pants off him. God, I can't even picture it. Remind me never to walk in here without knocking when you're home."

"Oh, ha-ha right back at you, you moron." Jessie wrinkled her nose and tilted her head back belligerently. "Would you rather I hit him with a can of peas? Or maybe something more deadly, like . . . oh, I know . . . the hefty can of spicy, diced tomatoes?"

"Yeah, Jessie, or bean him with a can of garbanzos! Hahahaha!"

"Don't you make fun of me, Bonham. You and Kevin always told me the best defense was a good offense." She grimaced. "Of course, when I tagged along, mostly you told me to go home."

"We were probably afraid of you," he said, roaring with laughter. Then he shook his head and reverted to using his best cop voice, "Ahem. Well, getting back to the business at hand. Do you have friends who know you walk every night? Would someone simply come in to wait for you?"

"And then run away like that when they heard me come home? No, I've only been here for a week, and I've been painting outdoors for the better part of every day."

"Well, you went to Denver. Maybe someone thought you were still gone."

"Not many people know I'm even back." She thought a minute, then continued, "Maybe Dad and Marty have close friends who would just come in and make themselves at home, but any of them would have turned on the light and raided the fridge."

"Got anybody in mind?"

She tilted her head back to look up at him. "Oh, wait," she said pointing an accusing finger at him, "The most likely suspect for that fridge raid would be you."

"I haven't seen your dad for a while." Russell said, averting his eyes. "And don't you know it's not good sense to trot around in the dark with your headphones on listening to a damn book? It's stupid. You can't even hear a car coming."

"What cars? I use the field access roads, not the highway, and at least *I* exercise. You're getting flabby. The closest you probably get to exercising is reading *Sports Illustrated*. Oh, wait, you only have to look at the pictures in that one, right? No reading required."

Russell stared at her. "I don't recall you being this mouthy when you were younger." He ignored Jessie's glare. "Well, if you walked in with your headphones on, you wouldn't have heard anything at first. How did you know someone was in the house?"

"I'd already taken my headphones off when I came in, and whoever it was made no noise. But I caught a hint of cigarette smoke." Jessie thought for a moment, eyes serious and the tip of her fingers against her mouth. "No, maybe a pipe. Not strong enough that I thought someone was smoking, but like someone whose clothing smelled strongly of smoke had walked through the kitchen seconds before I came in. You really notice the odor if you aren't blessed with the nasty habit yourself."

"Yeah, so I hear."

Jessie sniffed. A pleasant odor of musky aftershave clung to Russell. To her knowledge, he'd never smoked, but she was relieved all the same that he smelled good—too good, even—because it meant it wasn't him in the house earlier.

"I guess after the tire incident in Yellowstone and the broken window on the motorhome, I'm a little paranoid."

"No, I'm sorry I laughed at you, Jessie. I was relieved the incident seemed to have been pretty harmless. No damage. No injuries. But you're not paranoid. It's smart to be careful, Jessie. I still say you should have someone come and stay out here with you for a while. Someone seems to know where you're going and whether anyone's home or not. They could be searching for clues about the Morans. Or maybe they just hope they could find them here."

"Well, I hate it that some wacko is following me, ruining my tires, and breaking in when I'm gone. But I'm not having someone out here interfering with my work. End of subject."

She looked at him. A shiver of awareness turned her legs quivery. She'd always felt drawn to Russell, and several times she was sure he felt a strong spark of interest, too, but he'd never acknowledged it. Then Jessie felt a flash of anger.

What was she doing, forgetting that Russell married Kevin's fiancée almost before the body was buried—geez, was he so stupid he didn't realize what people would think? Or didn't he care?

Jessie turned away so Russell couldn't see her expression, and opened the refrigerator door. Looking at the soda cans, she pulled out a root beer. She cleared her throat. "Want something to drink? There's iced tea or there's pop."

When Jessie turned back to Russell, he was looking at her with a beat puppy expression, almost as though he'd known what she was thinking. She held out the can of root beer.

"Russell . . . ?"

"Oh. Um . . . no thanks. I have to be getting home. K. D. is probably asleep, but I had to call my neighbor, Janice Dahlberg, to come and stay with him until I got back. She just lives a minute or two down the road. The phone woke K. D., and he was hopping around in his room when I left, but Janice was going to try to get him to bed."

"You worried your sitter can't handle him?"

"Naw, she's a good egg, but I don't want to inconvenience her any more tonight." He strode toward the door. "Keep my number, keep your cell phone with you. If you have that 9mm pistol Dan gave you, keep it handy. Be sure to take it with you if you go out alone to paint. Go get a concealed carry permit for it."

Crap, Jessie thought. She had forgotten all about his little boy. He'd not only married Trish, they had a child. She felt foolish for thinking of Russell as anything other than a cop—a married cop, damn it, even if the wife didn't seem to be in the picture right now. No way Jessie was going to ask about her, either. It would be embarrassing if Russell knew how curious she was. She'd never liked Trish much. The girl had seemed immature to Jessie, and volatile, but she'd had Kevin wrapped around her finger as tight as duct tape.

"Idiot." Jessie winced. *Oh damn, had she said that out loud?*

"What?"

"Nothing. . . I just said, I'm not an idiot." She gave a small smile. "I already have the permit. And I like the gun much better than that hatchet. Now that scares me."

Russell looked at her and smiled back. "No, I don't think much scares you, Jessie. But be careful anyhow, will you? You should stop by the station to put in a report about the break in, even if nothing is missing. Give the whole place a better look before you come in, will you?"

He turned and was gone.

The phone rang several times before Arvid picked up, and before he said hello she heard him simper 'There you go. You're just daddy's little sweetheart, yes you are'. Then into the phone his gruff voice said, "Sorry, I was letting Esther's dang useless little dog out," he said. "Otherwise, I have to get up in the middle of the night to open the door and then wait until the little mutt comes back in. Can't leave it out in the yard with Bass, an owl might haul it off by its sorry little tuckus."

Remembering what Esther had told her about Minnow being Arvid's special baby, Jessie screwed up her face, trying not to laugh into the phone.

"Arvid, Russell just left, but I wanted to fill you in." She covered all the points of the break in and then said. "After he left, I thought about what that odd scraping sound that I heard when the person first stepped out of the front door. Arvid, it was the front door key being returned under the plant pot. That's how he got in. He knew where the key was kept. I'll ask Dad who would know about it, but the only person I come up with is Russell."

"Holy Ned," Arvid said. "Hmmm, just Russell, huh?"

"I'm afraid so, Arvid."

He paused, then said, "Aw, I'm not sure that's too important, Jessie. About everybody I know hides a key near the front door. Might be a fluke that the intruder found it. Odd though, for the burglar to put the key *back*. Don't touch the key, Jessie. I'll see if I can get a print off it."

"Okay," Jessie agreed.

"You said nothing was taken. They could have been looking for Amber's papers. Where do you keep them?"

"In Dad's big gun safe, and it's still locked. Since somebody shattered the Greyhawk window, I've been stacking Amber's research in the safe and locking it in unless I'm using it."

"That's a good idea, I'd keep on doing that. I'll see you in the morning if I'm still invited to help search through Amber's findings."

"Sure. Donuts are on Mr. FBI's to-do list, and I'll feed you lunch."

"Donuts, huh? I got a good feeling about this, Jessie. Hope he buys something other than just plain old cake ones."

"Me, too. Gooey, chocolate-frosted would be high on my list."

"Jelly filled," Arvid said. "If Amber found something all by her lonesome she thought was a good clue to the Morans, how can three enormous brains working on a sugar high miss it? See you tomorrow about nine."

After she'd hung up, Jessie thought about how thoroughly she'd searched the Greyhawk after the first break in. She took the flashlight from the kitchen drawer, and walked out to the barn. There was one place she hadn't looked for missing items. She opened the door to the motorhome and climbed in. Then she walked back to the compact kitchen area, opened the door of the refrigerator, and sucked in a surprised breath. The fridge was as empty as the day Jessie drove the Greyhawk off the sales lot. Jessie took a better inventory of the cupboards than she'd done the day the window was broken and noticed a large jar of peanut butter was missing, a box of crackers, maybe some pasta and a can or two of tuna, too.

Jessie thought. It was not cigarette or pipe smoke she smelled in the house this evening. It was the smell of a campfire, or maybe even a barbecue grill. Hmm. She thought about how much Arvid liked BBQ, then shook off the notion.

She locked up the motorhome and the barn door, jogged back to the house and decided not to bother Arvid again. She'd tell him and Russell in the morning. But whoever had entered the house tonight hadn't taken any food. How did that person know where to find the extra key? Jessie had no clue. And now she was wide awake. She decided to go down to the basement and hunt through the trunk Dan O'Bourne suggested was a possible hiding spot for Kate's second journal.

Chapter 32

Rural Montana, present day

Russell pulled out of O'Bourne's driveway and headed home. Halfway to his house, where his little boy was either in dreamland or waiting for Russell to tuck him in, he pulled into the driveway leading to a large highway maintenance building. He checked his watch. Then he tugged his wallet from his pocket and looked through it until he found the scrap of paper with the phone number he needed. Russell grabbed his cell phone and punched the number in.

"Yeah, it's me," he said to the deep voice that answered his call. "I know I'm a few minutes late phoning, and I can only talk a minute." The deep voice rumbled.

"Yes, I saw her," Russell said. "And no, I never told her."

He listened to the reply, then said, "No, we haven't found the paintings. Of course, we might not."

Russell dejectedly leaned back against the patrol car head rest as he listened, the phone pressed to his ear.

"Now we have a DEA man and an FBI agent hanging around complicating matters." The voice at the other end rumbled on at length. "No, I *don't* think I can take care of her," Russell said in an emphatic tone. "I don't trust myself to get it done. I'm sorry. I know it would be inconvenient for you, but you might have to come and do it yourself. I'll call you."

Russell rang off, put the phone on the passenger seat and started the engine.

When he pulled into his own driveway twenty minutes later, he saw with relief that K. D.'s bedroom window was dark. Janice Dahlgren had been able to get him back to bed. She was sitting patiently on the sofa reading a magazine when Russell walked in, her thinning grey hair pulled back into a knot, and reading glasses perched on her nose.

"Russell, that boy of yours is a wonder," she said, continuing with her usual non-stop stream of chatter. "When I put K. D. to bed I saw the new drawings up in his bedroom. The one of the llama he did with a marker makes me smile just to look at it. I taught school for thirty years when I lived in Wyoming, and never saw a child that could draw like that. Not as young as K.D. anyhow, that's for certain. I hope you have some of his drawings entered in the art competition at the Reuben White Gallery over in Baxter. In the youth categories, the prizes are big baskets of art supplies. Wouldn't he just love that?"

"Yes, he would. And so would I. Let me tell you, he goes through tablets and colored pencils like a teenager through movie popcorn."

"It has to be expensive, Russell."

"Yeah, it sure is, I've been spending money like water for paper, paints, markers and children's books about art. If he won a few art supplies, it would give my worn-out wallet a break." He smiled at her. "I'll sure think about entering his work, Janice. It was nice of you to remind me."

"Don't think long. My niece is entering. She mentioned that the deadline to register at the gallery and submit the child's work is this Saturday. Each child brings several drawings and then does a drawing or painting from a flower and fruit basket arranged on a table, and that result is judged right along with the ones the child brought in."

"The kid has to draw something right there at the gallery?"

"Yes. I'll bet they do it that way because too many parents 'help' their child. This way, if the child can do it on his own, it's evident. If the child can't, that is obvious, as well. All of the drawings are displayed, not just the winners. That's important to children, seeing their work appreciated enough to hang on a wall."

"Is Jessie O'Bourne doing the judging, do you know?"

"No. The gallery owner, Reuben White, chooses the awards in the children's art exhibition. Jessie O'Bourne is judging the adult work in the plein air category." She bent and picked up her purse from the sofa. "Russell, call the gallery and get the forms. Or, call me if you want me to get K.D. registered for you."

"I will."

"I'd be glad to do it. Now, I'd better get home."

"Thanks. You've bailed me out a lot since K. D. was born. Let me know when you need some more work done on your house. I owe you some handyman time."

"Seeing how that little boy is growing up is worth all the time I spend here. You make an old woman feel needed." She plucked at her frayed sweater cuff nervously. "But I do seem to have a leak in the garage roof, if you can get to it," she said in an apologetic tone. "I'm getting too old to climb that big ladder and I surely do hate to pay the high prices for repairmen when you do such a good job."

He patted her on the shoulder. "You stay off that ladder, Janice. I can come over in the morning before I go to work. The weatherman says we're getting some drizzle tomorrow afternoon."

She snorted. "You surely aren't taking old Koot's forecasts seriously? He hasn't been right all week. Just come in a couple days or so. No hurry."

Chapter 33

Sage Bluff, present day

Grant whistled softly to himself as he hung his jacket in the hotel room closet. As he turned around, his cell phone chirped. He grabbed it from the night stand and looked at it in disgust before answering.

"What is it now, Patricia?"

"Oh Grant, don't be such a sourpuss. What happened to 'hello'? Can't you be a little friendlier?"

"I think you've been friendly enough for both of us, Pat. And I don't have either the time or inclination to spend the rest of my evening on the phone. Whatever you need, I'm sure one of your many boyfriends can help you out."

"But the sink disposal in the condo isn't working, and you're so good at fixing my, well, you know . . . my plumbing," she crooned. "I miss you."

Grant rolled his eyes in exasperation.

"Pat, the divorce is final. I'm not interested in your plumbing. The condo is all yours and is now all your responsibility. You've got to quit calling me."

"But your tools are still here. Don't you want them? You can come and pick them up, and maybe while you're here, you can take a look at the disposal."

"I'm not in Boston. I'm in Montana on business. Call a plumber. But yeah, I would like my tools. I'll come and pick them up when I get back." He disconnected.

Five minutes later, his laptop was hooked to the hotel Wi-Fi and Grant was surfing the web. He was going to find several old masters' paintings with vivid morning skies before he worked through the stack of papers he'd checked out of the Sage Bluff police archives. His thoughts kept returning to a pair of laughing blue eyes.

Chapter 34

O'Bourne's ranch, present day
Jessie sat back on her heels by the antique trunk in the basement and opened the journal. Kate's second journal had been buried under a layer of outdated clothing, hand-sewn quilts and fabric her mother hadn't had time to use before she passed away. The thick notebook had a cobalt blue leather cover, and a satin ribbon was stitched into the binding for use as a book mark. On the inside cover of was written 'Kate Morgan – 1939'. *Nothing in between the old journal and 1939?*

Kate must have been too busy to keep writing when she was younger, or maybe her heart just wasn't in it. Kate had married, had a child, and then lost both her husband and little girl in the 1932 Long Beach earthquake in California, Jessie knew. Her eyes moistened at the thought.

She stood up, dusted off her jeans, closed the trunk and carried the journal up to the den. She switched on the brass lamp by the sofa, grabbed paper and pen for jotting down notes and sat, curled up with the journal on her lap. Jack pranced in, stood on his hind legs and put a tentative paw on her knee. After Jessie patted her thigh in invitation, he jumped up to join her. Immediately his loud motor went into overdrive, emitting a rumbling purr Jessie found companionable. She stroked the tom's silky back as she opened the journal.

On the first page a neat cursive hand had written simply 'Homecoming'. Jessie began reading the absorbing diary, a clear picture of her Aunt Kate filling her mind. *She was a good writer, too*, Jessie thought, as the life of Kate Morgan flowed from the pages and washed Jessie into the past.

Chapter 35

Kate's kitchen, Sage Bluff, Montana, 1939

A colorful ceramic cookie jar shaped like a plump hen sat in the center of the round oak table in the small rented apartment. The mute object was the only mediator between Kate and her brother, Nate. So far, it was doing a poor job. She'd hoped the cookies and the mug of coffee she'd poured would keep him too busy dunking his favorite snack to volunteer advice. Dressed in his work overalls and a green plaid flannel shirt with a missing button, Nate overflowed the kitchen chair and rested his work boot on the delicate, carved foot of the table leg.

I keep expecting him to rumble like his John Deere sitting on idle, Kate thought. *Hard to think of him as my 'little' brother. Course, he was a whole lot smaller when my folks brought him home.* She smiled to herself. *And maybe only half as opinionated.*

Perched on the dainty side chair, Kate glanced over at him. She sighed and slung her heavy braid of auburn hair over her shoulder. She lifted the cookie jar lid to fetch another square of shortbread, indicating with a gesture that "John Deere man" should help himself. Her brother reached a massive hand into the jar and withdrew several cookies.

Kate bit into her shortbread and looked expectantly at Nate. He glared back at her. His mouth was set in a thin line.

Yeah. He always gets that look when he wants to solve all my problems. Jeebers, I suppose I'm in for it, now.

"Good to have you home, Sis," Nate said, crunching into the first cookie, "Like I told you, movin' back was the best thing to do. Ye-ep,' he said, drawing two syllables from the word. "Best thing to do."

"It's done now." Kate grimaced, thinking of the two graves she left in San Francisco. "We'll see how things go."

"California's an outhouse of a place. Just an outhouse. First we worried about you bein' all alone in San Francisco going to art school, then, marrying a Navy man. Seemed like every time you wrote, Andy was out to sea." Nate gave his sister a sad look.

"He sure picked a bad day to drive down to Long Beach with your little one to see his parents—the wrong damn day."

Kate changed the subject. "When are you bringing Gemma for lessons? Giving art lessons to that talented little niece of mine is one reason I moved back home."

He looked toward the cookie jar and scowled. Then he scratched his head and went on. "Well, my Gemma is beyond the moon. Little monkey can't wait to learn to paint."

"Good."

"Saturday morning work for you? And what's this you said about working at the school?"

"Saturdays are fine." Kate said, ignoring the question. "Now give me that shirt. Doesn't your wife ever sew on your buttons?"

Nate looked chagrined, slipped out of the shirt and handed it to her, then reached again into the fat cookie jar, chewing the rich shortbread between muttered sentences. "You'd have to be working for that damn Matt. Not a good idea. Nope, not good."

"Oh, hush."

"Still a drinker. Don't look good for a school superintendent to always be in the suds. If so many men hadn't moved to the city looking for work, he'd of never got the job. Too many good men gone, that's why he got hired."

Kate shook her head in mute agreement, but wouldn't meet her brother's eyes. Her own eyes had filled with unshed tears.

Yes, too many good men gone . . . but why did one of them have to be mine?

She grabbed a button, needle and thread from her sewing box on the counter and slid open a drawer to find her scissors. Then she bit the bullet and filled her brother in on her plans.

"I'm going to work part-time at St. Benedict's after Christmas vacation," she said, running the needle through the fabric. "They need someone to finish the year for the math teacher—poor health, I guess. Just a few classes I feel confident I can teach."

Nate peered at her and scowled. Crumbs littered his undershirt, which she noticed had seen better days. Why hadn't his wife mended that? Noticing her glance, he looked down, brushing shortbread bits onto the floor with his meaty fingers.

Ignoring him, she whipped the thread through the button, attaching it firmly to Nate's shirt as she continued. "Since I'll be there at the school anyway, a few parents asked Matt to start a small art program. I need something to do. Teachers don't get paid much, but it'll pay for canvas and paint, if not much else."

Her brother glowered.

And now here we go. I'll have to hear all about Matt yet again, she thought. Blast Nate's hide. This looked to be a long session. Not looking at him, she pulled the last stitch through the green flannel, knotted the thread and snipped the end.

She handed the shirt to her brother, and got up to put another pot of coffee on. She busied herself scooping dark fragrant grounds from a canister into the basket of her percolator, using the chore to avoid looking at the giant dwarfing her table.

"So you've already seen Matt Ericson, huh? He left you bawling at the altar, looking like a gaffed fish. I don't want you working there." Nate drummed his fingers on the table. Then he chomped another cookie. "Don't need to be doin' nothin' for Matt, though. By god, he's a—"

"Oh hush, Nate." Kate snapped, turning from the stove, "Just listen to yourself. Of course I saw Matt. I couldn't

242

interview for the teaching position without seeing the superintendent, now could I?"

He ignored her. "Think he was fired from that last job he had in Great Falls. Gambling and drink," he said pointedly. "Bet he was embarrassed when he saw you were applying for the job." Nate thought about that. "Haw," he bellowed. "Haw. Haw."

She turned to the sink to fill the percolator with water, blocking Nate's view of her face. She grinned too, suppressing a chuckle.

Yeah, Matt had looked dumbstruck, absolutely mortified, when I walked through his office door.

That gratifying image quickly transformed into a memory of a young, charming Matt. He'd been so good looking. Tall, muscular, a lock of dark hair drooping over his forehead. But her brother had found him roaring drunk behind the church with another woman when he should have been saying wedding vows at the altar with Kate.

I'm lucky he screwed up on our wedding day, she mused. *Life with a drunk wouldn't have been pleasant.*

The next week, she'd left town. Funds from her Dad's investments in Burlington Northern and money inherited from her old mentor, Thomas Moran—money earmarked for art— paid for Kate's studies at the San Francisco Art Institute.

Then she had met Andy Morgan. Kate's hand shook holding the percolator. *Would she rather have had a drunk husband than a dead one?* She put the pot on the stove, turned up the heat, and turned to face her brother.

"Matt's good with the kids, though, for all his faults. Nate, don't worry, I'm not planning on getting involved with anyone. Especially not with some guy who left me waiting in the church. And looking *sooo* attractive, according to you. Not," she paused, then continued firmly, "that it's any of your business."

However, she *was* seeing Matt this evening, she reminded herself, not for old times' sake, but just to talk about the job. And she'd been having frequent dinners with Phillip Grayson, the new lawyer in town. His attention was flattering, especially since he must be at least eight or ten years younger than her. But Phillip was just a friend.

She glanced at the cookie jar. Kate swore it had a disbelieving expression in the black ceramic eyes. She gave the hen a dirty look and said with force, "Well, let's change the subject."

"Yeah, you know I don't like to butt into your business. Just not my style, even if you are my sister."

She gave an unladylike snort and looked at Nate in disbelief.

"I just worry about you." He looked contrite. "Besides, I'm supposed to behave myself. Gemma says I'm too bossy with her Aunt Kate." He pushed a button through the last buttonhole, and tugged the shirt over his middle. "Thanks."

"Gemma is very wise for her age."

"Maybe. Now, what about your painting? You should be doing some artwork for your galleries, not teaching other people."

Kate smacked his refilled coffee mug down on the table, sloshing golden liquid onto the table. "I'll find time to paint. I have a good place to do it, too. It'll do for both my living space and art studio. The best thing about it is the light from the high north windows, painter's light. It'll be perfect," Kate said with enthusiasm. "Guess where it is! Dad's letting me use the apartment he made over the barn. Going to help me move in?"

Nate made a choking sound. "I can't believe it. Do you know how many people asked to rent that apartment after he put heat and lights in? I think he hired men to work on it just to give them a bit of money since times have been so tough."

"That sounds like Daddy."

"But when it was finished, he wouldn't let anyone rent it. Man, someone's finally going to get some use out of that neat apartment."

Kate laughed. "Yep, and that someone is me. I love the bejeezus out of the place. That's where I'll teach Gemma."

"She'll love it."

"I can't work on scrubbing the school classroom until St. Benedict's Christmas vacation starts. Until then, Gemma and I will set up my studio and paint up a storm—a real tornado."

"But that school job . . ."

"Now, don't worry, Nate." Kate said. "It'll all work out."

She grabbed the hen by the neck and lifted the lid. "Want the last shortbread?"

Chapter 36

O'Bourne's ranch, present day

Jessie laughed out loud over several small sketches Kate had added to the notebook. A couple were of her niece Gemma at the drawing table, one with her tongue protruding in concentration while she drew, and one of Nate in his flannel shirt, buttons popped, tummy bulging.

Jessie had similar sketchbooks filled with drawings she'd made of the people in her own life. She wished she could go back in time to meet Kate, who she was certain would have been a kindred spirit. And she had a strange craving for shortbread. She took mental inventory of the butter in the fridge. *Might be enough to whip up a batch of maple shortbread.*

At this point in the journal there was still no mention of Kate finding the canvasses painted by Moran. Jessie chewed on the end of her pencil and thought about what she did know for certain. The people. She could list every person mentioned in Kate's writing.

As she read each chapter, Jessie opened a lined notebook and added to a scribbled list: Matt Ericson—once Kate's fiancée, Superintendent at St. Benedict's, drinking/gambling problem; Phillip Grayson—new, younger man in her life and a lawyer; Nate—the bossy adopted brother. Should she include him? It seemed wrong to do so, but without the tie of family, he would have been on the list. Jessie added Nate's name.

Then she put her list aside and turned the next page of Kate's journal. A pencil portrait of a man filled the page. Kate had written 'Phillip' in the margin. So that's the *younger man*. He looked strangely familiar.

Jessie stroked Jack's soft head, and began reading the new chapter.

Chapter 37

St. Benedict's Mission School, 1939

All morning Kate worked alone, scrubbing dingy classroom walls, listening to a small radio for company. She'd brought a full thermos of black coffee thick as mud and a paper sack that held a ham sandwich for lunch. Frequent coffee breaks kept her energy level up, the aroma of the strong brew a comforting scent and the heat of the mug a balm to her overworked, stiff fingers.

After lunch, things began looking up. Word had spread around the small town that Kate was fixing up a room at St. Benedicts' School over Christmas break to serve as a classroom for the first art courses ever offered at the school. Excited high school students, bundled against the cold, stopped by to help her. Introductions were made, coats and hats shed and piled on a bench in the hall, and a crew of loud teenagers filled the classroom.

With the exuberance of youth, the volume on the radio was cranked up and work on the schoolroom barreled ahead. Husky boys cleaned desks and then pushed each one against the back wall out of the way, flexing their biceps at each other. Two pretty girls pretended to ignore them while shyly talking to Kate, volunteering to wash the grimy windows and windowsills or sweep. One plump girl, Samantha Devon, shrugged on a jacket and ducked out mid-afternoon, returning soon afterwards shaking snow from her coat and carrying two dozen molasses cookies and a half-dozen bottles of root beer. Both pop and cookies disappeared like raindrops into a puddle.

Surrounded by youthful enthusiasm, Kate found herself smiling more during the afternoon than she had for months. By the end of the day, just one boy, Will Foster, remained to work alongside the slim, red-haired teacher. Kate had seen some of his sketches. Matt showed them to her when he offered her the job, a little bribe, most likely. He knew she couldn't resist helping anyone with such talent and desire to learn. It was obvious to Kate that Will Foster could draw anything. His drawings weren't just sketches, they were precise images of whatever he wanted to capture on paper.

The tall teen chattered non-stop about watercolor and oil painting. He was so anxious to learn that Kate grinned to herself at his enthusiasm.

Hope he picks it up as easily as my niece, Gemma. Her little paintings sing with vibrant color notes. If I can teach even one student to paint half as well, it'll be worth the effort.

With Will's help, she emptied the supply area and the shelves of an old kitchen cupboard crammed into the small space.

"Will, before you leave, help me move this monster out of the supply closet, please? It smells musty, but at least there haven't been mice living in it."

"Sure."

Pushing hard, they slid the unit forward, the wood creaking and groaning, until they were able to shove it through the open closet door and maneuver it into the classroom.

She grabbed the damp rag and attacked the cupboard with soapy water, using extra elbow grease on the inside shelves. Everything was so old it needed cleaning, painting or repair. The cupboard looked ancient. This could be the same cupboard we used at the old school, Kate decided. They must have kept it when they built the new school.

"The back is coming loose. It looks like kind of an amateur patch job," she said, pushing her hair back from her forehead.

"It needs a new coat of white enamel, and it would be good as new," Will said.

249

"You're right, but we sure aren't doing it right now. I'm exhausted. Let's shove it against the wall by the window so the wall supports the back, and that's enough for today."

When she finished cleaning she wanted to stop at Nate's and drop drawing paper off for Gemma. Phillip was taking her to dinner later, too, and she'd need to shower and change. As Kate turned to ask Will if he needed a ride home, a young woman appeared in the doorway holding Will's coat and beaming at him.

"Hey, Will, I have the pickup," the girl said. "If you're ready to come home, let's go."

"You have the truck?" An incredulous look crossed Will's face. "You got permission?" he asked in a suspicious tone.

The dark haired girl grinned slyly at him. Instead of answering, she cocked her hip against the doorway and glanced at Kate.

"I'm Gloria, Will's girlfriend. I hope he showed you a few of his drawings. You know, Will can draw an exact copy of anything. He's real good. Someday, he's going to be great—maybe famous."

Will looked embarrassed, but pleased with his girlfriend's praise. Gloria was dressed in thin clothes more suited to warmer weather, no gloves or hat. *She must be chilled to the bone.* The jacket she was wearing was worn and cheaply made, not like Will's heavy, warm coat, but the girl had a definite flair.

"It's nice to meet you. Yes, I know Will is very good." She turned to Will, who was blushing furiously. "Go ahead and take off now. And thanks, I really appreciate all your help."

Will took his coat, pulled gloves from the pocket and put on his winter gear, smiling as he walked toward the door. "If I see your car here tomorrow, I'll stop in and lend a hand again, Mrs. Morgan."

Kate heard the echo of excited chatter as the teens walked down the hallway and left the school. She frowned. Will seemed quite guileless, but there was something catlike and sleek about the girl. And the way she gazed around the room seemed almost sneaky.

Peering out the window, she saw them gleefully pitching snowballs at each other in the chill air before they hopped into a blue pickup and drove away. Will was in the driver's seat with Gloria's arm draped nonchalantly over his shoulder, the girl snuggled close in a very unladylike attitude. Boys were so oblivious sometimes. *There's something almost predatory about that girl,* Kate thought.

Chapter 38

O'Bourne's ranch, present day
Jessie added Will Foster, his girlfriend, Gloria, and Samantha Devon to her list. Any students Kate mentioned in her journal would be those she knew best. She went to the box of photos and found the group picture of the students with Kate at the school, wanting to put a face to the names.

Will, listed as William K. Foster, was a tall young man with an earnest expression. Jessie wondered if he'd ever done anything with his talent. Then she paused, thinking hard. Where had read the name Foster recently? It was somewhere other than the box of news articles and correspondence Amber had gathered. She would look through them tomorrow, keeping that name in mind. Meanwhile, she wondered if anything would come up online.

Jessie grabbed her laptop, connected to the internet and typed *William K. Foster* and *art* together into the search bar. There were multiple immediate hits but two caught her attention. One site covered the grand opening two years earlier of a newly renovated art gallery in the historic area of downtown Billings. The William K. Foster Gallery was high end, handling expensive deceased art such as paintings by Charlie Russell and Frederick Remington as well as the art of contemporary masters. The owner, Christian Foster. In the gallery description, it stated that the venue was named after the owner's grandfather, who had passed away years before.

In the second hit, a newspaper article dated only two weeks ago reported that a gas explosion in the basement had destroyed part of the facility, ruining multiple paintings and sculptures by well-known artists. The gallery owner was quoted as saying, ". . . we hope our insurance will cover the damage, but if not, we will cover the remainder of the ruined work. Those who consigned work with us will be compensated for any loss."

A list of destroyed paintings followed and Jessie scrolled down to read all the titles and view the corresponding images. Number eight was listed as having been in the owner's personal collection and was titled *A Whitetail Deer along the Missouri* by Thomas Moran.

Jessie gasped. The large painting sparkled with intense color, deep autumn reds and rich golds. Grazing under one of the trees was a deer that could only have been painted by someone working from the deer painting Thomas Moran had given her aunt Kate in 1918.

Jessie jumped up, put one arm in the air with her hand curled into a fist and whooped, "And the redhead has a Bingo!" She did a little dance around the room, spooking Jack, who beat a hasty retreat to the hallway, tail bushed.

Jessie leaned over, looking again at the computer screen. She said aloud to the cat, who peered back at her from the open door, "Oh, Grant's suspected forger had to have been Will Foster. I'd bet the ranch on it. The only way he could paint the large Moran copy was if he had access to the little original inscribed to Aunt Kate. The grandson, Christian, who now owns the damaged gallery, must be the one who called Christie's trying to sell the authentic painting."

She whooped again and Jack swayed back and forth, his mouth partway open and ears back, looking at Jessie. "Hfff," he said, then turned and stalked toward the back bedroom.

"I think Grant'll be going to Billings tomorrow instead of bringing donuts," she yelled.

She looked at her watch. 11:00. Dang! It was too late to call him, but now she was wide awake. Jessie did a little dance down the hall to the kitchen and peered into the refrigerator.

She reached in and grabbed a box of unsalted butter, shook a stick from the box and held it up like a microphone. Tossing her head back and striking a pose, she belted out, "Momma's little baby loves shortenin', shortenin'. Momma's little baby loves shortenin' bread!"

In honor of Kate, she was going to make a big, big batch.

Chapter 39

Sage Bluff, next morning

"Arvid, this is Grant. I'm going to drive to Billings to check out a lead Jessie found in the journal. There may be a connection to the small painting stolen from Kate Morgan, and to some other old Moran forgeries. So, no donuts for cops today, I'm afraid," Grant said, looking at his watch, which read 7:30 on the dot.

"Huh, had my heart set on jelly filled. You must've found something pretty good to drive all the way over to Billings."

"Jessie will fill you in, unless you've got time to ride along. If you can, I think I can promise it will prove interesting. Of course, if you go to Jessie's, I've been informed she baked a fresh batch of shortbread, whatever that is."

"Poop," Arvid said. "I sure would like to ride shotgun, but on top of Amber's murder, we have a missing person investigation here. Two, in fact. Not the normal type of case for Sage Bluff, so I'm flying by the seat of my pants. Think I'd better stick around. I'm not going to get to Jessie's today either. In fact, I'm just pulling into the station now."

"Really, a cop talking on the phone while driving? I believe that's against the law, Arvid," Grant's tone suspiciously cheerful. "Maybe I'll call Jessie back then and ask if she wants to ride along. I asked her earlier but she said she wanted to go through the files with you."

Arvid rang off in disgust. No donuts, no shortbread and no leads. All they'd found in Cassy's Fire Station locker after

255

using a bolt cutter on the lock had been an empty duffel bag and a pair of stained running shoes. They didn't even look like they'd fit Cassy, so all it gave them was another mystery.

Why lock a virtually empty locker?

Arvid had simply shut the locker, snapped a new lock on the door to replace the one they'd ruined, and pocketed the key.

I'm missing something. And so is Russell. Hope what I'm missing isn't something to do with Russell. Blast it all.

He steered into his parking place, got out of the patrol car and went into the station by way of the scarred and peeling back door.

Russell was standing by the door to Arvid's office with his hand ready to knock as Arvid hurried down the hall. He unclenched his hand and gave Arvid a wave. As he did so, Hurricane Blanche stormed from the other direction and descended on them like a fury. Today she wore a navy top and pink slacks made of stretchy material. A gaudy floral chiffon scarf floated around her neck. Her long strides brought her up to the two men.

"What have you done to find my niece, Russell?" She said, pointing her finger at Russell as she glared at him. Then she turned to Arvid. "How about you, Arvid?" She asked in a frigid tone.

"Uh . . ."

"My sister Violet is beside herself with worry. I promised I'd call her with a report, but I'm going to have to tell her I sure don't see any progress happening around here. Zip! And the night shift is no better." She snorted. "Bunch of morons. Do either of you have any idea where to start hunting for her?"

Arvid winced. He looked at Russell, and could tell by his expression that he planned to cut Blanche some slack. The poor woman was worried about her niece. Arvid got the uncomfortable feeling he had as a teen when his dad got tired of Arvid sliding by with average grades. He stopped listening to Blanche rant and instead heard his father's voice from the past.

256

"You can do better, son." He was telling Arvid. "See that you do, if you plan on doing any fishing during summer vacation. Otherwise, you'll spend the hot summer days with Daniel, and by gum, I mean Daniel Webster is who I mean. Get those grades up, or your momma and I will have you copying the dictionary in the hot summer sun instead of baiting a hook. The hot summer sun."

Arvid had buckled down and brought in a 3.8 grade point average on the next report card, but hard work wouldn't find Cassy or Travis Simpson. He had no leads to work on. He gave himself a swift mental kick in the tuckus.

"Calm down, Blanche. Tell your sister I'll be over this morning to go through Cassy's place again. Maybe there's something in her apartment we missed that will give us a clue to where she's gone. Have her phone me and I'll meet her there at her convenience."

Russell looked surprised, and Blanche looked unexpectedly taken aback at the suggestion. Then she shook her head, double chin quivering, and stretched up to her full height, eye to eye with the Norwegian, an annoyed expression on her face.

"Oh, puhleeease. That's the best you can do? Snoop through her apartment again? Again? It's a tiny apartment. The size of a pea! What do you think you missed in there, Arvid, airline tickets? I don't know if Violet will allow that. It would be an invasion of privacy, that's what it would be."

"Blanche . . ."

"What if she comes back and finds out we've been letting you men rummage in her underwear drawers and dig through her paperwork?"

"Blanche—"

"Violet already said she searched every inch of the place herself, and there was nothing at the apartment to show Cassy planned to go anywhere." She stopped for breath. "Besides, her suitcase is still there. Even you know you can't go very far without a change of clothes and a toothbrush, for God's sake."

"Blanche, do you want me to find her or don't you? I'm running out of options," Arvid said. "Nobody she works with has seen her. Her car is still parked at the apartment. She had no boyfriends anyone knows about."

"She didn't go off with a boyfriend!"

"And her girlfriends don't know where she is, and so on and so forth," Arvid continued. "I'm going to look again at places we've already explored because right now I can't think of a creative way to go about locating her. Maybe I'll get lucky. Maybe I missed something before."

"Lucky! I thought you and Russell were supposed to have all the answers. You aren't supposed to rely on luck. Luck! Luck, you say," Blanche snapped.

"Aw Blanche," Russell said.

She glared at him, then sniffed theatrically. "I wish Stendahl was here. He'd do something. If you can't think of anything better, I suppose I'll have to call my sister and see if she'll let you into Cassy's place to snoop. Again." She whirled around and headed back down the hall, muttering as she went. "Ought to just put on a uniform myself. Goodness knows I couldn't do any worse than this bunch."

Arvid and Russell watched her sashay down the hall, indignation evident in every step, the stretchy fabric of the pink slacks taut across her ample backside. Arvid looked at Russell, then back at Blanche's retreating form.

"Well, I guess we been reamed," he said. "Rightly so, I 'spose. And I gotta admit I feel like dog doo we can't find any leads on Travis or Cassy. But I gotta say, Russell, pink just ain't her color." Arvid shook his head. "Don't that look like two pigs fightin' in a sack?"

Russell stared down the hall. Then he erupted in a wheezy, silent chuckle, nearly doubling over.

"Uffda, don't you let her hear you laughing," Arvid muttered. "We don't want to hurt her feelings, but I'm just sayin'. Two pigs in a sack."

258

Chapter 40

Sage Bluff, present day

"I'd love to go to Billings, Grant, but I can't," Jessie said into the phone. "I promised the board for the plein air competition that we'd get together later this afternoon."

"Are you positive you don't want to come, Jessie? After all, it was your lead."

"I just can't. I've already postponed that meeting once because of Amber Reynolds and the Moran research. I don't dare do it again." She said. The gallery in Baxter sponsored two scholarships to the art workshop I'm giving here this coming fall—in September when there's gorgeous color— and the board received a flood of applications. Today, I'm going to choose who will receive them."

"Too bad. I'll call you if I find out anything," Grant said in a disappointed tone. "If your hunch pans out, this could be a major breakthrough in finding the Morans."

"That hunch is as good as the shortbread you're missing. Guess we'll see if the FBI deserves its stellar reputation," Jessie answered. "Tomorrow morning you and Arvid are invited for a do-over breakfast. I'll make my famous baked Chili Eggs and all the bacon you can steal from Jack. Then I'll let you both look through Amber's research."

"You've got a deal."

"Now, go find us a painting," Jessie encouraged.

Grant laughed and hung up, but as Jessie set the phone on the side table, she shook her head. She walked back into the kitchen and poured herself a cup of coffee, doused it with double cream and grabbed a piece of shortbread from the barrel shaped cookie jar. Plunking herself down on one of the kitchen chairs, she admitted she'd have enjoyed going with the gorgeous man to the William K. Foster Gallery. And taking that long drive to Billings to get to know him better.

Why did she find Grant so appealing? She pondered the question as she chewed the rich cookie. Ego, she decided. Grant appreciated her life's work. He understood that her painting was a major part of who she was. And he wasn't threatened that she was successful at it. He saw her in a way that Russell never had and never would.

Grant was better looking than Russell. More successful. Better company. *And as simple to grab as a free snack on a toothpick from the grocery store's Saturday samples, if she read the look in his eye correctly.*

At that thought, Jessie's stomach rumbled. She reached for another shortbread cookie and chewed it thoughtfully. Picking up her mug, she swallowed coffee without tasting it.

Who does Russell think he is, anyway? By God, someone ought to pry those eyelids of his open, she thought. He doesn't even notice how gorgeous the world is. *And what's with that ten years too late compliment about the piece of stained glass. He's sure never said one good thing about my paintings.* She gave a harsh laugh.

Now her dander was up. Jack unwisely chose that moment to jump onto Jessie's lap and begin kneading her thigh with his wide paws.

"What do you want now?" she snarled. Jack scrunched himself up, rubbed his head against her hand, and she reached down, immediately contrite, to stroke his wide orange forehead. "Aaaw, I'm sorry."

Jessie sat, sipping her now lukewarm coffee, gazing out the window at cotton ball clouds blowing in from the southwest. The top of the mass was outlined in vivid white, the underbelly shaded in warm grey with pink and mauve swirled through. She watched the sky, stroking the cat until his rumbling purr and the warmth of his soft body calmed her thoughts. She looked down at him and rubbed her thumb around his ear. He looked up at her and she saw transparent flecks of amber mixed with the yellow of Jack's eyes and the feline pupils gleaming with a deep blue black.

The world really is beautiful, she thought. *Russell misses so much.*

"If you're half the cat you're supposed to be, Jack Dempsey, next time he stops by you'll sink those claws right into the back of his ankle. Deep. Wake him up a bit, dammit." Aloud, in a voice imitating Arvid's rumble she said, "Huh. Pardon my Swedish."

She began to stand, picking Jack up as rose, squeezing the cat to her and nuzzling the soft fur with her cheek. Then, she chuckled and murmured, "It's a beautiful, beautiful day. Let's go paint something, fat boy."

It wasn't until Jessie had her easel set up and had a painting half-finished that the billowing clouds registered.

"It's in the cloud," she said in a thoughtful voice. "Even if we do find the iPad, I'll bet Amber has all her research stored in the digital cloud. And password protected, no doubt. "

Chapter 41

Sage Bluff Sheriff's Office, present day

Russell held the phone slightly away from his ear. The Miller teenager was obviously in some sort of trouble. Again. Tommy was yelling into the phone, his words tumbling over one another like pebbles washing downstream, pouring out such fear that dread slammed into Russell's gut with the force of a football quarterback.

"Tommy, calm down so I can understand you." Russell said in a commanding voice. "Take a deep breath." He heard the boy snuffle, then draw in a ragged gulp of air.

"Okay. Oh, god."

"Slowly and clearly now, kid." Russell said, enunciating each word with drillmaster precision. "Where are you? Do you need an ambulance?"

"An ambulance. That isn't gonna do squat, Deputy Bonham. You gave me your number. You said if I needed help, call you." His voice trailed off and then, almost whimpering, Tommy said, "The reservoir south of town. Over near the old barn on Fisher's bull ranch. For god's sake, come now!" Over the urgency in Tommy's voice, Russell heard someone losing their lunch.

"Calm down, Tommy. I'll be there in a few minutes", Russell said, as he swung the patrol car in a wide U-turn and headed south, siren screaming. He continued, "Tommy, you said 'we'. Who's with you and what's the problem?"

Dammit, Russell thought, *probably swimming in that dirty waterhole with friends and some dumbass kid might have drowned, as panicked as Tommy sounded.*

The reservoir was one of the hangouts kids used for Saturday night beer parties and date night privacy. When the kids got some liquor under their belts, some hotshot invariably wanted to take a swim. Just thinking about the brown, nasty water gave him the whim whams, but a kid with a beer in his belly had no common sense.

The reservoir was like a huge, stagnant, stewpot—full of abandoned vehicles and sharp, rusty metal—ready to slice into any teenager macho enough, or drunk enough, to dive in. He knew. He'd been one of those kids. After an inexpert belly flop of a dive, he'd come up from the water sliced wide open, an old fender doing the job like a butcher cutting beef. Still sported a puckered scar on his chest. Russell's badge of stupidity, his old man had called it. Of course, it was a given that his dad—had his liver lasted long enough to see it—wouldn't care much for the badge he wore now. Ah, well. Russell cleared his thoughts.

"You still there, Tommy?"

"Dead . . . too late . . . for an ambulance. Lisa Patterson. . . with me. . . and we. . . my battery. . . This crap phone!. . . cheap piece of. . .Dead!. . . can you hear me?" Tommy's voice became bursts of swearing sandwiched between static, then was quiet.

Russell stomped on the accelerator.

Chapter 42

St. Benedict's School, 1939

Kate examined the room. It was coming together and might turn into a great art classroom yet. Her gaze fell on the cupboard. Memories of her stay at St. Benedict's drew her back to the day she pulled the Moran paintings from the trash barrel and hid them.

While Sister walloped poor John Running Bear, Kate mustered her courage and raced to the nun's cabin. She pushed the wrapped paintings between the mattress and box spring of Sister Campbell's own bed. Kate smiled to herself. She'd known that crazy nun would never look in her own cabin for the paintings, even if she'd had second thoughts about pitching them in the trash.

Funny, she hadn't thought of Thomas' paintings in years. She still had the little notebook he'd given her, though. It was a prized possession.

A day or two after the artist rode out, her dad had come to pick her up. Kate smiled to herself, remembering how her dad had grinned and swung her high into the air, around and around. He sure wasn't kidding when he said there was a huge surprise waiting at home. Huge didn't begin to describe it, she thought with a grin. Her folks had adopted five-year-old Nate, a big boy even at that age.

Kate checked her watch. She'd better quit dwelling on the past and go home. But first, maybe she'd yank the broken back off that old cupboard. Then she'd call it a day. She picked up a screwdriver and stepped around to the loose backing. She wedged the tool under the thin alder covering the cupboard back and realized it wasn't actually coming apart, there was just an extra panel of wood protruding from under the backing.

Kate pushed the screwdriver into the crack with one hand and tried to grab the loose piece with the other hand to tug the piece out. A few inches of layered wooden panels pulled free and Kate saw it was actually two rectangles of thin wood bound together with a tattered bit of twine.

What the heck? She tugged harder. An edge of canvas fabric peeped out from between the hardboard panels. Even with just a small sliver of canvas, the pink roses were recognizable to Kate.

Omigosh, omigosh, omigosh! She careened out of the classroom and down the school hallway. Kate stopped in front of Matt's office door and pounded.

"Matt, are you still here? I need some muscle!"

Kate and Matt looked down at the two paintings that had been sandwiched between the thin alder wood panels. They nearly glowed! When she was a child she hadn't realized how truly beautiful they were.

"I just can't understand it. These are worth serious money. What could the priest have been thinking? Dad talked to John Running Bear after Father Mike died, and I know he gave the priest the paintings." Kate frowned. "Father Michael told John he was going to put them in a safe spot, so John thought he was taking them to a bank in town. After he died, and there was no sign of the artwork, we all assumed someone had taken the paintings." Kate shook her head. "I don't know. It's so odd. Father Michael could easily have found a buyer for these. For some reason, the priest chose to hide them in the cupboard at the school. Either he didn't have a chance to sell them before he died, or he thought that bidding at national auctions would reach higher prices once the influenza epidemic ran its course,"

"Yeah. Could be. But it's anybody's guess," Matt said with a shrug.

265

"Some of my past relatives believed he actually did put the paintings in a safe deposit box at the bank, and someone at the bank got away with both of them. Father Michael could have been returning to the school when he was killed, instead of on his way to town." She looked from the paintings to Matt.

He was staring at the paintings as though mesmerized.

Kate said, "Well, do you know how the new school was paid for, since neither of the paintings was sold to cover the land or building costs?"

"Uh huh. Copper. One of the wealthy 'Copper Kings', mine owners from Butte, paid for nearly all of it."

"Well, finding these paintings is a godsend," Kate said dreamily. "When we sell them, St. Benedict's should get enough money to start a trust fund—build another classroom and start new programs. There'd be money for teachers and supplies—"

"Wait a minute," Matt interrupted in a sharp tone. "Why should we tell anyone? This is like finding buried treasure. Like gold! Nobody but you and I know they've been found. And the school isn't in bad shape. It doesn't need the money. We could sell these ourselves."

Kate looked at him in incredulity. Then in fury.

"You'd better be joking." She crossed her arms across her chest. "If you aren't, I'm going to pretend I didn't hear you suggest such an awful thing. Surely you've grown up a little in the past twenty years. Don't you ever think of anyone but yourself? Or are you so far in debt from the gambling and booze you can't think straight? Is that it?"

Matt looked at her with a dumbfounded expression. She was standing by the window, her back stiff and small fists clenched. The early evening light gave her red hair a fiery shimmer. His expression softened.

"Aw, c'mon. Don't think of anyone but myself?" He tapped his index finger on the desk. "Listen, I haven't thought of anyone but you since you walked into the school and asked about the teaching job. In fact, I've hardly thought of anyone else since you left town. I lost you out of stupidity. I was stupid. Young and stupid." He stepped toward her.

266

Kate swung both palms up as though to push him back. The movement halted him in his tracks.

He scowled. "Everyone pushed us to get married, but we were so young! I was scared. I knew I needed more time, but instead of asking you to wait, I fooled around and blew it."

"That was a long time ago."

"I've changed since you came home." He held his hands out toward her in a placating manner. "No drinking, no gambling, not anymore. I love you. We could pick up where we left off. And if these paintings are half as valuable as you think they are, we could have a great new start. I'm thinking of us."

Kate glared at him, her face dark with disgust.

"Why, you scumbag. You forget I've known you all your life, Matthew Anderson. Good try, though."

Kate snatched up the paintings and her empty thermos. Giving him an angry look over her shoulder as she went through the door, she stomped out.

As soon as Kate walked into Nate's to show him the paintings, she realized something was drastically wrong at her brother's house. The roomy kitchen looked like nobody had cleaned it in weeks. Susan was usually meticulous. Then it hit her.

"Why in heaven's name didn't you tell me Susan left you, you big galoot? And poor Gemma. Girls that age need a woman around."

"Aw, Sis, we're working on it. Just like you always told me—Susan says I boss her around too much and she's not havin' it."

"It's bad enough you've been trying to do so much to take care of Dad. Here I was—off in California feeling sorry for myself, while you were trying to run the place and be both father and mother to Gemma. Honestly, did you really think I wouldn't come home to help out?"

"Like I said, Susan and me, we're talkin'. We're workin' on it. I'll get her back home, you'll see. And she's just in Baxter. Gemma stayed with me, so she wouldn't have to switch schools. The family wanted you to come home because you were ready,

267

not because we were whinin' around. You were doing so well with your paintings."

Kate sighed with exasperation. "Lord, what am I going to do with this whole lot of you? Family always, always comes first. I would have come home."

He looked contrite.

"Well, we'll talk about it later." Her eyes filled even as she held up the wrapped masterpieces. "Right now, I have something to show you. Call Gemma, too."

Still upset when she pulled the truck into the yard at her studio, Kate bit her lip to stop the trembling. She was livid with her sister-in-law for leaving instead of fighting it out with Nate and making things work. A bit of arguing cleared the air. That always worked best with him, and Susan should know that. She was worried about their happiness.

And she was worried about the paintings. She didn't put it past Matt to come looking for the two Moran landscapes. She'd been able to read that greedy look of his since they were children. He wanted them, and he meant to have them. When they were young, he always wheedled her into giving up the infrequent treats or toys, often cheating at games.

I loved him anyway. And I always let him get away with it. But not this time.

She parked in the yard and hurried up to the apartment with her coffee thermos and the paintings. She stared at the two canvases. Perhaps she'd send the one of the Yellowstone River breaks to be appraised. The one with all those wild roses. It was definitely her favorite. She'd be careful who she told about them, but she could get some advice from Phillip tonight. A lawyer should have some good input.

On second thought, she knew exactly what to do. She had two unframed paintings of her own ready to send to a gallery in Boston. Kenneth Worth, who owned the Boston gallery, was one person she trusted implicitly. He also knew someone at Christie's auction house in London, and that contact would know where the pieces would bring the best price. She ran to her studio space and slit open the box she'd previously packed, addressed to the Worth Gallery, slipping both Moran paintings between her own canvases and the triple layer of protective cardboard.

Then she grabbed notepaper and pen and wrote a quick note asking Kenneth to send the Moran paintings to the best person possible to handle authentication and appraisals and have them send her the bill. As an afterthought, she added a note about a special framing idea she had and requested he should send them back to her in care of her father, Jim O'Bourne. Kate put her letter into an envelope, added it to the box and resealed the package.

She breathed a sigh of relief. Having them sent to her dad would keep the paintings safe if Matt comes looking for them. She glanced about her apartment. The small painting of deer that Thomas Moran had given her when she was a child caught her eye. It hung on the wall near her easel. On the easel was a small, newly finished landscape she'd done during one of Gemma's lessons. Funny . . . she hadn't realized how much her own work looked like Thomas'.

Phillip would arrive in less than half an hour to pick her up, and Kate's thoughts went to the problem of what to wear to dinner. She opened her closet and chose a blue and black checked woolen skirt and black pullover sweater. She walked to the bathroom, undressed and showered quickly, trying not to get her hair wet. Then she untwisted the thick braid and slipped into the clothing. A touch of lip gloss, dash of perfume, a brush through her hair and she was ready to go. Her hair hung loose around her shoulders in a tumble of auburn.

Looking out the window, past the silhouettes of the cottonwood trees against the dusky sky, she saw headlights winding their way down the lane. She walked down the stairs with her package, opened her truck door, placed the box on the seat and locked the cab. *Problem solved.* Turning, she was just in time to greet Phillip.

Matt slumped miserably to a seated position on one of the school desks after Kate stormed out of the classroom, his head in his hands. A quick rap on the door made him sit up straight and call, "Yes?"

"Hi, Mr. Anderson. Have you seen Mrs. Morgan? We want to show her some more of Willis's drawings and see if she'd critique them before she left," Gloria said, looking around the room.

Willis looked down and shuffled his feet, appearing tremendously uncomfortable. Matt grimaced inwardly. He wondered how much of the argument between Kate and him they must have overheard. Sound carried so well in the empty school corridors. Damn, it was not only embarrassing, but he'd prefer the discovery of the Moran paintings to be just between Kate and him for now.

"She left, Gloria. Why not bring them in tomorrow, Willis? I'm sure she'll be glad to look at them. Right now, you'd better take off, so I can lock up."

The next day, Kate added two containers of turpentine to the art supplies in the old white cupboard and checked her list. Yes, she was sure she had everything she needed to start the art class the following week. She had enough books for twenty students: canvas, paints, brushes and paper. Every item was checked off.

She was surprised Willis hadn't shown up to lend a hand, but things worked out fine. Matt had strolled in looking like butter wouldn't melt in his mouth to give her a huge apology and offer to carry a stack of history books out of the art room and deliver them to the correct classroom. While he was gone, Samantha stopped to see if she could do anything to help. It was great timing. She didn't want Matt to see her with the package she had prepared. He might suspect the paintings were inside. *And he'd be right. But, I could send them with Samantha.* She walked out to her pickup, retrieved the package of paintings and handed it to Samantha with enough money to ship the box to Boston.

By the time Kate hopped in her old truck and started back to her apartment, she was exhausted and unsettled. Matt had tried again to talk to her. He'd agreed to let her handle the

Moran paintings, looking so sincere. Her heart ached with the realization she wasn't sure if she could trust his sincerity.

Pulling into the darkened driveway, she parked in her usual spot and got out. She got out and slowly climbed the stairs. With a twist of the key, she opened the door to her apartment and flipped on the light and let out a shriek. Her studio—her beautiful studio—was trashed.

The furniture was topsy-turvy, cushions tossed, art paper ripped and thrown on the floor. Her canvasses were pulled out of the shelves and pitched into a pile. A wail escaped her lips when she saw her easel was tipped over, and her new painting was gone.

She searched frantically for the small painting in the pile of blank canvasses. It was the best one she'd ever done. Then she noticed the empty hanger on the wall. The small painting of the deer, her precious gift from Thomas Moran, was missing, too.

She raised a hand to her mouth, stifling a sob. Her eyes hardened as she ran down the steps, jumped into her truck, and roared out of the driveway.

Wait until I get my hands on that greedy little so and so. If he isn't home, he'll be at the school. I'm gonna clobber him. I'm gonna clobber the bejeezus outta that Matt Anderson . . .

Kate entered the corridor and headed for Matt's office. Nobody had answered her knock at his home. The ten-minute drive to the schoolhouse had given her time to cool down. It didn't make sense Matt would take her new painting. And she didn't think he would have recognized the small one as a Moran. She glanced down the hallway.

That's strange—the light's on in the art room. She quietly opened the door, walked softly in and immediately heard hushed voices coming from the storage closet. Kate wrenched the door open.

"What the . . . what on earth are *you* doing here?" Two figures turned to Kate. One of them picked up the large claw hammer.

Chapter 43

Sage Bluff reservoir, present day

Russell punched number three on his speed dial and barked at Arvid when he answered. He filled him in, ending with, "Just get here. Fast." He handed Tommy his cellphone, instructing him to call his parents and then Lisa's home.

"Tell them you're both with the police, not in trouble, but helping at the scene of an accident by the reservoir."

"An accident? You're kidding, right? Can't you talk to them?"

"Tommy, just say what I told you and tell them I'll call as soon as I can."

For the umpteenth time, Russell wished Arvid hadn't been out fishing when the Sheriff suffered his heart attack. Then this would've landed in the big Norwegian's capable hands instead of his own. *Arvid is worth two of Stendahl, anyhow. And three of me.*

He couldn't focus. He tilted his head, pressing his right hand over his eyes.

What if it had been Jessie in the car? He'd only needed a quick glance into the vehicle to know it was a bloody mess. A feeling of panic tightened in his chest.

Russell noticed Tommy eyeing him expectantly and Russell wiped the back of his hand across his forehead, catching beads of sweat.

Well, I'm the only one here right now, this minute. Just buck the hell up, Bonham.

He was surprised at Tommy's backbone now that the kid had pulled himself together. The kid was all right. The girl, though, had emptied her stomach and couldn't stop crying.

Lisa Patterson was a petite brunette wearing blue shorts, a pink T-shirt and a vivid pink ball cap decorated with silver sequins in the shape of a skull. She sat on the grass with her head down, hugging her drawn up knees, shoulders shaking. The silver skull on the cap bobbed grotesquely up and down as she wept.

Russell groaned, and motioned to Tommy. He gave the boy a meaningful look and pointed toward the girl.

Then Russell squared his shoulders, went to his patrol car and opened the back door. He rummaged through a duffel bag. He found a light jacket and thin pair of gloves and donned both. With a handkerchief held over his mouth and nose, he once again approached the car Tommy and Lisa had discovered.

Even with the cloth pressed over his nose, the pungent odor assaulted him. It was a smell he associated with his neighbor's farm a week or two after the old codger butchered the annual steer. The old man would dump the offal in the field for carrion birds and other wildlife, but since he hated Russell's dad, he'd dump it on the fence line as close to the Bonham place as he could.

Just as Russell used to hear the swarms of bluebottles around the rotting mass, he heard the buzzing of flies from the blue Ford Taurus, the Taurus with Travis Simpson's license number.

As he steeled himself and bent to peer in, a magpie fluttered out the driver's side window, startling Russell. He flung his arm up defensively. He gagged, covered his nose again with the clean cloth and opened the car door.

The two bodies were strapped in as though going for a Sunday drive. Yellow-jackets had carved fist sized chunks from their faces, the voracious wasps crawling over one another to reach the feast. A blackness of flies flew random circles in the interior. He leaned in slowly, ever so slowly, to remove a brown purse from between the bodies. As he grabbed it, and began to cautiously ease it out, an irritated wasp bounced twice off the exposed wrist area between his glove and jacket cuff, stinging him both times.

He winced and staggered backward several steps, before he straightened. God, he hated those things. He opened the purse, and searched for the owner's ID. Locating the driver's license, he read the name. Even without ID, the clothing and hair had been enough for him to realize the search for Cassy Adams and Travis Simpson was over.

And he didn't like the ending one damn bit.

The situation was getting worse and worse. First Kevin's death, then Amber Reynolds, and now this horrific killing of the EMT and undercover agent. Could they all be related somehow? Nobody kills over some stupid paintings, do they?

He ticked items off a mental list: call Samuelson, the DEA agent. It seemed logical to ask for FBI help on this as soon as possible. Then, he'd call Doc Vickerson, who doubled as the county coroner. He shook his head, clamping his teeth over his bottom lip.

Gruesome.

Nothing an ambulance could do except remove the bodies. And a crime team should search the whole area before the ambulance can even do that. Arvid and Samuelson need to have a good look first, as well.

Russell massaged his bitten wrist as he walked over to retrieve his cell phone from Tommy. The teen sat with his arm around the girl, murmuring calming words near her ear. Russell hit the speed dial button again and spoke the moment it was answered.

"Arvid, make sure you have some crime scene gloves with you—something that fits those big Norwegian mitts of yours. And stop at Mickelsohn's Hardware as you head by. Pick up a couple cans of wasp spray."

Chapter 44

Sage Bluff Sheriff's Office, present day
Russell and Arvid stood by in helpless sympathy in her living room as Violet Adams wailed.

The door flew open and Blanche, dressed in exercise clothes and tennis shoes, barreled in, dropped her large tote bag on the floor and hurrying to her sister's side. "I just heard! I'm so sorry! You poor thing . . . and my poor niece. Cassy dead? I just can't believe it." She began murmuring to Violet, looking accusingly at Arvid and Russell.

Arvid cleared his throat. Whatever was happening in Sage Bluff seemed to be escalating: Amber Reynolds, Cassy Adams, Travis Simpson. And Williston had phoned the station just this morning. Jake Ward had been stabbed to death at the jailhouse in North Dakota. He needed to call and find out if they had any new info on that knifing. Sure strange Ward was killed right after he told the authorities there that he'd be willing to give a list of stops and contacts from memory. Jake said he thought his route had something to do with Amber's death, and by God, he was going to get even. How soon after Williston called the Sage Bluff station with that news had Ward been knifed? Someone had passed that info on to the wrong person.

Arvid, lost in his own thoughts, became dimly aware that Blanche was haranguing them. Rightly so, he figured. His stomach clenched.

". . . poor job of finding out what's going on." Blanche was saying. "And while you're at it, maybe you should take a good look at Jessie O'Bourne. And I don't mean just that pretty face of hers."

"What are you getting at, Blanche?" Russell asked.

"She doesn't have an alibi for Amber Reynolds' death, and there's no evidence of any break- in at her house. Not from either time she reported one. She told you herself nothing was missing. You two go running out there every time she calls. She could be scamming both of you. Probably scamming that pretty boy FBI agent, too."

"That's just crazy talk," Russell folded his arms across his chest.

"Maybe she found the paintings years ago. Maybe that's what Amber Reynolds found out. After all, Jessie went to a fancy art school, and look how she lives—like she's rich!"

"Blanche," Arvid chimed in. "You're just upset."

She gave Arvid a dirty look, and squatted down to open the large tote she'd dropped. Pulling out a packet of tissue, she shut the bag and set the tissues next to her sister.

Violet put her face in her hands and continued to weep, rocking side to side.

"And how would that have anything to do with Cassy or Travis Simpson getting shot, Blanche?" Arvid asked.

"That's your job to figure out, Arvid." Blanche sat down on the sofa and put her arm around Violet, making soothing sounds. She glanced up and continued in a more subdued tone of voice, "I think you can both go."

Russell nodded. "Are you sure, Blanche?"

"Yes, I can take care of my sister." Blanche sighed. "Your time is better spent figuring out what's going on."

Russell squatted by the sofa and awkwardly patted Violet's hand. "We're going to do the best we can to find the bastard who did this to your daughter. I promise." He stood and, after a quick glance at Blanche, nodded to Arvid.

As he opened the door to leave, they heard Blanche say, "What you need is a good hot cup of coffee, dear. I'm going to fix you some right now."

Russell stepped through and closed the door softly behind him. Then he looked at Arvid and they both shook their heads.

Chapter 45

Reuben White Gallery, Baxter, Montana, present day

They had renovated the façade since Jessie's last visit to the gallery. Now it was clean and contemporary, a definite improvement from the crumbling brickwork of yesteryear. She pulled open the door and stepped into a tasteful interior that was not only welcoming, but spacious. A small bell jingled as the door closed, and she looked around expecting to see Reuben or his assistant.

"Hello?" When nobody answered, Jessie found a rubber doorstep by the entrance, opened the door and pushed the stopper under it with the toe of her shoe. Then she returned to the pickup parked by the curb and lifted her first box of paintings from the truck bed. She carried it through the gallery entrance and set it down carefully by three panels she saw had been designated for her display. The freestanding, movable walls sported her name in a swirling font, the metallic lettering on black signage adhered at the top of the middle panel. A pedestal nearby held a stack of printed copies of Jessie's biography.

Scattered around the large room, more freestanding walls painted in an assortment of deep oranges and reds added hanging space that would be needed when the plein air paintings started trickling in. The gallery would also frame many of the pieces.

"Jessie!" The welcoming voice came from a petite brunette woman in a form fitting black sheath dress and impossibly tall heels.

"Hi, Denise." She gave the woman a quick hug. "Where's Reuben?"

"He had to handle an unexpected plumbing emergency at his father's home. He'll be here shortly." Denise smiled. "Would you like to look through the workshop applications while we wait, or go ahead and hang your work?"

"Actually, I still need frames for three pieces. Let me bring them in first and maybe you can choose frames for them while I go through the applications. Eight of the pieces are relatively small this time, as you requested."

"No problem about the frames," Denise said. "We love getting the business. And little paintings? Super! Sight unseen, I know those babies will be easy to find a buyer for." She smiled broadly at Jessie and gave her a thumbs up.

"Two of the tiny ones are still wet. Sorry." Jessie grimaced. "It's been a hectic week." She went once more to the pickup, returning with a wooden carrier that held several wet canvasses. She put the case on the counter at the back of the gallery.

"Let's take a look," Denise said. She slid the first painting from the container. It was the early morning painting Jessie had been working on the day she found Amber.

"Oh, I love the light on this one. 11 x 14?"

At Jessie's nod, the gallery owner turned to the display rack behind her and lifted down a simple gilded frame. "Something not too ornate, I think. We'll let the detail in the painting have the importance."

"Hmm. Yes, I agree. It's perfect. I'm glad you ordered so many of the standard sizes to have available for the event. Otherwise, I would have been up the proverbial creek without a paddle."

The back door of the gallery slammed, and a balding middle-aged man strode in, grabbing Jessie into a bear hug. "Good to see you, girl! What did you bring us?"

"Oh, Reuben." Denise laughed. "You sound as bad as our grandkids when they come to visit us. But, you'll be tickled to know Jessie did bring some small ones this time!"

"Superb," he bellowed. "I have a waiting list of potential buyers for her minis. Let me at 'em."

Two hours later, Jessie's art was arranged and hung on the panels. She heaved a sigh of relief. Fourteen pieces of new work. The display looked good. Two pieces sported red dots on their labels, which meant they'd already sold. Reuben, bless his heart, had called several special clients. Two men had rushed to the gallery to meet the artist and choose a painting.

One collector, Samuel Biermann, who asked to be notified of available small work, fell in love with Jessie's largest piece, *Bell Rock Sunset*. It was a painting of a red rock formation near Sedona, Arizona, with a background of a striking lavender and orange sunset.

"I have to have this one," Biermann had insisted. "My wife and I used to live in that area. We'll be celebrating our fiftieth anniversary next week. It's a perfect gift—a reminder of happy times."

Jessie told him it was a new piece, painted only several weeks before while visiting friends. After a short conversation, she'd made arrangements to contact him within the next year so the painting could be varnished. It was best to wait at least six months for the oil paint to fully cure. Before leaving the gallery, he proudly agreed to leave the painting on display until after the plein air event. A small red dot was affixed to the panel next to the painting, and a new tag made that read "SOLD - In the collection of Mr. and Mrs. Samuel Biermann".

Maybe Grant is right after all . . . about the vivid sunsets, Jessie mused after Biermann left, gazing at the welcome red dot. The thought of Grant filled her with an unexpected feeling of warmth. She smiled to herself, then went to thank Reuben for handling the lucrative sales.

Later, Denise handed her the stack of workshop forms, and showed her to a comfortable chair and table in the gallery's back room where she could spread out the workshop applications and sort through them. The three day intermediate oil painting workshop was full and registration was now closed.

"Be sure to look through the children's contest entries when you're done. You can't imagine how much fun some of them are," Denise said.

"I'd love to," Jessie sorted through the scholarship applications and chose two recipients. Then she picked up the rest of the workshop applications and began skimming through them, counting how many of her students were beginners, how many intermediate or advanced. She would plan her curriculum for the class to fit the expertise of the participants.

Each completed form included several photographs of the person's work, as she had requested. The images helped her evaluate artistic strengths, as well as weak areas where she might help them improve. Her classes always covered a multitude of painting topics such as color harmony, composition, understanding light.

An extra page added to the form gave a student the opportunity to tell her a little about themselves if they wished. She read through each person's registration sheets. It looked like it would be a great class.

Finally, Jessie stood and stretched, stifling a yawn. She put her chair away, and, as she did, saw the children's drawings on the next table. Reuben would judge them next week.

Denise had placed each work of art into a clear acrylic sheet, clipped all of the drawings by the same child together, and, if the child was too young to write, had stapled an envelope with the submission form filled out by the parent or teacher onto the last sheet. Then she placed them into bins according to the child's age.

A sketch of a laughing blue llama atop the thickest stack of submissions made Jessie grin. The top corner was marked "ENTRY 22". She checked the bin's label. Age group 4-6.

She stared at it. The drawing had a childlike spontaneity she didn't think any adult could pull off. It had definitely been done by a youngster. And it was fabulous.

She thought back to the drawings she'd made at the same age, drawings her parents still kept. *Somewhere. Probably still in the box up in the attic.* Hundreds of horses, she remembered, because she had wanted to be a cowgirl back then.

Still smiling, and now curious, she carefully slipped the other pages out of the submission folder. Besides the llama sketch, the child had submitted a fire hydrant with a large smile and feet, and a vivid drawing of three dancing chickens, feathers fluttering in sure strokes of red, green and blue marker. All three drawings had the same quirky style, meticulous accuracy, and tons of personality. *And all done with colored markers. Not even erasable.* She put them back in the folder.

Jessie thumbed through the completed "*done at the gallery*" still life entries until she found the numbered drawing that corresponded to the llama sketch.

Entry 22 had removed all of the fruit except the lemons, scattering them on the table in front of the flowers. Then the young artist had drawn each lemon a face with a puckered, sour expression. Several of the flowers in the vase appeared to be winking. She threw her head back and erupted in laughter. The little drawing was darling, and it showed an advanced grasp of realistic shading and light, tossed together with the twist of childlike imagination. *And I bet this child is filled to the gills with good old downright joy of living.*

The envelope paper-clipped to the entry taunted her. Jessie knew it would include the artist's name and information. She carefully opened the envelope and saw it also contained a photo. The picture was of a smiling, red-headed boy proudly holding the llama drawing. He bore a marked resemblance to Kevin O'Bourne when Jessie's brother was five.

Her eyes swam with tears.

The child had printed his own name on the form. Kevin Daniel Bonham. K.D.

Chapter 46

Bonham's home, present day

Russell placed the pizza and breadsticks in the oven to warm. He was listening to the radio, waiting for the six o'clock news and weather report as he washed a head of lettuce and tore pieces into a bowl. He'd have to throw together a side salad before supper, or serve the pepperoni pie with a huge helping of guilt. K.D. had been getting fed too much fast food this month.

Who was he kidding? This month? *Every month.* Man, he needed to buy a couple cook books and maybe stock the small freezer in the garage with healthier stuff.

Russell grated a carrot, diced a stick of celery, and tossed both onto the torn lettuce. He placed K.D.'s portion on a bright yellow plate, adding a dollop of ranch dressing. He set a glass of chocolate milk by the plate and was heading toward the stairway to call K.D. down to dinner when he saw the beat up Ford pull in and park in his driveway. Jessie stepped out. As she headed up the walk, a resolute expression on her face, she lugged a huge box. When she reached the top step, she plunked it down.

Russell's mind went blank. From the kitchen radio, he heard Koot Lundgren's deep voice say "Expect a thunderstorm this evening in Sage County." *Man, Koot finally hit a home run. Storm, heck, she looks mad as a tornado.*

He took a deep breath and opened the door.

"Jessie. Uh . . ." He turned his head to stare apprehensively up the stairs towards K.D.'s open door. Then he turned back to face Jessie.

"Why, Russell?" Jessie's face was stony, her voice quiet. Quiet like the eye of a hurricane.

"Why what?" *Oh, no, no, no, no,* he thought. *Not this too, after the day I've had.*

"WHY, Russell? I want to know why you kept Kevin's son from Dad and me. And I want to see him." Her lip quivered and her eyes were dark with anger. She set the heavy box down with a thump. "I would like to see him. Now."

"Oh, Jess. It's complicated."

"So simplify it, Russell."

"I wouldn't have let you leave Sage Bluff without telling you. I planned to talk to you. That's why I came over the other day."

"You've had about six years to tell me, Russ. Was there just not the right—gee, I don't know—moment? One moment, in six years? You know, sixty-some months?"

"Seventy two. There's seventy two months in six years, Jess."

"Seventy two blasted months?" She roared. "And not one right moment?"

"Daddy? Daddy?" A small voice came from the stairway landing. "What's wrong, Daddy?"

"It's okay, K.D.," Russell yelled up the steps.

"But . . . who's yelling?"

"It's your aunt Jess, K.D.. She yells a lot, but you'll like her. I promise."

"I gotta aunt?"

"Come on down. It's about time you met." Russell glanced quickly at Jessie and said in an undertone, "No yelling in front of my son."

"Your son, huh?"

"My son."

"Okay," Jessie breathed, her stony gaze still locked with his. She lowered her voice even more. "We'll do this your way. I'll let you hide behind the boy, you coward. I'll meet K.D., and then we'll talk." She stuck her index finger near his face. "But you hear me, Bonham. It will be a cold day in Hell before I forgive you for this—no matter what explanation you give me."

"I can explain."

"A cold day in H – e – double – ell. There can't possibly be a good excuse for this. I hope you realize that, Russell Stewart Bonham."

He stared at her. He wished he could just erase the six years. But then, he wouldn't have K.D. He turned his face away from hers and chewed on his bottom lip. He shook his right leg nervously, bouncing the knee. Looking with apprehension up the steps, he saw K.D. bounding down.

Jessie was watching the boy. Her eyes glistened with tears.

"You want some dinner, Jess?" He cleared his throat. "I . . . um . . .I cooked."

They sat together on the rickety wicker porch swing. "You were in school, Jess. Kevin would have wanted you to stay in France. What good would it have done if you'd come home?" He spoke softly. He'd tucked K.D. into bed shortly after dinner with the promise the next morning they'd open the big box Jessie had brought and assemble the child's easel it contained.

"Maybe I could have—"

"No. You couldn't have. If I had told you K.D. was Kevin's son, you'd have come home and trashed your year at the Paris Academy."

"But what about Trish? All this time I've thought . . ."

Jessie let the thought hang in the air like a spider dangling in a web. The swing moved gently forward and back, the rasping metal on metal sound doing its best to fill the silence. Finally, Russell sighed and spoke.

"Trish has been gone since K.D. was a month old. By that time, we were thinking about making it a real marriage. Instead, she took off."

"But . . . oh, Russell. That's awful! Why did she—"

"It isn't a pretty story, but you're determined to hear it, so let me talk. Please. Can you just sit and listen for a minute?"

Jessie took a deep breath and gestured for Russell to go ahead.

"Kevin was hooked on Trish, all right. But Trish was hooked on something totally different. Drugs. Mostly Oxycodone. Heck, maybe other drugs, too, but Oxycodone was the big one."

"Oh, my god." Jessie's foot stopped the movement of the swing as she stiffened. "I didn't know. I had no idea."

"Nobody did. Her addiction took even Kevin by surprise. He said it seemed like one day she was fine, the next he was engaged to a drug addict. He made the mistake of telling me. Me. A cop. We had a terrific argument over getting her into rehab. I told him if she wouldn't go, I'd eventually catch her out—arrest her for possession."

She looked up at him, a startled expression on her face. "Oh, please. You're trying to tell me Kevin didn't want her in rehab?"

"Well, yeah, he did. But he couldn't force her, and she wouldn't go voluntarily. He practically hounded her about it, and she wouldn't budge. Finally, he gave up. Said he would try to handle it. Get her clean himself." Russell snorted. "Yeah, like that was going to work. Oxycodone is horrible, just horrible, to kick. I pressed Trish so hard to give up her supplier that she finally agreed to rehab, if I agreed not to haul her in for possession."

"Oh . . ."

"But she didn't follow through right away. And she still wouldn't give me the name of her supplier. She was scared, Jessie. Real scared."

"Afraid? Of going to jail?"

"No. She thought someone would come after her—hurt her, maybe kill her—if they even suspected she'd turned them in."

"What about K.D.?"

"The day after your brother's accident, Trish realized she was pregnant. She was a mess. Terrible withdrawal

286

symptoms, and grief. But that was the turning point. She was determined to stay clean for the health of the unborn baby."

"So you married her because she was pregnant?"

"I'm getting to that. After Kevin's funeral, I took personal leave. I drove her directly to a rehab center in Las Vegas and stayed until she got through the worst of the withdrawal." He gave a small grin. "Turned out to be a longer leave than I'd planned. The Sheriff wasn't happy. I was lucky he took me back."

"Keep talking."

"The deal was, I would help her every way I could until the baby was born and she'd have time to make some hard decisions. It wasn't a real marriage, but it made me the legal father." He plucked at his shirt cuff with nervous fingers. "The rehab facility wiped out my savings. But Trish didn't have any relatives to help her, or to take K.D."

"But Kevin did, Russell. He had family."

"I was raised in your family, too. I felt like part of it. But your dad was a mess, Jessie. He couldn't get past the two deaths so close together - Kevin's, then your mom's. He was depressed. He took lousy care of himself. For a long time, there was no way he could even help take care of a baby. Every time you came home, he pretended to be feeling better than he really did. Then he'd fall apart again, soon as you left. It was only after he met Marty that he started pepping up."

"But I didn't know things were so bad. I could have . . ."

"Just listen, okay?" Russell said in irritation. "Will you just listen? This was Trish's baby, too, not just your brother's. I thought what Trish wanted for the baby had to count, and she wanted him with me. But shortly after K. D. was born, she skipped out. No word. No note. Nothing."

"She left her baby? That's terrible. And no note? Most women, even if they were leaving, would leave a letter behind for that baby. And why would she want her baby left with a man? Why not find a woman? Or even an adoptive family?"

"Because she thought since I was a policeman, I could protect her and the baby."

"Oh." Jessie sat in silence for so long Russell thought his heart would stop, waiting to hear what she would ask next.

"Okay . . . but then why leave without any notice? Could something have happened to her?"

"Nah. All her makeup. All that crap you women use. And shoes—more shoes than anybody could ever wear—every stitch of clothing she owned—it was all gone. Every ridiculous thing she bought with my money."

The expression on Jessie's face grew annoyed and Russell waved his hand in the air as though he could make the comment disappear. "You didn't know Trish that well, Jess. A lot of stuff she bought just because she was bored. And I haven't heard from her since. But every birthday, Kevin gets a nice package and a card—no return address—in the mail. It has to be from Trish. It makes me crazy that she can't just call once in a while."

"Didn't you try to find her, Russell?"

He snorted. "Try? Heck, I beat every bush with a stick from Vegas to Canada, and got absolutely no leads. Put out inquiries over the internet. Had buddies from other police stations do the same. I didn't turn up a single hint of her. Zip."

"Still, you should have let me know what was happening."

"Your dad said you were so happy, Jess. You were putting out fabulous work, and you weren't even out of the Paris Academy yet. I think he might have suspected the baby was Kevin's, but he never asked."

"Never asked? And you haven't seen fit to tell him? It's his grandson we're talking about. Dad's the kind of guy who would find not telling him a very big lapse, Russell."

"You know, Dan went into such a depression after losing Hannah he wouldn't even have been grandfather material."

"Oh, puh-leez," Jessie drawled sarcastically. "He'd be a fabulous grandpa and you know it. Knowing Kevin left a son would have been just the thing to raise his spirits, you dolt. I'm not even going to argue with you over that. And the past few years, I could have been home a lot to help, regardless of my art school. And regardless of the art shows I do."

He stiffened. "We don't need part-time people in his life, Jessie," he said angrily.

"Now you're just being ridiculous."

"Am I? You never wanted to stay in Sage Bluff, but I'm here for the long haul. I wanted a home for K.D. where he never had to wonder if the people he relied on were coming home or flying God knows where following their . . . art. " Russell made air quotes with his fingers.

Jessie glowered at him. "That's a really ignorant thing to say, Russell Bonham. Lots of people do have children and jobs that require travel, and they do make it work. My art is a job. A *great* job, actually. And it's good for children to have other relatives in their life, not just parents."

"K.D and I are fine by ourselves. Besides, Kevin was like a brother. Taking care of K.D. and Trish was something I could do for both him and Dan. I owed your dad that. He was the one that raised me, not that sorry excuse for a father that I . . . well, never mind."

"You think you owed Dad? Really?" Her voice dripped sarcasm. "So you repaid him by not telling him he has a grandson?"

"It wasn't like that."

"Then how was it?"

He heaved a deep sigh. "After K.D. was born, the days just slipped away. The days turned into months and the months into years." He looked down at his feet. "The longer I went without telling him, the harder it seemed to finally come clean. And I guess I got really possessive of K.D. I never really had much of a family of my own, but I hadn't set out to keep him to myself."

"But my Dad, Russell . . . I don't understand why you didn't at least tell him."

"Jessie—"

"Don't 'Jessie' me. You've stolen six years of his grandson's life away from Dad. And six years of knowing I had a nephew, a living part of Kevin, away from me. And it should have been my choice to come home or not and help. Nobody gave me a choice Russell. What is it with men that they think they can just make choices for any woman in their lives? It's going to take me a long time to forgive—"

"Jessie, hear me out."

"Then say something worth listening to."

"I didn't tell you because I was afraid you'd come home."

Her eyes widened.

"I was afraid you'd come home out of a sense of duty— or worse—pity." He grimaced. "If I'd told you, what would you have done?"

"Russell, I don't know. Until today I didn't know K.D. was . . . I thought . . . I didn't expect . . . ."

"Trish bailed. And she was his mother. His *mother*. I know what that's like. Good thing he wasn't old enough for it to hurt. I didn't want you to come home, let him get attached to you, and then have you leave again, Jess."

"Oh for . . . ." Jessie pressed her lips tightly together and crossed her arms across her chest. "I'd have come home to help out."

"Yeah. For a month? A year?" His leaned forward. "You could come home now, Jessie. Help raise your nephew. Give up the painting. Come home."

"Russell . . ." She closed her eyes and when she opened them her eyes blazed. "Give up my painting? Gee, how about you give up being a cop? If the shoe were on the other foot, how fair would that sound to you?"

"That's totally different."

Jessie gave a rueful chuckle. "No. No, it isn't. You can't ask me to give up my life's work. That's just silly. And it's also unfair."

"I think it's damn fair, Jess," His voice was as sharp as barbed wire, "You're a butterfly—you're like my mother—can't stay where God put you."

"A butterfly? A butterfly? Are you crazy? Do you have any idea how hard I work? Painting is work—every day rain or shine work—and I'm darn good at it. I make a good living."

"Ah, you make some money, and I know you're good—real good—but work? You just play around with it, Jess. It isn't like a real job."

"Why you . . . you . . . just because I enjoy it doesn't mean it isn't—"

"Work. Some work." Russell made a raspberry noise. "And a kid's better off in a stable environment, not with a momma who's gadabouting all over."

Jessie jumped up from the swing and stood looking down at him, shaking her head. "K.D. would be better off knowing his grandpa—knowing he has other family who care about him, not just one person."

"I . . . I kept thinking Trish might come back, that we'd tell Dan together. Then he met Marty and he seemed happy for a change. But it was hard for me to see him with someone other than Hannah. And he never seemed to be home. I know K.D. needs his Granddad. And Dan needs to know about Kevin. But, up to now, we've been fine." He leveled his gaze at her. "We're fine."

"No. You're not. And I want to be part of K.D.'s life whenever I can."

"Oh, gee. Thanks. Whenever you can? Maybe you can send him postcards from the crazy places you wind up with your . . . work."

"Why you . . . you sorry sack of egotistical, self-important, selfish, condescending . . ."

"Well, don't hold back, Jess girl." Russell stood, crossed his arms over his chest, mimicking her stance, and looked down at her with narrowed eyes.

Swinging her head, she flipped a wave of hair over her shoulder, and uncrossed her arms. "I can't even put how I feel into words, Russ. You might not want my help now, but I guarantee you'll want it later. I've seen the drawings K.D. made for the competition. They're fabulous. He is going to need—and want—the drawing and painting the same way I did. It will obsess him. He's going to be like me."

"I hope not." He waved his hand in a dismissive gesture. "But whatever he does, it's our business." Russell was quiet for

291

several minutes, then admitted quietly, "It's true. He's exactly like you. But you never come home, Jess."

Tears filled her eyes. "I . . . I've been home off and on. I just never let you know when I came. I was so mad and upset about your marriage that Dad probably never mentioned I'd been in Sage Bluff." Then her eyes flashed. "But any fool can see K.D. looks exactly like Kevin. If Dad saw him, he wouldn't just suspect he had a grandson, he'd know." Her gaze narrowed. "Six years. You haven't been going to see my Dad at all the past two or three years, have you?"

Russell's guilty expression was her answer.

"Oh, for . . . He lost Kevin, then Mom, and he must feel like he lost you, too, you idiot, if that's the case." She rubbed at her temples in an agitated motion, then wiped moisture from her face. "I can't believe you've done this. I thought . . . I thought you were a better man than this." She squeezed her eyes shut and then opened them, straightened her back and walked down the steps, hurrying toward her truck with tears streaming down her face.

"Jessie?" Russell called after her. "Jessie! Come back and talk. Don't be so damn stubborn."

She stopped and stood still, her back to him. The wetness glistened on her cheeks as she turned to face him. In the glint of the porch light he saw her eyes were as cold as an arctic sea.

"Russell, I listened to you. And I can simply look at you and know there's more you aren't telling me. And you're right. I'm stubborn. I've got a regular monopoly on stubborn. And I'm going to start digging. I'm going to figure out what kind of dirt is missing from your story. And you know what, Bonham?"

He stared at her as though he were seeing a stranger, but he said nothing.

"If you think I won't puzzle it out, you're not only less of a man than I thought, you're a fool." She swiveled, walked stiffly to the pickup, got in and gunned the engine, the wheels spitting rocks from the gravel driveway, the sound like popping corn as she pulled away.

Russell stood on the dimly lit porch watching the little pickup churn gravel until it disappeared.

"Well," he said aloud, "That went well."

* * *

Jessie drove mechanically, trying to calm herself. The boy was wonderful. She thought of the tousle-headed little man, chowing down on pizza and peering shyly at Jessie from under long reddish lashes. So like her brother's.

Then it hit her. The birthday presents K.D. received each year might mean more than an absent mother trying to assuage guilt. Birthdays—parties with cake, candles and presents—had been an important thing at O'Bourne's. She turned around and headed back to Russell's house.

Minutes later, he answered the door, a downcast expression on his face.

"About those packages you thought Trish sent—how were they wrapped?"

"What the . . .? You drove all the way back here to ask me something stupid like that?"

"What were they wrapped in? It's important."

"Uh, let me think." A sick expression washed over his face as understanding hit. "They were wrapped in newspaper, Jess. The comic section."

"Damn fool." Jessie turned around and stomped to the car, only turning as she opened the door to holler, "You're a damned fool, Russ."

His mouth dropped open. Then she saw realization dawn on his face. Russell looked sick.

"Trish didn't send any of those presents to K.D., did she?" he asked in a low voice.

"Nope."

At the O'Bourne house, any present from Dan was always wrapped in the Sunday funnies.

Chapter 47

Honolulu, Hawaii, present day

Dan O'Bourne stepped out of the shower and walked into the bedroom wearing nothing but a sunburn. Grabbing the phone from the walnut nightstand, he growled into the receiver.

"Hello?"

"So. Dad," Jessie began. "I won't keep you. I just have a couple questions."

"Hey, Jess girl! No, that's okay. Always glad to talk to my girl. 'Sides, my new bride must be out spending my moola on pineapples to ship back home to every godforsaken person she's ever met." He guffawed. "Better hope you're on her list, baby. They are gooood."

"Yeah. Hope so. Listen, Dad, I'm going to be very blunt. Have you seen Russell much the past couple years?"

"Uh . . . not a lot, Jess. Some," he admitted. "What's this about?"

"You see that little boy of his, you know, the little guy with the red hair? Looks like an O'Bourne family picture waiting to happen?"

"Uh . . . just a second, honey, I'm going to grab a towel or something. Just got out of the shower." Ducking back into the bathroom, he thought frantically. *Blast it. I got nothing. Nada. Zip.* He wrapped a thirsty terry-cloth robe around himself, courtesy of the Mauna Loa hotel. Then he went back out to take his lumps.

"Um . . ."

"Have you seen his son, Dad?" Her voice had a hacksaw edge to it that cut to the bone.

"Yeeah," he drawled. "I've seen him . . . just from a distance a few times. Saw him at the grocery store once. A few years back, I think. Cute little guy."

"Have you been sending him a nice package every birthday since he was born?"

Busted.

"Jessie, I can explain," Dan O'Bourne said.

"Oh, Dad," Jessie's voice caught on a sob. "You knew. You knew, but you didn't tell me. It would have been meant so much, knowing Kevin had a son. A little piece of him left behind."

"Aw, don't cry, Jessie. Calm down, honey. Please calm down."

"I don't want to calm down, Dad. I don't understand why neither you nor Russell let me know. And why aren't you over there being the grandpa that little boy needs?"

There was a minute of silence on the line. Then Dan cleared his throat.

"I kept waiting for Russell. Waiting for him to tell us. I had a hunch the boy was Kevin's, the red hair, you know. But it was only this past year that K.D. began to look like a mirror image of your brother at that age. O'Bournes always look sort of alike. Family resemblance—"

"Blast it, you should have told me," she interrupted. "Both you and Russell should have told me."

"Your art was going so good, though. I didn't want you to come home."

"Strange, isn't it? How nobody wanted me to come home? Nobody wanted to tell me? Everyone seems to think they know what's best for me. But nobody asks what I want."

"Aw, Jess girl . . ."

"Aw, Dad," she sniffed, "stuff a pineapple in it."

Chapter 48

O'Bourne's ranch, present day
Jessie's eyes were red-rimmed from the pity party she'd thrown the night before, but today—today she was determined to be cheerful when they read through Amber's notes. Look on the bright side, she told herself. You have a nephew. She took a bottle of maple syrup from the refrigerator, screwed off the metal cap and put the syrup in the microwave to warm.

She hummed as she cracked three eggs into a deep bowl and whisked them with a cup of milk, a teaspoon of maple flavoring and a capful of vanilla. Then she poured the mixture into a shallow pan and dropped slices of thick white bread into it, turning them over to moisten the opposite side before placing them one after the other onto the hot griddle.

The egg dish would have been plenty, but if she knew Arvid, he'd suck up French toast as well. Probably make comments about the French while he ate it. On the second burner, bacon sizzled. Watching it cook, inhaling the rich aroma filling the kitchen, Jessie took a satisfying swig of steaming coffee.

The hands of the wall clock hit seven as she opened the cupboard to pull down cheerful hand-painted, yellow plates from the shelf. She stacked them on the counter, planning to serve buffet style. Arvid and Grant would arrive at any minute.

And so would Jack, if the smell of browning bacon was any indicator. Jessie grabbed a mitt, opened the oven, and peeped in at her chili-baked eggs, one of her favorite Santa Fe breakfasts. The casserole was beginning to pull away from the edge of the pan, an indication it was almost done. She stepped back as she closed the oven door and her foot encountered something soft, squishy, and dependable as heat in summer.

"Yeoooww. Rwow."

Here's the bacon-loving Butter Tub, right on time.

Jack rubbed back and forth against her legs, continuing to sing the 'ain't got no bacon yet' blues. She grabbed the kitchen shears and snipped the end from one of the browning strips, lifted it out with the point of the scissors and placed it on a paper towel.

"It has to cool, Jack," She glanced down into reptilian yellow eyes. "And you're getting a whole piece, sweet baby, because you're the only male I like right now."

The tom began turning circles around her ankles, uttering insistent mewls.

She gently pushed him away with her foot, and reached for the control to turn down the heat on the burner. As she covered the pan, the doorbell rang and she hurried to open the door.

A beaming Arvid stood on the doorstep, followed by Grant, who carried a bubble-wrapped parcel. Jessie looked from Arvid, to Grant, to the package, then again to the smug expression on Grant's face.

She flung both arms in the air and pirouetted in joy.

"Yeah, baby!"

"Pretty spectacular start to the day." Arvid munched on a strip of bacon, glancing down at Jack, who had assessed the situation and decided the man was the most likely patsy. He lifted an orange paw and tapped Arvid on the leg. The end of the bacon strip slipped from beefy fingers to the waiting cat.

"Isn't it, though?" Jessie's smile was as wide as the Missouri River. "Who would have thought Grant would get both little pieces back on the same day?"

"Huh," Arvid grunted. "Well, that, too. But I was talking about this great breakfast." He patted his tummy. "The French are rightfully famous for their potatoes and toast, if you ask me. Yep, toast and spuds."

She grinned, gazing at the counter, where the little Moran deer painting and the small Kate Morgan landscape stood propped against a large wooden bread box. Grant had filled them both in on the visit to the William K. Foster Gallery and the letter Christian Foster had found after his aborted call to the auction house.

After his father's will was read, Christian had opened his dad's safe and found the small Moran. After calling the experts and receiving such a weird vibe from the woman on the phone, the poor guy had gone through records to check for a receipt, or letter of provenance. He'd discovered the damning information from his father. In a manila envelope were two letters marked *to be read only after my death.*

The first letter was from Christian's grandfather, Will. In it, he admitted his wife, Gloria, had stolen both the tiny Moran painting and one of Kate Morgan's when she was young and foolish. She'd taken them from Kate's studio, after overhearing a conversation between the school principal and Kate. Believing both paintings to be the work of Thomas Moran, she'd hoped the money they brought would enable her and Will to begin a great life together. Money that would allow her new husband to paint instead of work some hopeless 'hand to mouth' job when he had such talent. She hadn't disclosed the theft until after they'd married.

Will had refused to sell them, but was afraid to give them back, knowing that it would make his wife a suspect in Kate Morgan's murder. Instead, he'd kept them. He'd studied them. Learned from them.

Times became so tough over the years that, battling his conscience, he had turned to forgery. Will Foster had made his living—an exceptionally good one—from painting pieces that copied not only Moran's style of work, but other old masters as well.

The second letter was from Christian's father. It said only: *Son, I leave it to you to do what you feel is best with the two paintings. I couldn't face the embarrassment of doing what was right. Maybe you're stronger.*

"Who knows how many of Will's fakes grace the walls of collectors all over the world?" Grant said with irony. "And the funny thing is, Christian was afraid his gallery was so underinsured that once restitution was made to artists whose work was ruined, he might lose the gallery. Instead, he meets the reward criteria for the painting's return. Not the Moran—your aunt's."

"You mean the reward originally offered jointly by Burlington Northern and one of the copper kings?" Jessie asked. "They had both done business with Kate's father, Jim, and matched his offer of a reward. But, I know even with their matching funds, it raised the reward to only around ten thousand dollars. That wouldn't cover the loss of much artwork."

"Ah, but it was put into an interest bearing fund and never cancelled," Grant explained. "Christian is ecstatic. He has cooperated fully with the FBI and will come out smelling like a rose. The paintings will need to go back to D.C. for a complete professional appraisal so we can close the case, but you should get them back promptly after that."

"I know they're the real thing. I'll be glad to have them back in the family," Jessie smiled wide. "Wait until Dad hears."

Then her face clouded, her thoughts returning to her father and Russell's comments. Why hadn't her father asked her to stay home for a while after her mom's funeral? Or to come home later when he must have needed the company? She hated to think of him alone there, depressed, unable to pull himself out of the quagmire of grief.

Jessie looked toward the dining room window. A mass of clouds covered the sun for just an instant, causing the stained glass to look dull and opaque.

From the corner of her eye, she saw Grant looking at her with an odd expression, and she yanked herself back to the moment. He had been speaking to her.

"What'd you say, Grant?"

"I said that I have the librarian's findings in my car, too. She was kind enough to do the drudge work of searching newspaper files from the digital archives. She printed everything out that contained information on major crimes in the local area, between 1915 and 1930. There are numerous cases, both solved and unsolved."

"How kind of her."

"Nah," Arvid chimed in. "Grant did Cathy a kindness by asking for them. She gets bored there at the library."

"Well, anyway, I'll bring in the small box of files. We can spread them out on the table and maybe you two can help me search through them? Great minds, you know."

"Sure," Jessie and Arvid said together. Arvid rose and carried his plate and silverware to the dishwasher as Jessie picked up the syrup bottle and butter dish and returned both to the refrigerator. Jack followed in her wake, batting at her shoes.

"And breakfast was delicious. Thanks," Grant said with a grin as he disappeared through the kitchen door. He came back with a box of folders, and began spreading piles of paper over the glossy oak table. Jessie poured fresh mugs of coffee and they each scooped up a stack and began reading.

An hour later, Arvid asked, "How about this one? A bank was robbed."

"Yes! That's exactly what we need to be looking for. Amber said she'd found a tie in with a bank robbery." Grant beamed. "Let's hear it."

Arvid crowed, scanning the paper, "By gum, you're both going to like this one, then, but especially you Jessie, 'cause you're gonna recognize a name. Wait 'til you hear."

Mrs. Cal Potts, of Shelby, Montana, was arrested earlier this week and charged with complicity in the Helena bank robbery. Gordon Harris, who was grievously wounded when apprehended in May, recuperated enough to stand trial and stated that the woman agreed to meet him at an assignation point outside of town. She was to receive, then hide, the money from

the Helena Bank and Trust. Harris alleged
that the hand-off took place.

Harris claims the two were to meet
in Dillon three weeks later to split the
money, but his partner never arrived. The
money has not been located.

At the time of the robbery, Mrs.
Potts was not married. Gordon Harris
knew her as Virginia Grayson.

"Virginia Grayson!" Jessie exclaimed, "That's the name John Running Bear gave us for the fake nun in that old St. Benedict murder. Is there a photo?"

"Nup. But this is the same name, all right," he said, beaming. "Cold case," he said to Grant. "So cold it's frozen, in fact."

He passed the article to Jessie, and as she silently read it, Arvid gave Grant the high points of their interview with John Running Bear. When he finished speaking, Jessie handed the page to the FBI agent, who skimmed it with interest.

"Wonderful," Grant said enthusiastically, "This may actually have no bearing on the Moran paintings, but let's see if we can find any follow up articles about the trial."

Thirty minutes later, Jessie announced, "Acquitted."

"Really?" Arvid sounded surprised.

"The woman was lucky. Harris died before the trial, so there went the main witness. She had the jury believing Gordon Harris fabricated the story because he was a disgruntled boyfriend. Claimed he was just angry because she'd married Cal Potts. Her story stinks."

Jessie was looking at the two men with a twinkle in her eye. Waving the article in the air like a flag, she told them, "This is the woman who masqueraded as the nun. The write-up includes a photo, and I know where there's a match!"

A few minutes later, Jack wound figure eights around their ankles as the three of them stood at the kitchen table, their eyes transfixed at the two photographs placed side by side. One showed Kate O'Bourne as a young girl in front of the St. Benedict School. In the doorway behind the little girl stood a scowling, wide-faced nun. The other picture was the black and white newspaper image of Virginia Grayson.

"It's her," Arvid said with satisfaction. "The nun and the woman in the article are the same woman."

"Yes," Grant agreed, looking up. "I agree. It's clearly Virginia Grayson Potts. All these years, and I finally see a clue—a small possible lead to the Morans."

"Think we can find out if Grayson went back to her maiden name? And had a son named Philipp?" Jessie fingered the article about the robbery.

"Of course," Grant said. "Why?"

"Kate says in her journal that the man who she was going to dinner with, Phillip Grayson, was a lot younger. She was flattered that he showed her so much attention. Maybe he was just trying to get in her good graces, to see if he could find out anything about the missing paintings. Even when Moran gave them to the school, they were valuable. Because if that was Virginia Grayson's son, I'll bet he's the one who killed Aunt Kate."

Grant stroked his chin, listening intently. "Yes, we can do a complete background check. See if she had a son. And if so, see if he lived in the area."

"By the time Kate supposedly located them for the second time, they would have been priceless. Kate was killed right after she found them. She must have spoken to someone about them. My money says she decided to ask Phillip what to do about the paintings. He was a lawyer, if I remember right."

"And with Virginia Grayson being a crook, taking the nun's place, I'll bet she was responsible for the old murder of Sister Mary Campbell," Arvid said. "You know, Jessie, I don't like this. I don't mean this." He gestured to the pile of photos. "I mean the situation."

Jessie looked at him inquiringly. Arvid met her gaze, his eyes serious in the wide, sincere face.

"I mean Amber dying after figuring this out. Then, Tommy Miller finding the two bodies at the reservoir—linked

302

to either a drug ring or someone determined to find the two paintings—and both maybe linked to Amber Reynolds. I think you should borrow my dog."

"Your dog?" Jessie laughed.

Grant did not. Grant looked at Arvid with an appreciative expression. "It's a good idea. What kind of dog is it, Arvid? And is it trained?"

"Big. And yup."

"Big and nope. I don't want a dog here with Jack. That monster of yours would have my cat for a snack." She turned to the FBI agent. "That dog is huge, Grant. And when I say huge, I mean big as a tank."

Grant grinned. "Sounds like a good plan, my man." He gave Arvid a high five.

"Oh, give it up, you two." Jessie put her hands on her hips and scowled at them. "I'm making us a new pot of coffee, feeding you some shortbread and then I'm booting you both out. You can consider yourselves wined, dined, and evicted."

Grant had driven off, after spouting what Arvid thought was utterly incomprehensible nonsense at Jessie. She laughed.

"Inside joke," Jessie told Arvid. "Grant was listing the titles of paintings with morning skies."

"Huh. And what are you going to be up to this afternoon? You got time to stop by for some target practice?" Arvid looked concerned. "If you won't take the dog, at least brush up on your shooting."

"Yeah, maybe so. I'll follow you home now, and give it an hour. Then I have a canvas calling my name. I'm going to get a small painting done if it kills me."

And then . . . then she thought she might hit the grocery store and pick up one of those *Montana Homes for Sale* brochures the realtors stacked near the carts. See if anything was listed near Russell's. Something with studio space.

Chapter 49

O'Bourne's ranch, present day
Jessie answered the insistent ringing of the front doorbell to find
Arvid on the front stoop, dressed in a plaid, short-sleeved shirt
and khaki trousers, both liberally stained with Rorschak blots
of caramel-colored paint. Jessie grinned at him by way of
greeting and stepped out onto the porch.

"Well," he said, "You shot pretty good this afternoon,
but I'm glad you changed your mind about the dog. Let's get 'er
done. I got to get back and put a second coat on the spare
bedroom. Soon's you left, Esther got me painting it what she
calls 'mocha'."

"Sounds nice. It should be easy to live with."

"Ah, looks like plain light brown to me. Kinda makes
me want a cup of coffee, but what the heck. Gotta keep her
happy. I'm slapping it on fast, since we're working on those
reservoir murders."

"I can imagine. Are you making any progress?"

"Yeah, on the walls. But on the murders, we're all
running around looking busy but nobody's coming up with
nothing."

He walked over, opened the door of his truck and an
excited Bass tumbled out. Before Arvid could grab the beast's
trailing leash, the dog bounded to greet Jessie where she stood
near the front door of the O'Bourne home. He stood on hind
legs, planted huge paws on her shoulders and slathered her

cheek with one swipe of his huge tongue before leaping backward with a puppy-like wriggle.

Grimacing, she wiped her hand across her face. "Ugh! Omigod, that's just nasty! Ick . . . liver breath. That's about changed my mind right there."

"Sorry," Arvid's contrite words didn't match his amused expression. "Your new bodyguard is a mite enthusiastic. Next time remember the commands we covered, and don't let the big guy get the upper hand. Er, paw. If Bass knocks you tuckus over teakettle . . . boy howdy, it's gonna hurt."

"Geez, I thought he was trained."

Arvid looked hurt. "Well, he is. And trained well. But he's still young, and a bit rowdy."

Jessie pulled a paper from her pocket and looked at it. "Don't worry. Next time I'll be ready. I just spaced the command for 'down' a second too long." She scanned the list of words Arvid had given her. "Hmm, yeah. Well, I'll keep the list handy until I have them down pat."

She looked up to see Bass barreling through the yard, his wondrous journey from scent to scent ending abruptly at the hollyhocks along the barn where Jack liked to hunt. He snuffed, jowls flapping, spittle flying. Nose to the ground, he tracked the tomcat back to the house and stood expectantly on the doorstep. Arvid hurriedly grabbed his leash and wrapped it several times around his tree trunk-like wrist.

"Don't we need to let him run off a bit more steam before we make the introductions?" Jessie asked.

"No, I think we're good to go. He's socialized around other animals, including cats. No worries. I won't let him get out of line."

Jessie humphed.

"I'm tellin' ya, Bass is used to our barn cats. He won't hurt Jack."

"He'd better not," Jessie said, her eyes darting to Bass's gargantuan, wrinkly head. He looked back at her, panting. A long string of drool dropped at his feet.

"Oh, blech,"

"Ja, I know. It's his one bad habit. Most Neapolitan mastiffs drool like leaky faucets. Sorry."

"I'm still not sure I need a guard dog, anyway," Jessie reiterated, "Especially not one this big that looks like he needs ironing." She looked at his resolute expression and sighed. Walking over, she opened the door and stepped into the house, followed by cop and canine. Bass and his owner reached the door at the same time, jockeying for position, each trying to squeeze through before the other. Jessie looked nervously around, hoping to locate Jack before the cat panicked.

Bass strained against the leash, toenails scrabbling on the hardwood floor, until Arvid snapped his fingers. The behemoth sat down with a solid thump, tail whipping back and forth excitedly on the oak floorboards. Then he abruptly stiffened and tilted his head, ears perked, a string of slobber hanging from the side of his mouth. He looked expectantly toward the dining room.

Through the arched doorway marched one very indignant, hissing tomcat. Jack's tail was puffed, his fur spiked up like porcupine quills, and his radar focused 100% on the home invader. "Hisssssssss."

Bass scooted backward on his rump until he bumped into Arvid's leg.

Growling, Jack came forward until he stood fearlessly in front of the dog, ears flattened against his head. He sniffed the air, mouth open, as though smelling something putrefied. Then he showed Bass his fangs and emitted a challenging, high-pitched shriek ending in several short huffs from his half-open mouth.

Bass twitched, slanting his head to avert his eyes from the cat. He leaned his wide head against his master's thigh, rolled his eyes until the whites showed, and answered Jack's yowl with a low, half-hearted, "Bufff!"

Jessie and Arvid spoke at the same instant.

"Well, I'll be damned," Arvid said.

"Jack! Behave yourself," Jessie ordered. "It's okay."

"Sssssssssssss . . . phhhhhh . . . eh, eh. . . "

"Jack, knock it off." Jessie's voice held warning.

306

The cat minced backward a short distance, eyes shifting from the dog, then to the traitorous mistress who'd allowed the interloper into his household. Jessie squatted and spoke to the big tom in low soothing tones.

"He'll be fine, I think."

Bass stood. He tilted his head upward to look at Arvid and then down to peer curiously at the cat. Jack again sniffed the air. His fur relaxed like a balloon releasing air. He purposefully walked a nonchalant, tail up semi-circle around the mastiff and his Norwegian master, then made a beeline for his food dish.

He reached the bowl, gave Jessie a last reproachful look, then hurriedly wolfed down the remaining dab of kibble.

Laughter burst from Jessie's throat.

"I don't think we have to worry about that big boy hurting my baby. In fact, Bass would get a clawful if he made a try for the cat chow."

"Huh." Arvid grunted. "You got that right. By god, that there's one intimidating ball of fur." Then he turned to Bass and patted his head, "What a wuss! Embarrassing! Totally embarrassing." Bass gave him a lolling doggy grin, plopped down on the floor with his head on his paws and peered across the kitchen at the cat.

Jack glared back through eyes closed into mere slits.

With relief, Arvid unwound some leash from his wrist, allowing Bass more slack and Bass stretched out to roll onto his back, exposing an expanse of snow-white belly flecked with pink. He rolled his head to look at Jack, and the cat sauntered over until he stood close enough to touch his small pink nose to the big black one. Then the orange tom turned his back and walked away with a haughty air, tail waving like a conquering general's flag.

"Well, all that drama, and now he's friendly?" Arvid scratched his head.

"His bowl's empty," Jessie said, grinning from ear to ear, "Nothing left to be too possessive about. And I'm starving, too, now that I think about it. How about a mid-afternoon sandwich? We sort of missed lunch." Still smiling, she turned away from Arvid. "If you'll bring in the dog food and Bass's bed, I'll make something to eat. Let's see . . . I have sweet potato chips and . . ."

Her voice trailed off as she opened the refrigerator door and pulled out dill pickles, succulent ham, lettuce and mayo, and set them on the counter. Then she grabbed a knife from the silverware drawer and opened the bread box.

"Hey, Arvid," she said with a chortle, "Do Norwegians eat Russian rye bread?

"That was pretty good shooting this afternoon," Arvid said between bites.

"It was fun. And I enjoyed watching you take Bass through his tricks."

"He's a great dog. Say, do you always shoot what they call 'cross-eye dominant'? Just now I noticed that you pour coffee and make sandwiches with your right hand, but out there shooting, I figured you for a southpaw."

"No, I'm right handed. But Dad taught me to shoot that way. My left eye wants to run the show and he said letting it would make me more accurate."

"I guess it's pretty common, people with a dominant left eye, shooting left-handed but using their right hand for nearly everything else."

"It must be. Our whole family is that way," Jessie handed him the plate of cut cheddar. "My brother Kevin had to close his right eye even to look through a spotting scope or pair of binoculars. He was right handed like me, but when it came to guns, he was such a lefty. Weird, huh?"

Arvid stopped chewing. In his mind, a loud click sounded as a missing puzzle piece snapped firmly into place.

Chapter 50

After a restless night, hearing Bass every time the dog turned over on the rug by the bed, Jessie woke groggily, with the morning stretching emptily ahead. Jessie mulled over painting possibilities near the ranch. There were picturesque areas, but the day was overcast. She wasn't in the mood for landscape painting today. What she had in mind was a portrait.

She couldn't get Minna Heron Woman out of her mind—the intelligence that radiated from the woman, her striking bone structure, the wizened face.

Jessie grabbed her camera bag, poured dog food into the massive bowl for Bass and locked him in the house. He was too big to haul in her little pickup. He'd have to stay and do guard duty.

"Deres!" She told him, hoping she had the correct Norwegian command for 'stay'. "Deres, Bass!" Probably Arvid should have given her the command for 'please, don't eat the house'.

She kidnapped Jack from the hollyhock patch, having decided it was cool enough to take him along. She carried him to her pickup, and hopped in.

On the way out of town, she stopped at the Delite Bakery and Deli and bought two loaves of artisanal bread, an assortment of cookies and a small hickory smoked ham, tossing the bags behind the driver's seat of the truck.

Forty-five minutes later, she had turned at the Bison Creek Buffalo Jerky sign, jounced over the rutted road to Minna's and congratulated herself for not getting lost as she finally pulled into the woman's driveway. Jessie waited politely in the pickup for several minutes until Minna appeared in the doorway. Then she stepped out of the truck holding a laden grocery sack and called out, "Minna, it's Jessie O'Bourne. May I come in?"

"Of course, child." The old woman waved her hand toward the door. "Come in before it rains. It's going to be a gully washer. You'll need to leave fairly soon, or the roads will be slick as ice on your way home. Clay soil gets that way. I imagine you remember."

Jessie stared at the sky in puzzlement, seeing no hint of imminent rain. She opened both windows a crack for Jack, ignoring his yowled pleas for liberation, and glanced again at the sky. There did seem to be a feeling of heaviness in the air. And no Muggs barking at her today, she noticed. She walked the short distance to the house, stepped onto the small porch and reached for the door knob.

"Where's Muggs, Minna?"

"My granddaughter took him for a short run. Thunder and lightning scare him, but if Trula runs his short little legs into exhaustion before a storm hits, then Muggs doesn't hide under the bed." She laughed.

Jessie laughed too, and then told Minna what was in the grocery bag. "I can put one of the loaves of bread in your freezer," she offered. "I brought sugar cookies and a couple raisin-filled bars. You have to taste one of those. Mmmm, they're wonderful. Besides, they'll soften you up for the favor I want to ask," Jessie said with a smile in her voice.

She looked around the room. The cabin had been thoroughly cleaned and organized since she visited with Arvid. Then her eyes narrowed. An iPad sat open on the side table, and next to the table on the floor was a leather bag, the kind she'd seen on Amber's motorcycle. A hoodie was draped over a chair—a hoodie with a recognizable logo. Jessie gave a small involuntary gasp, and Minna's rheumy eyes turned toward the sound.

"Thank you for the bread, dear, and I would love a cookie. Would you please hand me one?" Her eyes were squinting intently toward the table. "Um . . . Trula will put things away when she gets home, and she'll be here soon."

"Your granddaughter must be good help." Jessie said tightly, drawing a cookie from the sack and handing it to the old woman.

"She is. Such an angel." Minna's glance again swept the room, almost as if searching for the girl. Abruptly, her cloudy eyes swung back to Jessie. "What did you want to ask me?"

Jessie drew in a deep breath. "I wanted to ask if you'd mind if I took your photo, Minna. I would like to paint your portrait. Or perhaps do a study with you standing outside by your doorway and the red geranium pot." She paused, then added, "And I'd like to know if Monette Weber from Denver is the 'granddaughter' you have staying here."

"Why on earth would you ask that, dear?"

"There's a Denver Broncos sweatshirt draped over your chair."

"Oh, crap," Minna said in disgust. "The girl does tend to scatter her things everywhere. I thought that was a jacket, but these old eyes just couldn't see whether it was Trula's or Monette's." In a resigned tone, she added, "Well . . . take your photos first, Jessie. When they get back, we'll visit. It's Monette's story to tell, and I think it's high time she should tell it."

"All right." Jessie stood for a minute staring at the sedate old woman. She breathed slowly in and out, trying to calm herself. Then, red head temperament running true to form, she blew like Mt. St. Helens.

"Listen . . . I found a dead body on Dad's farm. I had to give up my painting time to make police statements. The window shattered on my Greyhawk, which is, by the way, my pride and joy. Our family home has been broken into, and right now I am living with a drooling dog the size of a city bus. Arvid and I have wasted a lot of time hunting for that woman and she

311

was here all the time. By god, someone is going to tell me something helpful for a change!"

She looked at Minna. The woman's mouth was hanging open in surprise, but she said nothing. Then, she closed her mouth. Her lips began to twitch.

"And on that note," Jessie went on, "I believe I'll eat the last raisin cookie. Specifically, I want you to know, so that Monette can't." She opened the sack and yanked it out, tapping her foot and stuffing large bites of filled cookie into her mouth. When the last crumb disappeared, she heaved a sigh and gave Minna a slight smile, the sudden tantrum over.

Minna smiled widely back. "They're better with hot tea, dear. Savored in small bites."

Jessie nodded sheepishly. "Hmph. Are you sure you're comfortable with my painting your picture?"

"Ehh. It doesn't matter." She cocked her head and peered birdlike at Jessie. "In fact, I'm flattered. Send an 8 x 10 of one of the photos to that old goat, John Running Bear," she said, throwing her head back and cackling uproariously. "Tell him that's all of me he's ever going to get."

Jessie began to laugh. Finally, she wiped moisture from her eyes with the tail of her T-shirt. She drew a deep breath, the tension broken. She gave Minna a tentative smile and picked up her camera.

After numerous indoor photos, the two women went outside to pose Minna by the blossoming bucket of flowers. As they stepped up on the porch to go back inside, all hell broke loose.

Muggs returned with a vengeance. He spotted Jack sitting high on the back of Jessie's driver seat and the big headed dog broadcast his discovery with Hound of the Baskerville wails.

Jack returned fire with yowls and caterwauling, interspersed with a solo of hissing as loud as punctured tractor tires.

A young Indian girl ran around and around the pickup, trying to grab Muggs the Magnificent - Protector of the

Universe. A very slight, chocolate-box pretty, blond woman stood looking unhappily toward the house, staring at Jessie.

"I think you should come in, Monette," Jessie said firmly. "And, Trula, do not let that cat out of the truck, or Jack will eat that little dog like a wafer cookie."

"And then," Monette said, "Minna told me there could be a flash flood in the gully where I was dry camping, so I needed to move. She offered me a place to stay until I decided what to do." She gestured to the girl sitting cross-legged on the floor, petting Muggs. "Trula doesn't live here. She only comes to visit after school when Minna needs her. I've tried to help out some to pay for my room and board."

"And is the iPad on the table Amber's?" Jessie asked.

"No. It's mine. But I do have Amber's. I have all her things." She sniffled and blew her nose loudly into a tissue. "Well, not her phone. I don't have her phone. I have everything that wasn't on the motorcycle. But I . . . well . . . I couldn't decide whether to bring her things to the Sheriff's Department. It seemed so dangerous."

"Why did you think going to the police was dangerous?" Jessie asked. "Are you in trouble with the cops?"

"Of course not." The blonde shot Jessie an intense look. She picked up a sugar cookie but didn't bite into it.

Minna looked calm and relaxed in her recliner. The old woman had her head tilted toward the open window, a slight look of anticipation on her face.

"Better wrap it up girls," she said softly. "Rain's coming. And it's really going to be a gully washer. Jessie has to get on the road so she can beat it back to the highway. "But, Monette, she needs to hear your story. And I think you need to tell it."

Monette sat rigidly for a minute, a stubborn expression on her face. Finally, she heaved a sigh. "Okay," she said in a quavery voice. "I'm going to trust you because Minna does, and because it might help find out who hurt Amber." Her voice caught, and her gaze locked with the old woman's. "Amber was like my sister. But telling you means I'll have to . . . well, find somewhere new to stay. I don't want to keep hiding out like a criminal, but I'm afraid to go home. And, I don't want to hang out here and make it unsafe for Minna."

"Please tell me what happened. Everything you know," Jessie said.

Monette paused, still appearing nervous. Then in her little girl voice, she began, "The night Amber was hurt, I was exhausted. I'd pulled a couple all-nighters studying for a test I had the week we left for the trip. I fell asleep at the Bed and Breakfast, and Amber didn't wake me up to go with her to the O'Bourne place." Tears filled her eyes. "I didn't even know she was going that night. She'd said she'd make an appointment for the next day."

Minna offered encouragement. "Go on, dear."

"When I finally dragged myself out of bed, I called her and it went right to voicemail. I thought maybe I hadn't heard her come in, and she'd actually gone out before I even woke up. But all day—nothing. Then I noticed I had two missed calls. There were two voicemails from her the night before. The first message said she'd found something exciting and was on her way to O'Bournes," Monette said.

"Did she say what?" Jessie asked.

Monette shook her head. "No. The next time she called, she said she'd been practically run off the road by some crazy hick town cop. Then she laughed and said, 'You'll probably have to come bail me out in the morning, Web.' Then, 'Oh Christ, it's the same cop who—' and that's where the message ended." Her breath caught, and she gulped. "I can play it for you later."

"That would be great."

"And Amber never came back to the B&B! I never saw her again. I was afraid to go to the police. I figure it's got to be a cop who killed her."

Her delicate hands covered her face and she began to sob. Her tiny frame trembled.

Compassion surged through Jessie. "I'm so sorry about your friend, Monette. It was a truly awful thing that happened to her." Then Jessie continued in a steely voice. "And I'm sorry about Amber, but you're just going to have to cowgirl up and help find out who's responsible."

Surprise rounded the girl's eyes at Jessie's tone. It was the same look of incredulity Jessie had seen before on the faces of spoiled, lovely women used to getting their own way, and were shocked when their charms didn't work. That 'poor helpless little me' look probably worked ninety-nine percent of the time on the opposite sex.

"Surely you don't think I can go to the police, Jessie."

"Yeah, I do. Not to the Sheriff's Department, though. I have a good friend who's a cop. We're both going to have to trust him, Monette," Jessie said firmly. Then she thought of Grant. "Actually, I have two friends. One is FBI."

"FBI?"

"Yes." Jessie stood. She glanced at Minna, who nodded her head slightly. "I am assuming Monette's motorcycle is in your back shed. Can she leave it there for a few days?"

When Minna nodded her assent, Jessie looked back at the tiny blonde. "Get your bag."

Shortly after the little red truck pulled out of Minna's driveway, the grumble and growl of distant thunder sounded and the plop of fat raindrops hitting the windshield and truck roof followed. Soon, the rain began to slough down like buckets of water tossed from a second story window.

Jessie silently cussed the weatherman.

That darn old Koot Lundgren. I'm gonna paint his portrait with him as an old bulldog holding an umbrella on a sunny day.

She gave a slow, easy press to the brake, to judge how slick the road had become. The truck's rear gave a slight fishtail, and Jessie pulled it back into the right lane. Bad. It was getting bad. Ten minutes later, the rural road had become as slick as ice.

"It's a dirt road," Monette said, "Why is it so slippery?"

"Well, there's dirt roads and there's gravel roads in rural Montana, and believe me, they are worlds apart when it comes to safe driving in wet weather. This road's just hard packed dirt."

"Why don't they fix it?"

"The reservation doesn't have enough money for good maintenance, so they haven't put much gravel on it. No gravel— no tire traction." Gaze centered on the road, she continued, "Rain doesn't absorb very fast into the clay surface, so instead of getting a muddy road, we get a slimy skating rink."

"It's scary."

"Yes. I hate driving on them when they're like this." Jessie clenched her jaw.

"Better you than me." Monette shuddered.

"Ooh," Jessie said, her voice oozing sarcasm "Thanks."

"I've never driven on a road quite like this. I'm so glad I'm not trying it on my motorcycle."

"Don't worry, we'll be fine," Jessie said with a confidence she didn't feel. *I hate these snotty roads! Please Lord, please, please, let me get to the highway without a disaster.*

Her hands white-knuckled on the steering wheel, Jessie saw a cattle-truck coming from the other direction, and she groaned inwardly. As it approached, she instinctively steered the pickup slightly farther toward the right side of the wet road. Her right tires spun onto the slime-thick shoulder, and Monette squealed. Jack hissed.

Jessie held the little pickup straight, straddling the side of the road and edge of the barrow pit until she could slowly encourage it back onto the useless road.

She furrowed her brow as she tried to remember any washes or gullies between their present location and the beginning of the state highway. Water could fill those dips in the terrain with little or no warning in this area, the rain swelling and overflowing creek beds until flash floods whipped through the low spots like water directed into a gutter off a sloping roof. People who didn't respect the forces of nature had been swept away in their vehicles. Some had drowned.

With relief, Jessie realized she had already traversed the worst low spots, albeit with more fishtails than you'd find at Fisherman's Wharf in San Francisco. She forced herself to relax. Glancing to the side, she gave a reassuring smile to the

316

tiny blonde buckled into the passenger seat. Monette was practically squeezing the life out of a complaining Jack.

"I think you'd better ease up a little on the cat. You're giving poor Jack a waistline."

Monette flushed and released her hold on the tom, who then settled without rancor onto her lap and began to knead her thighs with his front paws.

"Sorry. It's been a tense week," she said in a tremulous voice.

"I imagine so," Jessie said, "We're lucky there aren't any cows on the road today. My dad says they know when a big storm is coming and head for higher ground. They have more smarts than folks give them credit for." She shrugged her shoulders. "Or maybe just good instincts."

"I'm so glad I didn't stay camped in the gully." Monette stared out the passenger window at the deluge. "It's probably flooding. I probably owe Minna my life."

"Could be. Now, help me keep an eye out for livestock. This is 'free-range'. That means the stock isn't confined by fences on the reservation. There's a giant of a bull roaming loose in the hills around here, too, a monster that I'd sure hate to run into. He'd flatten us like a tortilla."

Ten minutes later the rain had stopped and the truck pulled onto nice, solid asphalt. Jessie gratefully turned the little vehicle back toward Sage Bluff. She hadn't realized she'd actually been holding her breath until she let it out with a deep, relieved sigh.

The sky was phenomenal, dusky blues and stormy grey swirling into a maelstrom of color. Her fingers itched for a canvas and brushes, but she forced her mind away from the distraction and kept her eyes on the road. By the time she pulled the Ford pickup into O'Bourne's barn and folded the seat forward to help Monette retrieve her bag and the leather satchel, the satchel that held Amber's iPad and extra research, the sky was beginning to clear.

Monette and Jack walked out of the barn and waited as Jessie grabbed the new padlock from a hook near the open doorway. She stepped through, slid the barn door shut and pushed it hard, until the heavy duty hasp could be slipped over the U-shaped connection. Slipping the padlock on, she snicked it closed and yanked, making sure it had locked.

They walked to the house with Jack padding behind, the odor of rain-soaked earth and the sweet smell of sage redolent in the air.

Chapter 51

Arvid sat behind his oversized oak desk. After leaving Jessie's, he'd hit the speed dial for Russell and asked him to meet him at the station. He had walked to his office with a heavy heart, went directly to his filing cabinet and pulled the folder he'd kept that covered Kevin O'Bourne's accident. He opened it and looked at the photos. Then, without hesitation, he pulled his pistol, thumbed the safety off, sat, and placed it on his lap out of sight.

Russell walked in and Arvid motioned for the younger man to sit.

"What the heck? You've been out running around all day when we're trying to solve this Cassy Adams case, and now here you are sitting in the office on your big behind." Russell was only half joking. Then the grave look on his partner's face registered. Russell dropped into the extra chair. "You were going out to Jessie's this morning. Is she—"

"Jessie's fine."

"K.D.?"

"Everybody's fine."

"Then what's up?"

Arvid slid the folder across the desk. Russell opened it. "Kevin? I'm certain that Chief Phillips closed that case and—"

"So let's talk hypothetically, Russell. Let's go back a few years and revisit that barn out at O'Bourne's. You see, I learned a few new things about Kevin O'Bourne this week. The first is

319

that he left a son behind. One that has a smile just like his sister Jessie's."

"But—"

"Let me talk. The most important thing I learned was something I found out just today."

"Just spit it out, then," Russell said angrily.

"Kevin was right handed, but he shot like a southpaw."

Russell sat perfectly still. The anger vanished from his face. Then he jumped to his feet, his face ashen. "No, that can't be!" Then he froze.

Arvid had the semi-automatic pistol leveled at his chest.

"You know, you've been like a son to me. But you're going to sit down again. We're going to have us a confab. And until I'm satisfied with what you have to say, you ought to sit very still and make no sudden moves. In fact, take your gun belt off carefully, put it on the floor and slide it slowly under the desk with your foot."

Russell did so, then eased back into the seat.

"I didn't hurt him. And that just can't be. Kevin—"

"Ask Jessie. She told me once when we were just gabbing, that target shooting was the one thing Dan O'Bourne never taught you. You must've learned it all during your police training."

"Yeah." Russell said huskily, then cleared his throat. "Yes, that's true."

"And today, Jess O'Bourne sat across from me at the table and we were talking target shooting, and she says to me, 'My brother was right-handed, but with anything involving guns, he was a southpaw'."

Russell looked dumbstruck. "Good Lord. Cross-eye dominant. He must have been cross-eye dominant."

"Yep. That is correct. Now, let's talk. Do you need to look at the photos from Kevin's 'accident'? To refresh your memory? The photos that show Kevin shot in his right temple, the gun flung from his right hand, as though he'd fallen and shot himself, accidental like? "

Russell covered his face with his hands. "Oh, God."

"We can make it hypothetical if you want. Hypothetically, if someone wanted murder to look like an accident, of course, it would be smart to place the weapon by the correct hand."

Behind his hands, Russell made a gagging sound.

"Now," Arvid went on, "The photos of Kevin show that he could have shot himself, if he had just been a right-handed shooter. But nope. He wasn't. So, hypothetically, what do you think?

Russell sat still as stone. Then he lowered his hands and shuddered. He took a deep breath and then heaved a sigh.

"Hypothetically, maybe a good friend, maybe even a cop who thought of Kevin as a brother, could have found him dead in the barn. It looked like an obvious suicide. Maybe that cop could have altered the scene. Made it look accidental. An accident is a tragedy, but suicide . . . now, suicide is something altogether different. It's not only heart wrenching, but a parent and sibling always wonder if they failed that person."

"Of course, tampering with evidence would be illegal," Arvid said. "It would ruin that person's career if it was ever found out."

"Hypothetically, maybe that person put Hannah and Dan and, yes, Jessie O'Bourne before that career. And that cop made a mistake fixing it to look like an accident, because he found the gun in the wrong hand and didn't know Kevin shot like a southpaw." Russell gulped.

"No, son. You're not quite following my train of thought here. If that weapon was already placed by the wrong side of Kevin's body, it was originally a *murder* made to look like a suicide.

Russell gaped at him. "No, Arvid. Oh, no. Murder?"

"Yeah. So by moving the weapon yet again, the murder was made to look like an accident," Arvid said. "And now the trail is colder than an Eskimo's bare behind on a snowy day. But at least that hypothetical cop isn't a murderer."

Russell stared at him in mute misery.

Arvid heaved a deep sigh, stood, put the safety on and holstered his gun. "But why? Why did you think Kevin capable of suicide?"

"He was depressed because of Trish and Hannah. It was the only reason I could think of."

"Hannah?"

"Drugs. Kevin had just found out Trish was hooked on prescription drugs and so was Hannah. Oxycodone. Kevin blamed himself because it was his girlfriend who got his mother hooked on the drug, supplying it for her long after Hannah's doctor refused to write a prescription. Hannah broke her collarbone and injured her rotator cuff the year before. She'd been on pain pills and was finding it hard to get off of them. Harder and harder, she told me." He paused. "I took a pill from her prescription bottle once and took it in to the pharmacist. I asked him what the dose was."

"And?"

"God, Arvid. It was twice what was listed on the pill bottle. Hannah denied that she knew. She said that dosage couldn't possibly be correct. She told Kevin that Trish had picked up her last few prescriptions for her."

"Ah, hell."

"When Kevin heard Trish been supplying his mother with the Oxycodone, he went ballistic. He swung by and picked me up and we went right to Trish and confronted her. She wouldn't tell us who gave her the drugs, but she admitted that she hadn't gotten them from a pharmacy. Her own drug supplier threatened to cut her off if she didn't follow orders, and her orders were to keep getting Hannah her filled bottles of Oxy. Kevin and I asked her why. And Trish said we'd never understand. It was someone unbalanced who hated Kevin's mother."

Arvid scowled, but motioned for Russell to continue.

"We had a huge fight over getting them both, Hannah and Trish, into rehab. Kevin was more upset than I'd ever seen him. Later, he told me that when he talked to Trish in private, she said something that made him think whoever gave her the drugs set out to specifically make Hannah an addict. Even after

322

that, Kevin blamed himself." Russell stared at Arvid, his eyes full of sorrow.

"Go on, Russell."

"When I found him, I was horrified. It looked like suicide. I'm so, so sorry. I couldn't let Dan and Hannah . . . I couldn't let Jess . . ." He put his face in his hands. "Six years. Because of me, someone got away with murder for six years. "

Arvid stood, picking up the folder from the desk. He stared at it, slapping it into his hand a couple times, chewing his lip as he did so.

"What are you going to do?"

"It was just a hypothetical conversation, like I said. After all, the case is closed." He pulled open the drawer of the filing cabinet and shoved the paperwork in. Then he bent down, pulled Russell's gun belt from under the desk and handed it to him.

Russell looked at the big Norwegian, a hopeful expression on his face.

"But just because it's closed, don't mean that person ain't still out there. Something to solve, whether the case is hypothetical or not," Arvid growled.

Russell's voice was raspy. "You aren't turning me in?"

"I think you acted like a damn fool. But I don't think you could afford K.D.'s drawing paper if I turned you in. So no. I don't guess so. I'm going to trust my gut on this one. I always tell Esther that what's legal isn't always ethical and what's ethical ain't always legal. I got to say that in your case, that seems to fit."

Russell looked down at his shoes and heaved a sigh of relief. Then he put his palms up, covered his face again, and muffled a sob.

"But somehow, this is tied together with what's been happening lately," Arvid was mumbling, rubbing a hand over the stubble on his chin, giving Russell a chance to pull himself together. "I just can't get a handle on why I think that, but I do. Kevin, Amber, Cassy, Travis Simpson, the paintings and the drugs. It's all about money."

Russell raised his head, eyes wet. "And Hannah, too. And Trish. They're also connected, I think. I've been more of a fool than you know, Arvid. Dan O'Bourne called me today."

"So?"

"Jess found out about K.D. and called Dan. Then Dan called me. He suspected K.D. was his grandson from the very first, and he just wanted me to know he's been sending K.D. a birthday present every year."

"What's that mean? You trying to tell me something? If you are, spit it out."

"I thought Trish was sending those packages. Now that I know different, I wonder if we need to add Trish to the list."

"The list of deaths?"

"I'm afraid so. She was so nervous after K.D. was born. I just figured it was normal for women to be emotional after having a baby. I mean, what the heck do I know about it? Trish planned to leave K.D. with me all along. We discussed it."

"Hmph. A new baby, and she was planning on just leaving it?"

"It wasn't exactly a motherly attitude was it? But, since that's what we'd planned, why sneak off? Why not just say goodbye and get on a bus? I couldn't find any inkling of how she left town, Arvid. Not a whisper."

"She have any money?"

"I think she only had a few bucks. I'd just given her some and she'd blown it on girl stuff. You know, a manicure, clothes. But don't get me wrong, it wasn't a lot. She was afraid of what she'd spend it on if I gave her much. After the rehab, she really did want to stay clean. She just didn't trust herself to do it if she had the money for drugs."

"Huh," Arvid said.

"She promised she'd check in once in a while and find out how K.D. was doing. Looking back, it was silly of me to assume those packages were from her. Every year I wondered why there was no note. Why didn't she include anything personal in the package? How come she didn't let me know she was okay? Or at least ask about K.D.?"

Russell pushed his fingers through his brown hair in agitation. "Now that we suspect someone fixed Kevin's murder to look like suicide, I wonder if Trish ran off after all. Someone could have made it appear that way. Arvid, I don't want to even say it."

"She might be dead."

"Yeah," Russell said softly. "She's probably dead."

They sat, regarding each other in silence. "You didn't have a real marriage, then, did you, Russ?"

Russell threw his head up, startled at the question.

"Hey, I'm not trying to pry, but where'd she sleep? Where'd she keep her things?"

"Spare room," Russell said sheepishly. "Actually, we weren't even very good friends, let alone lovers. We had tolerated each other because of Kevin, but she knew how I felt about druggies."

"If someone else cleared out her stuff, any chance there might still be some fingerprints? Fingerprints can last thirty years if they're on the right surface."

Russell's expression brightened. "Arvid, you genius! I'm a lousy housekeeper. Trish had the small room that connected to K.D.'s. I've been using it as a storeroom for outgrown clothes and toys ever since she took off. I never saw anybody else at the house, but we could check her room for prints. You never know."

"A genius, huh? Maybe I got me one of those Mensa IQs. Yeah, I'd better get a bigger cap to keep all these brains in."

Russell looked at his watch. "We're supposed to meet Samuelson and another DEA man in half an hour to go over everything we've found about the reservoir murders. Actually, not found. Our results have been pretty much diddly. It will be more of a brainstorming session. I asked them to meet us in my office. You were planning to be there, weren't you?"

"Yup."

Russell nodded. "I'll get through the meeting, but after work I'm going to take time to treat that little room at the house as a fresh 'missing person' scene. Will you help me dust it for prints?"

"Sure."

"And Arvid," Russell said looking embarrassed. "Getting that hypothetical issue off my chest has given me a new lease on life. I'm sorry. I'm so sorry . . . and I . . . thank you for giving me a second chance to make this right. I know it isn't what I deserve."

"Is this mess why you've never made an effort with Jessie, Russ? I'm Norwegian, not blind, you know. Any fool can see how you feel about her."

"There are so many reasons. The main reason is that I haven't been able to get a proper divorce, because I can't find Trish. But that was only one of them," Russell said quietly. "I was afraid I'd somehow let something slip, and Jessie would find out that Kevin's death was a suicide. Or that her mother was addicted to Oxycodone. Besides, she wouldn't be satisfied to live in Sage Bluff."

Arvid listened, but said nothing.

"And now it's murder. How can I tell her Kevin was murdered? How can I admit that I screwed up so bad that the trail is not just cold, but so cold it's icy?" Russell's eyes were again moist with tears. "He was like a brother, and now I understand just how badly I failed him. Not just him. The whole family. And I promised Dan I wouldn't let Jessie know about Hannah's trouble."

The air in the room was still, humid. Even after more than a week, the pungent aroma of varnish lingered to remind those who entered that there were still such things as real wood floors. The two men sat in silence.

Then Arvid said, "That was dumb. That was almost as dumb as tampering with evidence. Do you and Dan O'Bourne really think so little of Jessie, Russ?"

"So little? No, we both think the world of Jess."

"Huh. You both sell her short, is what you do. That girl's made of good, strong stuff. And I'm thinking you love her. Or maybe you only think you do."

"Yeah, I won't deny it. But she's too sensitive to everything around her. She'd break apart like high-tempered glass dropped on concrete trying to cope with something like that."

Arvid snorted and looked at Russell with an expression bordering on disgust.

"Seems to me that you're the one who broke apart, Russ. You gave up your ethics. Even if it was in a misguided attempt to protect people you care about. You give up your self-respect when your ethics go out the window."

Russell looked down at his boots, a shamefaced expression on his face. "I know. You're right. I've despised myself for the past six years, wondered how to fix things, but I was afraid whatever I did would mean I'd lose K.D. And Jessie—"

"Hogwash. I'm going to say it once, then I'm not going to bring it up again. That redheaded gal is stronger than most people and you're doing her a disservice by not being straight with her. And so is Dan O'Bourne."

"You don't know her—"

"I do," Arvid interrupted, "I do know her. Hmph. Strange how I only met her a week or so ago, and I'm thinkin' I know her better than either one of you."

He levered his bulk out of the chair and stood, shaking his head at Russell's surprised look.

"I'm going for coffee. Some decent stuff, not Blanche's hogwash. I'll bring back four go-cups and a bag of donuts and haul 'em to your office. Should be right on time to meet Samuelson."

Russell was half out of his chair when the phone rang on Arvid's desk.

Arvid snagged it, automatically answering with a gruff, "Sage Bluff Sheriff's Office. Abrahmsen speaking."

His mouth dropped open as he listened.

"Uh huh. Uh huh. Well, I'll be damned. Thank you. Yes, we'll be down." Stunned, he replaced the receiver. Then he did a little twisting dance and pumped his fist in the air. Then he

327

grabbed the phone again and furiously began to punch in numbers.

"What is it? What's happened?"

"I've gotta call Esther. Won't know 'til next week if we won, but we're finalists in the mailbox contest!"

Arvid set the tray of coffee and donuts on Russell's massive, oak desk as Samuelson made the introductions.

"This is Mark Brookes. He'll be helping with the case."

Brookes was a short man whose receding hairline gave his forehead the appearance of an empty stage with the curtain rising. He nodded to both lawmen, shaking each of their hands formally before sitting down.

"Looks like we might need as much help as we can round up," Arvid began.

Samuelson grimaced. "Not a lot to go on, is there? I'd hoped there'd be more progress by now."

"Yes," Brookes agreed. "We hoped for more."

Russell nodded. "All we know for certain is that the bullet was from a 22 pistol. We think Cassy and Travis knew the person who shot them. At least one of them knew the shooter. The crime scene showed no sign of a struggle. Ballistics and blood spatter both indicate that Cassy and Travis were just sitting there and someone in the back seat blew a hole in first Cassy's head, then swung the pistol and shot Travis in the forehead as he turned toward the backseat. We suspect it was pure surprise, but we have no way of knowing."

"One shot for each person," Samuelson said thoughtfully. "Pretty efficient. Yes, perhaps someone they trusted." He looked at the file on his lap, reading through the notes on Arvid's interview with Jensen at the firehouse. "My guess is the shooter was probably known to Cassy Adams, since Travis hadn't been in the area long."

"Has the reservoir been searched for the pistol?" Brookes chimed in.

"Yeah," Russell said. "A recovery diver drove down from Billings. He had a nasty job to do, believe me, since the reservoir is full of old scrap metal. If it's in there, the diver didn't find it."

"Your report states that the fingerprints found match those of Travis, Cassy and a couple of her relatives. Did any of the handles look wiped?"

"Yep, both back door handles were clean of prints, if you check the next page," Russell said. "Wiped for sure."

"Hmmm," Samuelson rubbed the back of his neck. "Both handles. Could have been two people involved in the shooting then."

Brookes nodded.

"Possible, yes." Arvid reached for a donut. "In fact, I'd bet on it.

"What about those shoes found in the Fire Station locker? You say they were too large to be Cassy's? That's odd. I don't like odd." Samuelson's shrewd eyes looked up from the file. "But odd might give us a lead."

Brookes, a bobble-head doll of a man, again nodded his agreement. Both he and Samuelson looked at Arvid.

"I went down to the Fire Station after the bodies were found and removed them. Baker photographed the items, and she and Lenny are looking into it. Shoes are shoes. Nobody pays much attention. The labels were too worn to tell if they're men's or women's. We're guessing women's because of the silver charm found in one of them."

"Charm? I didn't see the shoes, or the photos yet. Arvid," Russell said. "You have the pics there?"

"In the file here," Samuelson said, turning pages while he listened to Arvid.

"The charm was wrapped in tissue and stuffed into the toe of one of the shoes. It's in the evidence locker if you want to see it," Arvid said to Samuelson. "What our small town station calls an evidence locker, anyway. It's actually a spare closet. Best we can do. Anyway, it's a large, heart shaped charm. It's—"

"You never mentioned that before," Russell interrupted. "Let me see those photos." He reached for the folder, practically snatching it from Samuelson's hands as the FBI agent and other two men looked at him in surprise.

"A heart shaped charm—" Russell flipped through the folder until he came to the page that listed the photos. "Where're the other pictures?" he asked frantically.

"Baker has them. She's making duplicates so she and Lenny can take them around to Cassy's acquaintances to see if anyone recognizes them."

"I've been working from the Travis Simpson angle. What size are the shoes, Arvid? You say they're tennis shoes?"

"Yep. Running shoes. Large. There's a stain on them we missed before. We sent them to the lab to see if the stain was blood. It was."

"Were they in a duffel bag?" Russell's voice was strained, intense.

"Yeah, like a gal might carry to a laundromat or pack for an overnight stay."

"Color? What color is the bag?"

"Pink, and—"

Russell was on his feet and walking quickly out the door. Samuelson, Arvid and Brookes looked at each other, brows raised, then stood and followed him down the hall. Russell headed for the spare room with the evidence closet and yanked a key from the jangle on his keychain. He unlocked the door and stepped in, looking at the shelf where a pink duffle bag sat, encased in a large, clear sack. Next to the duffle was a pair of shoes, likewise bagged. Russell ignored the shoes and looked at the last sack containing the silver charm.

"Oh, no," Russell groaned, putting a hand on his head and pushing his fingers through his hair. "Oh, no. Oh, no."

Arvid gripped his shoulder. "You okay?"

"These were Trish's. Not the shoes, but the duffel and charm.""

"Aw, Russ," Arvid said doubtfully. "How can you be sure? It's been over six years since you even saw her, let alone any of her things."

"No, I'm sure. It's Trish's charm. I was with Kevin when he bought it for her. She wore it all the time, not on a chain around her neck. She wore it slipped onto her tennis shoe laces."

"A lot of women might've had the same charm."

"The duffel looks like the one she had, too. I don't think she abandoned K.D., after all."

"Who exactly is Trish? And what's going on?" Samuelson asked.

"Well," Arvid said. "It's a long story. I sure can't see how it ties in but let's go back to the office, and we'll fill you in."

"Some perps like to use the same locations," Brookes said. "If you think these items definitely belonged to your wife, perhaps it would be a good idea to have a cadaver dog search the reservoir area where the body of our agent was found."

"Give me a break, Agent Brookes," Russell said. "It's been years since Trish disappeared. It's way too late for something like that."

"No," Samuelson broke in, "Brookes has a point. Some well-trained dogs can find remains even thirty years later. That's a proven fact. If your hunch is right and the deaths of the EMT and Travis Simpson are linked to the past, it may be worth the expense of hiring a handler and cadaver dog. Why would Miss Adams have clothes—the clothing of someone who supposedly left the area years ago—locked up in her personal space at the firehouse?"

"Well, that's the million dollar question, isn't it?" Russell looked thoughtful.

"Heck, we don't have any good leads on the current deaths, either, Russ," Arvid said. "Why not give it a shot?"

"In fact, DEA will pick up the expense of the dog since we're working on the murder of one of our own," Samuelson offered. "You need Tony Fiske out of Ogden. He's got a dog that is outstanding. Big golden retriever." He pulled out his cell phone, punched in some numbers and handed the phone to Russell.

"Piece of cake for a good cadaver dog, but I can't get there until the day after tomorrow," Fiske said. "Sorry." The groan of heavy machinery working in the background nearly drowned out the handler's voice.

"We don't even know if it's worthwhile to search the reservoir area. She disappeared nearly six years ago," Russell said. "I guess the search can wait until Friday. Is it still possible to locate remains after that long?"

"Man, didn't I just say that? This dog can find anyone—after thirty years—more than ten feet down. No sweat, man. If she's there, Kaz will find her."

"Then we'll see you and your dog at Sage Bluff's Sheriff's Office on Friday," Russell said. "You're almost as far as Salt Lake City, aren't you?"

"Yeah. A little less. I'll probably fly out of Salt Lake though."

"Can you make it by early afternoon?"

"Yeah, that's cool," Fiske said, "Damn. Gotta go. They found a kid."

A shiver ran down Russell's spine as he handed the cell phone back to the DEA agent.

"Thanks. I appreciate your help with this, Agent Samuelson. We don't have anyone local for such specialized tasks. We have a couple people we can call for search and rescue operations, but none trained in cadaver hunts."

"Let's drop the 'agent this' and 'agent that'," Samuelson said. "Just plain Ron and Mark will do."

"Fine by me," Russell said. "Russell, or Russ, is good."

"Arvid," Arvid said.

"Aaah, a good old-fashioned, Swedish name," Brookes said.

"Hmph," Arvid said with disgust. "Nup. Not quite."

Chapter 52

Sage Bluff, Montana, present day

"Follow the thread," Grant Kennedy said into the phone. "Find out if there are relatives in the area. Find out if there was a subsequent charge of any kind against her."

"And? Or is that all?" The woman on the other end sighed. She was used to Grant's overconfidence in her abilities. She looked up at the clock. Nearly six, D.C. time. *Makes it only four in the afternoon there in Montana. The hunk probably spaced the time difference—again. It would be sheer bliss to be able to go home on time for a change, maybe soak in a hot bath with a glass of moscato.*

"No, Kara. Try to find out whether any of the money ever surfaced."

"Well, that might be asking the impossible. It's been so long."

"Do your best. I know it isn't likely you can discover that after all these years, but it's worth a shot. Oh . . . and find out if Virginia Grayson had a son."

So much for the hot bath and vino, she thought. *At least it was a job for a sweet guy like Grant instead of the wrinkled old Mr. Fletcher. Fletcher, the lecher. Hmmm. Now, if their attitudes were only reversed . . . oh well.*

"And Kara?" Kennedy asked.

"Yes?"

"Thanks so much. I forgot about the time difference. I imagine you were ready to call it a night."

"Oh, not at all, Mr. Kennedy," she lied. "Not at all." She rubbed her temples. *Ah, but those bubbles and bubbly are so calling my name.*

"I owe you one, then, Kara. Next time I get to D.C., I'll bring you a bottle of five star wine from the vineyard in Missoula. Get this . . . they're located on Rattlesnake Drive. Hilarious address, but the wine is superb. Award winning."

"I look forward to that, sir." *Montana wine from Rattlesnake Drive*, she thought. *The smart-aleck. Who does he think he's kidding?*

Chapter 53

O'Bourne's ranch, present day

Grant wasn't pleased. He held up Amber's iPad. "I feel like an idiot. Jessie mentioned cloud storage quite some time ago. I should have had one of our tech guys hack into Amber's account even before we found the iPad. "

"Yes," Monette swung her head, giving her hair a flirty flip. "The cloud storage should have it all. Her notes. Her schedule. Where she went. Who she interviewed. Everything from this past trip. Amber put everything, even audio interviews she did using her iPhone, into cloud storage."

The introduction of Monette to Arvid and Grant had taken place over breakfast. It had not been a great meeting. Arvid was upset she hadn't come forward earlier, and in his blunt way, read her the riot act. Monette was so busy trying to charm Grant that it was hard for her to stay on topic.

Jessie sat, stroking Jack's fur and curiously watching the woman interact with the two men. Monette was, as Shelly Reynolds had said, a man-killer. She was the kind of woman who wore jeans with sparkly bling on the back pockets. You couldn't trust women who drew bulls-eyes on their tush, Jessie decided. She sure didn't fit the image of the computer geek she was purported to be. And you would think, since the Web had so recently lost her best friend, that she could concentrate on finding out who killed her instead of putting so much energy into flirting.

335

"Just so we're clear, I got no clue what you two brains are talking about," Arvid was saying. "I fish. I don't play on the computer. So give me a run-down in plain English."

Monette batted long lashes at him. "Think of it like a bank's safe-deposit box. Instead of being stored on her own computer, Amber's data is stored at an internet site—a hosting company." Monette wiggled long, delicate fingers. "In the cloud." She glanced at Grant. "I can figure out her ID and password, I think." She sashayed over to the coffee pot and poured herself half a cup of deep mountain roast, sparkles swaying as she walked by the FBI agent.

"I imagine her account will be password protected, though, right?" Jessie tried to keep the annoyance out of her voice.

"Yes, but Amber was pretty predictable. I can make some educated guesses. If it works, I can save you some time. If I can't figure it out, ask one of Grant's FBI geeks to use software to unencrypt and display her password." Monette sat on the edge of a chair, crossed her legs and swung her sandal-clad foot. Her toenails were polished the color of huckleberry jam, the shoe studded with rhinestones.

The mannerism made Jessie think of a cobra, mesmerizing its potential victim. Back and forth, up and down. Grant, she noticed, could not keep his eyes off that tiny, swinging foot.

"Of course, we could use my phone to locate hers if you want." Monette looked smug.

"Well, jeez Louise." Arvid crossed his arms over his broad chest. "Why didn't you say something before?"

Monette gave him a contemptuous look. "Nobody asked me. How was I supposed to know the cops didn't have her stored research or her phone? Or even wanted it? Her phone wasn't at the B&B when I gathered her things, and I knew she'd taken it along when she left. I figured the cops had it, but anyone even slightly competent on the computer would know to check the cloud." She looked apologetically at Grant. "The phone and laptop sync. Amber has them set to share important information like scheduled meetings. You know, like her calendar."

Arvid grimaced. "She might not have had time to make a record of the last day, I guess, either."

"Well, let's take a look." Monette put her mug on the table and held out her hand for Amber's iPad. "I'm sure her email will be the ID. If I can't guess the password, we can have a link sent to that email address and use that link to change her password. Let's see if it still has a charge."

"Wait a minute. You said they sync?" Arvid held up his hand, palm out. "Don't touch it, Monette. I think we'd better hope the battery's dead. We need to think about this. Will her iPad display the last time the files were accessed?"

"Yes." Monette stared at Arvid with grudging respect.

Grant rubbed his chin thoughtfully. "Someone must have her phone. Now, if we access schedules and files on her iPad, they'll know we've found the iPad, probably know we found you, too. And they'll suspect we know who she saw on that last day."

"That's right." Her face was pale. "Thank you for stopping me."

"Do you know if Amber's iPad uses software that would locate her phone?"

"No, it doesn't." Monette smiled. "But mine does . . . Amber was always misplacing her phone and used the 'find my friends' app on mine to find it."

Arvid half stood in alarm. "I hope that they haven't already started tracking you."

"We're good. I don't keep that feature turned on." She grinned. "Too many snoops."

"Great! We can take your phone to the station, turn that feature on, and search for hers. Before we go, let's hear that message you said was on your phone, Monette."

The voice of Amber Reynolds came across as clearly as though she sat next to them at the O'Bourne's kitchen table. They huddled, their chairs pulled close together, listening to the voicemail message. The last few words were garbled.

"One. She's saying 'one'," Arvid insisted.

337

"Or 'bum'," Grant suggested. "Maybe even 'dumb'."

"No. Turn it up and play it again." Jessie leaned forward. "I think the men are wrong. But the last word sounds like 'curly' to me."

"Geez." Arvid scratched his head. "I hope it's not Lenny. His hair's curly. 'Course, Lenny ain't so big. She definitely says the cop is big."

"Maybe it isn't anyone from the Sage Bluff's Sheriff's Office," Grant said. "What other law enforcement do you have out here?"

"State Highway Patrol, but we hardly ever even see them," Arvid said. "We have some reservists that work for the Sheriff's Office, but none of them are big men. Baxter might have some big fellows on their payroll, though, too. Might not be anyone from our own office." He sighed.

"Hmm." Grant tapped his finger on the table. "Monette, thanks for coming forward with this. You knew Amber's voice. We don't. What do you think she is saying at the end of the message?"

"Well, yeah, I knew her voice, but I still can't tell. She must have taken off her helmet."

Grant looked at her quizzically. "So?"

"It was Bluetooth compatible. Her phone might even have been in her pocket. She didn't have to be holding it near her mouth to be heard. You know, like a car recognizes a Bluetooth phone?"

"Too advanced for this electronic dinosaur," Arvid grumbled.

Monette sent Arvid a glance full of pity and exasperation. Then she shook her head, the blond curls shimmering with a life of their own. She leaned over, adjusted the volume, then again touched the play arrow.

'Monette, I know you're wasted after the long drive, so I didn't want to wake you, but I found out something important. I'm on my way to O'Bourne's right now hoping someone's home. I can hardly wait to tell you—

What the hell? Someone's trying to run me off the road . . . Oh, flashers—for god's sake, it's some hick town cop! I don't think

338

I was speeding, but I'd better pull over. Yeah, it IS a cop. You'll probably have to come and bail me out in the morning. Christ, it's that same big . . . one . . . curly . . . weird. What the—"

Jessie looked at Arvid. The big Norwegian had become a solid friend in the short time she'd known him. But he *was* big. Surely her instincts weren't that far off. Besides, Arvid had been out of town. A chill crawled up Jessie's spine. No, she thought. Not Arvid. But something stuck in the back of her mind, a niggling feeling that she was missing something important.

"One more time, please, Monette. Then I'll dish coffee cake and ice cream."

Monette pressed play and everyone tensed their shoulders and leaned in toward the voice. Again, each thought they heard a different word.

"It's hopeless." Monette threw her hands in the air. "I give up."

The other listeners nodded, their expressions echoing Monette's frustrated tone.

"Grant, you said you know someone who can enhance the sound." Jessie's gaze swiveled to Arvid. "Can he borrow the phone?"

Arvid gave a grunt. "Nup. Evidence in an ongoing investigation. And since any cop may be a suspect, and since Monette trusted me with it, nobody else on the Sage Bluff force is hearing this either."

"But how about Russ?"

Arvid swiveled his head and gave Jessie the fish-eye. "Oh, for Pete's sake," she said in a disgusted tone, glaring back at him.

"No, Jessie, he's right." Grant was staring at Arvid. "So. You don't want any of the other Sage Bluff cops to hear that message. At least not until there is a viable suspect. What if we forward it to my tech guy and to Samuelson, with a request to keep it under wraps, and you keep possession of a recording of the original?" Grant asked.

Arvid leaned back in his chair, closing his eyes and crossing his arms. "Yeah. I guess. Let's do it. But I keep the original. Your guy only gets a copy."

With a slight nod of acquiescence toward the big cop, Grant rose to help Jessie. He pulled the dessert plates from a high cupboard shelf, while she cut generous slices of Cowboy Coffee Cake. As she stood at the counter, Jack did a figure eight around Jessie's ankles and then posed expectantly by his food dish. Bass rolled his eyes to focus on the cat, but his massive head continued to rest on his master's boot.

"I'd be glad to write out a receipt for it—straight from the FBI to Sage Bluff's P.D.," Grant offered. "That help?"

"Yeah. Maybe." Arvid glowered at the phone. "I guess that would be best. I'll file it. I suppose I should call Sheriff Stendahl."

Grant raised an eyebrow in inquiry.

"Aw, he's still down in San Diego, recuperating at his son's place. Last time we spoke he said to keep him in the loop. Probably basking in the sun, the lucky stiff," Arvid said in disgust. "Poop. I wish I hadn't even heard the voice message. It ain't right that I'm sitting here like a big doofus, not telling anybody we found Monette. Not sharing this message with Russell. Or the other cops." His eyes took on a faraway look. "But hearing Amber's own voice tell it—it has to be a cop that hit her. A cop. Right from the horse's mouth." He waved his hand in the air as though shooing away a fly. "Someone I know, damn it all." He turned to Monette. "Sorry. Pardon my Swedish."

Bass stood, sensing Arvid's agitation, and dropped his head onto the big man's lap. Arvid scratched behind the dog's ears, a mournful expression on his face.

Jessie had her back to the group, topping the cake slices with whipped cream. As she turned with a laden plate in her hand, Monette demanded, "What on earth is that cat doing? He ate what was in his bowl, but now he keeps pawing under the stove."

Arvid gazed at Jessie with eyes full of mirth. She tightened her lips and gave an almost imperceptible shake of her head.

"Um . . . one of his toys probably rolled under there." Jessie glaring at the yellow tom. She set the dessert down in front of the blonde. "I'll fish it out later."

A flick of grey flashed for a millisecond, then disappeared under the stove. Jessie sighed, then turned to the group and gave them a wide smile, fake and shiny as a silver Christmas tree. She placed a delicate, china dessert plate in front of each person, dumped a handful of kibble into Jack's bowl, and sat. She changed the subject. "Say, Grant, how soon do you expect to hear from the woman in D.C. who was trying to find out more about the old bank robbery here?"

"Soon. Maybe tomorrow. And while I'm thinking about tomorrow, you were going to sing at the Wild Bull, weren't you?

"Yeah, I guess so." Jessie turned to Monette. "The chef at the Wild Bull restaurant is sponsoring a talent show night."

"Pretty pricey?"

"No, it's cheap to get in. Couple dollars. Donations are appreciated, though. Those funds go to buy paint for the High Butte Assisted Living Center. And any center residents who want to come, get in free. You were at the center to talk to John Running Bear. Did you ever see more depressing halls? "

"They're awful. I hope I never end up in a place so sad. And you're going to sing? I thought you were a painter."

"I am, but I like to belt out a good song, and they need a few people to stand up and make fools of themselves. When I paint in the studio, I paint to rock or blues, anything fast that keeps me slapping paint on the canvas. I sing along, so I know a lot of songs by heart. Singing's a hobby. It's fun, but I'm strictly amateur."

"What are you going to sing?" Monette and Grant asked in unison.

"Who knows? I think they have a really good band to accompany anyone who wants to sing. I'll talk to Chef Perry tomorrow and find out." She grinned and wrinkled her nose. "If

341

I don't know any of the songs they can play, I'll have to beg off."

"Oh, no you don't. I been looking forward to it all week." A red flush crept up Arvid's neck. "Uh . . . hmm . . ." He patted his belly. "Good dinners at them benefits. Don't know what Chef Perry has planned. Might even be prime rib."

"Yes," Grant chimed in, lending Arvid his support. "They're probably counting on you to show, Jessie."

"They probably wouldn't miss me, Grant. With all the fuss the Wild Bull has made about this fund-raiser, they must have gotten quite a few volunteers." Jessie rose to gather the small plates and walk to the dishwasher. "Heck, it's not like I'm the only one singing."

"Of course, you *did* promise," Arvid reminded her.

The men's eyes met, an unspoken message dangling like a fine cobweb between them. Monette tilted her head and started to open her mouth. Arvid put his finger to his lips. He had spoken to Chef Perry, and the Chef had told him he and Grant had better deliver Jessie to the stage. She was the only act.

"Yep," he said. "Maybe prime rib. Ought to be good."

"Omigod!" Monette's scream was high-pitched and quavery. "A mouse!"

Much later, as Jessie pulled on turquoise silk pajama bottoms and yanked a white tank top over her head, she chuckled. *Poor Monette.* No matter how graceful one was, there just wasn't a sexy way to scramble onto a chair and then slip, plopping your blingy jeaned behind right onto your uneaten coffee cake. Jessie threw back her head and laughed until Jack trotted in, perplexed at the sound she was making, and wound his tawny body around and around her legs.

Then she remembered Arvid's call, to tell her the missing phone had been located in deep grass quite some distance from the gate at her dad's field. They'd missed it at the crime scene. She thought again about Amber's voice message. In her mind, Jessie heard the last broken sentence. *Burly?*

Curly? Surely not. Then, she reminded herself just how valuable the Moran's were. Her stomach knotted.

Oh, no. But, it doesn't make sense. There would have to be an accomplice. I don't want to cast suspicion on anyone and be wrong. I'll look through the box of files again tomorrow.

She closed her eyes, mentally scanning photo after photo from Amber's research. *Yes,* she thought. *It does make sense.* She was nearly certain she knew who had killed Amber, or at least who one of the people involved in the girl's attack was. Especially if Amber was killed because of the Morans, not because of the drug route. But she had to be sure. She caught her lower lip between her teeth. *Hmmm.*

Worried, she checked the downstairs locks for the third time, then went back upstairs and locked the door of her bedroom as well. Jack jumped into his accustomed place on the bed, and stood on the patterned comforter, looking at her with unblinking eyes. She scratched behind his ears. Then, she grabbed the shotgun from the corner of the room, checked it, and slid it carefully under the bed where she could grab it even from a prone position. Finally satisfied, she snuggled into the cool linen sheets. Jack padded to her side, stretched and plunked down. She reached over, ruffled the tomcat's fur, and closed her eyes.

Sweet dreams, Mouse Boy.

Chapter 54

Rural Montana, present day
"I am so sorry, Chef Perry. I've been painting all afternoon and the time just got away from me." *Probably sunburned as well as embarrassed. Doggone it, my freckles will have freckles.* She rubbed her right shoulder.

"Come anyway. So you missed practice. It doesn't matter. This is a great band. They'll play whatever you know by heart."

"I'm way out in the boonies. I don't think I even have time to go home and change if I need to make it in time for your first set."

"That center is counting on you to bring in donations, Jessie O'Bourne. We promised the crowd some singers. Just get here. We'll figure out what to do about clothes when we see you," Chef Perry said in a harried voice. "Please! We really need you."

"Oh, all right. You guilted me into it. I'm on my way." Jessie wiped a hand across her forehead to brush away a drop of sweat. As her arm came up, she sniffed. *Yuck. I reckon. If I take a shortcut through Henblom's property and take the cut across Finnigan's, I can make it. Maybe with time for a sponge bath. Good thing I left Jack home minding the hollyhock patch. At least I don't have to detour to drop him home.*

* * *

"Take her, Sarah." Chef Perry handed the teen a key. "Go across the alley to my house and wait while she takes a

344

quick shower." He patted Jessie's arm. "Sarah went to school with my Melinda. You look about the same size. Sarah's going to raid my daughter's closet for you while you clean up. The band will keep the crowd busy. Now, hurry!"

Twenty minutes later, Jessie was in the back room at the Wild Bull Restaurant peering over the band leader's notebook of song choices. Her hair had pitched a fit about the humidity of the shower and tumbled down to her shoulders in an unmanageable halo of red curls. Sarah had applied too much makeup to her eyes, claiming "stage makeup" was the way to go. Hooker makeup is more like it, Jessie thought.

Melinda's shimmery, dark green dress was cut way lower than Jessie would've preferred. She squirmed. It was snug. Too snug. So snug she could hardly breathe the sigh of relief she felt when she saw several songs on the list that she knew by heart. As she reached for the door knob, the door burst open and Sarah collided with her, knocking Jessie onto the floor with a yelp.

"Omigosh! Are you okay?" The girl looked stricken.

Jessie pushed herself to a sitting position, groaned and then stood. She put a hand to the small of her back.

"Yeah, I'm good. I hope this wasn't Melinda's favorite dress, though." They both stared. The edge of the band notebook had snagged the filmy material and ripped a wide gash in the front of the skirt. The momentum of the fall had opened one side seam from hem to mid-thigh. She stretched and rolled her shoulders, feeling a lightning bolt of pain. "I'm afraid I won't be singing tonight. They'll have to put someone else on."

"They can't! Oh no, they just can't. See, here's the thing." Her voice was small. "Chef couldn't find anyone else. You're the only one."

"What? You have to be kidding. Did he even look?"

Sarah shrugged. "Uh, yeah. I think so. I don't know. But if you can't sing, he's gonna kill me. It's just you." Sarah sniffed. She stooped to pick up the heavy music folder. "The benefit will be ruined, and it's all my fault."

Jessie rubbed the back of her neck. She remembered the walk down the depressing halls of the High Butte Senior Living

Center—the dingy white walls, the lack of comfort and cheer that she, herself, would hope for in old age.

"Well, I guess if I'm it," she said, smiling at Sarah, "I'd better make it enough."

It was at that moment she saw the row of hooks, each one holding an apron similar to those she wore for painting. Only these were an almost neon yellow and emblazoned with the restaurant logo, the head of a red-eyed snorting bull. She grinned.

"Hey." Snagging the nearest one, she wrapped it around herself and tied it. "We're good to go." She patted the teary-eyed teen on the shoulder, steeled her resolve and pushed open the door.

"I had a little wardrobe mishap tonight, folks," Jessie began, leaning into the microphone. "So this is what you get." She threw her head back and raised her arms in the air. At the sight of the Wild Bull apron, the band and all the wait staff hooted and whooped. "And if I can sing—dressed in an outfit with a big old bull on it—I hope you folks out there can open your wallets and throw something in the kitty to dress up the retirement center!"

The drummer gave a quick drum roll ending with a bang of cymbal.

"The band is donating their time," Jessie said, gesturing to the four musicians, "And Koot Lundgren just informed me that he is making a fifty-dollar donation for every Friday that he misses the forecast for the next two months." Jessie turned to the tall balding man by her side and gave him a big hug.

"Make it a hundred, Koot! I still got wet hay on the ground from when you missed it last week," a voice in the audience yelled. The crowd roared.

"Ah hell, seventy-five then. Wilt, you're a whiner," Koot yelled back. "What kind of brother are you?"

Jessie turned to the band and gave them two thumbs up. They had a list of the songs she knew by heart, a mix of old blues and new country. A stoic expression had settled on the drummer's face, the look of someone watching an oncoming disaster but unable to prevent it. A dubious look passed between the piano player and guitarist as well, and she winced inwardly.

She swallowed hard. The air in the dimly lit room was filled with the smell of charred Angus and spilled Bud. Her stomach churned, protesting the lack of lunch and overload of jitters.

Chef Perry stepped in front of the mike for a quick announcement—directing the customers that the back of every seat held an envelope for their gift to the cause. "Make 'em big folks! Prime rib don't come cheap!"

While he spoke, Jessie shaded her eyes with her hand, searching the crowd for someone, anyone, she knew, but the back of the room was too dark to recognize individual faces. And with the dazzling colored spotlights over the band, the clothing on the first couple rows of restaurant customers blurred into blocks of color, a faceless kaleidoscope.

Then she saw John Running Bear seated in a wheelchair by an exit door, the illuminated sign casting a red glow over the prominent bones in his wrinkled face. He cackled something Jessie couldn't quite hear but what she thought was "Go, Red!" She gave him a little wave and blew him a kiss. Her shoulders relaxed. This was what the whole evening was about.

As Perry gestured for her to take her place at the microphone, Jessie felt another swirl of butterflies in her stomach. But as the band began to play the intro to *Me and Bobby McGee* Jessie leaned back, tilted her head, and her body swayed of its own volition to the beat. She began, "Busted flat in Baton Rouge . . .waitin' for a train . . . . " and with every line, she slipped out of herself and into the music. The guitar. The wailing lament of the harmonica. Her own voice. The beat of her heart. That's all there was.

In the back row, Grant Kennedy watched transfixed as Jessie transformed. When she first tipped her head back and let loose—that throaty, rich voice pouring out like flames whipping the music into a wildfire—half the people in the room, himself included, rose to their feet. The redhead blazing onstage, her eyes nearly closed, arms outstretched and palms with fingers splayed, never noticed, but the band went crazy, huge smiles on their faces. By the time she rasped, ". . . holding Bobby's body close to mine", her voice dropping to a sultry tone and her splayed fingers running seductively from her chest to the hollow of her throat, Grant felt a jolt of electricity akin to jamming his finger in a light socket and an irrational anger at his parents for not naming him Bobby. He leaned forward, yearning to reach the woman on stage.

Jessie sang song after song. When she began an intro saying, "Now, one of my favorite singers, a fine lady named Tina, would introduce this next song by saying, "This one is about Mary . . ." the room cheered. The band began the intro, giving it a softness while Jessie went on, "And first, I'm gonna do it easy. Then—I'm gonna do it. . . . rough." The band picked up tempo, and Jessie ignited the crowd with her version of *Proud Mary*, the entire room roaring and stomping their feet, little old ladies and youngsters alike waving their hands above their heads like backup singers while she wailed the music, moving in a Tina Turner frenzy.

Then *Ode to Billy Joe* poured heartache over her listeners before a rocked up version of *Amazing Grace* made every atheist in the room weep to accept religion.

After the old gospel song, she said into the microphone, "If you're enjoying the music—if that song made you feel charitable, reach deep into those pockets and," Jessie raised her hands over her head, causing the tight dress to ride high, and yelled, "pony up folks!" Money came out of jeans' pockets and purses and slipped into the white envelopes.

By then, the side seam of Jessie's dress had ripped to her hip, giving an enticing glimpse of slim leg as she moved to the music. Sexy as hell, Grant thought. But it wasn't only her sensual quality that revved the crowd. The woman on stage was awake—alive in a way most people never experience. She pulled you in, opened her soul, and became the song. Grant hoped someone was taping it. *Does that elusive quality even show up on tape?*

He understood why Arvid hated to miss Jessie's performance. *Oh, poor Arvid. And what a lucky draw for me. Probably a good thing we couldn't get Jessie on the phone this afternoon to let her know about the stake-out. She might have been too worried to get into the music.*

All around Grant, women hooted and cheered, yelling, "Oh, yeeeah, baby!" Jessie had launched into Carrie Underwood's *Before He Cheats*. As she reached the last chorus, his cell phone vibrated, dosing him with reality. He checked caller ID. *There's the big Norwegian now.*

Rising reluctantly from his seat, he moved through the crowd. He handed his donation envelope to a waiter as he stepped outside to answer the call.

"Did anyone try to hit O'Bourne's, Arvid? . . . Too bad. We'll have to work out a better plan." Grant listened to the grumbling at the other end of the line, then said, "No, Jessie's fine. She's ending the last song now. You weren't kidding when you said that woman can belt out a song." Louder grumbling peppered with mumbled "Swedish". Grant laughed

From his place by the door, he saw an old station wagon pull into the well-lit parking lot. Russell got out, K.D. in tow. An enormous, middle-aged man wearing a gaudy Hawaiian shirt tagged along. Russell nodded at Grant as he passed. Grant gave him a casual, two finger salute.

Bet they're ready to call it a night and collect the donations. Russell's going to hit Jessie's last song right at the tail end, if at all, Grant thought. He didn't stop to think why that gave him a sense of satisfaction.

"Dad!" Jessie threw her arms around him and squeezed hard. She released him and looked with surprise at the sight of Russell and K.D. by his side.

Dan O'Bourne beamed at her. "Sorry we missed your songs, cupcake."

Russell looked glumly at the musicians unplugging amps, packing away guitars, and rolling extension cords.

"Bet they were real nice," Dan went on, "but my flight was delayed."

"Uh oh. You came without Marty?"

"Yeah. My lovely bride has gotten herself obsessed with winning a women's golf tournament."

349

"And?"

"I told her she should go ahead and play, and I'd be back in three or four days. Then, I bribed her by extending the honeymoon a week, so's we could tour the other islands. She's as happy as a cowboy who just won the bull riding competition."

K.D. tugged on Russell's hand. "I'm thirsty, Dad."

Russell looked apologetically at Dan. "I'll take him to a table and order him a quick snack and glass of milk before I head home. Sorry we missed your show, Jessie." He nodded to her. "I'll let you two talk." He walked off toward the back of the restaurant with K.D.'s hand held firmly in his.

Jessie's gaze followed him, the beat from the evening's song metamorphosing once more into her biological Big Ben. Then she turned back to her father.

"Why didn't you let me know you were coming, Dad?"

"Knew you'd tell me not to come, honey. Don't be upset. A few days ago, Russell called and told me I should get my butt home and take care of you. Said he didn't feel he could do it. Stretched too thin.'

"Oh, for—"

"Hear me out. Whatever's going on here isn't any fault of Russell's. He thinks you need protecting, and I'm the easy answer for that. We'll hash it all out at the house."

"But how did you get here from the Billings airport?"

"Russ came and got me. And brought my grandson with him. About time we were introduced. 'Course, the little one slept most all the way back to Sage Bluff. He's a cutie, isn't he?"

"Don't think you're off the hook for not telling me about him. I am so mad at you."

Dan looked shamefaced. "Let's talk about it at home. It'll have to wait for morning, though."

"Okay, I'll let you off the hook 'til then, but only because you must be exhausted after the trip home."

"Well, yeah, but actually it's because we have company. Arvid and some DEA agent named Samuelson are waiting for us. I was instructed not to mention it to Russell. I still can't believe you and Arvid, of all people, are suspicious of—"

350

"Dad, why are they at the house? And how'd they get in?"

"They couldn't reach you, so they phoned me. I told them where to find the spare key. If you were out painting all day, I suppose you had your phone off again."

"Yeah, sorry. Guilty as charged. But why did they want in?"

"It was a last minute plan to watch the place. Arvid still thinks that girl's killer is after her research, and knows you have it. He said everyone knew you were singing at the Wild Bull, and it would be the perfect time to break in and hunt for the files. Or the Morans. People are so stupid. Like, 'poof', all of a sudden those paintings are going to appear after going missing for so many years? Nah. Anyway, Samuelson and Arvid thought your singing at the Wild Bull was like baiting a bear trap. So they took Monette over to stay with Esther for the evening, and then they staked out the place."

"Actually, that's a good plan. Did anyone show up?"

"Nah. But that FBI fellow, Grant, said he got some research today that you'd want to see. Hey, did you get a prize tonight, Jessie?"

"Nope."

"Never mind, honey, he said in a consoling tone." He hugged her shoulders. "Maybe next time."

"Sure," Jessie said, with a crooked grin. "Maybe next time. Shall we head home? I'll introduce you to our so-called security team. They're lucky I didn't come home early and shoot them myself, mistaking them for burglars."

"Ain't it the truth? And poor Arvid was pretty upset that he drew the short straw."

"Short straw?"

"Yeah, I guess the guys drew straws to see who would go to your talent show and who would stay and watch the house. Agent Kennedy won."

"Oh . . . I didn't see him there."

"Aren't you going to take off the apron? What happened, you get stuck waiting tables?"

"Something like that, yeah. But Chef Perry said I could keep the apron."

"Good thing, Jess girl, 'cause you got a big rip in that dress. The whole side seam's split out."

"I fell."

"Geez, girl. Now that I look at you, all that hooker goo on your face, and that dress. You look . . . sorry, honey but you look positively indecent!"

"Stage makeup, Dad. Not hooker goo. And I'm not hurt, thanks for asking."

"But—"

"Try not to think about it, Dad."

"You didn't sing *Amazing Grace* in that get-up, did you?

"Uh . . . I thought about it, but no," Jessie fibbed.

"Good thing." Dan shook his head. "All that hooker goo on your face and that dress, God mighta struck you dead, right there on the stage."

"Yeah. I probably had a close call, Dad."

Chapter 55

O'Bourne's ranch, present day

A huge, form lumbered out of the darkness toward Jessie's Ford as they pulled into the yard. "Good Lord, what is that thing?" Dan yelled. "It's a bear!"

Jessie laughed. "That's Bass. It's Arvid's dog. He's my bodyguard. Or he was until you came home. And I don't see how they could stake the place out if he's been running free in the yard. No thief in his right mind would try to break in once they caught sight of him. They must've let him out just now."

"Dog, huh? Didn't know they made 'em that big. That's a lot of D-O-G."

Jessie parked, and got out to ruffle Bass's big head. "How are you, baby? How's my big, drooly boy?" Bass trembled all over, his body aquiver with excitement. As Dan stepped out of the truck, the dog issued a low, rumbling inquiry.

"Whoa, now, hold on there, boy." Dan backed up.

"Good boy, Bass." Jessie grabbed his collar and scratched behind his ears. "It's okay, fellah."

"Hope that big guy is well-trained. He could really do some damage." He reached into the pickup bed and grabbed his suitcase.

"You can't imagine the tricks he knows. Well-trained doesn't begin to cover it. Have Arvid show you sometime. He'll probably be taking him home now that you're here."

"Nup," came Arvid's voice from the doorway, "Maybe not just yet." He held his hand out to Dan. "How you been?"

353

After Grant and Samuelson were introduced, the men brought Dan up to speed. Samuelson called Brookes to ask for a lift back to his hotel. Once the DEA agent said goodnight, the conversation drifted onto bad airplane food and the skimpy servings of said food. Dan sent longing looks at the refrigerator, and the trio decided that pastrami and cheese sandwiches would give them strength to go through the information Kara had overnighted to Grant.

"We looked through it this morning while Jessie was out. We can't see anything in it we can use." Arvid spread lavish mayo and mustard on a piece of sourdough. "I'll make you one of my special double-layered Dagwoods, Jessie, if you want."

She nodded. Her face was freshly scrubbed and the disreputable dress had been exchanged for blue jeans and her 'Starry Night' tee. She sat at the table sipping a cup of hot Earl Grey while she looked through newspaper articles and printouts of research spread out over the oak table. They included background on Gordon Harris, the bank robber, and witness statements taken at the robbery scene. None of the research mentioned a son named Phillip, but the complete arrest report of Virginia Grayson Potts was included, and Jessie marveled at the efficiency and resourcefulness of Grant's girl Friday. Indicated on the arrest sheet were "brown hair, green eyes". Not many people have green eyes, she thought.

Taking a bite of the pastrami and gooey cheddar concoction Arvid had put together and then nuked for her, she moaned in pleasure, the sound resonating deep in her throat, then realized Grant was gaping at her. She stopped, the sandwich half-way to her mouth.

"You want one, Grant? You can still change your mind."

"Uh, no. No. Thanks." Grant looked away.

"This is heavenly, Arvid. Just heavenly." She looked closer at the photo. It was clearer than the one Grant had located earlier in the newspaper archives. It reminded her of someone. But who? She might have to sleep on it. Then, "Oh!"

Jessie's quick intake of breath made Bass bound to his feet. She gave a whoop. Jack, who'd been sitting near her feet, hissed and arched his back as the dog strode toward the table, stopping the dog in mid-stride. The men stopped talking to stare at her.

Jessie explained her idea. "Everything is tied together. Maybe all the way to St. Benedict's, I think. And I'm not convinced a patrol car was involved. You wouldn't need a cop car to pull Amber over. Just one of those . . . What do they call them, Arvid? Bull something?"

"Bull blasters."

Dan looked puzzled.

"You know, those portable light and siren systems— they're magnetic and you just pop 'em on the top of your car. Our EMTs here in town use one. But you'd still need a uniform, Jessie."

"Uniforms can be faked, bought or stolen. I couldn't sleep last night, so I got up and worked up an outline of what I'm going to call "the Moran deaths"." She left the room and came back with a sheet of paper. "I think I see how they all connect."

Dan O'Bourne scratched his head, looking at the list. "Maybe."

"Curiouser and curiouser." Arvid wrinkled his forehead. "There might be something in your theory, but I don't think this explains everything. Especially not since Cassy was killed. Why kill her?"

"People kill friends and relatives, husbands and wives all the time."

"I know, they do. But, nup. This doesn't figure in Jake Ward's drug route. I just can't see it. Say, do you mind if I make another sandwich?"

"Go for it," Dan said. "Leave the fixings out. I'll make another one, too. Grant?"

"No, thanks. I had that great prime rib dinner at the Wild Bull before I watched your daughter's fine performance. I'm still stuffed."

Arvid looked up and gave him a look that could kill a chicken in its tracks. "Huh," He said. "Samuelson and I should've gone over there to eat before Esther dropped me off here."

Jessie was disappointed. The men didn't appreciate her theory. They just wanted to eat, eat, and eat some more. Arvid was the first man she'd seen that could keep up with her Dad in that regard.

She watched the men layering slices of meat and cheese, meat and cheese. Arvid was making his *third* double-layered Dagwood. *Double layered.* She thought about the receipt she'd found in Kate's old pochade box. The one that billed for 'double framing'.

She stood and hurried to her father's bedroom, returning a few minutes later with one of the Kate Morgan landscapes that had graced Dan and Hannah's home for years. Grant and Arvid looked at her questioningly. Dan O'Bourne just shook his head.

"I know what you're thinking, cupcake, but don't waste your time. Kate didn't hide any old masterpieces with her own work. Those pieces never even came back from the framer until a month or two after Kate died." He turned to Grant and Arvid to explain, "Granddad said Nate told him that when those paintings showed up in the mail, Kate's dad nearly cried they were such a welcome sight, something to remember his daughter by. Nate inherited them, then left them to me in his will. It was with the stipulation they stay in the family. They can't be sold, only passed on."

"Humor me, Dad."

Jessie lifted the first painting and put it face down on the table. She ripped old, brown, paper backing from the frame. A layer of wood had also been attached to the frame, using tiny screws.

"Is there a flat-head screwdriver handy?"

Dan stepped into the garage and came back with the tool. "You're wasting your time. And be careful with those, will you?"

After Jessie laid the first screw on the table, Arvid reached into his pocket and pulled out a Swiss army knife, swiveling the small screwdriver tool free. He went to work on another of the screw heads. Several minutes later, Jessie lifted the wood backing and gently took hold of Kate's painting. It was prepared as most oil paintings are today, linen canvas pulled tightly over a framework to keep the canvas taut. She carefully peeled back an edge of canvas to see if a second canvas was underneath.

Nothing.

"I told you so, little girl."

Jessie ignored him, picking up the wooden backing. A framer didn't need to back a stretched canvas. Normally, with an oil painting stretched onto stretcher bars, the back of the frame was simply left open so the canvas could "breathe". She examined the edge of the wood, before looking up at her disappointed audience.

"I think this is actually two thin pieces of wood sandwiched together. Aunt Kate had two pieces framed. And there were two missing Moran's the same week. You can't ignore the coincidence. All these years, I'll bet they were right under everyone's noses."

The three men leaned over the table and stared. Jessie worked the flat head of the screwdriver gently into an area at the corner of the wooden backing, a spot where it appeared as though the old wood was separating.

Gently. Gently. She pried.

The upper layer finally began to lift. Jessie ran the edge of the screwdriver sideways along the rift, working to one corner, then the next, as though slitting open a large wooden envelope. When she reached the corner of the third side, she carefully levered the screwdriver upward. The thin wood buckled and lifted. She pushed her fingers into the crevice and pulled the pieces apart.

A sheet of paper and a flat canvas fluttered to the table. The canvas was face down. On it was scrawled in sepia brush, *Spring on the Yellowstone.* Jessie reached out and turned the canvas over. Cottonwood trees. Deep red willow. The river winding through. It was exactly as described in Kate's journal.

Moran's signature began with an almost crude large "M" with a "T" struck across, ending in an arrow. She looked at the paper that had fluttered out along with the masterpiece. It was yellowed and brittle. Instead of touching it, she let it lay on the table, peering closely to read the faint, flowing cursive:

"Dear Kate, you are absolutely correct in your assertion that this is a genuine Thomas Moran. If you have opened this, I am assuming you have spoken to St. Benedict's and are ready to consign it to the auction house on their behalf—"

Jessie read no further.

"YES!" She threw her arms in the air and did a pirouette. As she swiveled around, Grant caught her in a hug and lifted her from the ground. Her dad took a turn, and then Arvid swung her into a bear hug and Grant grabbed her again.

As he set her gently back on the ground, his phone began to sing a repeated chorus of *Sweet Caroline.* "That's Kara. She must be burning the midnight oil. It's around two in the morning in D.C. Maybe she's got something."

He nodded his head while he listened, ended the call and his face lit with a huge smile. "Jessie, you nailed it, at least part of it. Virginia Grayson had a son named Phillip. A large ranch was purchased under the name Phillip Potts four years after the bank robbery. He could have changed his name back to Grayson later."

"Did Kara get anything else?"

"No, and she's heading home. It's just too late to do anymore tonight. If and when she finds anything else, a possible relative of Virginia or Phillip, she'll text or call. Maybe tomorrow." He looked at the old oak table.

Dan was finishing the last few screws on the back of the second landscape.

Several minutes later, a second canvas joined the first. They gathered around, peering at the vibrant painting in mute admiration.

"They really are gorgeous, aren't they?" Grant touched a corner of the second painting reverently. "But I have to say, these two beautiful pieces have been nothing but death on canvas."

Chapter 56

O'Bourne's ranch, present day

It was a dreary morning, with the sky threatening to dump buckets from a dense blanket of grey. Even the stained glass window couldn't pitch any brightness into O'Bourne's kitchen. Jessie hugged Jack to her chest, looking nervous. Arvid looked as guilty as a puppy who'd been caught peeing on the rug. Grant, Samuelson and Brookes looked stony. Dan's face, though bristled from lack of a razor, having had no time to shave before Russell knocked on the door, looked simply smug.

"Y'all should've had more faith in the boy," he said, as he opened the door to admit Russell. "I told them," Dan said. "I told Arvid and Jessie both that you wouldn't have anything to do with any part of the mess."

Russell swept his gaze around the room, the hurt on his face as raw as January wind. His gaze landed on Jessie and stayed. "You didn't trust me, Jess," he said with a bitter, self-effacing laugh. "First, you thought I could have hurt Kev, and now what I'm hearing is you thought I had it in me to bash some poor unsuspecting city girl over the head. You—"

"Uh uh, we're not discussing this. Look at me, Russell," Jessie broke in angrily. "Look me in the eye and tell me you had nothing, nothing whatsoever, to do with Kevin's death."

Russell looked away, glancing at Arvid. He started to open his mouth.

The big detective raised his hand, palm out. "We're gonna put that on the back burner for now, you two. Right now

359

we need to handle one thing at a time. And Russ, I'm sorry to admit that we didn't want to bring you in on this now, either. There could be more than one person involved. There's no proof yet of who Cassy and Travis's killer might be.

Russell glared openly at Jessie. "I suppose you think I murdered Cassy and Travis Simpson, too. Is that it?"

Arvid broke in gruffly. "Can it! Amber's schedule showed that she planned to stop at the Sheriff's Department the day she was attacked, Russell," Arvid said. "We aren't sure if she went to the building. But if she did, nobody admits to having seen or spoken to her. We're just trying to be careful by keeping as few people in the loop as possible. Besides, those are Sheriff Stendahl's orders."

Samuelson went on. "It could be someone who doesn't know or care the paintings exist, but we've got to see if Jessie's theory is valid. We talked to Sheriff Stendahl yesterday, and he asked us to bring you in on the trap we're setting."

"Stendahl knew I had my day booked." Russell almost spit the words out. "And Arvid was apprised of those plans, too."

Everyone's attention was riveted on Russell.

"I'm meeting the dog handler at the station."

Arvid slapped a palm to his forehead. "Plum forgot. I'm so sorry. Samuelson, we took your recommendation that we have a cadaver dog go over the reservoir grounds. They're coming all the way up from Salt Lake today. Still, it's really a long shot that they'll find Trish buried there."

Samuelson thought a minute, then said calmly, "I'm sorry, Bonham. Like I said, Stendahl wants another local man involved in today's plan. We can't logically rule out anyone else on the force as the killer's accomplice, so you're the best fit. How about if we send Brookes to work with the dog handler? He is familiar with that process and will let us know immediately if something is found. Best I can do. Now, let's get organized. The plan is as basic as they come. We're going to ask Blanche to leak a false story. She'll say the Morans have been moved to Arvid's place and will be there for the afternoon, before they're transferred to D.C. for appraisal tomorrow. We'll spend the rest of the day at Arvid's."

"See what fish rises to the bait," Arvid added, and pantomimed reeling in a catch.

"Where will the paintings be?"

Samuelson nodded. "We hadn't discussed it, but my idea is to leave the Morans here, in Dan's gun safe. Miss Weber will be stashed out at Minna Heron Woman's place. That will keep her out of the way and safe. Brookes can take her now, then go meet your cadaver dog team."

From the hallway, Monette sauntered into the kitchen. "I heard my name mentioned," she drawled. "I hope y'all were saying something sweet about me."

She wore a deep, rose-pink tank top and jeans that looked airbrushed on. She teetered on sandals with high cork heels, her hair styled in an intentional windblown style. When Monette caught sight of Russell, her eyes glittered like a fox spotting a quail, and she lifted her chin. She glided over to him and put her hand on his arm.

Russell, who'd been staring at Jessie, felt Monette's touch and wrenched his gaze away to look down at the petite blonde.

"Why, you must be Russell," she cooed. "You poor thing. It must have been awful for you, just awful, being shut out of an investigation in your own town." She wagged a finger at Jessie. "Now, you never told me he was so good looking. If I'd known, I'd have turned myself in to the Sage Bluff Sheriff's Department days earlier."

She turned toward the kitchen counter and headed to the coffee pot, working the sparkling billboard on the back of her jeans, a heart design of fake gems, for all she was worth. She turned her head coquettishly over her shoulder and said sweetly to Russell, "I'm just *sooo* sorry for all the trouble."

Russell was gaping open-mouthed.

Pole-axed, Jessie thought. *Damn the woman.*

Today, her own hair was pulled up into a ponytail, and she wore a plain, yellow tee, covered by a brown artist's apron sporting the Jerry's Art Store logo. Jessie swept her gaze downward, contrasting her own tennis shoes and serviceable jeans with Monette's fashion statement. She noticed a splotch of blue paint near the knee of her slacks and frowned.

Monette glided past.

"Just like a big, blinking, highway sign," Jessie grumbled under her breath. She saw Grant raise his eyebrows as though perplexed. She realized the FBI agent was the only man in the room not watching Monette pour her coffee. *Even Dad is gawking*, she thought in disgust. *But Grant has been staring at me all morning, instead. What's with that?*

"So," Samuelson said, pulling his gaze back to the group as Monette disappeared through the kitchen door with her coffee mug. He cleared his throat. "Like I said, Miss Weber will be taken to Minna Heron Woman's home. Kennedy, Bonham, Arvid and I will be at the Abrahmsen's house, waiting to see if anyone attempts to—"

"I could come, too." Dan interrupted. "I wouldn't mind getting in on the action, since the paintings were part of the family history for so long."

"No go. You're a civilian, Dan. Stay here and catch up with Jessie," Grant said. "You haven't even had time to talk."

Dan looked apprehensively at his daughter, remembering her threat to have a heartfelt talk. "She has her day pretty well planned, already."

"I want to do some plein air studies of the old barn. Dad's thinking about painting it white, so I wanted to take some good photos, and do a couple small paintings, just in case. Something to work from in the studio."

"Isn't it pretty gloomy today for that," Grant asked, peering out at the overcast sky.

"Doesn't matter. Sometimes flat lighting makes an interesting painting."

Dan watched Russell frown at the exchange between Grant and Jessie, then glanced again at the FBI agent and narrowed his eyes. Dan scratched his chin thoughtfully.

Abruptly, Russell smacked his coffee cup down by the sink and said to Dan. "Like Grant says, you're not law enforcement. Besides, you came home to take care of Jess. You should stay here."

"Yeah, I guess I ought." He smiled at Russell. "That's why Arvid brought you in to help, you know. When I told him you wanted me to come home and protect Jessie, it confirmed his gut feeling that you were clean."

"It's settled, then," Grant interrupted. "I do have a problem. I have no gun with me. When I came out to Sage Bluff originally to meet with Amber Reynolds, it was to be simply an interview."

"Can you shoot?" Dan O'Bourne asked skeptically.

"Of course. FBI training is comprehensive. Just because I'm in the art theft division doesn't mean I don't need to use a gun periodically, either." He looked around the room. "Would someone be kind enough to loan me one?"

"You can use the 9mm pistol I normally keep in my easel box," Jessie offered. "I'll go get it from the Greyhawk."

"Let's head out then," Samuelson barked. "Grant, I'll ride with you. Bonham, you and Arvid take your truck. There's room in Abrahmsen's garage, so both vehicles will be out of sight. We'll put out a fake call later that makes it appear Arvid had to take the patrol car out to an accident on Highway 89. If there is a dirty cop at the Sage Bluff Office, he'll think you're away from home, leaving a clear field to grab the paintings."

Brookes held the door open for Jessie, as she came back in carrying her pistol. He gave her a sweet smile, and she thanked him. Then she handed the gun and a loaded magazine to Grant.

Dan and Jessie stood on the porch, watching the two vehicles as they drove away. "You know, cupcake. Something about this just doesn't feel right."

"What Arvid would call 'fishy as trout for dinner', Dad," Jessie agreed. "I think he has an idea who's involved with the drug route and is playing it close to his chest. Or he's protecting someone, but I'm not sure why. I think all we can do is trust him to handle it." Bass stuck his big muzzle into her hand. She reached into the pocket of her painting apron, pulled out a dog treat and commanded, "Dekk!"

363

Bass flopped down and looked hopeful. "Good boy," she said, flipping him the small dog biscuit. He took it, walked over to the lilac bush near the front door, and disappeared under the overhanging branches into the cavern he'd excavated.

"What the—"

"I know. He's a digger. He's got a hole there you could put a cow in. I'll fill it in after Arvid takes him home."

"Hmph. Okay, then."

She kissed him lightly on the cheek. "I'm going to go paint, unless you want me to come in and make you something."

"Nah, I'm not hungry. Think I'll go in and send Marty an email. Ask her how the golf game is going. Later, I'll go up to the studio and see if I can fix that broken light you were complaining about. I'll take the shotgun up with me. And by the way, Jessie—"

"I know, I know. I saw your face when I said I'd loan Grant my pistol. You always said, 'Don't let anyone else use your gun.' But I'm not sure that loaning it to an FBI agent counts."

Chapter 57

Abrahmsen's home, present day

"I think we've wasted our afternoon," Samuelson said resignedly. The men stood spaced around the Abrahmsen's picture window, arranged so that they couldn't be seen from the driveway. "Let's give it another hour, but I tend to think we've missed something—some key piece of evidence. I told Blanche that Grant would be picking up the Morans at five-thirty. That fake call for Arvid to meet Russell at the reservoir went out two hours ago. If anyone was coming, they'd have tried something by now. Then he looked out the window at the long lane from the house to the Abrahmsens' turn-in. "Wait, someone just turned into the lane."

Just then, Russell's phone vibrated. "Hello?" His face paled. He looked over at Arvid.

"Russell?" Arvid asked.

"The cadaver dog has hit on an area near the copse of trees at the reservoir. They've started digging."

The sound of tires crunched on the gravel driveway. Samuelson flattened against the wall and carefully peered out, hand on his holster. "Jeep", Samuelson said.

Arvid had mimicked his action, but then relaxed. "Aw, it's just Sheriff Stendahl. He did say he thought he felt good enough to fly in. He hated missing the action and wanted to be here if it turned out he had a dirty cop in what he calls his 'family'."

The jeep Cherokee's door opened and a tall, rangy man got out. He wore a blue polo shirt and khaki pants. His brown hair was a crew cut, buzzed nearly to the point of baldness, and he carried himself as though his body was near collapse. Stendahl lifted his hand in a wave of greeting.

Russell put his gun in his holster, opened the door and greeted Stendahl, who came in as Russell was going out. "Hey, you're looking good. Come on in. I was just leaving, sir. Arvid will fill you in. If you'll give me your keys, I'll hurry and pull your jeep into the garage as soon as I back out."

Arvid introduced Samuelson, and Samuelson again took up his station near the window. The Sheriff headed for the sofa near the grand piano and sank gratefully down. Esther appeared in the kitchen doorway, holding a coffee pot and mug. She held up the pot and looked inquiringly at the Sheriff. He shook his head.

"She's not supposed to be here," Stendahl grumbled as she retreated into the kitchen.

"I know, sir. Sorry," Arvid said. "Esther's waiting for a call from her music publisher. We turned the ringer volume way down. I tried to get her to go to her sister's, but . . . ," he looked apprehensively at the kitchen door, "she's a stubborn woman. But we're about to give it up, anyway. I think our trap is a bust." He moved back to the window as the phone rang softly in the kitchen and they heard Esther pick up.

"Hello . . . . well, isn't that good news!"

Chapter 58

O'Bourne's ranch, present day

Jessie listened to Eric Clapton through her headphones as she blocked in the beginning of *Red Barn - Study One*. Her French easel was set up between the house and barn, and she happily slapped paint onto the canvas, periodically rocking out to Clapton's guitar. Jack was at his usual post, guarding the hollyhocks when she saw him suddenly run from the tall flowers and duck into the barn. It was only then that she registered realized a motorcycle was barreling down the driveway.

"Crap," she said aloud. "This can't be good."

Jessie looked past the large rider on the motorcycle and saw a grey compact car also turning into the lane. She ripped the headphones off, tossing them onto the small table placed beside the easel to hold her paints. She reached into her paint box, expecting to put her hand on the 9mm pistol, only to recall Grant had borrowed it.

And the motorcycle was coming in fast, giving her no time to get to the house.

Oh no, this REALLY isn't going according to plan. Wonder if I can bluff? At least give Dad some time to realize what was happening.

Then she remembered the dog. She yelled at the top of her lungs.

"Bass! Bli Klar! Get ready! Bli Klar!"

She saw a rustling in the lower branches of the lilac near the porch.

The cyclist ground the bike to a stop near Jessie and got off the bike. The big rider was dressed in leathers and was reaching to pull off a fancy helmet. When the helmet was removed, Jessie's stomach clenched at the sight of the tight curly hair.

Play it cool. Give Dad time.

"Hello, Blanche," Jessie said breezily. "What brings you out all this way? Do you have time for something to drink?"

"You know why I'm here, Jessie. You aren't stupid. I want those Morans." Blanche reached behind her back. Her arm swung around, and her hand was now holding a gun. Pointing it at Jessie, she said, "Move toward the house. Now. Unless the Morans are in that fancy motorhome of yours."

"The Morans are at Arvid's, Blanche," Jessie said firmly. "They're going to be sold to build a new wing on St. Benedict's. It's high time, don't you think?"

"Your Aunt cheated my grandma out of those paintings years ago, Jessie. And I'm in the loop. I know they aren't at Arvid's, so they must be somewhere here. But you'll tell me. You'll tell me eventually. They're part of my family's legacy."

"How do you figure that?"

The grey car had parked behind Blanche's motorcycle. A Honda Civic. Jessie saw the woman, a stranger, just sitting behind the wheel with the window halfway down. The driver didn't seem inclined to get out, and she was crying.

Blanche glanced over and rolled her eyes. She shook her head disgustedly and turned back to Jessie.

"My grandmother was at St. Benedict's when Moran came through. Just like your aunt Kate. It bothered her until the end of her days that she'd missed the opportunity to get the paintings. Your aunt Kate cheated her out of them."

"Your grandma was Virginia Grayson, right?"

Blanche's green eyes flashed, but she gave a contemptuous shrug. "It doesn't surprise me that you know that, Jessie. I've been kept well-informed of the investigation."

"I imagine Virginia killed the nun at St. Benedict's to give herself a place to hide out, then probably killed the priest because she was trying to find the paintings," Jessie said, rambling on. She slipped her hand behind to the side and gave Bass a two-fingered 'wait for it' sign. "And later, she killed my aunt Kate when the paintings resurfaced. Your grandmother was a thief. A cold hearted killer. Guess your old man was, too, if he was part of Kate's murder."

"Sticks and stones," Blanche said. "Grandma Virginia wasn't afraid to do what was necessary. She knew how to make money. She actually started with very little—the money from the bank really wasn't that huge an amount. When she got old, I took care of her. I'm pretty good at making money, myself. I started the drug route when I was just a pharmaceutical sales rep. And it's grown into the largest in this region. The sale of those paintings will let me expand my syndicate into Canada."

Jessie gave a start. "*Your* drug route? You were the head of Jake Ward's truck route?"

"Poor Jake. He was pretty broken up about Amber. What a coincidence that she wound up here in Sage Bluff. Amber was a clever girl. She came to the station and wanted to let the Sheriff know she'd found a photographic link between a cold case murder in Sage Bluff at St. Benedict's School and a bank robbery suspect named Virginia Grayson."

"You couldn't have her spreading that around, I suppose?" Jessie said.

"It was already around six o'clock when she stopped. I told her everyone had gone for the day and to come back early morning. When she asked for directions out to O'Bournes, I gave her a long, roundabout way to get here. It was easy to catch up with her near your dad's place and pull her over," Blanch bragged. "I had a gun along, but that fencing tool of your dad's, hanging right there near the gate, was just too handy. Saw it in the headlights as I pulled off to the side."

"Where did you get the cop's uniform? And I'm assuming you had a Bull blaster."

"Arvid's spare uniform was in the store room, while his floors were being varnished. Fit me like a glove. I grabbed the portable siren from Cassy's car on the way out of town. She needed it sometimes when she was on her EMT shift. My niece never locked her car."

"That was pretty clever, for a spur of the moment plan," Jessie said. Blanche motioned toward the house and Jessie obeyed, edging slowly to the left, keeping her eyes on the gun.

"You killed Cassy, too, didn't you?"

Blanche flinched, looking nervously back at the Honda. A plump woman in tan stretch pants and a floral shirt was getting out.

"Go home, Violet," Blanche yelled. "This doesn't concern you. Once I get the paintings, I'll disappear and run things from some other little hick town."

"Answer the question, Blanche," the little woman demanded. "I want to know if you killed my baby. I came to the station today. You and the Sheriff were in the coffee room. I was just reaching to open the door when I heard you say something about your drug shipment. Your drug route."

Jessie jolted as though Blanche had already shot her. *Russell was acting Sheriff. Russell was dirty after all. And Arvid was with Russell.* She heard a moan and was startled to realize it had come from her own throat. *Russell.*

"Go home, Violet. Eavesdropping was always one of your worst faults."

Violet shook her head emphatically. "At first, I couldn't figure out what you were talking about, but I knew it was important. I heard enough to know that whatever's going on, you're both in on it together," Violet accused, tears coursing down her face, her nose running. "I heard you say you were coming to O'Bournes'."

"Violet, you don't know what you're talking about."

"I went back down the hall as quiet as I could, and sat in the car. While I waited for you to come out, I figured it all out. I remember how much like Grandma you were. She was a mean, vindictive, sly woman. She disgraced the family. And I can't let you hurt anyone else, Blanche."

"Stay out of this, Violet. Go home."

Violet wiped her nose with the back of her hand. "Either you or Sheriff Stendahl shot my daughter and left her at the reservoir to rot. Sweet Jesus. Her face—"

"Stendahl?" Jessie stammered. "But—" *Thank god . . . . Stendahl, not Russell.*

Blanch looked at her watch. "Stendahl's over at Abrahmsen's getting rid of Arvid and Russell right now." She waved the gun at Jessie, motioning her toward the house. Over her shoulder she said, "Get a grip, Violet. Do you really think I would shoot my own niece?"

"So it *is* your drug route—or is it Stendahl's?" Jessie asked.

"Of course it's mine. Stendahl's just a hired hand. He took a little leave of absence to go on a procurement trip for me. He's as healthy as you. Now where are they, Jessie? The Morans?"

"They're . . . they're in Dad's gun safe in the basement," Jessie tried to sound hesitant.

"It takes money, you know, to bring in good people—to buy the trucks—the prescriptions. To pay off the doctors. Doctors like Doc Turner. You know," She gave Jessie a nasty grin and added slyly, "Your *mother's* doctor."

"My mother's—"

"Oh, honey," Blanche's voice was saccharine. "You mean Kevin never told you that your mom was hooked on Oxycodone? When she broke her collar bone, she was in pain— a *lot* of pain. I had Doc Turner give her, and keep on giving her, just a bit too much pain killer. Hannah thought Trish was so helpful, driving to town, filling the prescriptions for her. But Trish didn't go to the pharmacy. We'd switch the pills for stronger ones before they ever reached the house. Just a little gift from our house to yours."

"My mother?" Jessie's mind raced. "But why? And Trish?" A memory surfaced of her Dad encouraging her to stay at school over the holidays. Kevin telling her Hannah was ill.

"Did you ever look at your mother, Jessie?" Blanche looked disgusted. "We went to school together. To put it simply, she was popular. She was beautiful. And I was not. In those

371

days, I had a thing for Jules Nielson, but Hannah had Jules wrapped around her little finger. Even after she married Dan, he wouldn't look at me. God, how I hated that woman. And Trish . . . well, she loved your brother, but she was weak. When your brother found out Trish had been giving Hannah the Oxycodone, it fair broke his heart." Blanche snickered. "He asked too many questions. I think he was beginning to suspect I was the supplier." She gestured with the gun. "I couldn't have that."

"What do you mean?"

"She had him killed, Jessie," Violet choked out. "Or killed him herself. And Trish. And the girl from Denver." She turned and screamed at Blanche. "Did you kill my beautiful Cassy, too, Blanche? Did you?"

"Violet, that's silly talk. Get back in the car. This doesn't concern you."

Violet strode closer. Her little hands were balled into fists.

Jessie glanced toward the lilac bush. Saw a glimmer of big white dog. She gave a 'wait' hand gesture. Again . . . 'wait for the command'.

Please God, let me be getting the commands right. Please don't let me be saying 'get your toy'.

"Ironic, isn't it?" Blanche ignored Violet's distress. "Kevin asked Stendahl to come out and talk to him. He didn't want to come to the station because he wanted to make an end run around me. He asked Stendahl to investigate me. Me. So the Sheriff shot him. He arranged it to look like a suicide." She grinned malevolently at Jessie. "Suicide is so sad, isn't it? So very sad. But poor Russell found the body."

Jessie's mind went blank. "Suicide?"

"Obviously, that damn Russell wanted to save Dan and Hannah what heartbreak he could. Russell thought Kevin actually *had* committed suicide. He must've been the one who rearranged Kevin's body again, to look like an accident."

Jessie stopped walking. Her mouth fell open.

The guilty look on Russell's face. Yes, Blanche's words have a ring of truth. What could be more awful for a good cop than to know you've tampered with evidence?

"Move!" Blanche waved the gun again, encouraging Jessie on.

"Why kill Cassy?" Jessie asked.

"Cassy. You killed my Cassy," Violet blubbered.

"I didn't." Blanche turned halfway toward her sister and screamed, "I didn't!" Then she went on calmly, as though nothing had happened. "Cassy rode with Amber Reynolds when the girl was airlifted to Billings. Before she died, the Reynolds girl mumbled. Mostly gibberish, but she said the cop who hit her worked the desk. Cassy went to my house and snooped. She found my shoes—still with a little blood on them. She went through the whole house . . . snooping." She turned again towards Violet. "But I didn't kill her! I should have killed the little snoop, but I didn't. She even snooped through my jewelry box."

"Is that where the charm in Cassy's locker at the Fire Station came from?" Jessie asked. "It was Trish's, wasn't it?"

Keep her talking. Stall. Where's Dad? She gave Bass a 'ready' signal.

"Yes. I had gotten rid of Trish's things, so Russell would think she'd left town. But I kept the charm as a little souvenir. Cassy found it in my jewelry box. She used to have a spinning class with Trish and she remembered how Trish wore it threaded through her tennis shoe laces. I never thought to look at the Fire Station."

"What about Travis?"

"He was unimportant. But I didn't kill either of them."

"I don't believe you, Blanche," Violet was weeping uncontrollably, swaying and repeating over and over, "My baby. My baby."

Jessie turned and began trudging the last few steps toward the house, carefully giving a 'wait' hand gesture as she passed the lilac.

As she neared the porch, Jessie made a cutting motion with her hand and screamed.

373

"Bass! Ta ned! Take down!"

A blur of white burst from under the lilac bush like a 747 lifting its nose off the runway. Violet screamed and threw herself to the left. Blanche turned away from Jessie to face the dog.

"Whump!" Bass hit her in the center of her torso. As the gun went flying from her hand, she slammed down like a felled oak. She landed with Bass covering her from chest to knee, the breath knocked out of her.

The gun landed next to Violet.

"You're going to pay for this, Blanche," Violet shrieked. Her eyes fell on the pistol. As the squat woman bent to pick it up, Jessie dived, slid her palms across the ground, and grabbed the gun.

"Shoot her!" Violet screamed. "Shoot her or give me the gun!" When Jessie ignored her, the woman fell to her knees, rocking with her hands over her face, weeping.

As Jessie brought her hand up with the gun, she realized her Dad was already there.

He stood above Blanche's prostrate form with a shotgun pointed down at her head. The arm holding the shotgun was trembling. Bass's face was inches from Blanche's chin and he was giving her his best snarl, teeth bared, a large string of drool hanging from his mouth.

"What the hell is this thing?" Blanche screamed. "Get it off me! Get it off!"

"It's just Arvid's dog, Blanche," Jessie said quietly. "And I wouldn't move if I were you. At least not until I look up the command for 'Get Off'. It's slipped my mind."

"Snuck around the back as soon as I heard the yelling," Dan said. "I couldn't hear all she was saying, but I heard enough to wish I had the guts to simply pull the trigger. My sweet Hannah . . . my boy." His eyes were moist. "And now I almost lost you. I told you before, Jess girl," he said, shaking his head at her, his voice shaky, "Don't ever loan your gun out."

"I know. I had a close call." Tears streamed down Jessie's face. "Don't shoot her, Dad."

374

"I . . . I won't. Now go call Abrahmsen's. Then get that dog a big treat."

Chapter 59

Esther answered on the first ring. "Hello? Esther Abrahmsen speaking."

"Esther, this is Jessie. Pretend it's someone else. Is Stendahl there? He's the missing link."

"Oh, yes. Well, isn't that good news?"

"He's in on the drug trafficking, and he's probably the one who shot Cassy and the DEA agent. Dad is holding a shotgun on Blanche here. Bass took her down. But, Esther, Stendahl is there to kill Arvid and Russell."

Esther said smoothly, "Oh, my. You're such a sweetheart. Thanks so much for letting me know."

"I take it the men are in the other room. I'm calling Russell right now so he can send the cavalry. Is there something there in the kitchen you can use as a weapon?"

"Hmmm? Oh, sure. I'm looking at it right now," Esther said. Her eyes fell on the cast iron skillet. "See you later."

Esther looked into the living room. From her vantage point she could see that Stendahl had his hand under a throw pillow, and she suspected it held a weapon. He was biding his time, waiting to strike. She picked up the skillet and held it by her side. Then Esther walked casually into the living room and stopped by the sofa, standing near Stendahl, but with her body turned slightly away.

"Guess what, Arvid?" Esther gave him a slight grin, winked, and gave a tiny inclination of her head toward the man on the sofa. Arvid's eyes widened.

"Good news, Esther?"

"That was one of your friends, Arvid. He wanted me to tell you the Bass are biting. Oh, and . . . ," she turned and looked at the Sheriff, "you're probably not a fishing enthusiast. That actually means Blanche just tagged you."

Stendahl's hand came up from the pillow holding a gun aimed at Samuelson, but Esther was faster. She slammed the skillet down hard, connecting not only with the hand holding the pistol, but continuing on to bounce firmly off the Sheriff's kneecap. He bent over and let out a blood-curdling shriek.

In seconds, Arvid, Grant, and Samuelson all had their weapons trained on the screaming man. He held his injured hand curled into his chest and his good hand over his knee, rocking in agony.

"Good job, Esther," Arvid said, grinning from ear to ear. "That's my girl."

"Is everyone okay at O'Bourne's?" Grant asked worriedly, as Samuelson grabbed both Stendahl's wrists and secured them with cuffs.

"Right as rain," Esther told him. "You had her pistol, but fortunately, she had the dog." She smiled. "It's like owning a rocket launcher."

Grant and Samuelson began to laugh.

"By the way, Arvid. Jessie can't seem to call Bass off. There's nothing on her list that means 'get off'."

"Poop," Arvid said. "It's not on her list, 'cause it isn't one Bass knows. Call her back. Ask her if she has a piece of baloney."

Chapter 60

Jessie leaned on Russell's desk. She'd brought him a new desk blotter and a large box of drawing supplies for K.D..

"I'm so sorry about Trish," she said softly. Trish had indeed been buried at the reservoir. Fiske and his cadaver dog found her remains. "And I'm sorry I doubted you about Kevin. What you tried to do for Mom and Dad—"

"Please don't mention it. I screwed everything up. If I'd left well enough alone, maybe we'd have figured out sooner that Kevin was murdered."

"Was Mom really addicted to the Oxy—"

He grimaced. "Yes. But she was trying to get a handle on it."

Jessie gave him a sorrowful look.

"Blanche was a great actress. Who could've known that she was so vindictive and that she hated your family so much?"

"At least she didn't kill her own niece. Stendahl admitted that Duane from the gas station was coerced into calling Cassy. He claimed his friend had nearly drowned out at the reservoir and he needed help. It was Simpson's bad luck that Cassy Adams grabbed him to go out there with her. He must have offered to drive."

"Poor guy. So nobody actually figured out he was a DEA agent."

"No. When they got to the reservoir, two of Blanche's goons were there, dressed in swim trunks. They said their buddy had been taken to the hospital by another pair of paramedics and when they hopped into their pickup to follow them to town, their vehicle wouldn't start. Of course, Cassy and Travis offered them a ride to town."

"So they shot them from the back seat. Cassy and Travis probably didn't have time to react."

"No time at all. We suspect the killers had Travis call in to work and say he had a family emergency. Just to delay any search for him. They likely told him to call both the Fire Station and the hospital, since he was supposed to have a shift that day at both locations. Instead of calling the hospital, he dialed the DEA office number."

"But why didn't they have Cassy call?"

"Stendahl says they weren't supposed to kill her—just scare her into silence. After all, she was the ringleader's niece. Cassy must have been uncooperative."

"I can't imagine how awful it must be for Violet to know that Blanche was involved, even if she didn't pull the trigger. And what about Jake Ward?"

"Stendahl claims it was Blanche who put out the hit on Jake Ward. She overheard Arvid and me talking about Ward planning to turn state's evidence. Duane got word to Jake at the prison that Blanche was the one who killed Amber. Ward was determined to take her down for that. He really loved that girl."

"Duane had more nerve than I would have thought. He must have thought he could notify Ward without Blanche finding out, but figured he couldn't turn her in without implicating himself."

"Yeah. Especially since Blanche kept threatening to hurt his little sister if he didn't play by her rules. Of course, Duane was probably afraid he'd be next, and hoped Jake would bust the whole thing wide open—let the chips fall where they may. He claims he didn't know that when he phoned Cassy, Blanche had two goons out there at the reservoir ready to kill her. He thought he was just sending Cassy on a wild goose chase so they could search her apartment. When he heard around town that Cassy and Travis Simpson went missing, he complained to Blanche. Stendahl had his hired help work him over as a warning. Nobody takes credit for damaging your tire. I think it was just one of those things—some random nut case."

Russell picked up the box Jessie had brought. "So, what's this?"

"It's for K.D., but you may as well open it."

Russell cut the tape holding the box closed, and spread the children's art supplies across the desk. He gave Jessie a thumbs up.

"I appreciate these. And K.D. will be ecstatic. Thanks."

"You're welcome."

"Anyway, getting back to Blanche's mess. We still haven't found out who was searching your dad's house that night. Some other poor schmuck under her thumb, I suppose. Arvid suspects it's someone who works at the Wild Bull. There are several questionable guys who run those outside grills. Might account for the smoky smell you mentioned."

"That's a possibility, Russ. I'll bet their clothing reeks of it by the end of a shift."

"It'll take some time before we get all of the people involved rounded up—if ever."

Jessie nodded. "Grant hand-carried the three Morans to an expert in Boston. I'm sure they'll be verified as authentic. Our family will keep our small one, but I know the money the two large landscapes will bring at auction will be a great boost to the school here in town."

"Talking about painting, how did the plein air event go, Jess?"

"Good. It went great." She paused. "I'll be back in the fall to teach a workshop."

"Jessie . . . ," Russell began. "Will you think about coming home for good . . . maybe give you and me a chance?"

"And give up painting like you mentioned before, you mean, Russell? No." She looked at him, her eyes dark. "I'll come often enough to give K.D. some lessons, though. We can work in Kate's old studio."

"You know I don't want a wife who needs to travel. You could sing instead, Jess. Hey, get hooked up with the band that played at the Wild Bull."

"And you can put a cork in it, Russell. I don't want a husband who feels I'm not good enough as I am, Russ. Someone who doesn't care if I'm doing what I love. I deserve better. And I guess I'll keep looking until I find it. I've told you before, I'm not like your mother."

"That isn't—"

"Yeah. It is. You've never gotten past the way your mom left. Somehow, you think a wife needs to be right there at home. Well, the 1950s have come and gone, Russell."

He didn't answer.

"By the way, Monette's looking for a job here in Sage Bluff. She's already talked to the owner of the new computer store and has an interview. Dad's having her house sit until they get back. He flew back to Maui to finish his extended honeymoon. I have an art show in Fredericksburg, and I can't stay any longer."

Russell gave her a mournful look. He stood and came around the desk to wrap his arms around her. She leaned into the hug for a minute and then disentangled herself.

"She likes you, Russell. You might give her some thought."

Jessie turned and started toward the open door. She could feel Russell's gaze on her as she walked away. She'd taken a leaf from Monette's book and bought herself a pair of those blingy jeans.

Russell sat down heavily behind his desk and stared into space. The decisive click of the shutting door threatened to smother him, made it difficult to draw breath. For nearly fifteen minutes, he sat motionless. His mind was a merry-go-round of disjointed thoughts

Was she right?

He thought back to when Jessie was studying at the Paris Academy, how he'd decided he'd had enough of Dan O'Bourne telling him how poorly suited they were. How he'd rashly purchased an airline ticket and the biggest diamond he could afford. It would have meant he'd have to be the one to compromise, to leave Sage Bluff. But, he'd planned to go to

France, tell Jessie in person how much he loved her and ask if they could build a life together.

What had happened to that younger Russell, the one with the courage to risk it all?

He rocked back in his chair, leaning precariously on the back legs. Kevin's death and Trish's dilemma changed Russell's flight plans. Now, he had a second chance. She was here, within reach. And he was letting her go.

Who does she think she is, trying to fob me off on Monette? Monette, of all people. Could she possibly be more different from Jessie?

He pictured the two women in his mind. The little, flirty blonde, and the tall redhead. When he thought of Jessie, he remembered how she'd looked standing near the stained glass window, the light filtering colors across her face. And he realized, it wasn't the warmth of color that made her so beautiful to him at that moment. He was a damned fool.

It was love.

In a flash, he was out of the building, running down the street, searching frantically for the Hawk. Jessie was gone. He rushed back to his office and picked up the phone, punching in her number.

Jessie tracked Arvid down at the Calico Café.

I should've known to look here first. It's huckleberry pie Wednesday again.

"Hey, Arvid." She slid into the booth.

"Hey, yourself. Want a piece?"

"Yeah, but I'm going to get mine to go. I'll stick it in the Greyhawk fridge until I hit Yellowstone. I'm heading out, and I wanted to stop and give you a hug goodbye."

Arvid waved a waitress over and gave him Jessie's pie order, telling her to add it to his bill.

"You tell Russell, 'no dice'? He loves you, you know."

"Yeah. I know, Arvid. But I finally realized that we aren't suited. Dad used to tell me so, and I finally realized how right he was. All of the O'Bournes are stubborn, so it took me a while to give up on Russell."

"That Grant Kennedy was getting pretty sweet on you, Jess. He gets a certain look in his eyes when he even hears your name. I heard him tell you he'd like to stay in touch. Boston's a long way, but you might give him a call."

"I did, Arvid. Yesterday."

"And?"

"Some woman . . . ," Jessie cleared her suddenly tight throat. "A woman named Pat answered. Said she was his wife, and asked me if I wanted to leave a message."

Arvid looked startled. "Poop. Well, if that don't beat all."

"It does," she said, her voice catching. A dull feeling settled in her chest, and she recognized it as the deep loneliness she'd become accustomed to. She'd become very fond of Grant. In fact, she'd hoped Grant might be 'the one'. She'd certainly never suspected he was a player. That biological clock of hers had better just shut up. Reaching into the tote she'd carried in, she brought out a small, flat package. It was wrapped in the Sunday comics.

"I brought you a little thank-you gift for the loan of the D-O-G."

"You didn't have to do that." A wide smile brightened his face. He unwrapped the package to find a small oil painting of Bass, with Jack curled up by the dog's side. "It's priceless, Jess. Thanks!"

"I didn't make up the pose. One night I got up to get a drink, and they were snuggled up on Bass's bed like two hot dogs in a bun."

"You talked to John Running Bear, didn't you?'

"Yeah. Blast his wrinkly old hide. He could've saved us a lot of time. He finally admitted that he'd seen Virginia dump Sister Mary Catherine in the river. He didn't let on at the time. Had to stay there, he says, and make sure the younger kids were okay. When Moran came to the school, he thought the painter was too old and frail to be of help. Then, when the body was found, he spoke up, but everyone thought he was lying. Hungry for attention, they told him. John's parents told him to keep quiet and let the white folks sort it out."

383

"Oh, man. He must have been terrified."

"Yeah. The poor little kid. Seems funny to say that, now that he's so old."

The waitress reappeared and set a white Styrofoam box on the Formica table in front of Jessie. She picked it up and slid from the booth, then leaned over and gave Arvid a light kiss on the cheek.

"You and Esther come down to Santa Fe anytime you want a vacation." She gave him a brief hug. "Drive down in that new motorhome of yours and park it in the driveway as long as you want, you hear? Congratulations again, Arvid. I'll bet that horse trailer you won in the mail-box contest made a great trade-in."

"Yep. Made a big dent in the down payment. Esther and I already got a big fishing trip in the works. She's going to write her music while I catch us dinner."

Jessie turned and was walking away when Arvid said, "Hey, Jess!"

She looked back.

He gave her two thumbs up. "Killer jeans!"

She gave him a little salute and a wink. A few minutes later, she opened the door of the Greyhawk, stowed the pie, and slipped behind the wheel. Jack was sitting in the passenger seat, kneading the upholstery into submission and purring in satisfaction, ready to hit the road.

Her phone buzzed. When she checked the caller I.D., Jessie's heart lurched.

Russell.

Abruptly, she turned the phone off and dropped it into the glove compartment. She stared out the windshield, scanning the nearly empty streets of her beloved hometown. She felt the urge to go somewhere. Anywhere. And put brush to canvas.

"I'm just not in the mood for any long drawn out goodbyes," Jessie said, scratching Jack behind the ears. "So, I guess it's just you and me, Butter Tub."

She started the engine, put the radio on, and pulled onto the cracked, asphalt road leading out of Sage Bluff.

"Let's go paint something."

384

END

ABOUT THE AUTHOR

Mary Ann Cherry is a professional artist, much like her heroine, Jessie O'Bourne. She was raised in rural Montana in an area similar to the fictitious town of Sage Bluff. She now lives in rural Idaho with her husband and several pudgy cats.

Cherry and her husband travel to art shows, where she exhibits her work professionally. She takes part in 'quick draws' at the shows, producing a painting in about an hour's time from start to finish. Her work is in the permanent collection of several art museums, and she is a Master Signature member of the Women Artists of the West.

Usually you can find her painting in her home studio, or writing at a desk situated on an upper floor landing—one that affords a lovely view of a grassy yard and lush golden willow tree during the summer, and frost covered branches and snow during those cold Idaho winters. Wherever she is working, the coffee pot is always on and the brew is of the good strong Norwegian variety that holds up the spoon.

Jack is patterned after the big orange tomcat Cherry's father owned, who was indeed named after the old time boxer, Jack Dempsey. In his youth, Jack would growl at pickups going past the yard and stand between Cherry's feet to welcome visitors with a snarl when the doorbell rang. Such a charmer!

I hope you have enjoyed this novel. Thank you for being a Jessie O'Bourne art mystery reader.

If you enjoyed "Death on Canvas" and want to continue your friendship with Jessie, Jack (that rascal) and Arvid, please continue reading. Here is a free sample of Book Two of the Jessie O'Bourne Art Mystery series, "Death at Crooked Creek". Enjoy!

Please check the website: www.maryanncherry.net for the availability date.

Prologue

September - Nielson's farm near Crooked Creek, Montana

Adele Nielson stood with her hands on her slender hips and gave her father her best teenage stink-eye. *Is he the most stubborn man on the planet? He's as bullheaded as that big Angus bull in Fergusen's back paddock.*

Berg Nielson avoided her gaze. He sat in his favorite chair, his normally bronzed face as pale as white bread and his eyes rheumy. He looked bone-weary. Adele knew the chemo had stomped the stuffing out of him. *Thank God he's through with the barrage of treatments,* she thought. According to the oncologist, the chemo been superbly successful. Even so, Doc warned her Berg would feel as useful as an old work boot for several weeks—one with no laces, holes in the sole, and shredded lining.

She stiffened her spine and prepared to do battle. Adele knew that to grow a successful crop come spring, winter wheat should be planted at least six weeks before the ground froze. Eight weeks was even better. Worn out as he was, her dad was nonetheless determined he could do the planting himself.

"You know you aren't up to it. Not yet." She gave him a stern look. "Besides, Jeff Benson came over yesterday and loaded the planter with seed. The John Deere's all ready to go, and my evening shift at work doesn't start 'til six. I can at least get the north field planted."

She looked at her watch and frowned. Maybe she'd be a few minutes late to work. She loved her job at the library, but the world wouldn't stop spinning if people waited fifteen minutes to check out a Louise Penny or Dan Brown novel. Of course, Mrs. Madsen, that gossipy old biddy, might feel out of sorts if her interlibrary loan had come in and Adele wasn't behind the desk the second the hour hand hit six so Mrs. Madsen could pick it up. For some reason, she came only when she knew Adele would be working the desk. *Could the woman be curious about her Dad?* Adele gave a shudder. But, she was in her early sixties, about the same age as Berg, and since Adele's mother, Vi, passed away, the Madsen woman always inquired about Berg's health. *Oh, well. It doesn't bear thinking about.*

Adele twisted a lock of her shoulder-length brown hair and gave her dad a look that would wither steel. "And tomorrow's Saturday. I have all weekend to do winter wheat."

Without further discussion, she walked to the entryway closet and pulled out his coveralls, holding them against her body to judge the size. She realized with a wince how long it had been since she'd pulled her own weight on the farm. Grimacing, she gave Berg's large coveralls a critical glance. While she was nowhere near her dad's breadth, she *was* tall. And hippy. Maybe she could manage with them for a day. It would save her jeans. Every time she worked in the barn or drove the old John Deere, she managed to wipe oil on her jeans.

Hmmmm. Dominic was more her size. Maybe she should go up to her brother's old bedroom and borrow some work clothes. Goodness knows, he won't need them back until he comes home from his deployment. Still, she hated to just help herself to his things.

Her Dad gave her a critical look. "You'll be swimming in those, Addy." Then he stared out the window at the unseeded fields with a wistful expression. "You sure you can do it? You don't mind?"

"I don't mind," she insisted. "It'll be fun." Smiling to herself, she realized she meant it. In fact, she felt a little skip in her step at the thought of having something substantial she could help with, instead of sitting by helplessly and worrying about her Dad's health. She gave the heavy coveralls a shake. "And these'll do fine."

"Okay, okay. But not unless you sit and have a good breakfast before you start."

She wasn't hungry, but she hesitated. She knew he didn't feel up to cooking for himself. And he still didn't have his appetite back. He'd skip eating unless she made him a meal and watched him chow down.

"That's a great idea. I'm hungry as heck for bacon and eggs. But I'm only fixing them if you'll eat, too." She draped the coveralls over the back of a chair, went to the kitchen and took a frying pan off the hanging pot rack. Humming, Adele bustled around the cheerful room, pulling a loaf of sourdough from the wooden bread box and setting out ingredients for French toast, scrambled eggs and bacon. Soon, the mouthwatering smell of frying bacon made her glad she'd decided to postpone the fieldwork and cook. She plopped the French toast into another pan, and while it sizzled, she quickly packed drinks and snacks into a cooler to take along in the tractor.

Half an hour later, she sat at the kitchen table across from her father. He looked better. The hot breakfast had been a good idea. They argued too much lately—especially about her choice of boyfriends—and sharing a companionable breakfast took the edge off the irritation they felt toward each other.

She tried to cut him some slack, knowing the chemo made him cranky as an old grizzly, but he seemed to be mighty opinionated about college. About girls who married too young. About jobs. The boredom of the snack shop job she'd tried before landing the position at the library proved he was right about *that* job. College *was* a good idea. She shivered inwardly. Not marriage. Not at nineteen. She wasn't ready, even though at first it had sounded like fun to have her own place. If she ever did get married, she hoped it would be because she couldn't be happy without one specific man. *A man*. Not a boy. And right now, she was pretty sure she was the only adult in her relationship even though her boyfriend had four years on her. She stood and began clearing the table.

When her father got sick, she'd grown up a little— actually, a lot—learning how easy it was to *want* to take care of someone you loved, but how hard it was to *do* it. It must be even harder to take care of kids, she mused. She didn't want to give her dad the satisfaction of telling him he'd been right all along, though. Grinning, she guessed it all broke down to wanting to argue for the sake of stating her own mind, letting him know she was all grown up. Making her own decisions.

"What are you smiling at, girl? Thinking of that damn kid, I'll bet. That engagement ring he offered you had a diamond about the size of a pinhead. You know what that fellow has most of, don'tcha?"

"No, but I'll bet you're going to tell me," she said in a combative tone, egging him on. She chewed her bottom lip. *Heck, that brought a little color to his cheeks. I need to remember he's been sick. Stomp on my tongue a little. Besides, he's a lot older than my friend's folks. Old enough to be my grandpa instead of my dad. Man, Dom and I must have been the classic afterthoughts.*

"Bull. That man is full of it. Pure bull. Never heard the like." He guffawed, the laugh ending in a short cough. "Why, he's full of more bull than old Johnson's big Aberdeen Angus. And he's too old for you, that's for sure."

Adele put the last plate in the dishwasher and grabbed the coveralls, slipping the baggy legs over her jeans. It was a bit nippy out and the heater in the cab of the tractor wasn't working. She reached into the hall closet again to take one of Berg's blue knit caps off the shelf.

"You could be right, Dad." Tucking her hair under the hat, she grabbed the cooler, pecked the surprised man on the cheek and headed out the door. "Love you!" she called over her shoulder.

Partway to the tractor she heard the door to the house open and Berg call after her, "I love you too, Addy!"

———

"Ugh." She'd forgotten how mind-numbingly boring seeding could be. Row after row after row at five miles an hour. How could she have thought it might be fun? It was getting towards eleven when she began obsessing about lunch. Even though she'd munched all the snacks from the cooler, her stomach rumbled like an approaching train. The music pounding through the cab helped the boredom but didn't do squat for the hunger pangs. She wished she'd packed more in the cooler. Was there at least one of those cardboard-tasting granola bars left? Continuing her slow pace down the row, she reached an arm to the right, flipped open the small insulated bag and rifled through wrappers and napkins. An apple core. A plastic fork.

She leaned to the left as her fingers found the last peanut butter and honey bar. There was a distant pop and something sharp stung the side of her neck. She slapped her hand at it, yanking off the knit cap in the process. She gasped when she saw that the hat, and her fingers, were crimson with blood. A spider web crack blossomed across the front windshield. The John Deere lurched across the field as she wiped the back of her neck in horror. She twisted around and saw a neat round hole in the back window.

A bullet. It must've just grazed me.

Adele's head swung around, her eyes scanning the field. Nothing. She pulled the tractor to a stop and put it in park. Then she looked toward the far ridge. Next to a parked pickup, someone stood there holding a rifle.

"What the hell? What's he—"

As she saw the man raise the rifle to take aim again, she stiffened in horror. Adele threw herself to the floor a fraction of a second too late.

———

Out at the highway, the shooter lowered the rifle. "Oh, God! No, no, no. Not Addy."

He swore aloud in disgust and disbelief. Just as the girl turned her head—just after he'd squeezed off the second shot— he'd realized it wasn't Berg. The knit hat had come off. Damn! She'd been wearing her dad's knit cap. *Damn, damn, damn, damn, damn!*

He let the rifle drop to the ground and covered his face with his hands. He squinted his eyes shut, seeing the bullet plowing its way through that lovely face in his mind's eye. That sweet, beautiful girl. His stomach roiled. He couldn't let himself vomit. *DNA*, he thought. *If you can get it from hair, you can sure get DNA from someone's lost lunch.*

Addy . . . Oh, Addy.

He should have planned better. His stomach threatened to erupt. He ejected the shell casing and put it into his pocket. Then, looking frantically around, he spotted the first empty casing. He grabbed it and picked up the rifle. He ran to his pickup, jumped in and stomped on the gas. He had to get out of there. As he headed over the hill, his eyes filled, making it difficult to see the road. Without bothering to wipe the tears away, he headed toward town. Reason reasserted itself. *Don't be stupid. Follow the original plan*, he thought. He hit the gas. When he got to town, he'd stop in at the gas station on the other side of Main. Then get a cup of coffee from the diner. Make it hard for people to remember just what time he'd stopped by.

His mind churned into overdrive.

"Think, you idiot!" he bellowed aloud. "Think!

He forced himself to be calm. He had to concentrate. He might have killed her later, but he wasn't prepared to deal with it so soon. And now, his scheme had to be revamped. Totally revamped. His upset stomach threatened to ruin his focus. Glancing at the passenger seat, he saw the fast food sack from his morning run through the Quik Stop. At the time, he thought he could eat, but he'd been so nervous he hadn't swallowed more than a bite. His stomach did another heave. He pulled the pickup over and stopped on the edge of the gravel road. He snatched the bag and opened it to be met with the nauseating odor of a greasy breakfast burrito.

"Oh, God," he groaned. He leaned over the paper sack and retched.

Chapter One

Following March - Crooked Creek Resort

Jessie O'Bourne brushed her red hair back from her face, pulled on her knit gloves and gathered her strength. Then she grabbed the handle of the unwieldy hand-truck and dragged it backward. The handcart loaded with paintings threatened to spill as she waded through six-inch deep snow to the service entrance of the majestic Crooked Creek Lodge. The Hawk, her beloved motor home, sat double-parked as close as she'd been able to manage, with her orange tom wailing like a tortured soul in the cat carrier while she unloaded. She couldn't chance Jack getting loose—and lost—while she took trip after trip into the building.

Unlike the well-lit, welcoming front entrance of the hotel where she'd checked in, the artists' parking area remained unplowed. Numerous tracks through the snow testified that many artists had already slogged through the deep snow to carry their paintings and display panels into their reserved rooms—rooms where each painter or sculptor would exhibit for the four days of the annual Crooked Creek Art Expo.

"Why the heck didn't they plow and shovel back here?" Jessie grumbled aloud. With the snow still coming down, whoever responsible for snow removal must plan to wait until the heavy white stuff quit falling. Under her breath, she muttered several of Arvid's favorite four-letter words. Her Norwegian friend, Detective Sergeant Arvid Abrahmsen, from the Sage Bluff, Montana, Sheriff's Office, had some choice expletives he liked to blame on the Swedes.

"Drek," Jessie said aloud, trying out another choice Arvidism. Then her heel caught the edge of the buried sidewalk and she lost her grip on the hand-truck handle. She stumbled, overcompensated for the weight of the cumbersome cart, and tumbled backward into the dirty wet snow, her behind settling squishily into the slush just as she heard the door behind her open with a loud squeak. She swore again.

"Let me help you." The voice was amused and deeply masculine.

End of sample…

24785860R00224

Made in the USA
San Bernardino, CA
07 February 2019